Reverence

Reawakening

by

Duralle S. Hare

DORRANCE
PUBLISHING CO
EST. 1920
PITTSBURGH, PENNSYLVANIA 15238

Dorrance Publishing Co
585 Alpha Drive
Pittsburgh, PA 15238
Visit our website at *www.dorrancebookstore.com*

ISBN: 979-8-8860-4382-2
eISBN: 979-8-8860-4475-1

Falling Star

Witnessing a shooting star is one of those magical moments you never forget. You know how the story goes: when you see one, make a wish and hope that one day it will come true. This was just one of the little things that illuminated our childhoods. Little did we know that shooting stars were much more miraculous.

July 24th, 2019, at 11:05 P.M., somewhere over the west coast of America, a falling star was spotted. Many who gazed at its wonder closed their eyes to make a wish as the luminescent object flew through the sky.

Though this bright object streaking through the atmosphere appeared to be the same as the others, this particular falling star was different from the others. In fact, it wasn't the dusty space rock many thought it to be.

The "falling star" finally reached the ground, creating a smaller crater than one would've expected for its size. The crash wasn't loud enough to catch many people's attention either, as the landing site was a few miles from any locals.

As the dust cleared around the crater, the object that fell from the sky finally became clearer to view. The dust revealed that the object appeared to be that of a young girl. It didn't take long for her to come to after the landing.

She scrunched her closed eyelids a few times as she sat up. Though she behaved as if she were hurt, her body was fine. When she finally opened her eyes, she only opened them partly. It didn't seem as if she was weak or had dust in her eyes. Rather, her expression seemed more distressed. It was as if she were upset about something.

She quickly stood up and faced the sky.

"How rude! You could've been gentler! AND I DIDN'T DO ANYTHING!"

She threw a mini tantrum and kicked around the dirt in the crater. This 6'0 tall girl appeared to be in her twenties. Her skin was as brown as the dirt around her and her hair a dark violet, which would make it difficult to see her at this time of night. That is, if it weren't for her eerie eyes, which were mostly black. Her irises were a golden yellow and shone brightly in the darkness.

Her spooky eyes lowered to an odd circular object she must've kicked up. She bent down to pick it up, and once it was in her hands, she let out a stressed sigh. The object in her hand was fluorescent in a red-violet glow. The glow around it seemed rather dim and was growing less radiant over time.

"Great, and now I'm losing my powers," she mumbled to herself, "This is so goofy..."

The girl stood back up and hovered the ring over her head to see if it would stay. Once she let it go, it levitated for a few seconds, but it didn't last long at all. The ring's light went completely out, and it fell down and around her neck. She jumped a little when it landed on her shoulders. She started to lift it up again, but instead decided to keep it around her neck.

"Well, at least it looks a bit stylish like this," she told herself.

"Good to see you're taking things rather well already."

The sudden voice startled the girl again. She was under the impression that she was the only one there. After recollecting herself, she looked up at the ridge of the crater to see who was talking to her. A hooded figure loomed over the opening, peering down at her, who was in the middle.

"Don't scare me like that!" the girl shot at him.

The hooded figure cocked his head to the side.

"Scared? You? Really?"

The girl looked annoyed. She quickly hopped to the same level as him to let him have a piece of her mind.

"Um, yes!? Who else?"

The hooded figure leaned back, as the girl got up in his grill.

"Well, I mean, seeing that you're an angel and all... I just knew a being that was not taught fear would be perfectly fine with me walking up to say hello."

The girl looked dumfounded and disgusted all at once.

"Oh lord, you're one of those types."

"Hey now! We're not supposed to use the Lord's name in vain, remember?"

Feeling a bit guilty, the girl turned around and out of the hooded figure's face.

"Sh-shush! Leave me alone, I'm a bit discombobulated!"

The hooded figure stood back up straight.

"I'm afraid I cannot do that, my dear."

The girl peered over her shoulder.

"And why is that?"

"Well because I was put in charge of guiding you."

"Guiding me?" the girl questioned. She then turned a little more to face the hooded figure. Now that she wasn't focused on getting on his case, she could see who she was talking to better.

The figure's hood was covering his green glowing skull, which seemed to only add to his creepy outfit. His clothes were a dead green color and long as if they were a robe. The ends looked ragged as if they were drug through jagged terrain. Two bands of cloth wrapped around him and formed an 'X' across his chest. There were also two rings wrapped around his shoulders, one on each side. They appeared to be just like the girl's halo around her neck, but unlike hers, they were glowing. They radiated a slightly green-ish tint. As he stood tall before the girl, he kept his arms crossed behind his back. It was apparent to her that he was also an angel.

"I see now," she responded. "So, you're the one they were talking about."

"I'm glad you understand now," he said.

"Well, I'm just telling you now, I didn't do anything, so you'll be wasting your time —whatever you're gonna do."

"Is that so?" the hooded guy said, mocking her. "Well, can I at least have the name of the legendary 'fallen angel' who 'didn't do anything?'"

The girl mean-mugged him, once again annoyed with the sass she was getting from him. She was honestly debating whether she would tell him her name or not, but she ultimately did.

"Viugra is my name," she said, "At least, that's the name they gave me before chucking me down here."

"I see. Do you happen to know your real name?"

"Well, yeah it's…"

As Viugra spoke, she found her memory running to a dead end. The hooded angel chuckled.

"Heh… I didn't think so."

"If you knew I didn't know, then why'd ya ask?" Viugra shot back, annoyed, "What's your name anyways? Since we're introducing ourselves here."

"My name is Moriel, but I prefer Mori," he responded.

"Cool, cool," Viugra responded quickly. She then asked the question that was bothering her since the moment she recognized him.

"So, um, why's your face bony like that? You aren't a demon, are you?"

Mori pretended to be a bit embarrassed about his face and covered it with his also bony hands.

"Oh, don't judge me! I always looked like this! What, does an angel have to look like a perfectly fleshed out being?"

Viugra almost felt bad, but she realized his sarcasm.

"Please. I know the 'legendary' angel Mori isn't embarrassed of his looks!"

Mori chuckled behinds his hands, then removed them from his face and stood straight.

"Well played, Viugra! I think we'll get along just fine."

"I guess," Viugra said. She finally got tired of the back and forth and decided to ask Mori what the game plan was.

"Alright, enough of that. What exactly am I doing?"

Mori, sensing Viugra's seriousness, also focused in on their business.

"Well, it's simple really: you're gonna live life as a human while you're down here." Viugra shrugged her shoulders.

"Seems simple enough. No problem at all! I don't see the point."

Mori then looked at Viugra, but his countenance was much grimmer.

"The human race is more complicated than you may think, Viugra. Your journey is going to be filled with a plethora of complex experiences you've never seen before."

"Is that so?" Viugra responded. "Well, we'll see about that. I don't really have a choice here but to listen to you, so show me the way!"

Mori nodded.

"Certainly. But before we go, I want you to take a look around this place. Do you know where we are?"

Viugra raised an eyebrow, then slowly panned her vision across the land. The moon shone bright as the clouds passed it by. It's calming light gradually brightened the area up so that Viugra could see better. Cut stone was planted into the ground in rows and columns for many yards out. Some were shaped differently than others, some of which were in the shape of a cross. Viugra then recognized where they were. Though a human would've freaked out about showing up here at night, Viugra was calm.

"We're in a cemetery. I think I saw someone get buried here not that long ago."

"Precisely," Mori stated, "This cemetery has been a frequent of mine as of late."

"You hang out in cemeteries?" Viugra questioned, placing a hand on her hip as she turned towards him.

"Well, yes," Mori started, glancing over the tombstones, "And no. Not like you think anyways."

"Well, what should I think?" Viugra asked.

Mori's head sunk a little. Viugra noticed this, thinking it odd that an angel would appear depressed.

"Um…" She started. Before she could ask what was wrong, Mori continued on as if nothing happened.

"You'll understand one day," Mori started, "Right now, we're starting off easy."

"What?" Viugra nearly yelled,"You can't tell me? I don't mean to come off prideful, but I'll have you know that I understand lots of things! They did teach me up there!"

"It's different!" Mori yelled back. Even with the short time they've had to know each other, Viugra knew that Mori was serious. In fact, she could sense the hurt in his voice. Something must've happened recently that really bothered him.

Realizing he raised his voice at her, he turned around and apologized.

"I'm sorry, Viugra. I didn't mean to…"

"It's okay," she interrupted, "You don't have to apologize. I would like to know if something's bothering you though. It's not good to keep it in."

Mori thought for a moment.

"…no. I know you're right, but now's not the time. I will tell you when the time is right."

Viugra was feeling a little disappointed, but she respected his decision. Even so, she couldn't help but be a bit playful to try and cheer him up.

"Alright fine. But just know, I'm gonna keep asking you until you tell me."

"Oh no," Mori mumbled, "Don't tell me you're one of them…"

"Yep! So, prepare thy self!" Viugra teased, sticking her tongue out at him.

Mori looked at Viugra intently. He knew what she was trying to do, and he appreciated it.

"Heh, you really are a Charity Angel, aren't you?"

"Well, yeah!" Viugra exclaimed, "You know our purpose is to promote love. We're very empathetic creatures. I just wanted to cheer you up."

"By teasing me?" Mori said, with a slightly skeptic tone. This didn't faze Viugra one bit.

"Of course! I could tell from when I first spoke to you back there that one of your love languages is harmless banter! You can't deny it!"

Viugra pointed at Mori with this accusation, as if she had solved a case with little effort. Mori chuckled, but then it turned into full-blown laughter.

"Hahaha! There's not much that gets past you, huh? Well done, Viugra!"

Viugra noticed his word choice here was a bit odd. Why 'well done'? She inquired about this.

"Wait, why well done? This is just what I do."

"True," Mori said, now talking with the brighter tone he had earlier, "And that was your first test. You passed!"

Viugra's eyes widened.

"Wait, YOU WERE TESTING ME?"

"Yup," Mori said casually, "You pass."

Viugra was feeling happy, but she was also feeling deceived.

"Wooooow. I can't believe you were testing me without even telling me! That was sneaky!"

Mori chuckled.

"Oh, dear Viugra. You know just as well as I do that some things are better learned through experience over explanation. Someone I recently observed said 'I can show you better than I can tell you.' It's a great saying, honestly."

Viugra's cheeks puffed up as she admitted to his point.

"Yeah, you're right I guess…"

"But seriously," Mori cut in, "It is important you remember your purpose as we move forward. It's the first step to redemption for you."

"Like I said, I didn't do anything," Viugra stated, "I don't really understand why I'm here. I didn't sin or nothin'. If I didn't know any better, I'd almost feel like they're picking on me."

If Mori had eyes, they would've narrowed at this.

"Viugra, it's vital to prevent the act of sin before you get close to committing it. I don't know exactly what you did up there, but something you did suggested that you might succumb to temptation. At least, that's what Azariel put in the report."

"What, because I asked them about my parents?" Viugra raised an eyebrow, starting to become frustrated, "I feel that angels are no different than humans in that they'd like to know more about them, right?"

Mori thought to himself at this statement.

Wait, so they didn't tell her? I wonder if they expect her to figure it out on her own while she's down here. If so, I feel like they're making my job harder than it should be.

"I suppose you could be right," Mori said. He glanced up at the night sky and noticed the position of the moon had shifted. It seemed like thirty minutes had passed as they were talking.

"Welp, how about we get moving? We've got a long journey ahead of us."

"Really?" Viugra asked, "It can't be that long. We can just fly there, can't we?"

"Nah," Mori responded. Viugra was shocked.

"Wha…? What do you mean… 'Nah'?"

"I mean 'Nah'," Mori said, looking back at Viugra with his head cocked to the side again. "Do you not understand what 'Nah' means?"

"I know what it means! I just don't understand why we can't fly!"

"Well... you can give it a try if you want to," Mori said. Viugra looked at him skeptically, then began to position herself to take off. She squatted down and looked to the sky. Without hesitation, she jumped with all her might into the air. The leap alone had enough force to get her up several feet in the air, just above the trees. Then suddenly, she sprouted a pair of huge, dove like wings from her upper back. She then proceeded to flap them, but soon realized why she couldn't fly: her wings were unresponsive!

Viugra felt her body descending to the Earth, which incited a little bit of panic and haste. She tried frantically to move her wings but to no avail. She simply didn't have enough power to do so, as most of her strength was sapped from her fall from the heavens.

Mori stood with hands behind his back as he watched her fall to the ground. Viugra wailed in pain.

"AAAAAAaaagh!"

"See?" Mori said. "You don't have enough power to use your wings right now. Certainly, you could tell that from how faintly your halo's glowing, no?"

"Oh hush!" Viugra screamed, still groveling in pain, "You could've at least caught me!"

"Huh," Mori pondered, "I guess I could've. That way you wouldn't have an incentive to trust my word. Makes sense."

"I feel like there's a better way to do that," Viugra steamed, now finally able to stand up.

Mori chuckled, but Viugra didn't laugh.

"Great, so my wings are useless. And I love my wings..."

"The best way for you to gain your flight again is to pass the upcoming tests," Mori informed her, as he began to walk through the cemetery, "The more you prove yourself, the more strength you'll regain."

Viugra still felt that this was all unnecessary, as she only wanted to learn more about her parents. Any child who wasn't raised by their biological parents would at least wonder, right? So why is she condemned for simply asking questions? That is the frustration Viugra is dealing with.

Regardless of her feelings, she knew she had to cooperate.

"Alright then. Have it your way. Let's go then."

"Certainly," Mori said. "We're off!"

Sin City

Almost an entire hour passed before Mori and Viugra made it to the city that they were heading to. They had to head through the cemetery and through the woods by foot, which proved to be an arduous journey for Viugra. Since she fell to Earth, her power had diminished little to none. As a consequence, their trek on foot was tiresome. By the time they got out of the forest, Viugra was starting to get fed up.

"Geez, Mori! Why didn't you tell me it would be this bad?" Viugra complained, picking leaves out of her hair, "I didn't think losing this much power would make me this weak!"

"You didn't?" Mori asked, "Well, what did you think it would do to you?"

"I don't know," Viugra responded, finally pulling the last leaf out of her hair, walking closer to Mori. "I was pretty strong. Even with a small amount of my power, this 'walk' should've been a piece of cake."

"Is that so?" Mori said, now being playful with Viugra. Even so, Viugra was actually quite serious in her questioning. When Mori realized this, he cleared his bony throat and decided to answer straight.

"They really didn't explain anything to you, huh? Well... I'll tell you this much. The reason your strength is as low as it is right now, even though you're very powerful, is because those who sent you here put a special seal on your power."

"A seal, huh?" Viugra said. She looked down at the halo around her neck as Mori continued.

"Yes, a seal. With that on your power, you can't use your strength like you used to. In order to regain your strength, you must continue to prove yourself. And to prove yourself, you must pass each trial that lies ahead for you."

"Seems simple enough," Viugra said, "Like I said before, they did teach me up there."

"Knowing and doing are two different things my dear," Mori said. He turned to face the edge of the cliff.

"Now, take a look out that way."

Viugra walked up next to Mori and looked in the direction he instructed her to look. Just shy of a couple of miles from the cliff was a large urban city. The city was aglow with lights in the windows and car headlights and taillights in the streets below. Though it was after midnight, the city appeared to be well awake.

"Wow," Viugra said.

"It's beautiful, isn't it?" Mori asked.

"Well, yeah I guess..." Viugra answered, not sounding very satisfied.

"Well, that's not convincing. Is something wrong?" Mori asked.

"No, not really," Viugra started. "It's just that... well... I like nature."

"Ah, I see," Mori said, "The city life must seem a bit artificial to you."

"Well, that's one way to put it," Viugra confirmed, "Don't get me wrong, it is quite the sight. I just like nature more though. It is part of his creation after all."

"True dat," Mori agreed, "But don't worry. It's not as bad as you might think. Just give it a chance."

"Alright," Viugra said with a sigh.

"Good! Now on to the city full of thugs and crime!"

Viugra looked at Mori crazy.

"What!? Didn't you just say it's not that bad? Why would you say that?"

"Oh V," Mori started, "Is it ok for me to call you V?"

"Sure, whatever," Viugra said, keeping focus on the topic at hand, "Now why did you say what you said?"

Mori turned to look at the city.

"Certainly, you know that humanity is not without fault. No matter where we go in this world, there's bound to be wrongdoing. This city's no different."

Viugra raised an eyebrow.

"I know that. We angels…"

"Fallen Angels," Mori corrected. Viugra glared at him straight-faced. If Mori had flesh on his bones, he would be smiling like a goofball. Clearly, he was still being petty.

"Yeah, yeah — FALLEN Angels," Viugra continued, "It just seems weird that you'd state the obvious like that. You sure you weren't emphasizing how bad it really is down there?"

Mori's head sunk a little. The tone of his voice also changed as he made his response.

"My, my. You're quite perceptive, Viugra."

Mori headed over to Viugra. He had noticed some extra leaves and twigs sticking out of her wings and went to pull them out for her. Viugra caught on to what he was doing, then turned around for him to get them out. As he did this, he continued to explain what was going on in the city.

"You are right, Viugra. I was emphasizing the problems in this city. While there is crime and sin everywhere, Nerezza is one of the worst places on the west coast."

"Nerezza?" Viugra nearly shouted, "You're telling me this city is…"

"Yes," Mori said, as he plucked the last of the debris in her wings out. "This is the city of darkness, Nerezza."

Mori turned to look at the city once more.

"All sorts of crime happen in this city, most of which aren't natural."

"The demons," Viugra stated. Mori nodded.

"They've been causing this city problems for years now. When they've even influenced the mayor to rename the city something that literally means 'darkness,' you know it's bad."

"How come we haven't swooped in to take them out already?" Viugra asked, "It's not like we don't have the power to do so."

"Because V," Mori replied, "It's not our place to do so."

"But we're Angels," Viugra started.

"Fallen Angels," Mori said again.

"You know what?" Viugra said, annoyed by his pettiness, "Whatever, you know what I mean. Anyways, aren't we supposed to help protect them from sin?"

"Not exactly," Mori said, "You aren't exactly wrong, but…"

"But what?" Viugra cut in. She was actually getting frustrated for real. Mori could see the irritation in her face and hear it in her voice. Mori sighed.

"Well… that's something you'll have to learn through your trials."

"Oh, come on! That's a cop out answer!" Viugra growled.

"Call it what you may," Mori said, "But it's the truth. You will eventually learn why we can't just jump in and clean house like you want to."

Viugra was getting angry, but she knew that she had to calm down. Mori glanced at her from the side, then turned away.

I'm sorry Viugra, he thought to himself, *If I could just straight up tell you, I would. Things just aren't what they seem to you. I hope you get through this soon so you can get your answers.*

Mori broke away from his thoughts to move Viugra on to the next task.

"Alright, that's enough talk for now. What I need you to do right now is strip."

"Whoa! Excuse you?" Viugra snapped. Mori just laughed.

"I don't see what's so funny, Mori."

"I'm sorry," Mori said, "It's just that, you're so precious when you get mad."

Viugra looked as if she was about to break all of his bones.

"Relax, V. Surely you know I wouldn't mean it like that."

"I dunno," Viugra replied, "You are a *fallen* Angel after all."

"Ah," Mori said, "You're getting good at your comebacks. This really is gonna be a fun journey!"

Viugra smirked.

"Yeah, yeah. Anyways, why do you need me to change clothes?"

"To blend in, of course," Mori said, "You can't blend in while you're still wearing your angel garments. Not unless you want to look like a stage performer in these streets."

"Do I even have enough power to do something like that?"

"Yep!" Mori reassured her, "Why do you think I tested you so early? I knew you'd need some power to be able to do that. Even so..."

Mori sensed Viugra's current strength and noticed that she might not have enough to completely conceal her Angel appearance.

"You may only have enough to change clothes. I'm not sure if you'll be able to fully dismiss your wings and halo."

"Well, I can try something at least," Viugra said, "What's something they wear down there?"

Mori, using his own power, displayed a few different images of women's clothing that Viugra could try to imitate.

"I have several ideas for you! Let me give you the run-down!"

Quickly swiping the images around, Mori showed off a few different styles he's seen in his own time being down there. The options he had ranged from the casual street hoodie and jeans to fancy dresses, business suits, and many more. Viugra considered her options carefully, but she also didn't take very long to pick what she wanted.

"Okay, I know what I'll wear," she told Mori. She took a few steps backwards as Mori dispersed the projection he had up. Viugra spread her hands out to her sides, palms up. She raised her head up and closed her eyes, almost as if she were receiving a blessing from above. Suddenly, she began to glow in a white light. Her entire body was engulfed in radiance for a few seconds. Finally, the light dimmed down and she became visible again. Mori expressed delight in her choice of fashion.

"Ah! Very nice! I love it!"

Viugra's Angel attire was no more. Instead, she was clothed in attire fitting for the summertime. On her feet were white strapped sandals with straw soles. Her choice of pants were dark green cargos with a single pocket by the knee on each pant leg. Her top was a horizontally stripped tube-like tank top. Each stripe gradually changed from a very dark pink at the base of the shirt to a nearly white strip of pink at the top, and the stripes also grew from narrow to wide from the bottom up. There were no straps holding her shirt up. Instead, she had shrunk her wings down as much as she could and tucked their tips under the top of the shirt to help keep it pinned up. Her halo continued to rest around her neck.

"Not bad, huh?" Viugra said, proud of her choice of fashion. Mori nodded in agreement, but then paused when he realized something.

"Actually, you might want to do one more thing."

"Wait, really?" she asked, wondering what he was getting at.

Mori pointed to the eye sockets in his skull. Viugra cocked her head to the side and imitated his motions to try and figure out what he was on about. Then she remembered: her eyes look spooky right now. Walking around town with charcoal black eyes and yellow pupils would definitely freak someone out.

"Oh yeah. I guess I should do this then."

Luckily, Viugra had just enough strength left to fashion a pair of shades out of her clothing. A small light flashed around from behind her and hovered in front of her. She stuck out her hand and grabbed the shades that appeared from the light and placed them on her head.

"Better?" she asked Mori.

"Much better," he replied, "Can't have anyone confusing you for a demon, now can we?"

"Right," Viugra replied.

"Righty ho!" Mori continued, "Let us continue! We must meet up with the one you will be protecting."

"I'm protecting someone?" Viugra asked, "How can I do that? I just used most of my strength to change my clothes."

"I dunno," Mori said, "You tell me."

"Really?" Viugra replied, "Throw me a bone here! If this is part of my test, then don't you think it'll be a bit unfair?"

Mori shook his head.

"What, do you think you'll be fighting demons already, V? We know not to throw you into a fight you won't be able to handle yet. Besides, you fashioned your current attire out of your holy garments. It's not like you don't have some form of protection yourself. You'll be aight!"

Viugra huffed under her breath.

"You know, you can be a real smart a**..."

A shin bone flew through the air and clonked Viugra in the head.

"OW!" she screamed, "That HURT! What was that for?"

"You asked me to throw you a bone, right?" Mori taunted, "So, I threw you a bone. You don't want it?"

"You know that's not what I meant," she replied, picking his tibia up and flinging it back at him. Mori stuck his leg up and caught the bone midair, snapping it back into place. He then set his leg down into his foot bones to reconnect them all, then his cloak swung back over them.

"Also, refrain from cursing," he continued, "I get this weird twitch in my bones whenever someone does. Usually leads to me kicking at them. Not sure why."

"You know very well why," Viugra steamed.

"Besides," Mori continued, "It doesn't look good for a lady to use such foul language. 'specially an *angel* lady."

"Fine, fine," Viugra said, "I'll try not to let that slip again."

"Good," Mori said happily. He turned around to look to the city.

For her to be cussing like that, I wonder if this world's sin is already affecting her. I better keep an eye on that...

"So," Mori asked, ready to get a move on, "Are you ready to go now?"

"Sure," Viugra said, "Let's get this over with."

"You know it's not gonna be that quick, right? You've got a lot to do."

"Please," Viugra said, now making her way down the path leading to Nerezza, "If this test is fair, then it should be a piece of cake. Besides, I still need my questions answered. This test won't stop me from getting them."

As Viugra continued down the path, Mori shook his head.

You still don't get why you're here, do you, Viugra?

Beyond Castle Walls

Not long after changing, Viugra and Mori ended up in the city of Nerezza. As expected, the city night life was bustling. Parties and clubs were still pumping music and young people were still out having fun. Traffic was thick, but not as thick as it would be during the day. Buildings rose high to the clouds, towering over the populace below. People in the streets were dressed in clothes that were clearly pricy. Groups of families, friends, and others seemed to be enjoying their stroll through the night. The lights illuminated the city, and yet they could not mask the darkness Viugra and Mori could feel from the metropolis. Well, more so Mori than Viugra.

"Sheesh!" Viugra grumbled, "Being amongst all these people makes me feel a bit claustrophobic. It's waaaaaay different from seeing it high up."

"See?" Mori stated, "Experience and knowledge are two different things, V."

"Clearly," she responded, "So which way are we heading?"

"We keep heading south," Mori said, "We still have about 100 miles to go before we get there, so we better keep moving."

"Great," Viugra said, "Alright then, let's go."

"Fo sho," Mori responded, waving his hand at a random passerby. They continued on as if Mori hadn't actually waved at them at all. Viugra noticed him do this and felt like addressing it.

"It must be nice, not being seen like that by everyone."

"Yup," Mori said.

Viugra was referring to the fact that Mori was still in his grim looking clothes. Not only that, but of course his skeletal physique as well.

"Don't tell me you're getting jealous?" Mori teased. Viugra just waved him off.

"Please. Jealousy is beneath me. However..."

Viugra watched as some random men walked past her, goggling at her lustfully.

"It would help to keep people like that from looking at me so hungrily."

"Maybe they think you know how to cook?" Mori said, "Perhaps you should give them something to eat."

Viugra looked at Mori skeptically.

"Um, how 'bout no? They want to eat a dish I'll never serve to them."

"Never say never, V," Mori chuckled. Viugra knew he was being funny again.

About thirty minutes passed, and they were almost at their destination. The tall city buildings were now no more than four or five stories high and had a different look to them. They were moving toward the outer city now, where most people went home. This is also where crime was almost at its worst. This became very apparent to Viugra the further in they walked. Though there weren't as many people about, the kind of people that were around didn't look so kosher.

The locals around were very rough looking. Their clothes were more tattered than those who were in the urban part of Nerezza. Those that weren't still looked as if they were gang affiliated. Even some of the ladies standing around with what would've been fancy attire looked a bit beat up. The looks on some of their faces were also far less cheery than those in the inner city.

"Wow," Viugra said in a low sad voice, "There's so much hurt in these people's faces. What's going on here?"

"This is where the least wealthy reside," Mori said, "Those who struggle to survive on a daily and lead rather difficult lives are the kind of people you'll see around here."

"I see," Viugra responded. As they continued to walk, they passed some alleys where more people were. Some people were against walls and looked even more rough than those on the sidewalk, almost as if they had been thrown in the mud. Viugra noticed and quickly picked up on who they were.

"The homeless," she muttered.

"Yes," Mori confirmed, "They probably have the hardest time surviving in life out of any group of people around here."

Viugra stopped abruptly and made her way over to the homeless man sitting in the alley. Mori watched her and cocked his head to the side, but he didn't say anything. He just watched to see what would happen.

"Hmm," Viugra thought to herself, as she checked to see if he was okay. He didn't move at all, even though she was so close to him.

"Hello?" Viugra asked, "Sir, are you ok?"

Still no movement.

He must be very exhausted, Viugra thought to herself, *I wonder if he's homeless, if he's even eaten anything.*

Viugra reached her hand out to touch the homeless man. With her hand on his shoulder, she closed her eyes and let out some of her power. After a few seconds of this, she lifted her hand and stood up.

"It's not much, but that should help you to keep going," Viugra said, "I wish I could do more for you, but I can't right now. Stay strong, okay?"

With that, Viugra walked back towards Mori. As she walked, the homeless man came to life. He lifted his head up and towards Viugra with little effort. A look of surprise over his newfound energy washed over his face. With a gruff voice, he spoke out.

"Y-you... are you... an angel?"

Viugra stopped. She was about to answer him, but then she looked at Mori. Mori was shaking his head frantically. He was trying to tell her not to tell him what she really was. Viugra thought quickly for that split second, then turned around halfway.

"I'm just a blessing from the High One."

With that, Viugra continued to walk out of the alley. The homeless man remained in the alley. In fact, he laid down and went straight to sleep. Even though Viugra wasn't strong enough to know exactly what he was going through, she was able to guess what he was struggling with. He hadn't eaten much in days, and he was honestly on the verge of lying down for good. He was scared to go to sleep, for fear that he wouldn't wake up again. But because Viugra healed him and gave him a bit of energy, he went to sleep despite his hunger. As he dozed off, tears slowly began to roll down his face. Viugra felt the hope restored in his heart as she walked away, then she smiled.

Once she reached Mori, Mori gave her accolades.

"Well done, V! You're not as bad as they made you out to be, are ya?"

"Of course not," Viugra stated, happily, "I told you they were tripping."

"Maybe so," Mori said, "Buuuut… you'll have to do more than that to prove it."

"Huuuuuuugh," Viugra grunted, "You just can't be satisfied, can you bonehead?"

"But I can," Mori said playfully, "But the others though? Well… I don't know…"

"Right," Viugra agreed.

The two continued to walk towards their destination. They were almost there, about two miles away. As they walked, Viugra decided to question Mori. She was curious about why he was on Earth before she was.

"So…. Mori," Viugra started.

"Yeeeyah?" Mori responded goofily.

"Why were you here on Earth? Aren't most angels supposed to be in heaven most of the time?"

"Good question," Mori said, "Why am I here?"

"That's what I'm asking you!" Viugra rumbled.

"Why am I here, huh?" Mori said, "Well... I can't really tell you."

"Does it have something to do with that burial a few days ago?" Viugra continued to pry. If Mori had eyes, he would've side eyed her just then.

"I... can't tell you, V."

"Maybe it has something to do with the way you look?"

"Guuurl, you nosey as I don't know what!"

"What?" Viugra grinned, "I wanna know!"

"For what doh?" Mori questioned, still speaking rather funny.

"You just seemed so sad, so hurt for that one moment in the graveyard." Viugra said, trying to sympathize with him.

"Well, you're not wrong," he confirmed. "That still won't make me talk, V."

Suddenly, Mori's skull perked up as if he remembered something.

"What's up?" Viugra asked.

"Y'know, I forgot I had something important to take care of."

"What?"

Mori quickly materialized a piece of paper with an address on it. He gently slapped it onto Viugra's stomach. She nearly flinched, not expecting him to do that.

"H-hey!" Viugra yelled out of surprise.

"Shhh! You'll wake the locals!" Mori hushed. Then out of nowhere, he pulled out a rather flashy weapon. Viugra blinked in surprise.

"Whoa, big fella! What are you about to do?"

"Don't worry," Mori tried to reassure her. "Nothing crazy. I'll be back before you know it. Go on without me, aight?"

In the blink of an eye, Mori vanished. Viugra couldn't believe what she was seeing. He really left her! For a moment, she didn't care if the locals were sleeping.

"HEY! GET BACK HERE!"

It was too late. Wherever Mori had went, he left so quickly that her words never reached him. Although, they did reach the nearby group of guys across the street. And they weren't exactly friendly. Now locking on to Viugra, they began to approach her.

"Heeeah shweetcheeks! Whyya screamin' sho lhouh?" one guy, who appeared drunk, said.

Oh great, what have I done? Viugra thought.

"Somethin' we can do fo ya?"

"Not in the slightest," Viugra responded, "Please, go back to the other side of the street."

"And ignore a damsel in distress? That's just not in me," another guy said.

"I beg to differ," Viugra said, as she was able to sense his intentions. In fact, she was able to sense them much more clearly now than before.

I guess Mori was right. My strength slowly comes back to me after I do something good to prove myself.

"Why're y'all wastin' yer breaths?" a voice rang over the entire group, "Ain't it clear? She don' wanna be bother'd!"

A skinny guy who seemed to be in his early forties pushed past the guys to get closer to her. Viugra didn't let her guard down for a second. His heart was tainted, just like the others.

"At this point," he started. Then he reached his hand out to grab Viugra. Viugra slapped his hand away gently, but to him it felt like heated resistance. The man's expression turned angry. At this point, the horde had pretty much surrounded her. The wall of an apartment building they were by was a few inches behind Viugra. Despite her looking trapped, Viugra was calm. She wasn't worried at all. Though there was a dozen of them surrounding her, her posture was still confident. The drunk guy from earlier walked up some.

"Ch'mon Jhach, we jush wahn sum fuhn!"

Jack, the alleged leader of the pack, looked at him and the other goons surrounding her. Then he shook his head as he turned back around to her. He scanned her posture as he made his next comment.

"You idiots. You had to pick a confident one."

Then Jack smirked.

"Lucky fer y'all, she's my type."

Viugra sighed.

I don't have the strength to get out of here without exposing myself. I guess I'll have to fight then.

The goons eased in on her, lust practically oozing from their eyeballs. Viugra, who wasn't taking this too seriously, gave them one final goofy warning.

"Seems your hearts have led you to obliteration. Turn back now and you shall not be smote!"

The goons looked at one another, then busted out laughing at her Elizabethan speak. Jack laughed louder than any of them.

"Hahaha! She's even proper! Oh, we're gonna have fun with this one!"

"Get the f*** away from her."

A voice rang out over the crowd. Jack and his goons stopped everything they were doing. Viugra, who was also surprised, turned with them to the south side of the building they were by to see who had spoken up. Viugra couldn't see past some of the goons too well, but then she realized something.

That voice... it was a bit deeper than I expected, but if I'm not mistaken...

Before the goons stood a short girl who couldn't be more than 10 years old.

Bailey

Before the goons and Viugra stood a fair-skinned girl in black denim and a red undershirt. She also wore red and white chucks. Her curly chestnut-blonde hair was held back in a ponytail through a crimson scrunchie. Unlike Viugra, she stood a bit slouched. Though her posture may have suggested frailty, the look in her eyes said otherwise. Beyond the stressed eyelids of this girl was a calm but fierce glare, sharp enough to pierce your soul. The goons and Viugra picked up on this right away.

"A girl?" Jack questioned, looking at her more intensely. The girl's gaze remained stern. Jack could see that there was something different about her, something kind of unsettling. Even so, she only appeared as a young girl to him. Viugra, on the other hand, saw more than that.

The drunk began wobbling his way towards her. Viugra was now on alert, but not for her own safety. She was concerned about the drunk.

"Wait, don't go near her!"

Jack and some of his goons closed in on Viugra to keep her closed off. The others approached the little girl. Both Viugra and the girl didn't flinch.

"Oh, don't worry," Jack said, "I know it's past her bedtime. We'll make sure to put her to sleep. You just stay here for a moment, sweetcheeks."

Viugra briefly shifted her eyes to Jack. The look in her eyes was of genuine concern and of almost equal ferocity as that of the girl. Jack hadn't seen such a powerful look before now, which was enough to throw him off his game. If he wasn't nervous before, he was now.

As the three others approached the girl, Viugra glanced back at the girl and noticed her beginning to remove her left hand from behind her back. Without wasting another moment, Viugra suddenly charged through the goons who were fencing her off, pushing them to the ground. She delivered a chop to each of the goons' necks approaching the girl, knocking them unconscious. The three of them fell to the ground, just a few feet away from the little girl.

Jack and the remaining goons were in awe in what had just happened. Even the girl's glare softened out of surprise. Viugra's move was so fast, it was almost unreal for a normal human to pull off. Viugra was smart enough to know her limits, so she held back how fast she could really move, despite lacking her powers.

Without even turning back around to face the others, Viugra dashed after the girl and lifted her up and over her shoulder before anyone could react.

"Hey! Wh–" Jack started. He was so stunned that he couldn't even finish his thought. Before he could finish, Viugra was already a couple blocks away and headed down an alley with the girl pounding her fists on her back. With their victims gone, the crew all looked dumbfounded.

"Uh… Jack," one of the goons started, "What just happened?"

Jack, who was both frustrated and amazed, scanned the goons who had been knocked out on the ground and noticed that they hadn't really been unconscious, but weak from Viugra's blows. As they stood up rubbing the back of their necks, Jack did the same as he answered the goon.

"In't it obvious? We got played."

✵✵✵✵✵✵✵✵

Once Viugra saw that they were far away enough to avoid the gang, she stopped running. Though they weren't too far from where they were, she did go somewhere where they wouldn't bother trying to find them. When she figured the coast was clear, she sighed out of relief. Then she remembered the pounding feeling on her back. The girl was throwing some solid punches, but they weren't strong enough to hurt Viugra.

"I'LL KICK YOUR A** IF YOU DON'T PUT BE DOWN YOU B****! YOU BETTER NOT BE F***ING WITH ME. I WILL KILL YOU!"

Even when called such foul things, Viugra remained calm. She could kind of understand her frustration. After all, she was also a stranger. Even so, she didn't like the fact that she was such a potty mouth.

Viugra set her down like she wanted, but before the girl could run away, she smacked the mess out of her. The girl fell flat on her butt, but she was still conscious. She held the right side of her face as she glared at Viugra. Though the pain behind the slap was immense, the girl didn't even have tears in her eyes. Viugra noticed this.

She's really tough. I can't believe she's not at least in tears from that.

"Hand it to me," Viugra commanded. The girl's eyebrows scrunched together.

"I don't know what you're talking about."

"Don't play dumb," Viugra said calmly, "I know you have a weapon in your hand. Put it in my hand right now."

Viugra put her left hand out.

"I don't have a weapon!" the girl retaliated.

"I felt you beating my back with it. You can't lie to me."

The girl realized she couldn't lie about it anymore.

"Well, what if I don't?"

"I could just take it from you myself," Viugra shot back, "I'm giving you a chance to do what's right."

The girl was silent. She knew Viugra was right, but she wasn't willing to admit it. Even so, she reluctantly handed over the weapon in her hand. Jack and his goons were so blind from their lust that they didn't even notice this girl was packing heat. Luckily, Viugra noticed and acted quickly to keep the situation from escalating any further.

"I'm glad you didn't use this," Viugra said calmly but sternly, still locking her eyes with the girl's.

"I could handle them," the girl responded.

"You're missing the point," Viugra said, holding the 9mm down, "You could've gotten yourself in more trouble than you realize."

"So, what, I should've left you alone?" the girl shot back. Then she stopped and sneered sarcastically.

"Oh, my bad. You could've handled yourself, huh?"

If the girl would've known that Viugra could handle herself, she would've left her alone.

Viugra sighed and slowly approached the girl who was getting back on her feet now. Once up, she took a step backwards in protest. Viugra stopped when she did this and continued to voice her concern.

"Look, I know you were just trying to save me. And I know you think you can't trust me right now, on the off chance that I'm part of some setup..."

The girl's eyes narrowed. She wasn't letting up her guard for one second.

"...but please, look at the bigger picture here."

This statement seemed to trigger something in the girl.

"What do you think would've happened if you had shot him? Shot them if you can shoot that fast?"

"They would've died. Obviously."

In Viugra's mind, she facepalmed. She raised an eyebrow, still looking this girl in the eyes as she spoke.

"And your parents? What about them?"

The girl chuckled.

"What about them?"

I see, Viugra thought to herself, *Something must've happened to them. That or she's rebellious.*

The girl skeptically stared into Viugra's eyes. Luckily, Viugra's shades were still on, so the girl couldn't see her spooky eyes. But somehow, she seemed to know what Viugra was thinking about. Viugra felt this and thought it best to make her thoughts clear to her.

"I'm sure they're worried about you being out this late. No matter what might've happened between you, you shouldn't let them worry about you like this."

The girl's eyes narrowed. Viugra sensed a haughty spirit.

"...I can't stand people like you."

Just when I thought I was getting through to her, Viugra sighed.

"Always trying to save everyone, but not even concerned about themselves. It gets on my nerves," the girl continued.

Viugra was starting to get annoyed, but this time it was more genuine than when she was interacting with Mori. While her frustration was more so playful with Mori, it was now borderline anger. If anything could anger Viugra, it would be an ungrateful person. This girl was making that plain to her.

"Do you not care about your own life?"

The girl chuckled. She knew she was getting under Viugra's skin, and she was playing on that.

"Please. Just like you, I could've handled myself," she sneered.

Viugra was livid.

YOU COULD'VE BEEN KILLED, YOU BRAT!

Viugra almost let this slip, but she probably bit her tongue in half holding it in. The girl could see Viugra gripping the gun tighter. She let out one last chuckle, then turned around.

"Why don't you go find someone else to bother? I'm tired of hearing you lecture me, you hypocrite."

Viugra almost messed up. She was a split second away from hitting the girl again, which would've been to damage her instead of knocking sense into her like before. But she didn't. Viugra realized what this girl was trying to do.

"...You think you're slick, don't you?"

"What are you talking about now?" the girl groaned, clearly tired of all this talk.

"You're just trying to work me up, hoping that I just leave you alone."

The girl let out a low, shocked gasp, but Viugra still heard it.

"You knew I wasn't gonna let you walk away by yourself, so you figured you'd make me mad enough to leave you alone. Didn't you?"

The girl didn't respond, but she didn't have to. Viugra had her figured out. During their little staring contest, Viugra was trying to read her the entire time. Before she turned around, Viugra learned her real motives.

Viugra walked towards the girl to place her hand on her shoulder gently.

"You'll have to try harder than that to push me away, hun," she said in her Elizabethan accent. The girl smacked her hand away as she turned to face her.

"First, don't EVER touch me again. Second, don't think you have me figured out you B****."

Viugra was getting tired of being called that word. If anything was disrespectful to call her, it was that.

"Okay," Viugra said, "Let me add to that."

Viugra broke both rules immediately. She vaulted the girl over her shoulder and began to walk off. The girl began to beat on her back again, but Viugra was still unphased.

"Third," Viugra mocked. "Don't call me a B****."

✲✲✲✲✲✲✲

Somewhere several blocks away from where Viugra and the girl were located, several people lay flat on the cold night concrete in an alley. Beside them were the bodies of several demons. They were some of the most ferocious demons in the city. Luckily, they had been dealt with. Their bodies faded away, and the few people who must've been possessed came to. They looked at one another in confusion, wondering what had happened to them to be lying in an alley all together like that.

Standing above them on the edge of the rooftop was a hooded figure dressed in a green robe. The giant scythe that was in his hand disappeared, and he continued to watch from above. Two green rings slid up around his arms and rested over each of his shoulders, and he removed his hoodie.

"Those were A-class lust demons. Looks like someone might be after Viugra."

Red Robin Hood

Viugra walked out of the alley with the flailing girl still vaulted over her shoulder. Once she reached the sidewalk, she looked down the street to see where the gang that had surrounded her was. They seemed to have gone off somewhere. Odds are, they didn't want to be caught up with the feds, so they made their getaway as soon as possible.

Good, Viugra thought to herself.

"Let me GOOO!" the girl screamed. She opened her mouth and chomped down hard into Viugra's side. Viugra was barely phased. In fact, the girl didn't even draw blood. She almost drew her own blood and now reels in pain with ringing teeth.

"S***! What the F***?"

Viugra glanced over her shoulder.

"Biting me isn't going to work, y'know."

"Clearly!" the girl groaned loudly, "What are you made of, solid rubber?"

Viugra barely answered her as she tried to figure out what to do next.

"I'm just strong. So, where's your home?"

"I ain't 'bout to tell you!" the girl shot back.

"Mmm, okay then," Viugra started, now walking back north, "I'll just drop you off at the local police station. Of course, I'll have to tell them you were out past curfew and in possession of a firearm."

"You're a f***ing lie," she called her out.

"Y'know, you cuss a lot," Viugra said, "That isn't very attractive."

"Does it LOOK like I care?" the girl argued back.

"Nah. But you probably will once you realize I'm not joking."

The girl seemed to tense up from this. She knew that she would be in loads of trouble if Viugra meant this. Begrudgingly, she told Viugra where her home was.

"...it's that way. A block and a half down."

"Thank you. Was that so hard?" Viugra answered back.

"Harder than your love handles," the girl grumbled, "Those aren't even love handles, they're hate handles..."

"Nothing about me is hateful," Viugra said, now turning around to head south again. "Now let's get you home."

"Wait..." the girl started. Viugra paused.

"Hmm?"

"Please... just take me back to that alley. Just for a second."

Viugra would've contested, but she realized that maybe she would learn why the girl was out this late in the first place. She looked where the girl was pointing and saw that the alley she was talking about was where Viugra was being cornered.

"What's over there?" Viugra asked.

"My stuff," the girl answered, now feeling that she had no choice but to be honest in this situation, "I need it before I go home."

"Mmkay, sure," Viugra said.

She walked down the street to the alleyway. As they got closer, Viugra remembered feeling multiple presences down that way despite not actually looking down there. It was the same alley where the girl had emerged to try and rescue her. Once she reached the alley, she noticed that it was full of people. Homeless people.

"Can you put me down?" the girl pleaded.

"You won't try to run, will you?" Viugra asked, "I can catch you, you know."

"No S*** Sherlock," the girl responded, "I know that already. You gonna drop me or what?"

Viugra set the girl down and let her go to find her stuff. The girl calmly walked to the dumpster on the right side of the alley and leaned around the corner. She reached down and grabbed a rather dingy red backpack that seemed to be filled to the brim with something. Instead of throwing it over her shoulder and returning to Viugra, she glanced her way to see what she was doing. Viugra was standing with her hands clasped together behind her back, smiling tenderly. She noticed the girl was glancing at her, and she waved before returning to her stance.

She's playing with me, the girl thought to herself, *just who the h*** does she think she is?*

The girl turned around and walked further down the alley. Viugra didn't budge. She knew the girl had a good reason to walk down this way. There were about a dozen homeless people, all who were old, weak, and covered in barely warm clothes. The girl approached each one, pulling out an item from her bag for each one. She was giving them all a piece of a sub sandwich to eat. Viugra's smile seemed to grow a little as she witnessed this.

I knew it, she thought to herself, *This girl wasn't out this late for any bad reasons. She just wanted to help out the homeless. I bet there's not many around here with a heart like hers. Even so, it's not good for her to be out here alone like this. On top of that...*

Viugra looked at the gun she had confiscated from the girl.

She knows what kind of danger is out here. I could sense it earlier: she's been through something really tough. I don't know what yet, but for her to carry a gun like that...

"I'm done," the girl said, now walking back to Viugra. She noticed Viugra holding her pistol and examining it.

"You thinking about giving that back to me?"

"Thinking is a good way to put it," Viugra said, now putting the gun in the top of her pants on the side.

"You know, if you don't give it back, it would be considered stealing right?"

"You mean like you did?" Viugra shot back. The girl scrunched her eyebrows, irritated at her accusation.

"What makes you think I stole that?"

"Well, why would a girl your age have one? I'm pretty sure you're too young to be buying guns."

"Whatever," the girl responded, looping the straps of her backpack over her arms, "Let's go already."

She didn't even answer me, Viugra thought.

Viugra noticed that the girl didn't even move, even though she said she was ready to go.

"Well?" Viugra said, throwing her hands out in front of her to say, 'go ahead.' The girl laughed.

"Oh, my bad. I thought you were gonna hurl me over your shoulder again."

"Nah," Viugra said, "I think you get the idea now."

The two walked away from the alley and towards the girl's home. Once they reached the block her home was on, the girl stopped. Viugra stopped behind her.

"Are you home?" Viugra asked. The girl nodded.

"Yeah. This is where I live."

Viugra looked up at the ranch style home. It was rather clean compared to the other houses on the block. The girl's parents must keep their living space as clean as possible.

"Alrighty then. But before you go, I need to ask you something."

"Oh great. What now?"

"What's your name?"

"My name?" the girl responded.

"Yes, your name. I would like to know it."

The girl looked at Viugra skeptically, then turned around.

"I don't tell strangers my name."

I guess that's fair, Viugra thought to herself, *But it's not like I can do anything with that information.*

"...Bailey."

Viugra was a bit shocked. She thought this girl really wouldn't tell her.

"Huh?"

"You asked for my name, right? Well, listen then!" Bailey snapped.

"I did hear you," Viugra said. But in her mind, she thought something else.

Raise your voice at me again, little girl. I'll put you to sleep before you set foot back in the house!

"I'm still a stranger to you. Why'd you decide to tell me your name?"

Bailey looked over her shoulder. Viugra sensed a change in Bailey's aura. It seemed like she was more solemn and relaxed than before. Even her facial expression was more peaceful than it had been all night.

"Well, to me, you're not strange."

Then she walked up the driveway to the house. Before digging in her backpack to look for the key to the door, she looked back at Viugra who was watching her enter. Viugra smiled and waved at her. Bailey began to raise her hand to wave back, but then she remembered something. In her remembrance, she stepped away from the door and headed back to Viugra. Viugra blinked a few times, wondering what was wrong.

Uhh... okay?

"Give me the gun," Bailey demanded.

"Sheesh," Viugra responded, "What's the magic word?"

"Don't play with me. Give me the gun... uh..."

Bailey had forgotten to ask Viugra for her name. She caught on and filled Bailey's statement for her.

"Viugra."

"Viugra?" Bailey repeated, somewhat disgusted, "What the h*** kind of name is that?"

Viugra was a bit offended.

"Ugh! Clearly the one my parents gave me."

"Your parents need help," Bailey said, "Viugra sounds like that drug used for sex or something. Was that what was on his mind when they had you?"

"I can't believe you just said that!" Viugra said, now starting to lose her cool a bit. Bailey must've run Viugra's patience down.

"Relax, I'm just joking."

"No, you weren't," Viugra shot back, hands spread out to the side, "I know when someone is serious or not. My father never named me after some poison used to increase lustful desires. What do you...?"

Bailey managed to get Viugra worked up enough to get her guard down. In that moment, she jetted her hand out quickly to swipe the gun away from Viugra. She almost succeeded in nabbing it, but unfortunately for her, Viugra was way too fast for her. Bailey barely touched the gun before Viugra seemed to vanish behind her. Bailey's body weight carried her forward and nearly sent her crashing into the street.

"Aahh!" Bailey shouted.

"Gotcha!"

Viugra caught Bailey by the waist just in time.

"Hey, let me go!" Bailey argued.

"Well, if you insist," Viugra said in her Elizabethan accent. She let Bailey go and she fell to the ground. Bailey braced herself for the impact this time, keeping from bruising herself up from the pavement.

"You tried to get me worked up again, didn't you?" Viugra said, as Bailey got up from the ground.

"Not really," Bailey said, feeling a bit embarrassed and confused, "I'm just an opportunist. More importantly..."

Bailey pointed at Viugra.

"How the h***'d you do that?"

"Do what?" Viugra said, sticking her tongue out.

"Don't play stupid with me B****," Bailey shot back. "You vanished or something. What was that?"

"All I did was sidestep around you," Viugra said, "It's not that complicated."

"No way!" Bailey shouted, now irritated herself.

"Shhhh!" Viugra hushed her, "You'll wake the neighborhood!"

"Hahaha. I really don't care," Bailey responded, laughing while still peeved. She really was reaching a point of not caring.

Suddenly, Viugra perked up. She was alerted by something.

"Would you stop playing around and give me the gun already? I can't go home without it."

"Sure, here," Viugra said quickly. Bailey was a bit shocked. Viugra grabbed Bailey's hand and placed the gun gently in her palm. Bailey almost jerked away until she noticed what Viugra was doing. She was all confused again.

"Wait, that was too easy. What are you...?"

"I don't have time to talk anymore," Viugra said calmly with a smile, "It's time for you to go home."

"Hey!"

Viugra picked up Bailey and ran her up to the porch of her house. She set her down on her feet, then ran back down the driveway and east to the next street. Bailey watched her the entire time, this time stunned at what just happened.

Damnation

Viugra had run just a few blocks away before wall jumping and hopping up to the rooftops of the buildings. She paused briefly, looking around for whatever seemed to be keeping her on alert. Whatever it was, she couldn't fully sense it. Her intuition was that whoever is after her might be stronger than her.

Now above ground, she used her real strength to hop far away with ease. Apparently, she was doing enough good things to loosen the seal on her powers because when she jumped, she went so high that the buildings looked like floor tiles below her. She used her barely-moveable wings as gliders to lengthen her jump.

I need to get somewhere where there aren't too many people, and soon, Viugra thought to herself, *Whoever is following me is dangerous and they're closing in fast. They're most likely a demon. And they brought guests.*

Viugra scanned the ground as she was gliding down on her descent. She was already fifty feet above ground when she noticed a park with no one around.

An open space, she thought, *Good. Let's see what this is all about.*

Viugra angled her wings so that she would hasten her drop. She landed softly on the ground and waited. As she waited, she realized something.

If I got more of my strength back, I wonder…

Viugra held out her hand and focused her energy in her palm. A light began to shine from it, manifesting into several objects that appeared to be daggers. Viugra regained enough of her power to materialize weapons out of light. Despite regaining this ability, Viugra seemed disappointed.

"Figures. Guess this'll have to do for now. At least I won't have to punch them to death..."

Not long after she said this, three figures landed around her. She jumped into a fighting stance, ready to defend herself. Her hunch was correct: she was surrounded by demons. However, they appeared to be simple imps. Imps are low-class demons with the appearance of deranged children, with bat wings and devil tails.

"Just as I thought," She spoke. Even though she was surrounded, she eased her stance.

Without saying anything, the three demons lunged at Viugra. Viugra gracefully slid to her right, letting the demons clash into each other. Using her momentum and her right foot as a pivot, she did one graceful ballerina spin counterclockwise and flung three of her six daggers into the bunched up demons. Each dagger struck each demon clean in their heads. They fell to the ground, writhing and squealing from pain. Viugra finished her spin, then approached the demons. The daggers dissipated, reforming themselves between Viugra's knuckles right before she reached them. She bent down and grabbed one of the demons. The demon screeched something indistinct, but Viugra could understand what it was saying.

"Well, that's what you get for attacking a girl in the night," Viugra responded. The demon looked up at her, then ceased its squealing. Instead, it reached for Viugra with hearts in its eyes. It muttered something else, this time causing Viugra to react in disgust.

"Eww, no!" Viugra responded, now speaking Elizabethan again, "Have ye no decorum? To blatantly demand a favor of such perversion! The nerve!"

As the other imp demons seemed to recover, Viugra tossed the one in her hand into them hard, knocking them down once more.

"You all have two options," Viugra spoke, now back to normal. She wanted to make sure what she said next was taken seriously, "You can change your selfish desires to something positive for everyone, or I can send you back to Hell. You get one chance."

Viugra was giving them a look similar to the one she gave Jack earlier. This time, however, she took off her shades. Her eyes glowed in a warm magenta-colored light. The demons squealed once more, but one of them calmed down. Viugra smirked.

"Seems you all have made your decisions."

Viugra tossed two daggers at the demons, both headshots. A white ring formed from the puncture point on both of their heads, growing and traveling across their bodies in a single instant. The demons froze, then moments later they vaporized into thin air. The remaining demon jumped in terror after seeing his once-allied demons vanish. Viugra approached the remaining demon and placed her hand on its head.

"I'm glad you decided to turn your life around, little guy," Viugra said, smiling, "This new path won't be easy for you, but you will find better relationships than with those you were just with. You already know what comes next. Are you ready to repent?"

The demon nodded, tears filling its eyes.

Viugra then used her power again to transform the demon. A bright light burst from its body, engulfing a few yards of the park in a white glow. After a few seconds of this, the light dimmed and faded away. Viugra removed her hand and watched the once-demon flap its wings. Though he was a fallen angel, his appearance had become that of a little boy with dove wings. The expression on his face is also more pleasant compared to that of his demon form. Before he took off for the heavens, he flew up to Viugra and uttered a joyful noise.

"You don't have to thank me," Viugra said to him, "Just make sure you strive to do better from now on, ok? And no more perverted friends."

After their short embrace, he shot up far into the night sky. Viugra watched his ascent until he was no longer visible.

"Well, that takes care of that," Viugra said to herself, "I didn't expect one of them to actually have a change of heart though."

Viugra continued to look at the sky. Her expression turned skeptical, as she muttered under her breath.

"That's why I don't understand why y'all put me on this test. I think I'm doing pretty good so far. We're just wasting time."

Viugra lowered her head and closed her eyes. Despite the statement she muttered to herself, there was something bothering her.

Still... something's off. I only felt three demons, but it seems like there was one more for some reason...

Without warning, something came and completely swept Viugra off the ground. In an instant, Viugra found herself flying across Nerezza with a death grip around her throat. Her eyes shot wide open in total shock and pain. She grabbed the hand choking her with her left, trying to free up some air. The thumbnail of the hand choking her grew and punctured the space between her chin and neck a little, causing her to groan in agony.

"Ah, ah, ah," a mysterious, yet alluring feminine voice warned her, "You don't want me to slip do you?"

This girl! Viugra thought to herself, slightly panicked, *Not only can I not free up some space to breathe, but she's also holding my head back with just the tip of her thumb?*

Viugra managed to shift her eyes towards her attacker's face. Though it was hard to see, she could make out a few of her features. She appeared to be wearing something black. Her skin was also dark. Her hair was dark, short and feathery with a few points sticking out of her head. Behind her were two huge black objects, but at this point things were getting blurry for Viugra to see clearly.

I'm... starting to... lose consciousness. Gotta... act now...!

With as much energy as she could muster, Viugra focused her energy into her right hand, nearly limp from her being choked. She swung and slapped the woman across her face. The woman barely even moved.

"Is that all? Love taps won't get you anywhere honey."

Viugra closed her eyes, no longer able to breathe. Suddenly, an intricate looking circle formed on the woman's face. She noticed it's increasing glow.

"Ah, clever."

The circle dispersed in a wave of green electricity, spreading about the woman's body. The electrocution caused her to seize up for a split second, simultaneously placing a temporary seal on her strength. The sudden seize caused her to snap Viugra's neck a bit. The two, now well outside of Nerezza, plummeted from the clouds to the ground below.

☼☼☼☼☼☼☼

Meanwhile, back in Nerezza, Mori continued to fight off the lust demons. Before he could catch up to Viugra, their numbers had increased to over 100. Though he was stronger than them, they were powerful enough and plentiful in numbers to keep him held up from reaching Viugra. After reaping a few of them with his scythe, he sensed Viugra's energy fading.

Oh no, he thought, *I've been here too long. If I don't get over there soon, she'll…*

Another demon forced Mori to block, breaking his thoughts as well. In one motion, he pushed it back and cleaved it in half. It's remains fell to the ground, vaporizing before making contact.

Mori lifted his head up to view the demons still trying to distract him. He sighed heavily, then lowered his head.

There's still so many of them. I didn't want to use that power, but if I don't, Viugra will fail her test. Guess this is what I get for being the good guy…

Without raising his head, Mori addressed the demons surrounding him.

"Y'know, I really don't like bullies."

Mori's energy flared immensely, causing some of the demons to flinch from just his aura. He lifted his head, but his skull looked more jagged and ferocious than before. His eye sockets were even slanted to make him appear more aggressive.

"Just remember one thing on your way back to Hell. You brought this out of me."

✲✲✲✲✲✲✲

Viugra and her attacker had landed in the graveyard, north of Nerezza. She was almost unconscious at this point, struggling to hold on to life. Though she could breathe again, her neck was still snapped. With a snapped neck and little to no power to heal and fight at this point, things were looking bad for her. Viugra coughed as she tried to get back some air, adding to her pain. Though she could sit up a little, standing wasn't even an option. It was hard enough for her to prop up on one hand and hold her neck with the other.

While continuing to cough and gasp for air, she looked up and saw a figure emerging from the dust cloud from where they landed. It was the woman again, and this time Viugra could make out her appearance. She has a slim figure, about the same height as Viugra, and dark skin with an eerie hint of red. She wore a long, square patterned black trench coat and all black leather pants that conformed to her womanly shape. The leather leggings were like biker pants, but the left pant leg cut off mid-thigh. The rest of that leg was covered by a red and black plaid stocking. Instead of a shirt under her trench coat, she only wore a stylish black brassiere with red trimmings. She was also wearing black boots; the right boot was short and the left halfway up her shin. Her hair was blood red, and her eyes black as the night with ominous amber pupils. Two horns were sprouted from her head and angled backwards. Two black tails were looped through the belt rings on her trench coat, keeping it from blowing everywhere. The rings around each horn glowed with a similar color to Viugra's halo, however they glowed with a darker shade of violet than hers.

"See what you did?" the demon started; body still engulfed in green electricity, "You made me slip."

Viugra, with no time to be conscious of her energy usage, healed her neck before the woman was standing above her.

"This could'a been easier on both of us girl," the demon started. She then broke the unique seal Viugra had placed on her with little effort. Then she slinked down to Viugra before she could even protest. The demon started to feel her up along her arm and to her neck.

"That's aight. We gon' make this work."

"There's nothing to work out," Viugra growled, shuddering at this woman's creepiness. She then pushed her off and scooched away.

"Oooh, so feisty. I like when my prey fights back," the demon said. Viugra's eyes locked on the hand that was feeling her up, the same one that was choking her before. The nails had all retracted, and her hands looked normal again. That's what she was worried about.

"What do you want from me," Viugra asked in a firm tone. Despite the way she asked, the demon knew how she was really feeling.

"You can stop acting tough around me," she said.

The demon extended her hand to Viugra. Viugra leaned back some more.

"Chiara," she introduced.

"...Viugra," Viugra replied hesitantly. Chiara smiled.

"I see. You don't remember your name yet either?"

"Yeah, what of it?" Viugra said.

"You just won't drop the tough girl act, huh?" Chiara sighed. Then she smiled malevolently, mouth stretching abnormally wide for her face. Viugra noticed that her teeth were jagged.

"What if I told you a secret?"

"Secrets from the underworld? Boy, I really want to know those," Viugra said sarcastically, "It's not like I learned about it in holy school."

"Good!" Chiara continued, disregarding her sarcasm. She leaned in close to Viugra's face when she said this, "Because the secrets I know ain't in your history books."

Viugra, finding enough strength to stand up, did so and tried her best not to stumble backwards. Still, she ended up leaning against a nearby tree. Chiara stood up, her face retracting back to normal. Viugra glared at Chiara skeptically.

"You're a demon. Why should I trust anything you say?"

"A demon, huh?" Chiara said, "You guys still putting labels on people?"

"It's not labeling if that's what you are," Viugra shot back, "Nothing you say will convince me otherwise."

"Really," Chiara said, closing her eyes. She smirked again, but this time it was different.

"What if it came from Xerasel?"

Viugra's expression lit up. Chiara opened her eyes, looking directly at Viugra. Viugra looked away as soon as she did. Whether or not she would admit it, Chiara had Viugra's attention.

"I don't like what you're hinting at."

"You don't have to, honey," Chiara said, "You just gave me what I wanted."

Viugra flinched. Just as soon as she said this, Viugra knew what she meant. The biggest vulnerability of a Charity Angel is their deepest inner desires, and Viugra just revealed it to her!

*D*** it!* Viugra thought.

What happened next transpired within a single second. Chiara dashed towards Viugra in the blink of an eye. Her demonic energy surrounded her hand, which was distorted like before when she was choking Viugra. She was so fast that Viugra hadn't even noticed when the palm of her hand was just an inch from her chest.

In that same second, something imbued in a bright green flame flew from Nerezza and past the trees. It was just as close to Chiara as she was to Viugra. Only Chiara's middle finger reached Viugra's chest before the flame-engulfed figure took hold of Chiara. All of Chiara's momentum was negated as this green figure charged her.

From Viugra's perspective, all she could see was Chiara's silhouette disappear. As soon as it did, the ground exploded to her left. Viugra wasn't prepared for it and jumped at the sound of the explosion. The tailwind from the flaming object finally caught up, shaking the trees violently and toppling Viugra in the process. She grabbed the grass by the tree to keep from being blown away in that single powerful gust of wind.

When everything subsided, Viugra let go of the grass.

"Ugh... what just... happened?"

She rolled over on her back and sat up to face the crater. For a few seconds, nothing happened. It was oddly quiet. Viugra then stumbled to her feet. She decided to walk over to the crater to see what had happened. With each step, she could feel her confidence diminishing and her fear intensifying. Viugra tried to process what was going on, but it seemed like her emotions only distracted her, as they were all over the place.

Was that Chiara? Viugra thought to herself, *What did she... oh god, am I about to die? I... I don't know what to do! No... I can't think like that! Why am I thinking like that? I don't worry! That's... not me, right? Ugh... I don't... feel right...*

Mid thought, Viugra reached the edge of the crater. She slumped down to her knees. Moments later, a shadow flew up into the air. Startled, Viugra's head shot up. Chiara, who now looked severely beat up, had flown up into the air as if to get away from something. She also looked pissed.

"D*** it!" She said aloud, "I thought I had more time than this."

"You thought wrong," a familiar voice spoke from the crater. Viugra knew who it was immediately.

"Mori?" Viugra exclaimed, struggling to hold back her relief and tears. This whole ordeal with Chiara and the demons proved to be trying for Viugra. She had never been put in a situation like this before, where she didn't know what to do. There was always an out, an answer for each problem. Up until a moment ago, she had run out of options. She was vulnerable and had no ability to change what would've happened next. But Mori's intervention was right on time. He was the answer Viugra needed in that moment!

"Are you ok, V?" Mori asked, not turning his head.

"I... I don't know..." Viugra responded. She looked down. Mori's power was surging throughout the graveyard, but Viugra couldn't tell. All she knew was that he was glowing in an intense green flame. She had no idea just how much power he was exuding right now.

"You went through a lot of trouble just to separate us," Mori spoke to Chiara, "Why didn't ya just ask if you wanted to spend some time with her?"

Chiara chuckled to herself.

"We both know how that would've gone, Mr. Skellington."

Mori's head narrowed.

"What do you want with Viugra?"

"Me?" Chiara started, "Well, I just wanted to see what I was working with here. Frankly..."

She looked down at Viugra, who was still fighting to hold her composure.

"...She still has some maturing to do."

"Are you serious?" Mori questioned.

"Yes," Chiara responded, extending her hand towards Viugra, "That's why I was going to invite her to visit Xerasel."

"Xerasel?" Mori repeated, shocked to hear her mention him.

"Boy, aren't you the one liner legend?" Chiara teased. She then shifted her eyes to Viugra's. Viugra was watching her the whole time, but she seemed to have a glazed look in her eyes. Chiara smirked.

"Don't you want to come with me to meet your father?"

"Sure," Viugra blurted. Mori couldn't believe what he had heard.

"Viugra! Have you lost your mind? She's a demon! The only thing she wants is for her own personal gain! Why would you go with her, let alone believe what she says?"

Viugra, somewhat snapping out of her odd lull, absorbed the words Mori spoke to her.

"Oh! I-I mean... no! I would never go with the likes of you, you demon!" Viugra responded. She almost slipped and spoke in her Elizabethan accent. Mori turned and cocked his head at her. If he had flesh, he would be looking at her extremely crazy right now. Viugra scratched her head as she saw his gesture. She looked extremely stressed, as if she was juggling multiple emotions at once. At the same time, Viugra noticed Mori's face had changed.

"Wait, what happened to your..." She started.

"Not now, V!" Mori interrupted, abruptly turning back around. Chiara's smirk stretched out into her abnormal grin once more.

"No worries," Chiara finally said, lowering her hand, "You'll change your mind soon enough, Viugra."

Chiara turned around as she prepared to take off.

"What, is that all?" Mori asked, surprised that she was leaving so soon.

"Yep," Chiara responded, "I'll give her some time to grow. She'll make an excellent addition to our ranks! Ahahahahah!"

As Chiara laughed to herself, she vanished in a cloud of darkness. Viugra sighed, but not one of relief. It was almost as if she regretted something. She didn't have time to figure out what it could be before Mori flew out of the crater and in Viugra's face.

"WHAT THE H*** WERE YOU THINKING?"

"WAAAAAAH!" Viugra responded in utter shock.

"Why would you even entertain going along with a demon? You know how tricky they are!" Mori fumed. At this point, he was back in his usual form.

"I-I'm sorry," Viugra pleaded, "I don't know..."

"You don't know?" Mori nearly exploded a second time. What kept him from doing this was Viugra embracing him. It was his turn to be shocked.

"I... I don't know what happened to me," Viugra started, now sobbing, "I know it's not something I would do, honest! I tried to fight her off, she nearly killed me, she made me feel weird, and..."

"Shhhhh..." Mori hushed, now speaking much more calmly, "Calm down, calm down."

Viugra continued to cry in Mori's shoulder. Although he hadn't known Viugra but for a few hours, he could tell that she wasn't herself.

"Look, I'm sorry for yelling at you. I just don't understand why you would say what you did. Look at me, V."

Viugra lifted her head up to Mori, staring in the holes in his head.

"Why did you say what you did?"

Viugra wiped her face, thinking about what happened around that moment. Then it finally came to her.

"Mori, I... I don't know who I am anymore."

"Whoa, V," Mori started, "That's a bit extreme. It can't be that bad."

"No, seriously!" Viugra stated, "I mean, I know who I am, but I don't at the same time."

"Huh?" Mori said, holding Viugra back a distance.

"It's hard to explain..." Viugra said, dropping her head,"I just know that something's not right with... huh?"

When Viugra looked down at her chest, she noticed something there that wasn't there before.

"Mori... what is this?"

"What is what?" Mori asked. He looked at where she was pointing. Right below her neck was an eerie looking eye symbol. It glowed with a dark magenta hue, and in the center of the pupil was an upside down five-point star. Once Mori saw it, it was clear to him what was wrong with Viugra.

"Oh no…"

"What?" Viugra asked, growing concerned.

Mori looked Viugra in the eyes. She couldn't tell, but he was very worried about her. What was on her chest would make her journey and trials much harder to pass, and Mori knew this more than she did at the moment.

"Viugra, you've been cursed."

Neutralized

"Cursed?"

Mori did not respond right away.

"What are you talking about, Mori?" Viugra continued to question,"That doesn't make sense. I can't be cursed."

Mori let go of Viugra and hung his head. Viugra didn't understand his gesture or what he was alluding to, which was uncomfortable for her.

"I can't tell what you're thinking," Viugra said, a little quieter, "That's... not right..."

As Mori hung his head, he quietly prayed. Viugra, who would normally ask him what's wrong or even speak on what's on his mind, couldn't tell if he was ignoring her or praying. Because of this, she did something completely out of character. She smacked him.

"Ow!" Mori yelped. He looked up at Viugra immediately. She didn't even have an expression on her face.

"What do you mean by cursed, Mori?" Viugra repeated now that she had his attention.

"Why'd you do that?" Mori whined, holding his face, "I was praying!"

"Oh," Viugra said, dryly, "Sorry? I just figured it would get your attention. Are you gonna answer my question though?"

Mori, appalled by Viugra's rather offensive action, had to doubletake, and center himself.

Relax, Mori. Remember, she's cursed...

Mori decided to sit down in the grass. Viugra looked at him confused, now starting to get a bit frustrated by him not answering.

Before she would decide to do something else to him, Mori finally addressed her.

"Sit, V," he said in a gentle but firm tone.

"So, you're not gonna explain yourself?" Viugra asked.

"No, I will," Mori said, still adjusting to her lack of intuition,"That's why I'm asking you to come and sit with me."

Viugra made her way over to Mori and sat next to him. Once she was settled, Mori looked up into the night sky. The quarter moon shone brightly through the night, illuminating the forest around them. If it weren't for the half of it reflecting light, they would be in deep darkness. While keeping his gaze upon the moon, Mori began to explain himself.

"Viugra, you've lived in the heavens most of your life, right?"

"Yeah," said Viugra, "Everyone pretty much pitched in to help raise me."

"Do you know why?"

"Well according to the other angels, my father fell in battle," Viugra responded, becoming slightly skeptical at his questioning, "Ever since, the High One delegated Angels from each race to see over my growth."

Mori's head was still lifted to the sky, his gaze fixated on the moon still.

"This is all true."

"Why are you asking me about that?" Viugra finally asked a question back, "I don't see how this is connected to me being cursed."

"V," Mori started, figuring something else out as they talked, "I say this out of love: The kind of curse you have shouldn't affect your intelligence. And yet, you still haven't connected the dots?"

"Uh... well..." Viugra mumbled. Truth is, she didn't seem to understand herself. This was all still new to her. However, Mori knew what was going on.

"V... you've been relying on your powers this whole time, haven't you?"

"Huh?" Viugra said, surprised, "Have I?"

"Hoh lawd," Mori said, putting his hand over his skull, "Why didn't Azariel warn me about this? This is going to be harder than I thought..."

"Hey!" Viugra shouted, now feeling offended, "Don't talk as if there's no hope for me! And I thought you told me not to use the lord's name in vain? You did it again!"

"Oh," Mori said, surprised, "Did I?"

"Yes, you did!" Viugra responded. Clearly, Mori's back-sass went clear over her head. Mori hung his head, disappointed.

She didn't even catch that? Aww, it's getting worse by the minute!

"And will you get to the point?" Viugra said, now irritated by Mori's dodginess, "You still haven't said anything about this curse! I'm this close to beating it out of you!"

Viugra expressed how little patience she had left with him with her fingers. Mori looked at Viugra, now legitimately shocked at her response.

"V, relax. There's no need to get worked up. I was just about to tell you. You do realize you aren't acting like yourself lately, right?"

Viugra, realizing that she just blew up on Mori, took a deep breath and sighed.

"I'm sorry, Mori. I… I can't believe I got worked up so easily. But please get to the point. I need to know what this is all about."

Viugra pointed to her chest as she stated this, the curse mark still illuminated. Mori sighed and nodded his head.

"Alright, Viugra. No more games. I'll get to the point."

"Thank you," Viugra responded. She repositioned herself to face Mori. Mori did the same. Without wasting any more time, Mori finally unveiled the ominous truth about Viugra's family.

"Viugra, you aren't a real angel."

"What?" she responded, more so appalled than shocked, "How could you say-?"

"No, listen," Mori cut in, not giving her a chance to get worked up again, "You do have angel blood in your veins. But that's not all."

Viugra listened silently, heart beating faster in anticipation.

"You also have the blood of a human. You're... a Nephilim."

"A... Nephilim...?"

Viugra's heart seemed to stop at this. Though she didn't really know what this meant, for some reason her heart seemed to.

"...Wh-what does that mean exactly?"

"You should know, V," Mori continued, "Nephilim are the offspring of both an angel and a human being, most commonly a male angel and a female person."

"You... can't be serious, right?" Viugra responded. She held her chest, as her heart seemed to be hurting at this breaking news.

"I am," Mori said, "Not only is this the reason why you are cursed, but also the reason you're going through your trial."

"I can't believe this..." Viugra muttered to herself. Mori noticed how heartbroken she was but continued to explain the rest.

"Do you know why you're going through this trial?"

"...I thought I did..." Viugra said in a low tone. Mori could tell that Viugra was starting to get it, but just to clear it up, he explained it anyways.

"Well, I'll tell you. The rules for angel and human relationships are strict, and an angel sleeping with a human is a big taboo. Those who have slept with humans are condemned, stripped of their holy powers, and cast into Hell, reborn as their demon counterpart. In the event that a child will be conceived, they are taken by heavenly hosts and raised as such until they reach the age of accountability. They are then put through the Trial of Reverence to test their morality. If they succeed, they are allowed to keep their angelic powers and reside in the heavens. But if they are to fail, they must live the rest of their life as a human with little to no powers remaining."

Viugra remained silent as Mori finished his explanation. Mori could tell that she was having a hard time taking in everything.

"...you ok, V?"

"...I'm sorry, Mori," Viugra responded. She stood up and began to walk away.

"H-hey!" he started, gracefully hopping to his feet as well, "Where are you about to go, V?"

"I need some time alone," Viugra responded without turning around.

"You aren't going to do something crazy, are you?" Mori asked out of concern.

"No," Viugra answered, "Please, just let me be alone."

Before he could protest, Viugra ran off. Mori was stuck reaching out for her. He could have easily caught her and tried to calm her, but he didn't. For some reason, he felt that she would be alright. Instead, he sat and waited, clasping his bony hands together with a sense of conviction.

I'm sorry, V. I know how hard this is on you. Maybe I should've waited to tell you. But I promise, you aren't alone. I'm going to help you get through this trial no matter what it takes. I won't fail again.

✲✲✲✲✲✲✲✲

Several hours passed and the sun was starting to rise. Viugra hadn't returned.

In the midst of his waiting, Mori ended up repairing the land where he had grounded Chiara earlier that morning. As he was patching up the ground, he had his left forearm bone in his right hand with the attached hand balled into a fist. He was singing into it like a microphone. Of course, his vocals left much to be desired.

"Fallen stars from the heavens above, you'll one day return to respite."

He flicked his hand out as if throwing something at one of the craters in the ground. It instantly returned to its former appearance. He continued to sing to himself as he pranced over to another hole.

"But stray away from the luminous void..."

"...yield not to the alluring black light."

Mori nearly jumped out of his angel robes when he heard a voice finish his verse. He turned around and realized that Viugra had finally returned. She looked way better than she did when she first left.

"Viugra!?" Mori exclaimed. He reattached his bones to his arm with haste, and Viugra laughed to herself. It seemed like she was getting a kick out of seeing him flustered.

"H-how long have you been there?"

"Long enough to know what you were singing."

Viugra bent over with her right fist up to her mouth as if she were singing in a microphone.

"Fallen stars from the heavens above!"

Then she flung her hand out towards the ground as if she were patching up holes like he was. Clearly, she was making fun of him. Mori couldn't believe what he was seeing.

"V... you're acting like a child..."

"What? Too much?" Viugra asked. She was starting to feel like she had offended him.

"Oh no!" Mori responded quickly, "It's not that. You weren't like this earlier this morning."

Viugra smiled.

"I know. There was a lot of things I had to process last night alone. I'm sorry I ran away from you like that."

"Don't worry about it," Mori said, "I'm just glad you seem to be doing better." "Something like that," Viugra said.

"Well, if you don't mind me asking," Mori began to question, "What did you do when you left?"

"Well," Viugra started, "I ran some distance out and fell out in the grass for a while. To be honest, I was in tears. I hadn't felt a heartache like that ever in my life."

"Hmm... I bet..." Mori responded, starting to feel bad again.

"I started to think about my dad," Viugra continued, "I thought about the stories one of the angels used to tell me about him. He was the leader of the Charity Angels for a long time, since he had acquired Archangel status. He had won many battles against demons trying to corrupt humanity for decades, maybe even centuries. Everyone regarded him as the most powerful angel under the High One."

"Right."

"It was hard for me to picture someone so honorable falling so far. I tried to believe that what you told me wasn't true. I know you wouldn't lie to me, but that's how I felt earlier."

"Don't worry," Mori assured, "I might've thought you were lying to me if I were in your shoes."

"Thanks for understanding," Viugra continued, "But you know, while I kept trying to hold on to the way I viewed my father, I realized something."

"And what was that?"

"...I was falling asleep."

Mori fell over. He wasn't expecting her to say this.

"You were falling asleep. That was your big revelation?"

"Yep," Viugra said, "So, I fell asleep."

"Congratulations, V," Mori played along, "You learned the importance of sleep. I'm so glad you were enlightened by this!"

"Most definitely," Viugra continued. Mori put his hand over his face, forgetting that she was still dense. Or... at least he thought.

"SIKE!" Viugra exclaimed, "I knew you were being sarcastic!"

"Whaaaaat!?" Mori yelped in surprise. Viugra laughed to herself.

"I gotcha good, didn't I?"

"Hahahah," Mori laughed, still a bit confused, "Yeeeah, ya got me. How did you change from yesterday?"

"I might've been joking, but I was also serious," Viugra said, now walking over to Mori to help him up, "I needed sleep."

At first, Mori wasn't understanding. But it didn't take him but a second to figure it out.

"Oh, right! I forgot; you are drained of most of your power right now."

"Exactly," Viugra continued, "I used up a lot of my energy fighting Chiara, and after she cursed me, I was pretty much as vulnerable as a human. Still am, honestly."

"On top of that," Mori added, "You were emotionally drained from everything you heard between her and I, correct?"

"Indeed," Viugra responded, this time in her Elizabethan accent.

"That makes all the sense," Mori agreed, "I'm sorry I overwhelmed you like that, V."

"Don't sweat it," she responded normally.

The two looked at each other cheerfully, then watched as the sun was continuing to rise. After a few moments of silence, Mori thought of something and turned to Viugra to ask her.

"If you feel comfortable talking about it now, may I ask you something?"

"Sure."

"What will you do now, now that you know more about your father?"

Viugra thought for a moment, then turned to Mori to answer him.

"I'm going to find him and ask him what happened."

Mori cocked his head to the side, more so from concern.

"V, you do know what that means right?"

"Yeah," she said, "It means I'm probably going to have to go to Hell to do that."

"That's a very risky thing to try," Mori said, "You could easily end up turning into a demon and failing this trial."

"I know, I know," Viugra said, running her fingers through her hair, "But that's where my heart's leading me. It's always longed to finally meet my father one day. And now that I know where and what he is, I want to find him even more."

She turned to Mori as she spoke from her heart.

"He may be a demon now, but that doesn't change the fact that he was once an Archangel of the Charity Angels. I want to hear from him why he committed the taboo. I need to know what kind of angel he truly was."

Mori could see the conviction in Viugra's eyes. He could tell that she was truly back to her usual self, and yet he could see a foolish end. But this is the dangerous fate of a Charity Angel whose desires were tempted. Mori could see that there was no point in arguing with her about this. So, he improvised.

"Alright, V," he started, "I can see that there's no way of changing your mind. But I do have a proposal for you."

"A proposal?" Viugra asked.

"Yes," Mori started, putting his hand on her shoulder, "You must continue this trial. There's no positive outcome for you if you abandon this task. And if you do that, you will eventually meet someone who can help you find your father."

"Really?" Viugra said, getting a bit excited.

"Yep," Mori continued, "Once you pass enough of your trials, you will end up meeting your mother."

"My... mother?" Viugra said. This whole time, she was so concerned about meeting her father that she didn't even give a second thought about her mother.

"Wow... this whole time I hadn't even thought about her."

"Right?" Mori began to tease, "What kind of daughter are you?"

"A worthless one," Viugra said, now moping, "How could I forget my mama?"

"Now, now," Mori continued, "You are remorseful about it. I'll charge it to your mind and not your heart."

"Okay!" Viugra said, snapping right out of her trivial guilt. Mori shook his head.

"Well, that didn't last long."

"Let's go then!" Viugra continued, "I'm ready to get this over with. If I have to prove to them that I'm worthy enough to be an angel, then I'll do anything to get it done."

Yeah, that's what I'm worried about, Mori thought to himself.

"Alright then. You do remember where we were supposed to be heading right?"

"Do I remember?" Mori chuckled, "I'm the one guiding you. Of course, I do! And from what I can tell…"

Mori looked Viugra dead in her eyes. Viugra stepped back a bit, feeling a little creeped out. It seemed like he was staring into her soul.

"…You've already met her."

"I have?" Viugra said shocked. She thought about what happened last night, and immediately she knew who it was. Instantly, she began to feel regret.

"…Nooooooo…"

"Yeeeeeeeesssssss," Mori mocked, "You're gonna be the guardian angel of Bailey Rooke!"

The Demon Girl

"HUH?"

Bailey quickly raised her head from her desk, groggy from being awoken from a pleasant sleep. Hair in a frizz, she looked up at the blurry figure who called her name. A multitude of laughs and giggles erupted from all around her. She turned her head, scanning the room and scrunching her eyebrows as she was waking up.

"Enough, class!" the female teacher snapped, "I've been teaching this stuff all school year long and clearly few of you retained anything I've taught you. You need to learn to pay attention in life. Now..."

Bailey finally woke up enough to be coherent. It was Tuesday, the 25th of July, and finals were beginning tomorrow. She was too tired to really care about what her math teacher was talking about, so she took a nap. This was nothing new, as she had been doing this for the past few months now.

"...Bailey," the teacher continued, "Wake up and solve for x."

Bailey looked up at the board. They were reviewing for tomorrow's finals. As she studied the problem, she raised an eyebrow. The other students who were laughing at her before watched her in anticipation, seeing if she would get the answer this time. The problem looked like this:

$$6x*2 / 2x = 6$$

One of the male flunkies who hadn't been there for most of the semester leaned over to his friend.

"There's no way she'll get this. She never pays attention!"

"You still think that?" the other guy responded, *"I bet you ten bucks she will!"*

"You're on! And you better pay up too!" he responded.

"Two," Bailey finally answered. The class was holding their breath.

"Two is your answer?" the teacher asked.

"Yeah, yeah…" Bailey said, dropping her head back into her arms to sleep again.

"Two is the correct answer. Well done, Bailey," the teacher said, sighing.

"WHAAAAT? AWW COME. ON!" the class was in an outrage.

"ENOUGH SHOUTING!" the teacher roared. She pointed at several students.

"Vicky, John, and Sean! Go to the office!"

"But Mrs. Henry…!"

"No buts! Get *your* butts to the office!" Mrs. Henry said with heated sass, "I'm tired of telling you three specifically to pay attention and shut your mouths! And you three are the main ones distracting the class! Get out!"

The three grabbed their stuff and walked out of the room to the office. On the way out, John paused and turned around to Sean.

*"You owe me ten dollars,, B****."*

*"Man, F*** off!"*

"OUT!"

They finally exited the room. Some of the girls in the class were giggling.

"You'd best stop laughing or you'll be joining them, girls," Mrs. Henry warned. The girls went quiet immediately.

Mrs. Henry walked to her desk to contact the office about the three students she sent down there. As she was dialing the phone, the whole class was quiet.

"Every last one of you better be quiet while I'm on the phone. Study your guides until I'm done. If I even hear a whisper, you're gone too. Do you understand?"

"Yeeeesss Mrs. Henry," the class responded, half groaning. Everyone was looking ready to get out of that class. Everyone but a few students, a sleeping Bailey, and a boy two seats behind her. This boy's intense gaze was locked on Bailey ever since she answered that math problem.

How does she do that? She's always knocked out, don't never pay attention in class, and then just wakes up knowing the answer?

Bailey shifted her head to the other side in slumber.

...I gotta know. How does she do that?

Mrs. Henry finished her phone call and hung up the phone. She stood up and walked to the center of the classroom again. She glanced at the clock and realized that class would be over in less than a minute, so she sighed and gave her final remarks.

"Alright class. I've been very disappointed with a majority of you this year. Lots of you have been playing around instead of focusing in class. I know who's trying in class and who's not."

The class shuffled a bit.

I also know who doesn't need to try, Mrs. Henry thought to herself, looking at Bailey.

"You all have less than twenty-four hours to study your guides and be ready for your tests tomorrow. I'm genuinely scared of how you're doing in your other classes. If you don't pass your tests, you'll be seeing me for another year. If you don't want that, I suggest you all take this seriously. Also..."

The last few seconds of her speech was spoken in a much lighter tone.

"Make sure you get plenty of rest and eat a good breakfast before you come in tomorrow!"

As soon as she said tomorrow, the bell rang. Everybody in class got up immediately and rushed to the doors. Bailey woke up once more, realizing that the class period was over. She picked up her unopened backpack and began to glide her way out herself. She didn't even bother taking out her study guide.

At Duncan Middle School, everyone wore similar uniforms. They required all their students to dress up using the apparel available with a store they partnered with. Aside from a white shirt or blouse with the school logo on it, they allowed their students to change up the color of either their ties, skirts, or slacks. Sometimes the students would wear sweater vests with the school logo on it. In Bailey's case, she wore a white dress shirt, peach and teal striped tie, and teal slacks with peach and teal stripes along the sides. She didn't really like wearing skirts.

Before she could make it out of the classroom, Mrs. Henry stopped her.

"Come here for a minute, Bailey."

Bailey stopped and pivoted her body just enough to squint at Mrs. Henry.

"Don't look at me like that," Mrs. Henry started, "I won't be long."

Bailey made her way down to the front of the class. On her way, she felt eyes on her back. She quickly glanced over her shoulder. The boy who sat behind her was still there, packing up his stuff. His attire was similar to hers, but his dress shirt sleeves were full length. He also had on the black sweater vest with white trim and had blue instead of red in his tie and slacks. He had all kinds of homework, folders, and pencils sprawled out on his desk, so packing up was taking him a while. Prior to loading his backpack, he was staring at Bailey while she was heading up. He hoped she didn't see him staring. Mrs. Henry noticed her stop and realized he was still there.

"You know you can leave now, right Charles?"

"Yeah, I know," Charles responded, "I'm packing up."

Mrs. Henry gently smiled.

"Okay. Don't be late for your next class."

"I won't."

Bailey turned back towards Mrs. Henry and finished her journey between the desks to reach her.

"Bailey," Mrs. Henry began.

"Mmhmm," Bailey said, still waking up.

"That's not how you respond to me, Bailey," she corrected, "Listen. You are very smart Bailey. You get all As in class and pass every test. I don't need to tell you that.

Then why are we here…? Bailey thought to herself.

"I know this class is probably boring to you, but I needed you to help me help the class."

Bailey, fully awake now, scrunched her lips at this.

"I don't mean that literally," Mrs. Henry clarified, "You sleeping in class gives the other students the idea that they can goof off and still get their grades too. Whether or not you believe it, you're one of the leaders in this class."

I don't get that vibe from them, but ok, Bailey thought to herself.

"It doesn't really matter for my class what I'm telling you. But when you get to the High School, just think about that. You have more influence than you think. I know a leader when I see one Bailey. Just, please… try to act like one from now on."

"Sure, Mrs. Henry," Bailey responded.

Mrs. Henry sighed.

"I also know a liar when I see one."

Bailey smirked.

"Alright, Bailey. I won't bother you anymore for the rest of the week. I would say good luck tomorrow, but I know you'll pass. Go get lunch."

"Okie doke," Bailey responded.

Pointless talk, but whatever.

Bailey turned around and headed to the exit. She noticed Charles hadn't left yet still. He just finished loading his backpack by the time she was passing him. She side-eyed him as she walked by. Charles looked away. He made himself look way too obvious. Bailey didn't bother confronting him about it. She continued out the door to lunch and thought to herself.

Stalker.

☼☼☼☼☼☼☼☼

At Duncan Middle School, there were three lunch periods. Bailey had the second. It was about noon, and ten of her thirty minutes to eat were already used up. On her way to the cafeteria, there were students in the halls who needed to be in class. They were trying to skip. When Bailey walked past them, she could feel their whispers radiating negativity on her back.

Ain't that the demon girl? I thought she has lunch.

*Maybe she's up to something. You know she left a surprise in someone's locker for calling her a B****. Maybe she's doing it again?*

Wouldn't doubt it. She's aggressive.

She kinda cute tho. I'd smash.

*You idiot! You'd really sleep with the devil? You crazy as h***.*

Bailey turned around, coldly staring at the kids. She didn't know what they were saying exactly, but she didn't need to. She knew what it was about. The kids turned around quickly and began to walk away. Bailey caught up to them and placed her hands on two of the three's shoulders.

"...uuhhhh..." one of the boys stuttered, trying to think of a cover up, "Wh-what's good, Bethy?"

The girl who was ahead of them froze and turned her head around in fear. Turns out, it was the same three who were sent to the office. They were trying to avoid going.

"Bethy, huh?" Bailey said, "Cute. Too bad it ain't my name."

"Oh, word?" Sean was sweating, "My bad."

"Yeah, your bad," Bailey repeated.

"S-so, what's up?" John questioned, "Y-you tryna hang?"

"Oh no, not at all," Bailey said, letting the two go, "Just wanted to say hi."

"R-really...?" Vicky said, surprised.

Bailey turned around and smirked.

"...nope."

With her left hand on her hip, she knocked on a classroom door with her other. The three were terrified. Bailey just knocked on the door of one of the orneriest teachers in the school. She just set them up.

"Why would you do that?" John yelped. Sean and Vicky covered his mouth.

"Shut up! You're gonna get us exposed!"

"Who just knocked on my door?"

The door had flung open, and an older man stepped out. He immediately noticed the three kids outside his door. Vicky spoke up quickly.

"It wasn't us! It was-"

Before she could even point at her, Bailey was so far down the hall that the teacher wouldn't believe her if she told him. The three were astounded.

How did she run away so quickly? That was fast!

Sh-she was so quiet with it too!!

*She petty? H*** yeah! I'm on that a-*

"I'm writing all three of ya up!!!"

The three kids sulked as a triumphant Bailey walked off to lunch.

✡✡✡✡✡✡✡

At this point, Bailey only had about twelve minutes to get some food and eat. Realizing this, she made an effort to go straight for the lunch line. She was hungry too. Once in the cafeteria, her stomach growled at her in frustration. She was starting to feel a bit more irritable. Being tired and hungry is never a good combo.

Aside from the day's lunch special, there were other options to eat. Bosco sticks, wraps, and pretzels were a few of the options available. Unfortunately for Bailey, she didn't have enough to get the better options. She only had two bucks and some loose change on her. If she hadn't bought all that food for the homeless yesterday, she would've had enough to last for the week. Even so, she didn't complain. Instead of wishing on a better option, she settled for the watery mashed potatoes, rough green beans, and mystery meat that was served cheapest.

Eight minutes left. Bailey searched for a table to eat at. Most of them were full, as the second lunch (or B lunch) was the largest out of the three. There were a few seats open at three nearby tables, but Bailey really didn't want to sit next to those ungrateful brats. The way she was feeling, she knew she might haul off on one of them if they crossed her. Even so, she didn't have time to waste so she groaned as she plopped in the first open seat.

The volume at the table instantly went down a few decibels. It was a table full of girls. They all looked at Bailey from the sides of their faces. Bailey didn't even look at them.

If I didn't know better, I'd've thought you were being quiet for me to eat in peace. Too bad I do.

The girls gossiped amongst themselves, then returned to their conversation.

Three minutes left. Bailey was almost there. It was amazing that they hadn't pissed her off up to this point. She managed to finish her food before the lunch period was over with. Now she just had to wait until the food fully digested so she wouldn't be so irritable. She tossed her empty tray in the trash next to the table, then laid her head down until the bell rang. She could hear the other girl's conversation as she closed her eyes.

"This food's so nasty," one girl said, spooning up her soupy potatoes.

"I know right? Like, we need better chefs or something," said another girl.

"That's why I get Bosco sticks all the time."

"I just deal with it. I know I'm gonna be hungry eventually."

"Why didn't you get some Bosco sticks?" the third girl said, taking only the second bite out of her food.

"I don't have enough for it," the first girl said, miserably spooning up another bite of her potatoes. They weren't even seasoned. She nearly gagged on them.

"You can't afford to be eating Bosco sticks anyways, lumpy," the second girl teased.

Bailey breathed heavily. The other girls didn't even notice.

"Shut up!" the first girl said, angry and hurt from this statement. She was a little plump, but not enough to be called lumpy.

"Please, you ain't gonna do nothin'," the second girl said, "Just sit there and eat your veggies."

"Careful," the third girl said, taking her third bite, "You don't want her to bite your head off!"

The two girls laughed, getting up from the table and throwing their trays away. One and a half Bosco sticks, two apples, a half-eaten wrap, and two half-drunk pop bottles fell to the bottom of the can. As they hit the bottom, a powerful left hook hit the second girl straight in her jawline. The first girl watched in horror as the second girl fell and an even stronger right hook took out the third girl. Everyone nearby started to turn around and watch. One minute before lunch was over, and Bailey couldn't contain the seething rage within her.

The third girl was knocked out cold, but the second girl got back up and attempted to punch Bailey from the back. It didn't work. Bailey swayed to her left a bit, grabbed the girl's arm, then pulled her over her back, using the girl's momentum to flip her out in front and slam her on the ground next to the other one. The kids nearby lost their minds.

"DAAAAAYUM!"

"OH MY GOD!"

"BROOOO, WHAAAAT?"

The second girl Bailey flipped onto the ground reeled in agony. If Bailey wasn't short and as low to the ground as she was when she flipped her, she would've messed her back up severely. This kind of behavior is what earned her the label of "demon girl". She was merciless.

"Wasting F***ing food AND being a B**** to someone not up to your fake a** standards of beauty? I would've tossed you both in the trash if I could've! Pissed me off."

Several of the school's staff came in to see what all the commotion was about. They found Bailey standing over two girls sprawled out on the floor in misery. Bailey didn't look sorry for one second. She knew what she did and didn't deny it. The teachers looked at her and shook their heads.

"...this again, Bailey?"

Bailey just turned her head and huffed.

And then the bell rang.

The Miracle Child

At about 10 A.M., Mori and Viugra finally reached the outer part of Nerezza, where they were last night. It took Viugra longer to make the journey, as she was getting used to being human. Being without her angelic powers wasn't something she was used to. Despite her lack of power, she still had enough energy to get this far with minimal exhaustion.

The entire trip to Bailey's home was rather quiet compared to before, and Mori noticed this. It was clear to him that Viugra wasn't her usual self. She would've talked to him about something by now. Instead, she was deep in thought for most of the journey. This was causing Mori to grow concerned. The manipulation of the curse could potentially lead her down the path of failure. He didn't want that to happen. When they were just a few blocks away from the house, Mori decided to stop Viugra to check her state of mind.

"Hold on a sec, V," Mori spoke.

Viugra continued to walk. Mori cocked his head to the side.

Is… she ignoring me? I'm sure I spoke loud enough. Or is she just that deep in thought?

He tried again, a little louder this time.

"Viugra, wait up!"

She still continued to walk; arms crossed in thinking posture. She was definitely deep in thought.

Mori sighed, then zipped in front of her. Even then, she continued to walk until she bumped into him.

"Whoa!" Viugra finally spoke, "What the heck did I just bump into?"

"Um, me?" Mori said.

"Me?" Viugra repeated. The sound of Mori's voice cued recognition, "Mori?"

"Yes!" Mori responded, "You can't see me anymore, can you?"

"Nope," Viugra said, "I can only hear you."

Figures, Mori thought to himself, *The curse is getting worse...*

Viugra looked around for a moment, a bit confused.

"Why'd you stop me? This doesn't look like the place."

"Come with me for a moment."

"I still can't see you, y'know."

"Don't worry," Mori reassured, reaching around Viugra's shoulders. He guided her down a nearby alley. It wasn't the same one where the homeless people were, but not far from it. Once they were far away enough where no one would be looking, Mori let down his concealment arte.

"Does this have something to do with my dad?" Viugra asked.

"No, V. I just want to know something."

"Oooook," she said goofily, placing her hands on her waist, "What's up?"

"Do you have any idea what the Trial of Reverence is about?"

"To prove I can stay in the heavens, right?" she said, "That and find my father."

"Yes and, well, no," Mori said, "You're partially right. There's more to it than that."

"It doesn't have to do with my father?" Viugra asked, squinting and raising an eyebrow.

"Well... for you, it does."

"Ah, ok."

Geeze, Mori thought, *She's hell-bent on finding her father now. If she ends up thinking that she won't find her father by completing this trial, she won't want to do it. And given what the first trial for her is...*

"If that's all, can we go now?" Viugra asked.

"Hold on, V!" Mori said, "Patience is a virtue."

"I suppose," Viugra shrugged, "I just want to get this over with as soon as possible. The sooner I finish this trial, the sooner I find my parents."

Mori sighed.

"Look, V. If you don't understand what the purpose of the trial is, how do you expect to overcome it? You'll be one less step from reaching your dad."

She thought for a moment, then nodded in agreement.

"You're right, Mori," she said, folding her arms, "So then, since I apparently don't know, what *is* it about?"

Mori started to answer her but stopped just as quickly.

"I… you have to figure it out for yourself, Viugra."

"Seriously?" Viugra said, disappointed, "What, you don't know either or something?"

"No, it's not that," Mori said. He turned his head towards the sky.

"If I were to straight up tell you, I'd be giving you the answers to the test. I can't help you cheat, now can I?"

"Well, I don't see the problem," Viugra exclaimed, getting a bit annoyed, "Heck, why'd you even bring it up if you couldn't tell me?"

"I was hoping you'd already know," Mori said. Then Mori grew a bit suspicious.

"You did say they taught you all kinds of stuff up there, right. So how come you don't know that?"

"Simple: they never told me," Viugra shot back. Mori cocked his head.

"You sure?"

"No, why would I…" Viugra began, then paused as something came to mind, "…um, well…"

"Heh," Mori chuckled, "V, did you almost lie to me?"

"N-no!" Viugra stuttered, flustered, "Okay, I miiiiight've cut Azariel off when he started talking bad about my father. I didn't know he was explaining what this trial was about."

Mori could tell that she was speaking the truth.

"I appreciate your honesty, V." Mori said to her.

You might be losing your sense of right and wrong, but at least you still hold true to being honest. But even so, at this rate…

Mori raised his hand towards Viugra. Viugra blinked, trying to understand his gesture.

"Viugra," Mori began, asking in a serious tone, "Can I trust you to stay in this alley for about, I don't know, five-ish minutes?"

Viugra looked at him crazy.

"For what? I'm on a mission, Mori. We gotta get a move on!"

Mori sighed once again. Before she could even react, Mori created a man-sized arte circle that radically revolved and flipped around her. It then slowed down until eventually stopping in place, and with it, Viugra's movement halted as well.

H-Hey! Viugra tried to shout. But nothing came out. Her mouth was restrained as well.

"Sorry, V," Mori apologized, "You're just gonna have to trust me."

Suddenly, a bright blue circle with unique patterns around its circumference formed at the base of Mori's feet. Faster than the blink of an eye, Mori quietly disappeared in the glowing light that shot up from it. The light vanished before reaching a height noticeable by others walking down the street nearby.

Viugra was stuck in the middle of the alley, unable to move until Mori returned.

✲✲✲✲✲✲✲✲

When Mori reappeared, he was no longer surrounded by rundown buildings and broken streets. Instead, he appeared in a place brightly illuminated and yet gentle on the eyes. The ground beneath his feet wasn't ground at all, but rather white clouds so soft and loose-looking, you'd think he would fall through at any moment. In front of Mori was a stone platform with gold trim and marble tiling, shaped in the form of a circle about three meters in diameter, and at the center was a pedestal that closely resembled that of an altar.

Not long after he appeared, a bright light descended from above the platform and gracefully hovered above the pedestal. The light faded away peacefully, simultaneously revealing an angel clad in a pastel green armor. A magnificent longsword with a golden hilt dangled on his left waist, and a fancy buckler on his right. The man's left hand rested on his sword hilt while his right rested to his side. His four wings spread out behind him in a near "X" shape, one of the few displays signaling the presence of an Archangel. The medium skin-toned angel finally landed on the pedestal, his short blonde hair settling from the descent.

"Moriel," the angel spoke, "How dost thou?"

"Sup bro," Mori responded.

"Ugh, you messed it up!" the angel spoke, disappointed, "You were supposed to do it my way this time, remember?"

"Whoops! I guess I forgot," Mori said, rubbing the back of his head.

"Fret not," the angel continued, "Well, what brings you to the heavens today? Is it about your new protégé?"

"You read me like a book," Mori said, "Though, it wasn't that hard to figure out, was it?"

"I knew you'd come eventually," he said, "Has she been giving you a hard time already?"

"No," Mori said initially. But then he thought about the last few hours he spent with her.

"…Well… a lil."

"Well, speak your mind brother," the angel sat on the pedestal, "I'm always willing to let you vent to me."

"Where do I even begin, bro?" Mori started, also popping a squat.

Mori explained everything that happened since Viugra came to Earth. He talked about how she was a bold character and was pretty laid back about most things. Mori even mentioned how quickly they seemed to bond. Azariel laughed at some of the goofy moments Mori already had with Viugra. Mori also talked about the strong empathetic traits he felt from her helping the homeless man. Eventually, the conversation shifted to the reason Mori was there: Viugra's curse.

"I tried my best to reach her before anything happened, but I was a second too late."

Azariel was listening intently, fingers intertwined under his chin.

"This is why I've come to talk to you," Mori began his plea, "I wish to seek mercy on behalf of Viugra. Because of this unexpected interference, she's been put at an unintended disadvantage for completing the trial."

Azariel closed his eyes, then sat up from his thinking posture. He rested his clasped hands in his lap as he prepared to respond to Mori.

"I understand well what you have told me, brother. Surely, this is a misfortune upon Viugra's journey. It pains me to learn that the denizens of Hell seek malice upon our heavenly sister. However… "

Mori's head lowered a bit. He knew what Azariel would say next.

"…I, too, cannot interfere with her trial. Regardless of what may happen during her test, no angel can directly interfere with her trials. We may ask her questions or divulge minor hints, even protect her from certain dangers outside of those within the trials. But we cannot give her the answers, nor provide any divine assistance."

"But brother, surely there's some work around here!" Mori said. Azariel's eyes narrowed.

"You mean to manipulate the process?"

"No, of course not," Mori said, "Look — the way things are now, Viugra has little to no chance of even passing the first trial. And you know as well as I do that only a handful have ever passed the third trial, let alone complete the entire test."

"Certainly," Azariel confirmed, "We have had thousands of Nephilim undergo the Trials of Reverence, but less than 100 have passed the third trial. And the number of those who have completed the trials altogether is nine, two of which we know succeeded by an extremely narrow margin."

Azariel's tone sounded grim as he spoke of the statistics of the trial's success rate. Mori also seemed to exude an air of discomfort. He seemed to remember well how the two trials concluded, and the cost of the success behind each. Mori shook those thoughts and continued to plead his case.

"And that's not all. As you also know, the order of each trial is tailored to each Nephilim who partakes in them, ranging from the least difficult to the most. And Viugra has the hardest first trial out of all the options."

Azariel sighed and nodded in agreement. He knew well what she was up against.

"Viugra is no slouch, certainly. But even so, I want to help Viugra as much as I can, but I–"

"Enough, Moriel," Azariel interrupted with a calm yet commanding voice. A brief moment of silence followed. Mori leaned back, sighing in the process. He realized that he was getting a bit worked up.

"You seem more distraught about your new mentee this time, and you've barely spent a day with her. Are you, perhaps, having flashbacks?"

Mori remained silent at this. Azariel didn't press any further into it.

"Regardless, you'd do well to maintain your composure. You cannot afford to fail again."

"Yes... you're right, Azariel," Mori responded, somberly. Though Azariel was his brother, he was also his leader. For a moment, Mori had forgotten this. It was nothing against Mori for Azariel to correct him. It was only a matter of upholding order and respect. After Mori calmed down, Azariel sighed once more and eased himself.

"As I said before, we cannot directly intervene in any Trial of Reverence. Viugra must endure this trial by her own strength, skill, and will."

Mori gritted his teeth.

"I… understand."

Azariel smiled.

"…However… she has already insured a means of fighting the curse."

Mori seemed to gain hope.

"Truly?"

He spoke in a near Elizabethan accent.

"Heh," Azariel chuckled, "Now you decide to play along?"

Azariel stood up, closing his eyes as if he were praying. A few seconds later, he rose his right hand, palm facing up as if to receive something. A light with four points darted from another part of the heavens at an amazing speed. The sound of a child's voice singing happily rang through the air. After whirring around a bit, it finally hovered in Azariel's palm and became silent.

"Before she was cursed, Viugra left an Impression on this creature. Since she "impressed" him, he technically belongs to her. She is very fortunate that no one else claimed him before now."

"Ah, I see," Mori spoke, "And because he has her Impression, he also adopted the alignment and condition of her soul at the time!"

"Indeed," Azariel continued, "It is not much different from a newborn seeing its mother for the first time."

Azariel sent the light over to Mori, and Mori stood and received it into his own bony hands.

"Perhaps all she needs is a constant reminder of who she was. I cannot guarantee that this will work, but it does increase the odds.

Speaking of reminders, remind her to name him to officially gain guardianship over him. Have her find someone who can create a Particeps Reliquia; since she doesn't have any power to conduct the rite, she'll need it."

"Will do," Mori said.

"One more thing," Azariel spoke, "Keep an eye on it. It only recently converted from demon status. It will take about a week before it can maintain its alignment on its own."

"Makes sense," Mori said, "Thank you, brother."

"Thank not I," Azariel said, "Just be glad Viugra performed a self-miracle."

Mori glowed and vanished to return to Viugra on Earth. After he was gone, Azariel shifted to a thinking posture.

That Putto was very young. It seems almost deliberate that Chiara would bring a Cambion into a fight against one of Moriel's pupils. Chiara… what are you up to?

✲✲✲✲✲✲✲✲

Meanwhile, in the depths of Hell, Chiara made her way through a dark corridor which was barely lit at all. Her creepy smile stretched her face wide as she trekked to her destination. Though her pace was persistent, she was in agonizing pain. The heat in this realm was no ordinary scorcher. It was designed by the High One to punish those who were wicked in their ways. For this reason, agonizing screams could be heard throughout the entire circle she was in.

Eventually, Chiara reached a rather claustrophobic room that was only slightly more lit than the corridor that led up to it. Though it was hard to see, a figure in the back of the room stirred a bit when she entered.

"I'm back, my liege. Though, I'm still not sure I should call you that."

The figure weakly lifted his head and opened his eyes to view Chiara. His pupils were scarlet red, which were different from Chiara's amber glow. Not much else could be seen in this dark room.

"Chiara..." the man whispered, "How did it go?"

Chiara fell backwards and flapped her wings gently to hover in a relaxed position.

"So far, so good," Chiara answered, "Though it's a matter of perspective, really."

"Details, Chiara," the man growled.

"Oh relax. I groped her like you wanted. Now she's all confused. How long do you think it'll be before her preference changes?"

The dark figure released an immense amount of power from within himself. The wave of corrupted energy slammed Chiara against the wall in the back of the room. She let out a loud groan as the stone wall crumbled on top of her, revealing the outside world, full of countless demons flying about. Chiara climbed out of the rubble and dusted herself off. She then wiped the blood from her mouth as the figure continued to speak.

"I know you didn't complete the curse, B****. I can see it in your eyes."

"Well, if ya know so much, why'd ya ask?" Chiara retorted, still smiling as if she hadn't been thrown against the wall.

"To test your loyalty," the figure responded. He then stood up from where he was and walked towards her. He had two powerful restraint artes in the form of ethereal chains trying their best to barely hold him back. He walked as close as he could until he could push against the chain's restrictive powers no longer. You could faintly see the ragged and rent garbs on this man, eerily lit from the crimson glow of the flames from outside.

He grabbed Chiara by the neck and lifted her off the ground. Chiara grabbed his massive hand, struggling to ease his titanic grip for air. It was hard enough to breathe in Hell's heatwave.

"You came short of what I asked you to do, despite the legion of

Alpha class demons I sent with you. You have one more chance to tell me the truth; who stood in your way?"

He eased his grip to allow Chiara to speak.

"*ch*... th... the... Death... Angel..."

The demon dropped Chiara to the ground.

"Very good. I didn't have to pop your head off this time."

Chiara hacked and gasped for air as the mysterious man returned to his post.

"Moriel Bautista. I guess he was right," the man spoke to himself, "No matter. I will still achieve my goal regardless."

Chiara finally managed to stand.

"Spoken like a true villain. Let me guess what's next: you want me to go check on the little guy?"

The mysterious demon glared coldly at Chiara.

"Your mouth will bring you trouble, wench. As it has in the past."

"Oh please," Chiara shot back, "You're only so grumpy because it hasn't been pleasing you."

The mysterious demon closed his eyes and returned to his initial posture.

"Waste no more time. Find the girl and observe. When the time is right, you know what to do."

"Yeah, yeah," Chiara responded.

Chiara flexed her wings to stretch them, then proceeded down the corridor from which she came to enact the mysterious demon's plan.

Preparation

Back in the alleys of Nerezza, a stilled Viugra has caught the attention of several passersby ever since Mori left her there. They were all curious as to how she could stand so still for several hours like she had. Some asked if she was okay, but she couldn't answer them. And now, there was a group of immature boys poking at her, testing how long it would take her to jump at them out of frustration. Luckily for her, Mori finally came back a little after noon.

"Hey, V! I'm back!"

Viugra remained frozen, hands still on hips. The boys were still poking around her body to see if she would move.

"You look mad. Oh, is it because I froze you?" Mori asked.

Viugra remained still, though Mori could sense the fury radiating from her.

Hmm, Mori thought, *This might get intense...*

Mori snapped his fingers, and Viugra blinked. Instantly, her eyes crunched in rage. The boys who were about to take selfies with her rear-end jumped and ran away when they noticed her reanimating. Lucky for them, her rage wasn't meant for them. She marched quickly up to Mori and gave him a right hook to the jaw with all her strength. Mori's head jerked to the side with the punch.

"D***, Mori! Three HOURS? You said you'd be RIGHT BACK! That's three hours I could've been trying to find my dad!"

"Wow," Mori responded, now holding his face, "You didn't hold back this time. But to be fair, it was only a few minutes from my perspective."

"A few...?"

Viugra nearly lost it. She clenched her fists and began to storm away.

"Let's go. RIGHT NOW!"

As Viugra reached the end of the alley, she paused for a moment. She clenched her fists tighter and turned around.

"And for the record, I know time flows three times faster in the heavens. That leaves the question of why you didn't hurry up, Mr. Right Back."

"There's no need to be hasty, V," Mori finally responded, teleporting between her and the sidewalk. Viugra turned to face him again.

"And for the record, I also know that you know. That leaves the question of why you're in such a rush, Ms. Never-Told-Me."

Viugra, initially shocked to see him pop up by the sidewalk, squinted at Mori.

"...What are you getting at...?"

"Two things, V," Mori began, "One: patience. I know you can't help it, but rushing into things is only going to make things worse for you, you know. Two: You have all the time in the world to finish this trial. You could waste thirty years before you finished, and it'd be fine. Therefore, you have no reason to rush."

"Wait... what?" Viugra said, confused.

"Oh, didn't Azariel tell you?" Mori said playfully, turning towards the street, "Wait, lemme guess... you cut him off, didn't you?"

"I–" Viugra began to speak, but Mori cut her off somewhat mockingly.

"Iiiiii... don't wanna hear it, V. We already know the answer to that, don't we?"

Viugra sulked quietly. Mori paused for a moment, then turned around to finish speaking. His tone changed drastically to a gentle yet very serious one as he spoke his next line.

"And the more you let your desires take the wheel, the more likely they'll drive you off a cliff. And if that happens, you may lose the chance to meet your father. But you should already know this. Is that what you want?"

"N-no...," Viugra grumbled, body starting to quake from frustration.

"Then get a grip, V."

She couldn't even argue back with Mori on this. Everything he said was right. Even without the curse, she still wanted to see her father. And if she let her desires dictate what she'd do, she'd end up failing the trial. Even so, the curse caused her to question herself.

Is it really that bad? Viugra thought to herself, *I mean, if I fail the trial, I'll still be able to be with my father. Sure, I'd be a demon, but then I'd finally be with him, right?*

Mori noticed Viugra deep in thought, then sighed. There seemed to be some subtle disappointment in it.

"V, I know you're struggling to figure out what to do right now. My job isn't to tell you what to do aside from what the trials expect from you. It's on you whatever you decide to do. But consider this: What do you think the father figure you look up to would think about you making bad decisions just to see him?"

Viugra seemed to snap out of the curse's influence at this. Once again, Mori was right. All of the stories she heard from the other angels in the heavens about Xerasel are what inspired her to become the best angel she could. Hearing about how he fought for what was right and the demons he sent back to Hell captivated Viugra to a great degree. For her to choose to do wrong simply because it would help her find him would cause him to be ashamed, even if he were a demon now. That's just not what she wanted to believe he'd want from her.

With this in mind, Viugra relaxed and became a bit somber.

"...I... I'm sorry Mori," she spoke quietly, "You're right. My dad wouldn't want this. Not the one I know. I've got to try harder."

Mori nodded his head. If he could show it, he'd be smiling. But Viugra wasn't done.

"I'm sorry for hitting you too. I… think I realize that it wasn't called for. This curse is really messing with my mind. I'm… just not used to feeling like this. Overwhelmed by emotions, no more power, it's all… new to me."

Mori could sense Viugra's voice trembling a bit. She was getting vulnerable with him, and it was prevalent that one of the emotions she had been struggling with lately was fear.

"I'll admit, I'm scared. Ever since Chiara tossed me around a bit and cursed me, I have been. I've never felt that helpless before. I feel like, if I don't hurry, something might happen where I'll never see my dad and I don't want to lose that chance."

Mori turned around and placed his hand on Viugra's shoulder.

"Viugra, I understand your fear. Trust me, I've seen it enough to know. But you're forgetting what they taught you up there."

"What's that?" Viugra asked.

"…I'm sorry, V," Mori said, regretfully, "I can't tell you yet. You must prove that you understand what it is through the first trial."

"The trial, huh?" Viugra chuckled nervously, "When does this trial begin anyways?"

Mori removed his hand from her shoulder.

"It's already begun, Viugra. At the end of sunrise this morning."

Viugra seemed to grow a bit nervous.

"This morning? Why didn't you say something sooner? I could've messed up or something!"

"Oh relax, V," Mori said, "I tried to tell you on our way here. Besides, I've been monitoring the status of your morality since you woke up. You're not even completely neutralized like I thought."

"Huh?"

Mori began to make flashy gestures as he explained himself.

"The curse Chiara placed on you was certainly meant to set you to absolute zero. However! She didn't get the full curse off on you. Why? Because I was there! Just in the nick of time, I stopped her from fully cursing you. You are changed, no doubt. But the only thing really neutral about you right now is how you choose to do right. In other words, you're neutral good right now."

"Neutral good?" Viugra questioned. Mori groaned and his posture slunk a bit.

"Geez, V. I thought you paid attention in that class."

"Well, clearly not!" Viugra said, looking away in shame. Then in her Elizabethan accent, she said, "Now wouldst thou finish?"

"Neutral good just means you still choose to do what's right," Mori explained, "You don't really follow the rules to do so, but you don't necessarily break them either. You just like to do good."

"Ah, I see," Viugra responded, "And what about the other moralities?"

"You really want me to rehash a whole lesson you ought to remember? Seriously, V."

"Well, won't you?"

Mori cocked his head to the side.

"...Will I?"

Viugra glared at him coldly.

"You know what? Whatever."

"Good!" Mori delighted.

Viugra groaned loudly out of frustration. Some people walking by looked at her in the alley, vocalizing her frustrations. Mori was still invisible and inaudible to everyone else, leaving Viugra to look like she was going crazy. Even so, she didn't really pay them much attention.

"Whatever, Mori," Viugra continued. Then she thought about something he had said earlier.

"By the way, how did you know Chiara barely cursed me? You only got there as soon as she started to. You got some sort of far sight?"

"Far sight? No, don't be ridiculous," Mori waved the notion away. Viugra raised an eyebrow.

"It's not that ridiculous, you know. We are angels after all."

"Nephilim, my dear," Mori teased. Viugra blinked at his response.

"Huh?"

"I mean you, of course," Mori said.

"Sure…"

"I suppose I'll tell you. But let's walk and talk. By now, Bailey will probably be heading home."

Viugra was a bit puzzled at this statement, but she listened to Mori and followed him out of the alley. As they went down the street to Bailey's home, Mori explained his unique ability to Viugra.

"I have an ability that allows me to see the entire life of humans. When they were born, what they did, how they died, you name it. And ever since you were cursed and reverted to your human form, you fell within the rules of this power. As an angel, I couldn't see anything about your life. But now, I have a general idea of what happened and happens to you."

"So, you already know how this will end for me?" Viugra asked.

"Well… kind of," Mori continued, "I can't tell you how or when, since I'm not supposed to, but you do eventually get your angelic power back. When that happens, I actually can't see what happens to you beyond that."

"Interesting," Viugra said, "I don't think I've heard any angels having that power before. How'd you get it?"

"That's a secret, V."

"Oh really?" she inquired, "Does it have something to do with that graveyard?"

Mori opened his mouth, then closed it.

"It does, doesn't it?"

"I'm still not telling you."

"Doesn't matter. You didn't have to this time."

Viugra smiled hard, feeling accomplished that she was able to guess that. Mori sighed. He also realized something about her ever since they left the alley.

Funny. She's more like herself now, the self I first met anyways. Was a pep talk all she needed? Even so, I can sense that she's still struggling with the curse, but at least she's fighting it back a bit better now. I hope she'll keep that up.

It wasn't long before they reached Bailey's home. Once they were outside the house, Mori stopped Viugra before they walked up to the door.

"Okay, V. From this point forward, every decision you make is very important. You are still at a disadvantage with the curse, even though it's not as bad as it could've been. Do you think you're ready?"

"Honestly, I don't know," Viugra said, "But… I have to try."

"That's the spirit," Mori said, "Though the trial technically began already, we've been in the standby phase up until now. Once the final preparatory step has been taken, the true challenge will begin."

Then he remembered something else he wanted to tell her.

"Before I tell you what you need to do for this trial, there's something else I want you to know."

Mori turned to face Viugra.

"You will encounter many people on this journey, lots of which who will really test where you stand. Not just from here in Nerezza, either. From all over the world."

"Did you see that happening in my life?" Viugra questioned with a smirk.

"Actually, no," Mori said, "But I've been around the block to know."

"But the planet's round."

"Oh Viugra, you precious chocolate drop you," Mori teased.

"What's that supposed to mean?" Viugra responded, raising an eyebrow.

"Nothing," Mori responded quickly, "But listen. Humans are far more complex beings than you probably think. Things aren't always black and white with them, unlike most angels. Because of the sin in this world, many lines, which are clear to us, are the opposite to them. They may seem like a good person on the surface but be rotten to the core, and you may not know until they act. And vice versa."

"Hmm," Viugra said, looking at her curse mark, "I don't know if I'll be able to handle that."

"'Course you can!" Mori reassured, "Even though you forgot about the whole morality thing, which we won't bring up, you do have one natural advantage on your side. You're a Charity Angel, and Charity Angels are naturally empathetic creatures! Just relax and focus. You'll know what to do because it's in your nature."

Mori pointed at her heart.

"When the time comes when you feel lost, search your heart for the answers. And when you find the truth, follow it relentlessly. It'll keep you honest."

"But Mori... how can you be so sure?"

Mori chuckled.

"I just told you, V. Besides, I distinctly remember when we first met, you told me you already knew what to do."

"Wait, you believed me?" Viugra said, somewhat shocked.

"Um, yeah?" Mori responded with a funny tone, "Should I not've?"

"...kinda," Viugra responded, looking off.

"Geez, V. I was only–" Mori started. Then he realized she was only messing with him when he saw a smile crack on her face.

"Ha, you almost got me. You're using that curse to your advantage. That's hardly fair."

"Hey, if I'm gonna struggle with it, I might as well make it a little fun right?" Viugra said.

"True," Mori said, "Well... sort of. Just don't get too crazy, aight? It's still dangerous."

"Fair enough."

She then smirked at Mori.

"What's that look for, V?"

"I'll tell you in a moment," Viugra said, "First, tell me what the first trial is about."

"Okie doke," Mori began, "To kickstart your trial, you must find work and earn money to make a living as a human being."

"That it?" Viugra said, confidently, "That doesn't sound that hard honestly."

"You'd think that, wouldn't you?" Mori taunted, "Well, we'll see about that. Once you've proven that you understand the point of the trial, you will pass, and the next trial will begin."

"Sounds good to me."

"Also keep in mind that the answer to this trial does not solely lie within working alone. You will have other encounters that will constantly test you outside of work. It's up to you to figure out what they all mean."

"No probs."

"Glad to hear that confident vigor in your voice, V!" Mori delighted, "Now, what were you smirking about earlier?"

"Right," Viugra prepped, "Just wondering, but you sure it's okay for you to tell me all of that? Seems like you are tightrope-walking a dangerous line."

"Heheh," Mori chuckled, "Is that so?"

Mori handed Viugra an envelope he had prepared for her.

"It's fiiiine. I'm not really telling you what to do. Just some… friendly advice."

Viugra seemed a bit surprised, but she did begin to feel like she was growing closer to Mori. It amazed her since they only met within twenty-four hours and so much had already happened. Though, it's not hard or strange for angels to trust one another so quickly. After all, they're on the side of righteousness. Besides, she felt some comfort from Mori's words.

"Thanks, Mori," Viugra said gingerly.

Mori chuckled, but in a way that seemed like he was up to something. Viugra was beginning to regret her words.

"Don't thank me yet," he responded, "Once we're done with all of this setup, I'll be watching you from a distance until you complete the trial."

"Huh? But why?" Viugra asked, disappointed.

He tapped the envelope.

"I can't interfere with your progression once they receive this letter. That's just how things are, V. Sorry."

Way to ruin the moment, Mori, Viugra thought to herself.

She walked up to their mailbox to drop the envelope in.

There it goes, Mori thought to himself, *I did everything I could to help you. Well, short of getting your new buddy ready for ya. But we can get that later.*

Just as soon as Mori thought about this, he realized that he may have made a costly mistake. There wouldn't be a "later" for them to get the Reliquia like Azariel suggested. Mori just stated that once one of the Rookes opened the letter, he would have to watch over Viugra from afar. If he didn't get her Reliquia while he was still around, she wouldn't have her second chance and may end up failing the trial! With this in mind, Mori began to panic.

Oh… oh crap…!

Once it was in, she looked back at Mori, who was now wildly waving for her to come back.

What's up with him? She thought to herself.

Viugra made her way back to Mori down the drive.

"Now what?"

"I almost forgot!" Mori yelped, "There's somewhere I have to take you before they get that letter!"

"You forgot!?" Viugra nearly yelled, "How'd you–"

"I didn't forget!" Mori said, "I mean, I did but not like–"

Before he could finish, he noticed a particular car coming down the street towards them.

"No time to explain!" Mori said, grabbing Viugra's hand and bolting down the street. "They're almost home!"

Stressed

Not long after Viugra and Mori dashed off, a mid-sized sedan pulled into the driveway of the house. It was Bailey and her mother, who had to bring her home. After a long and rather fruitless talk with the principal, Bailey got suspended for the rest of the day. Though they didn't want to kick her out due to finals being this week, they couldn't let her get off easy for nearly breaking a girl's back on the floor either. It left everyone in awe that she could even do such a thing considering how young she was.

Mrs. Rooke was a lean, curvaceous woman with a similar appearance to Bailey. She had short bangs and wore the rest of her hair back in a ponytail. She also wore glasses. As she had left work, her attire was still business casual. She sported a blue-gray blazer jacket, slacks, and pumps with a white dress shirt underneath. You'd think she was a beautiful thirty-eight-year-old woman. However, you could see the stress of work in her face.

The whole ride home, Mrs. Rooke was giving her an entire lecture about behaving in school. Bailey quietly listened to her mother ripping her a new one, while simultaneously looking out the car window. Funny enough, she seemed more agitated with Bailey's behavior this time around than before. Possibly because it was the last week of school and she actually got suspended this time. It was only when they pulled into the drive that Mrs. Rooke finally started to change the subject.

"I don't even know why I waste my breath with you, child. No, I do, actually. I keep suffocating in the hopes that you'll one day understand that you can't always beat sense into people. You gotta let them figure it out on their own. Do you hear me, Bailey?"

"Yes mom," Bailey responded. She grabbed her backpack and opened the car door to get out. Mrs. Rooke followed suit, continuing as she got out of the car.

"Yeah, I know you're hearing me. You aren't listening, though, are you?"

Bailey cracked a sly smile but turned in a way where Mrs. Rooke couldn't see her. It didn't matter though because she already knew what Bailey would do.

"Stop smirking," Mrs. Rooke continued, as she passed Bailey and unlocked the front door, "I'm serious."

Before Mrs. Rooke finished opening the door, she noticed the mailbox had something in it.

"I forgot how early they run around here," she muttered to herself, aggressively snatching up its contents, "Seeing as I'd normally be at work."

There were several envelopes addressed to Melisende Rooke, and a couple of them addressed to Mr. & Mrs. Rooke. One of them was addressed as Mely Rooke, the nickname those close to her call her. She shuffled through them as she walked in. Most of the mail was junk, consisting of credit card companies, a couple of bills coming up, and a few letters for the upcoming polls. As she sifted through the mail, she stopped a few steps into the house when she came across one with an odd-looking seal on it.

"This looks different," Mrs. Rooke spoke to herself. The image in the seal seemed to be that of a shooting star with seven points and seven abstract figures dancing above each. She flipped the envelope around to the front, where there was no return address. She turned to Bailey, who was removing her shoes before she fully came in.

"Bailey, do you recognize this at all?" she asked.

Bailey slipped off her last shoe and walked up to her mother to look. She raised an eyebrow, not sure of what the seal meant.

"Nope. Looks like something important though."

"Right," Mrs. Rooke responded, sighing, "I'm not about to open it. It's probably junk."

"You haven't been talking to some other man, have you?" Bailey said, jokingly.

"Hush your mouth!" Mrs. Rooke told Bailey, "I would never! Don't joke like that!"

"Sorry mom," Bailey said, sarcastically, "Didn't mean to offend you."

"And if you keep on, I'm gonna be sorry about grounding you," she threatened, "You are already this close to losing your allowance tomorrow."

Bailey pretended not to care, slightly looking off from Mrs. Rooke. Even so, she immediately thought about the homeless people she had been sneaking food to. Not being able to bring food to the homeless did bother her.

While her mother continued to rant, Bailey felt a little pressure in her chest. She quickly pressed her hand over the right side of her chest. The pressure disappeared as soon as she did so.

Huh, Bailey thought, *I guess I'm alright. But I hope I didn't overdo it...*

"...and don't think I don't know what you did last night, young lady," Mrs. Rooke continued. She didn't seem to notice Bailey grab her chest.

Shocked, Bailey dropped her hands to her sides and looked at her mother from the corner her eye. Mrs. Rooke corrected that very quickly.

"Don't you look at me sideways like that! Straighten up!"

Bailey faced her mom all the way.

"I... don't know what you're talking about, mom."

"I know when you're playing stupid, Bailey," she started, "I know you went out while I was working over to go feed those homeless folk."

Bailey seemed a bit shocked.

How did she find out? I thought I covered all of my tracks?

"Someone I work with saw some RMC trying to assault a couple of girls last night on their way home. They told me one of them was wearing red and looked kind of like you."

RMC was an acronym for the Raiders Motorcycle Club, a notorious gang that's seen in the less fortunate areas of Nerezza. Mrs. Rooke was referring to Jack and the others who were surrounding Viugra.

Of course, Bailey thought to herself, growing frustrated with herself. *I should've just left that B**** alone. She could've taken care of herself anyways.*

"Honestly," Mrs. Rooke vented as she slapped the mail down on a nearby stand, "It's like dealing with stray cats. You keep feeding them, they keep coming back for more."

As soon as she said that, she gasped and looked at Bailey. The expression on Bailey's face had changed from frustrated to livid. Her widened eyes locked with Mrs. Rooke's. Mrs. Rooke realized that she said something uncalled for.

"Bailey… I didn't mean…"

"Shut up."

Bailey ran up the nearby stairs as her mother tried to stop her.

"Bailey!"

It was too late. Bailey already made it to her room and shut the door hard. Mrs. Rooke let out a stressed sigh and cursed under her breath.

"D*** it."

Bailey leaned up against her bedroom door. She tried her best to contain the rage building up in her, but to no avail. She searched her room for something to throw or punch. Her room was rather immaculate, as she did keep it clean. With nothing readily available to pummel, she ultimately screamed with no restraint.

"UUUUGGGGH!"

She ran and flopped on her bed; face burrowed in her soft red pillow.

*I can't believe she F***ing said that!* Bailey screamed in her pillow, *They ain't no d*** cats! They're humans! They need to eat just like us! And they can't even help themselves! God, I hate selfish people! God D-*

Before she could even finish her thought, she felt a sharp pain in the right side of her chest. She grabbed it, grimacing in pain. It felt like someone was driving a knife in her chest, as it continued to intensify.

"A-augh... s***..." Bailey grunted loudly. She sounded too out of breath to even scream in pain. She started to roll out of bed as she writhed, trying to fight the pain.

Not a moment too late, Mrs. Rooke busted into her room as she hit the floor holding her chest and grunting breathlessly.

"Bailey!"

She immediately dashed out of Bailey's room and into her own, which was two doors down and across from hers. Mrs. Rooke went straight to her dresser and opened up the first drawer, which had a bunch of medicine in it. She grabbed the one she needed, a water bottle on top of the dresser, and ran back to Bailey. At this point, the pain was getting intense enough to cause Bailey to pass out.

Mrs. Rooke dropped to the floor behind Bailey and carefully rolled her over and sat her up.

"Open your mouth!"

Bailey was growing weak from the pain, but the fight remained in her eyes. She weakly did so, still griped with pain.

Mrs. Rooke then shook a pill from the bottle she had and put it in Bailey's mouth. She opened the water bottle up and held it up to Bailey's mouth to get some water to swallow the pill. Bailey was already struggling to fight the pain, but she managed to tough it out a bit longer and swallow the medicine.

Bailey managed to get the pill down before coughing as a reflex from the pain. Mrs. Rooke laid Bailey's head in her lap and began to gently brush her hair back to comfort her until the medicine took effect.

The medicine began to work as soon as it hit Bailey's stomach, so after about thirty minutes, the pain began to subside. Mrs. Rooke noticed that Bailey was starting to calm down.

"Bailey, how are you feeling now?"

"Mom..." Bailey said. Though she was a bit exhausted from fighting the pain, she still had a bit of energy left to talk at least.

"I'm better now. Thanks."

"You don't need to thank me," Mrs. Rooke said, "I'm your mother. Taking care of you is automatic."

"But you really don't–" Bailey began.

"Shhhh," Mrs. Rooke hushed softly, "Just relax. It might start back up if you don't."

Bailey made a face, then laid her head back down on her mother's lap and stared at the ceiling. Mrs. Rooke seemed to know what Bailey was going to say and brushed her hair some more as she replied in a gentle tone.

"This is why I tell you what not to do, Bailey. Any excessive amounts of stress and lack of sleep will likely stir up your episodes. You being out late like you were and flipping girls probably caused you to flare up. You should know how your body works by now."

Bailey looked down at her chest and placed her hand over it as her mother continued to speak.

"You're a smart and strong little girl, but you can't handle everything. Sometimes you need to secure yourself before you go rescuing others out of hot water. Otherwise, they'll just yoink you in with them. Then you'll both be drowning in problems."

Bailey looked off as if these words burned her to hear them.

"You're my little rebel. It doesn't matter what the circumstances are because I'm gonna take care of you anyways. That's our promise."

Bailey looked over into her mother's glossy eyes, which were now focused on a picture on Bailey's dresser. There were three people in it: her, Bailey, and Bastian Rooke. Bastian Rooke was Bailey's father and Mrs. Rooke's husband. They had taken a picture near a military base where he had been stationed for almost four years now. Bailey was much smaller then than she is now. Though she was wearing somewhat decent clothes, her face seemed to be grungy in the picture. Compared to the picture, you wouldn't even know that she was only ten looking at her now.

Bailey started to feel bad. She knew her mother loved her and didn't mean what she said earlier.

"I'm... sorry."

"No. I should be apologizing this time," Mrs. Rooke said, "I should've known better not to agitate your condition. I should've known..."

Mrs. Rooke looked down at Bailey for a moment. Her eyes were starting to clear up now. Bailey smirked a bit.

*I didn't mean for her to worry like this. But still... I can't just stop helping the homeless now. At the same time, I'm stressing her out. D***...*

Suddenly, Mrs. Rooke's phone rang. She reached into her pocket, looked at the caller ID and realized that it was the lab. She worked at a Pharmaceutical Lab where she tested medication that may be available to the public. They were calling to see why she hadn't returned to work yet. Mrs. Rooke picked up the phone.

"Hello... yes... no, an emergency came up... I know, I know... yes, but... okay... sure... fine. I'll be back shortly..."

Mrs. Rooke hung up the phone. Bailey managed to sit all the way up now.

"Gotta go back, huh?"

"Of course," Mrs. Rooke replied, standing back up. Bailey noticed her mother holding her back as she got up on her feet.

"Will you be okay at home by yourself? You'll rest until I get home, right?"

"Yes, Mom," Bailey said. She stood up, gently holding her chest. Mrs. Rooke noticed her do this.

"Bailey, I hope you understand that you need to keep resting right now."

"I do, mom."

"Then make sure you do it. I don't want to come back home and see you sprawled out on the floor again, okay?"

"Okay."

With that, Mrs. Rooke got up and headed out of Bailey's room. On her way out, she told Bailey that there were leftovers in the fridge when she got hungry. She had to work overtime again, so she wouldn't be back home until late. Once she made it to the bottom of the stairs, she put her hands on her hips, sighed, then looked around the house for a moment.

Many homes in the outer parts of Nerezza weren't very well kept. The Rooke household was an exception. It was one of the remaining houses built from years ago in the city, long before it received its new name. Despite its older feel, the piping, wiring, furnace, and other various things you'd find in any house were replaced with up-to-date equipment that fell within modern standards and regulations. The house was trimmed with wooden finish, with a wooden table and chairs in the living room to the left of the main hallway and various other wooden cabinets and furniture. They all had elegant floral carvings in them to add character to them. There were also flowerless plants in various corners of the house for decoration.

Mrs. Rooke continued to think about Bailey and how she might decide to disobey again.

I can't keep doing this, she thought to herself, as she prepared to leave the house, *I need to find a way to keep an eye on her while I'm gone. This is starting to stress me out…*

Right before Mrs. Rooke opened the door to leave the house, she paused and looked at the pile of mail. For some reason, she felt the urge to check the mysterious mail that came in. Her gut was telling her to open it. She walked back to the stand where the mail was and sifted through the mail until she got the one with the star seal on it. She held it in her hands for a moment, then walked out the door.

✡✡✡✡✡✡✡

After about a few hours (around five o'clock or so), Bailey was out of bed. She wasn't doing anything too crazy, but she had decided to exercise. She just couldn't stay in bed anymore. She initially pulled out her phone and scoured the internet for a few minutes. Looking up new things to learn about the world was one of her favorite pass times. But after a while, she fell asleep. Being out as late as she had been caught up to her. It was only about ten minutes before that she had woken up and decided to exercise.

Bailey had switched out of her school uniform into a white tank top and exercise leggings. She had already done several push-ups and was now doing crunches and sit-ups. She managed to do 100 straight, then took a quick break.

She glanced up at the photo on her dresser while she rested. Her father was someone she really looked up to, which was one of her motivators for exercising.

If I'm gonna be like him, I have to keep getting stronger, Bailey thought to herself.

Once she caught some of her breath, she got back to her crunches. After another set, she decided to stop. She didn't want to overdo it and end up making her mother upset because she was on the floor again. Instead, she took a quick shower and prepared to grab something to eat. The clothes she had laid out to put on once she was done showering were some comfortable at-home clothes. Basically, a white shirt with red sleeves and some jeans. She kept her shoes off and wore socks to avoid messing up the carpet.

While she was dressing herself, she looked in the mirror and noticed something off with her hair. It was small and barely noticeable, but she saw it. At the roots of her hair, she noticed that it was beginning to turn black.

Great, she thought to herself, *Gonna have to dye it again soon…*

Bailey finished putting on her clothes, then made her way downstairs to get some food. The kitchen was just past the stairs. You would enter it if you walked straight forward after entering the house. Bailey headed to the fridge and opened it to see what she could eat.

"Let's see," she talked to herself.

The core essentials were in her fridge. Eggs, milk, breakfast meats, condiments, and some grapes lined the shelves inside. There were also cans of pop and other snackable items available as well. In addition to those, a pot of casserole from a couple of days ago remained. There was enough for one person to get full off. Mrs. Rooke hadn't been able to cook anything for a while due to work. Bailey would be able to find something to eat if leftovers weren't in there, but she would have to cook it if her mom wouldn't be home for a while.

Bailey pulled out the leftovers and grabbed a pop. She took a couple of steps to the other side of the kitchen to grab a plate and warm everything up in the microwave. By the time she got to it, she took a quick glance at the clock. It was just a few minutes to six.

"Geez," Bailey thought to herself, as she placed her plate in the microwave, "What the heck am I supposed to do for the next few hours? Staying inside is so boring."

While her food was warming up, she walked back over to the fridge and grabbed the bread from the top of it to get a slice. She waited until the last few seconds on the microwave to do this, and when it went off, she took her plate out to put her bread on. After this, she walked it over to the kitchen table.

Before she sat down, she went back to make sure everything was put back up or placed in the sink. She put the bread back on top of the fridge and placed the casserole pot in the sink to be washed later. There were a few dishes building up by now, so she knew she was going to have to wash them before she did anything else after eating.

"Well, that's one thing to do," Bailey said. As she turned around to go eat, she eyed the television in the living room nearby.

"Guess I'll cut the news on or something."

The way the dining room was set up, anyone could be eating at the table and watch shows or movies on the 50" flat screen television in the living room nearby. Bailey grabbed the remote and turned on the tv. It was already on the news channel. Bailey listened to the reporter as she made her way back to her seat.

"The reason behind those knocked out in the alley as well as the bizarre turbulent winds late last night still remains a mystery. But however mysterious, some say it's just another night in Nerezza. Back to you, Jeffrey."

Bailey took a bite of her casserole.

There's always some weird stuff going on around here. But they're always making it seem like some monsters or demons are behind it. How stupid.

"Thank you, Stacey. When we come back, we'll bring to you an update on the shooting star sighting last night that everyone says was 'bigger than life.' Also, an update on the new medication scientists claim will significantly reduce the number of flu cases that may flood the hospitals this year."

Just as the reporter finished making this statement, the doorbell rang. Bailey finished her last bite then drank some pop to help it go down. She then made her way to the door to see who it was.

"Hello?" she said.

Suddenly, Bailey's eyes went wide, and her mouth hung open. She couldn't believe who she was seeing at the door. Standing before her was a young black girl with a bag, a ridiculous looking necklace, and shades. It was Viugra!

"H-hey…! You're… Bailey, right?" Viugra started, trying to change her voice to sound different.

Oh Hell-o alright, Bailey thought to herself.

"What the h*** do you want?"

"Well, that's rude," Viugra responded, "I see why your mother called me."

"Huh?" Bailey said, shocked, "What are you talking ab–"

Bailey didn't even have to finish her question before she realized what was going on. Her eyes widened even more as she figured out why Viugra was there.

"No way..."

Viugra sighed, then placed her hands on her hips as she revealed the truth even she was dreading.

"Please, call me Valerie. I'm gonna be babysitting you here on out."

Animus

As Bailey let Viugra into the house, a wave of aggravation began to wash over her. Even though the six o'clock portion of the news filled the air, the silent but tense energy from her rang louder. But unlike the night before, Viugra didn't pick up on it.

Viugra attempted to talk to Bailey as they reached the living room, but Bailey didn't respond. Bailey sat back at the kitchen table and glared at Viugra, while Viugra sat in the living room where the television eventually grabbed her attention. She finally realized that Bailey didn't want to talk for some reason, so she just took her backpack off, sat up proper, hands crossed in her lap, and started watching the news.

While sulking at the table, Bailey made a full scan of Viugra. Everything about her was the same as last night. However, she did notice a couple of differences. Viugra didn't have the backpack before, for one. And for another, she had a strange marking on her chest just under her weird necklace.

Did I not see that before? Bailey thought to herself, *No, it can't be. But when did she get that? She didn't strike me as the type to get tattoos.*

After some time passed, a certain portion of the news caught Viugra's attention which eventually led to her breaking the silence.

"Last night, another incident involving the RMC and LL took southwest Nerezza near the docks by storm at around 2 P.M.. Rounds from various weapons rang through the streets and had several nearby residents fearing for their lives as the two gangs fought. One resident describes the noise as 'cacophonous'. Several individuals not directly involved with the shootout were injured, three of which are severe cases and are now in ICU fighting for their lives. Mayor Carnegie claims he would have planned to address the recent outbreak of gang violence this evening, but already has a conference setup to discuss the current status of the medication being developed for the Animus outbreak. More on that story next."

"Animus outbreak?" Viugra spoke out loud.

Bailey seemed to snap out of her frustration at this question.

"Huh?"

"The Animus outbreak," Viugra repeated, "What is that?"

Bailey couldn't believe what she was hearing.

"You seriously don't know?"

"Nope."

Bailey sat up at this. Clearly, she was both astonished and frustrated at this bit of news.

"How do you not know? Do you live under a rock? H***, do you even live in Nerezza?"

"I have my reasons, I don't live under a rock, and...," Viugra responded, counting her fingers for each question. The last question was one she had to be careful answering.

"...I do now, I guess."

"You guess?" Bailey questioned. She then remembered her frustration with Viugra even being in her house and decided to not ask anymore.

"Well, watch the d*** news. I don't have to tell you anything," Bailey said, facepalming.

"You know, it's not very ladylike to cuss so much," Viugra said, trying to ignore Bailey's attitude.

"It's nOt vERy lady liKe to cUss sO mUch," Bailey mocked.

"Yeah, that's what I said," Viugra said, "Also, what's wrong with your voice?"

"It's called mocking," Bailey said, now in disbelief. Despite how petty it sounded, Bailey couldn't tell if Viugra was serious or being funny.

What the heck? Bailey thought to herself. *Is she toying with me!? I swear to God...*

"...Now on to our developing story," The news continued, "The cerebral disease Animitis, also known as the Animus Disease, has become a major health concern for approximately ten percent of the 300,000-plus lives here in Nerezza. Of that percentage, half has died since the first reported case two months ago. The number of new cases is around thirty or less each day, leaving most hopeful and not as concerned as when it first appeared. However, health officials fear that if underestimated, the Animus may eventually affect everyone in the city. Animus deaths are still on the rise, as medical scientists are still scrambling day and night to develop a medication to combat the disease."

"Really..." Viugra thought out loud. She then looked at Bailey, who still looked like she was sulking.

"Sounds like this Animus is dangerous. Good thing I'm here to protect you, right?"

"Shut it and watch the news," Bailey grumbled.

"Shut what?"

"Your mouth! What else?" Bailey snapped.

From the sound of her response, Viugra could kind of tell Bailey was getting more frustrated. She didn't respond, but made an effort to not agitate her further as she continued to watch the news.

"...one of our reporters went live at the Manna Laboratories to learn more about the development of medication earlier today."

Bailey sat up a little more when she heard this. Viugra noticed but remained silent.

"Dr. Melisende Rooke, the lead scientist for the development against Animus joins us today. Please, share with us your current progress of drug discovery."

Bailey's mother appeared on tv, dressed in a unique lab coat. Viugra grew a bit more interested, now that she is getting a better look at the woman who accepted her babysitting services. She noted how saggy Melisende's face looked. Viugra could tell she was probably exhausted, but Bailey seemed to know exactly how stressed her mother was. As if to confirm it, Mrs. Rooke let out a hesitant, strained sigh before speaking to the reporter.

"As you know, the Animus Disease's origins are still unknown. We are still in the process of developing a new drug to combat, if not completely treat, this medical threat. Unfortunately, there is not much else I can speak on at the moment."

"...is there anything you can tell us about the origins of the Animus Disease?"

Mrs. Rooke seemed to restrain another sigh.

"The details regarding its origins are left to a separate research team and not mine. You would have to ask them, though they are having a harder time than we are right now."

"Okay. Well, do you know who is most likely to get the Animus, Dr. Rooke?"

Mrs. Rooke's face seemed to tense up a bit, but she fought her frustration and answered his next question.

"We are still gathering data to determine that. However, I have noticed an interesting correlation between confirmed cases and their previous underlying conditions."

"Is that so?" the reporter responded, "Will you share what that is with us?"

"Certainly," Mrs. Rooke spoke.

In that moment, the news seemed to glitch out for a split second. Bailey and Viugra noticed, but only Bailey paid it any mind.

"...that those with underlying mental conditions seem to be more likely to have Animus just three whole days' worth of time after exuding symptoms–"

It seemed like Dr. Rooke was continuing to talk, but the audio cut out before she could finish. The audio shifted back to the main news reporter who spoke earlier, then a scene switched back to the news reporter's desk followed in a rather jarring transition. Bailey gritted her teeth when this happened, and Viugra noticed a clearly angry expression on her face.

"The Animus continues to haunt the people of Nerezza as the scientists seem to continue searching for a cure, in what seems to be a fruitless endeavor."

As the reporter was continuing on with her report, Viugra grabbed the remote and cut the television off.

"Hey! What the f***, Viugra?" Bailey yelled

"I thought I told you my name was Valerie," Viugra responded calmly.

"Your name could be Vagisil for all I care," Bailey said, "Why the h*** did you cut that off? I was watching that!"

Viugra walked over to the kitchen table and sat down adjacent from Bailey.

"I think that's enough T.V. for you for now. Instead, let's talk a little."

Bailey looked at Viugra as if she were crazy.

"How 'bout no?"

Bailey got up and went for the remote. Viugra realized what she was doing and grabbed her arm to stop her.

"Now hold on a sec–" Viugra started. Bailey, out of pure reaction, quickly turned around and sank her teeth into Viugra's left forearm. And unlike before, Viugra felt every last one of her teeth powerfully sink into her flesh.

"OOOOOOOWWWW!"

Bailey jumped at the loud screech, simultaneously releasing her bite. To her amazement, Viugra was gripping her arm and reeling in pain. Bailey had drawn blood, contrary to what happened the last time she tried to bite her. Not only that, but she herself seemed to calm down from her growing anger faster than usual.

"Oh s***..."

"What the h...," Viugra started. But even in the midst of her pain, she knew not to cuss. Not like this.

"...hea-heaveeeeens was that for?"

"Isn't that worse to say?" Bailey tried to joke, but still shocked and a bit guilty.

The pain was starting to make Viugra pissed.

"Would you just help me?" she growled through gritted teeth.

"Hold on," Bailey said.

Bailey grabbed a towel for Viugra to hold against her wound until she came back with some bandages. After grabbing the first aid kit and some mouthwash to rinse her own mouth clean, she sat in her chair and proceeded to bandage Viugra's arm for her.

Bailey couldn't stop her amazement as she watched a once solid woman grimace in pain from a bite that didn't even leave a mark the first time. It continued to poke at her curiosity until she couldn't help but ask as she finished wrapping her arm.

"How did I do that?"

"What? Bite me?" Viugra asked.

"No, I mean, yes," Bailey said, still trying to understand what all had just happened. "Don't you remember? I couldn't do that yesterday."

"Oh yeah... heh, I guess you found my weak spot..." Viugra tried to play it off. Bailey wasn't buying it.

"Bulls***. There's no way you only bulked up your love handles and not the rest of your body. And also..."

Bailey squinted as she grew more skeptical of Viugra. Viugra was finding it hard to look away from Bailey.

"Why are you acting so slow? It's like, you don't recognize any of my hints. Not that I really mind."

"Slow?" Viugra started, tense with pressure, "I don't know what you mean."

"Yes, you do!" Bailey shot back, "It's like you're acting ignorant on purpose or something!"

"Huh?"

"Exactly that!" Bailey exclaimed, "What's wrong with you?"

"Eheh… I wonder," Viugra mumbled.

Geeze, she's sharp! Viugra thought to herself, *But she is right. I can't really understand her like I did before. Is it because I'm weaker now?*

"And one more thing before I make you answer me," Bailey said, now finishing and tightening the arm bandage.

"OW!" Viugra yelped.

"Sorry," Bailey mumbled.

"It's okay…"

"When you screamed," Bailey began asking her last question. "My whole attitude changed. It was like you screamed my anger away or something. How did you–?"

Bailey paused mid-questioning. Viugra wasn't sure why she stopped.

"How did I… what?"

"…y'know what? Never mind. Just answer the first two questions."

Viugra looked confused. Bailey gave her a warning look.

"What? I said answer the first two questions! Or I'll start pressing into your wound."

"Hold on now!" Viugra lit up, "N-no need for that!"

"Hmph."

Great, Viugra thought to herself, *If she's this sharp, does that mean she already knows my identity? I don't want to tell her unless I'm sure, but I also don't want to lie…*

"Alright," She huffed, "Truth is… I'm…"

At that moment, the front door started to click. Bailey looked up and realized that Mrs. Rooke must've been coming home early! She then looked at the clock on the microwave. 7:45pm.

What timing, Bailey thought to herself. She glared at Viugra as she stood up.

"Lucky a**. We'll continue this convo later. You will answer my questions. And trust and believe, I don't forget."

"Sure, sure," Viugra said, feeling a wave of relief.

☼☼☼☼☼☼☼☼

"You're home early, mom."

Mrs. Rooke had just hung up her coat and slipped out of her shoes when Bailey dropped this question. Viugra, standing behind Bailey in the hallway, finally got a good look at the lady who hired her. Compared to how she looked on television, her face was more obvious in showing stress.

"Yes, well... I needed to see how things were going."

She looked up at Viugra and took note of her attire. She also noticed what seemed like a tattoo below her neck.

"It's good to finally meet you in person, Valerie. I'm Mrs. Rooke if you hadn't already guessed. Before I continue, I must know something. Is that how you normally show up to work?"

"N-No," Viugra answered.

"If you expect to get hired for more work around the city, then it better not be. Be glad I'm not the type to judge first appearances."

Mrs. Rooke also noticed Viugra's fresh bandages.

"Did you hurt yourself recently?"

Viugra glanced at Bailey. Bailey held her breath, shaking her head in protest. Viugra could somewhat tell that Bailey didn't want her to say anything. That was one gesture she kind of remembered.

"Sort of," Viugra responded, trying to think of a way to answer without lying or giving it away, "Someone bit me today, so I had to patch myself up."

"Is that so?" Mrs. Rooke said, "And I suppose it didn't happen to be Bailey, did it?"

Bailey facepalmed. Of course, Mrs. Rooke would think it was Bailey. Biting is what she does. Viugra realized that she slipped up and that there was no point in trying to hide it.

"Yes," Viugra started, "But I was just trying to keep her from being aggravated by the news, Mrs. Rooke."

Bailey jerked her head as if to say, 'shut up,' but it was already too late.

"Bailey," Mrs. Rooke continued, "I thought we agreed that you would relax today? Unless you forgot what happened?"

"No mom," Bailey sighed, "But I had to watch the news. And they cut you off in that interview! That's… that's disrespectful!"

So that's why she was getting agitated, Viugra thought to herself, *But did they cut her off on purpose? If so, I wonder why…*

Mrs. Rooke sighed and gently placed her hand around Bailey. Bailey looked at her hand as if she didn't really want to be touched.

"I know, baby. But I told you before, the news will just make you madder. There's a reason I told you not to watch too much of it. That's also the reason why I took a risk and called Valerie here."

"Her?" Bailey questioned, looking at Viugra.

"Yes. I know how hardheaded you can be, Bailey. Normally, I wouldn't just hire someone for anything until I met them first. But I have too much on my plate to constantly keep an eye on you. Luckily, I knew I would be able to come home early today to check on things. That's why I gave Valerie a test. I told her that you have a condition that flares up whenever you get too stressed. If she could recognize when you were stressed and act accordingly, then I would give her a chance. And I had a feeling you'd do something that would frustrate you before I got home."

"I see," Bailey said, looking away.

Mrs. Rooke turned to Viugra again.

"You passed my little test. I still don't know how much I can trust you yet, but I'm willing to at least give you a chance to prove yourself."

Viugra tried her best not to show her excitement. Of course, it wasn't because she just wanted to babysit Bailey. Rather, it was the first step to completing the first trial and reaching her father.

Mrs. Rooke turned to Bailey.

"As for the interview, there are some things the media doesn't want the public to hear. I told you this before. But don't get so worked up. The truth will come out when the time is right."

"Are you talking about that second thing you were gonna say? I think they started to cut you off before you said it."

Mrs. Rooke smirked.

"You caught that, did you?" Mrs. Rooke said, "Lots of people here skim over the news and wouldn't even notice something like that. You're pretty perceptive, aren't you Valerie?"

Viugra rubbed the back of her neck.

I wouldn't say that... least, not how I am right now.

"Then again," Mrs. Rooke teased, "Maybe not. You did seem to have a hard time keeping up with our talk over the phone earlier."

"Oh, that?" Viugra nervously chuckled.

"Hmph," Mrs. Rooke continued, "But to answer your question: yes, there is a second correlation between the disease and those with underlying conditions. I assume you want to know?"

"Certainly."

Mrs. Rooke rubbed Bailey's shoulder. Bailey looked away. It was almost as if she knew what her mother would say but didn't agree with it.

"All Animus cases seem to lack a certain level of spirituality."

Test of Integrity

"A lack of spirituality?"

"Yes," Mrs. Rooke continued to explain, "Put simply, those who are not familiar with the supernatural."

"Interesting," Viugra responded. Everything Mrs. Rooke was explaining to her about the Animus not only seemed to make sense, but it also sounded familiar. Even so, Viugra couldn't seem to figure out why. It didn't help that she was starting to get an unusual headache trying to keep up with the details.

Something about this Animus reminds me of something. But what exactly…?

Mrs. Rooke noticed Viugra thinking and chuckled.

"I'm sorry. This must all sound ridiculous to you."

"N-no, not at all actually!" Viugra responded.

Mrs. Rooke chuckled again. She then dug into her pocket to grab her wallet while walking closer to Viugra.

"Valerie, can I call you Val for short?"

"Sure."

Mrs. Rooke pulled out $40.

"This is for you for watching Bailey. I really do appreciate what you did for me this evening."

"You're welcome," Viugra said with a smile.

"Although I'm willing to keep using your services, you'll have to earn my complete trust," Mrs. Rooke said, sighing, "I didn't even want to hire a babysitter in the first place, but it's getting harder balancing work with taking care of Bailey."

Mrs. Rooke glanced over her shoulder at Bailey. Bailey huffed and looked off. Knowing Bailey's usual persona, Mrs. Rooke realized that she was behaving a little differently.

"So, um," Viugra began, "You'll need me again tomorrow, right?"

"You need money, right?" Mrs. Rooke responded, raising her eyebrow.

"I guess so," Viugra said. Mrs. Rooke looked at her confused.

"You guess?"

"I-I mean yes! Of course, I do!"

"Then there's your answer."

Mrs. Rooke placed the money in Viugra's hand.

"Thank you very much, Mrs. Rooke," Viugra said happily.

"No problem, Val," Mrs. Rooke said, "Let's see how long you keep this up."

As Mrs. Rooke walked Viugra to the door, Bailey watched on in disbelief.

I can't believe this is happening.

After saying her goodbyes, Viugra left the Rooke's home and headed down the main road. As she was walking away, Mrs. Rooke and Bailey watched from their home. Once Viugra crossed the street, Mrs. Rooke turned to Bailey to talk about her.

"Be honest, what's your take on her?"

"My take?" Bailey asked, somewhat surprised. It was true, she didn't care for Viugra's meddling. However, as much as she didn't want to admit it, there was nothing bad to say about her.

"She's… alright… I guess…"

"Just 'alright' huh?" Mrs. Rooke said, looking a bit suspicious.

"Yeah," Bailey said, then abruptly changed the topic, "Don't you think you were a bit impulsive hiring someone you just met today? What if she tried to hurt me?"

Mrs. Rooke looked at Bailey, then reached into her pocket. After getting an appropriate hold on it, she peeked at the 9mm pistol Bailey swiped the other night.

Bailey was slightly surprised. She always knew her mom had a savage side. Mrs. Rooke dropped the gun back into her pocket as Bailey continued her skepticism.

"Oooookay... but there's no way you would've known–"

"I've been watching from outside this whole time."

This surprised Bailey. She looked over at the windows with semi-transparent curtains. Just beyond that, the dark silhouette of a chair could be seen just past the edge of the window. She didn't even notice her mother had been there all this time.

"Seriously...?"

"Yep," Mrs. Rooke confirmed, "I parked across the street just a few seconds after she walked in the house. After that, I sat in that chair observing from the outside. I saw everything that happened, including you biting her."

Mrs. Rooke closed and locked the front door.

"Those questions I asked her were a test. She almost failed."

"Why didn't she?" Bailey asked, trying not to sound too disappointed.

"A partial truth is no different than a partial lie in my book. She intentionally avoided snitching on you to save you from getting in trouble. Once I hinted that I knew it was you, she came clean. If not for that, then she would've failed."

"Heh," Bailey said, "Well, aren't you clever?"

Mrs. Rooke smirked.

"But since we're on the subject of honesty, it's your turn to fess up. You were with her the other night, weren't you?"

"Urk," Bailey uttered. The strained look on Bailey's face answered for her.

"I knew it."

"Am I that predictable?" Bailey asked, feeling a bit salty.

"You're not as sneaky as you think you are, Bailey," Mrs. Rooke said, "That's why I keep telling you to keep your butt in the house when I'm gone."

"Oh please!" Bailey growled.

Mrs. Rooke took a few steps towards the stairs.

"Don't 'oh please' me, Bailey! I have enough stress at work, let alone worrying about you. You need to remember who's in charge here!"

Bailey's face scrunched in frustration. Mrs. Rooke sighed.

"I care about your safety, Bailey. There's too much going on out here for you to be wandering the streets alone at night like that. You've been through enough as it is."

Bailey noticed the effects of stress on her mother's face once she brought it up. Bailey's frustration slowly disappeared from her face as she looked away. She knew her mother was right. But it bothers her greatly when others are on the street in need who don't have what she's got now.

"...I know, mom," Bailey sighed.

"Then show me," Mrs. Rooke said, "I better not hear about you being out at night while Valerie is here watching you."

"...You won't."

"Good," Mrs. Rooke said, now heading to her room. Bailey, feeling bested, made her way back to the kitchen. Halfway up the stairs, Mrs. Rooke paused on a thought, then turned to address Bailey once more.

"Y'know, you and Valerie could become friends," she chuckled, "You're both bad at cover-ups and both need friends."

"No, I'm not, and no I don't," Bailey firmly responded.

✲✲✲✲✲✲✲

It was just a few minutes after eight, and the scarlet sun was just starting to sink behind the buildings. The streets were still busy with people, unlike the period when Viugra first arrived.

Her next objective was to return to the place Mori dragged her off to before her trial officially began. Even so, she took a slight detour just to see what was around. Aside from curiosity, Viugra needed to decompress from dealing with Bailey. Plus, she was a bit hesitant about heading back right away. Something about that guy Mori introduced her to comes off rude.

Everyone around actually seemed pretty chill, whether they were hanging out outdoors at their favorite café or playing basketball at the craggy court. There were also plenty of people walking with their lovers or pets in the park. It was the same park that Viugra confronted the demons that had pursued her. Looking at the park during the day, she couldn't help but feel some disbelief about everything that had happened while being on Earth already.

Man, she thought to herself, *A lot happened just last night. I didn't expect this whole trial thing to start off so crazy like it did.*

After about 20 minutes of wandering, Viugra started to notice her energy levels dropping. She realized that she was getting tired, a sensation that occured more frequently than she was used to. She began to walk towards the westside of Nerezza, where the man Mori introduced her to resided. He was supposed to take her in during her trial. Despite being ready to head there, Viugra took her time. She was dreading having to go back already.

Man, being tired like this is upsetting, she thought to herself, *I want to explore some more. There's a lot I wanna learn about this city since I'm gonna be here for a while. Plus, I really don't want to deal with THAT guy right now. Seriously, how can an angel be that ornery? I'm getting a headache just thinking about it!*

She stopped on this thought for a moment. There was a bit of pressure in her head that was slowly becoming worse.

"I'm actually getting a headache!?" Viugra exclaimed. A few people eyed her as she blurted this out.

"Ehehe, good day," Viugra spoke to them, slightly embarrassed. The onlookers continued to walk away. Viugra sighed, then refocused on her headache. While thinking about this, she also realized another feeling in her stomach.

Geez, Viugra thought, *Why am I feeling all of this right now?*

She looked around to see if anyone was watching her awkwardly standing on the sidewalk. Fewer people were around now, and nobody was paying her much attention. She put her hands over her head and stomach and closed her eyes.

I feel… an emptiness, she analyzed, *A lack of energy, some pain in my stomach, this headache... I don't remember the curse making me feel like this before. It's definitely something else. But what?*

Just as she finished thinking this, a strange gurgling sound rumbled from her belly.

Growling?

That's when it finally hit her: she hadn't eaten anything since being human! It's a wonder she hadn't passed out by now.

"Oh no!" she spoke out, "I forgot humans have to eat! I'm about to die!"

As she spoke out, she noticed a rather skinny man in ragged clothing down a nearby alley. His shifty eyes were loosely focused on Viugra. He noticed her looking at him, then called out to her to come closer.

"Hey! Com'er a sec."

Viugra, seeing nothing wrong with approaching this stranger, walked into the alley to speak to him.

"Yes?"

"Ya got some dough?"

"Dough?" Viugra responded, "Liiiike… cookie dough?"

"No, not that dough!" the man said, "Y'know, money!"

"Oh!" Viugra said, "Yeah."

An awkward pause followed.

"Well?" the man asked.

"Well, what?" Viugra asked.

"What's it look like?" the man shouted.

"It looks green, I suppose?" Viugra responded. Though she wasn't trying to sound smart mouthed, she clearly didn't understand this man's motive.

"You smarta–" the man started. He caught himself before he messed up the game he was trying to play.

"Agh! Ne'ermind, just gimme your money!"

"I kind of need it though," Viugra responded, "I'm not feeling so great right now. If I don't get something to eat soon, I might die."

"How 'bout that, me too!" the man growled. He realized he was getting a bit aggressive when he saw Viugra's face looking at him crazy.

"Sorry! Sorry, I just... I need money ta eat. I get a lil crazy without food. So please, give me some money?"

"Sheesh," Viugra said. The man was giving her his best pouty face. Viugra, being the caring person that she is, bought into it.

"Okay, okay. Hold on a sec."

Viugra flipped her backpack around to rummage for the pay Mrs. Rooke gave her. As she was distracted, the guy quickly pulled out a solid object in his pocket to strike her with. With no hesitation, he swiftly lunged at her with it. Before he got anywhere near her head, he slowed down immensely. It was almost as if someone clicked slow-motion on his body.

Once Viugra remembered which pocket it was in, she reached in and grabbed one of the bills.

"Here it is!"

It was then that she finally lifted her head up and noticed the man on his tippy toes, just as he was about to leave the ground.

"OH SH–" Viugra shouted, shocked and surprised.

"Shut your mouth, Valerie!" A male voice cut in from behind her, "That kind of language is appalling. I don't even know where you learned to talk like that. The High One certainly wouldn't like that, now, would he?"

Viugra looked over her shoulder at the tall, muscular, and yet slender man. His muscles were slim but defined enough to know which one was which. He appeared to be someone from a workshop of some sort, as he was wearing a brown leather apron and a tool belt with it. There weren't any tools in the pouches, save a handy sledgehammer where his right hand rested atop of. Each hand was fitted with forearm long gloves with holes at the mid knuckles for breathability. He wore a dark navy tank top, dark brown jeans, and some resilient looking brown boots. Though his red-orange hair was mostly short, a good sum of it was banded at the back of his head and ran down his back midway. A rather vibrant crimson sweatband wrapped around his head just below his widow's peak. A pair of dark grey goggles covered his eyes, though his sharp, gold hazel eyes still gleamed through. His left hand was stretched out towards the guy who was moving in slow motion.

"What do you think you're doing? I've been trying to call you for a while now! Did you forget how to answer your phone or something?"

"Vulcanel Zelos," Viugra muttered. This is the man Mori brought her to earlier. She wasn't thrilled to see him at all.

"And I thought I told you to call me Van!" he snarled, now marching up to Viugra.

"Alright, alright!" Viugra spoke up, "Why are you in such a fit?

"Check your phone," Van said through barred teeth.

Viugra flipped her backpack to her front to rummage through it for her phone. The guy who tried to assail her reached his tipping point, resulting in a dead drop into the concrete face first. Neither Viugra nor Van paid him any attention.

"Here it is," Viugra said, pulling out a flip phone, "Let's see. Ooooooo…!"

As soon as she opened it, she noticed the twenty plus unopened messages and missed calls.

"Now you tell me, *why* am I in such a fit?"

"I-I just got these…," she stuttered, "Maybe something's wrong with it? Here, maybe you know!"

"I doubt that."

Viugra held the phone up to Van. He aggressively took hold of it and immediately noticed the slashed speaker icon at the top.

"Silenced? I told you to put the ringer on! You should've done that as soon as I told you to!"

"Alright already!" Viugra flinched, distress clearly in her face, "I-I'm sorry!"

Van was so close to Viugra that she could smell his surprisingly minty breath.

"Then do better!" Van said, still in her face.

"Okay!" Viugra pleaded, scrambling for words, and holding hands up between their faces, "I-I should've had my phone on! I f-forgot, okay? M-mori had r-rushed me along so fast I d-didn't even think about it until now."

"Don't you dare blame him," Van snapped again, but finally starting to calm down. He could see that Viugra was freaking out. In that same moment, he got a whiff of an unpleasant scent coming from her. He sniffed audibly, then glared at Viugra. Finally, he backed away and took a deep breath.

"At this rate, you're gonna be stuck with me for a while. Learn some responsibility, Valerie. You can start with lesson number one: personal hygiene."

"Wow," Viugra said, nervous but offended, "That's rude!"

"You clearly haven't smelled yourself lately," Van said, with a little sass, "If ya did, you'd understand why I said that."

"Preposterous!" Viugra said in her Elizabethan accent. She was clearly getting annoyed though. "You're just being mean now!"

She raised her arm up to smell herself just to prove her point. It didn't take long for her offensive B.O. to disrespect her nostrils. As Viugra cringed, the man on the ground slowly began to twist in a weird way as if he smelled it too.

"Uuuugh…woah," Viugra said, losing her accent in disgust, "That's rank."

"See?" Van confirmed. He finally noticed the man on the ground who was bleeding from his broken face. Van shook his head and tossed a towel near the man's head for him to wipe up the blood. He then turned towards the street.

"Let's go before that man who tried to swindle you comes to."

"Huh?" Viugra asked.

"Gaaah! Why do I need to explain everything to you?" Vulcanel snapped, "You're a Charity Angel, for Pete's sake!"

"Well, yes but… hey!"

He grabbed Viugra by the wrist, gently but firm, and rushed her out of the alley. As soon as they turned the corner, Vulcanel's spell wore off and the man on the ground rolled around in agony holding his bloody broken nose.

The "Why" Question

Later that night, a door opened to a bedroom in an attic. The night sky, tainted by light pollution from the inner city, dimly lit the room through a westward facing window with a beautiful iron-worked frame. In its caliginous glow, hazy silhouettes of a full-sized bed, a nightstand with a lamp on it, a well-crafted wardrobe, mirror, and other various boxes neatly lined the edges of the room.

In the doorway stood a hunched feminine, humanoid figure. After taking a couple of steps into the room, she allowed her backpack to slump from her back to the floor with a feeble thud. Weakly, she closed the door behind her. Walking to the bed, she removed a dimly lit hoop from around her neck and shades which hid her ominous, yet tired yellow eyes.

It was obvious that this figure, Viugra, was very tired. After setting down her halo and shades onto the nightstand next to the lamp, she flopped onto the bed in a supine position. She sighed and stared at the center of the attic ceiling. She was feeling exhausted, despite some lingering thoughts fueling her insomnia. With all that had happened since she left Bailey's house, only the most recent interaction with Van brought her to the question of why.

Two Hours Earlier

After about 10 minutes of sprint walking from the alley, Viugra and Vulcanel arrived at his ironsmith shop, VanHolly Works. The store was located close to the western shores of Nerezza's suburbs. This brick warehouse doubled as his home and his day job. Several miles north and you could see parts of a shipping port out in the water, with boats of varying sizes and designs. To the south, you could see the roads and buildings fading off into a more mountainous area with steeper cliffs along the coastline. There were a few buildings neighboring VanHolly. Due to the amount of noise, however, most shop and homeowners avoided setting up shop near it.

Before she even stepped foot in the place, Viugra acted as if she really didn't want to go in. Van knew why she was reluctant and began to push her through the doors anyways.

"H-hey!" Viugra yelped.

"As soon as you get up the stairs, you won't have to worry about the air," Van huffed, "So stop pouting!"

The shop inside was huge, with various equipment in monochrome colors staggered throughout. Forges, anvils, boilers, and other contraptions vital to ironworking were still being operated by workers. The workers were outfitted with special suits designed to protect them from any accidents that could possibly take place. Smoke fogging the air moved upwards and disappeared as they neared the ventilation ducts. Metals that glowed as brightly as a halo illuminated the shop as they were dumped into containers and hammered into shape by the employees. There were also a few steel stairs lined along the edges of the room to lead to small walkways where further maintenance and work took place in the ironwork process. Near the back of the shop, two huge garage doors with metal curtain-like filters were open to the coast for further ventilation. Next to those was another set of stairs that seem to lead to a second floor above the shop.

Though an amazing sight to some, Viugra couldn't help but feel sick from all of the smog. Vulcanel noticed, placed his hand on her shoulder, and proceeded to transform her clothes.

Before she could even protest, her outfit had completely changed to that of the workers in the shop.

"HEY!" she growled, examining herself, "You can't just change my clothes like that!"

"I'm not letting you walk through here with just a bubblegum tank top on," Vulcanel said, walking towards the stairs nearby, "I already explained that when you first came here."

"Hmph," Viugra huffed.

"Make your way to the stairs in the back. Dinner's about done, so my sister will take care of the rest when you get there. I need to send these folks home."

"Yeah, yeah," Viugra said.

"And watch your mouth! Or I'll cut your portions."

Viugra's stomach growled, as if to tell her to shut up for both their sakes. She made her way past the busybody workers, who were clothed in the same protective gear as her. Each of their fits were embroidered with wings on their backs and even their helmets were wrapped with a decorative ring.

Viugra recognized the ring's design. The jagged design reminiscent of the teeth of a cogwheel was the design of a well-seasoned Proficiency Angel's halo. Normally their halos would be thicker and have a hexagonal cutout in their centers, but they were transformed into their helmets to somewhat blend in as a human and be uniform with the VanHolly aesthetic.

Though Viugra's suit was basically the same, hers didn't have the same level of detail. The average Charity Angel would don a halo shaped as a double helix (similar to DNA, but without the connections in-between). In Viugra's case, it was a simple band with no color.

I guess I'll have to get my powers back if I want this to look more stylish, she thought to herself, watching the other workers as she walked, *I wonder how long that's going to take anyways. Sheesh…*

After a while, she reached the bottom of the stairs and began to make her way up to the second floor. While she climbed the stairs, she could hear Van over a PA speaking to the workers.

"THE WORKDAY IS OVER! I WILL SEE YOU ALL IN TWO DAYS. MAKE SURE YOU CLEAN UP YOUR AREAS. I BETTER NOT SEE ANYTHING OUT OF PLACE OR ANY WASTED

MATERIAL JUST LAYING ABOUT! WE WERE BORN TO WORK, NOT TO BE SLOUCHES!"

"YES SIR!" All the workers shouted in response. They scattered like ants, returning to their stations to shut down and clean up all that they needed to.

As Viugra climbed the tall staircase, she could feel her body growing weak on her. With tired muscles and heavy breathing, she found herself struggling to move about halfway up. The heat in the shop didn't seem to help her case either.

Geeze... she thought to herself, *It feels like Hell in here! My energy feels low. Even with this suit on, I feel like I'm burning up! I can't be this exhausted, can I?*

What Viugra failed to remember was that she had been walking miles all day, and since she was human, it exhausted her body's energy greatly. On top of that, she hadn't eaten anything since being on Earth. The only thing her body had forced her to do was sleep. It was a wonder she hadn't passed out yet from a lack of self-care. Even so, she could tell that her head was beginning to feel funny.

"...f...finally...," Viugra huffed, as she pulled herself up to the door to the second floor. Out of curiosity, she peeked over the railing to see how the shop looked from up high. That was a mistake, as she almost immediately felt dizzy. She quickly grabbed the rail to steady herself.

Holy crap... She thought to herself as she waited to regain her senses, *I should not have done that...*

Once stable, Viugra opened the second floor door and stepped in. The second floor was quite different than the first. There were a few rooms lining the hallway she was in, which stretched all the way to the front of the shop. There was one pretty big room in the middle of the second floor, filled with bandsaws, router tables, and other woodworking machines. Viugra could see them through plexiglass windows. Several worktables were in there as well, with drawers on the sides most likely for hand tools and equipment.

Viugra slowly made her way down the hall, holding onto the railing to keep from keeling over. Past the woodshop was the break room, where workers ate for lunch. It was more like a hall, as the room was pretty big for a break room.

"Ah, Valerie!" a voice called out to her. Viugra turned to a cheery face poking out from the kitchen in the break room.

"Are you okay? You don't look so good."

"Y-yeah..." Viugra confessed, "I'm not feeling so good."

"Oh, you poor thing!" the girl said, "I forgot; you probably haven't eaten anything since you've been here! You must be starving by now!"

"Probably," Viugra struggled to say.

The lady dashed back into the kitchen and quickly grabbed a couple of cooking utensils and a plate. She then began plopping a few of the things she finished cooking on it.

"Wash your hands then take a seat, please! I'll get you something to eat so you don't go dying on us!"

Dying? Viugra thought, *Well now that you mentioned it, it does feel like my soul's about to leave my body or something...*

Viugra washed her hands in a sink near the kitchen in the hall. Then she found a seat across from the kitchen counter and sat at the table. The intoxicating aroma coming from the food the girl was cooking was starting to make Viugra feel a bit sick. The food certainly smelled unbelievably scrumptious. However, this only made Viugra's stomach flail in frustration, as she still had to wait just a minute or two before she could soothe her ravenous hunger. Part of Viugra wanted to ransack the kitchen right then to get the food herself, but she figured it was the influence of the curse and fought to maintain the etiquette training that was drilled into her.

I can't let this... thing... get the best of me. But man... I want that food so bad...!

Moments later, the girl exited the kitchen with a plate of food for Viugra to eat. She gave Viugra a big piece of honey-glazed salmon, grilled asparagus, and herb roasted red potatoes. Viugra was so starved, she nearly snatched the plate from her. The girl was nearly startled by Viugra's suddenness, but soon relaxed in pity as she noticed the depravity in Viugra's face.

"I-I'm... sorry...," Viugra apologized.

"It's okay," the girl said, "I understand that you're hungry."

She handed Viugra a fork and knife to eat with.

"Thanks," Viugra smiled.

It didn't take long for Viugra to finish the plate. The salmon didn't stand a chance. The flavors blended so well in her mouth that Viugra hardly took her time to savor it. By the time Viugra finished it, the girl who was cooking in the kitchen came out to sit with her. She brought a pitcher of lemonade with her for the both of them to drink.

Viugra smiled as she watched her stomach's savior join her at the table. Hephasteya Zelos was her name, though she prefered to be called Holly. She was Van's fraternal twin, and yet she was far nicer than him.

Now that Viugra was calmer, she watched Holly as she sat down with such thankful eyes. Her semi-braided, curly red hair was bunched up in her hairnet. She was also wearing a blue and white apron with Greek designs on it, and a navy-blue tank top underneath. In addition to that, she had some brown cargo pants and black boots on as well. Several bracelets clacked together around her arms. Some were a single metal band, some had jewels encrusted in metal loops, a couple were made of wood beads, and more. She had enough of these to cover half of her forearms with.

She placed a glass of lemonade by Viugra's plate after she sat.

"Feeling better?"

"Yes Ma'am!" Viugra exclaimed, downing the lemonade gracefully.

"You've been so nice to me... I don't know what to say but thank you!"

"Think nothing of it! I love being hospitable is all!"

Holly looked around the break room.

"I didn't get to ask before, but what do you think of VanHolly?" Holly asked, "Van and I have worked hard for a long time to bring it together."

"It's… nice," Viugra hesitated. Holly noticed it.

"You don't have to spare my feelings, Val! If you don't like it here, it won't hurt me none."

"No, no!" Viugra said, "It really is amazing, honestly! It's just… well… I'm more accustomed to the outdoor air is all."

Viugra then realized that the air upstairs was different from below.

"Though come to think of it, the air here smells fresher. More natural."

Holly giggled.

"That's because I made sure Van didn't smog our home with his work. The way we designed the ventilation upstairs, you couldn't even smell the difference. On top of that, this is the woodshop floor of the building. You're probably smelling that cherry wood log I put in the fireplace."

"Amazing," Viugra said, looking behind her. True to her words, a fireplace in the back of the hall burned with the scent of cherrywood. Though it wasn't the outdoors, Viugra welcomed the aroma over the poison downstairs.

At that moment, the door which Viugra had come through earlier opened and closed. Immediately, Holly knew who it was and shifted her eyes to Viugra's empty plate.

"Oh no."

"Oh no?" Viugra asked.

"It's Van!"

"Vulcanel," Viugra disdainfully muttered in her Elizabethan accent, "No offense, but your brother has a rather dreadful attitude."

"I know, but let's not worried about that right now!" Holly panicked, "He's not going to like that I fed you early."

"Huh?" Viugra said, not understanding.

"Smells good, sis," Van said as he entered the break room, "I'm sure you're done now, so we can start ea–"

Van paused as he noticed the plate in front of Viugra with splotches of glaze still on it. Holly and Viugra were smiling nervously, as an enraged Van spoke his mind.

"YOU WERE SUPPOSED TO WAIT FOR ME! WE EAT AS ONE IN THIS HOUSEHOLD!"

"I'm sorry!" Both Holly and Viugra yelped.

✲✲✲✲✲✲✲✲

After a while, Van and Holly each fixed their own plates and sat down at the table with Viugra. Holly brought Viugra another plate of food to eat as well. What she gave Viugra earlier was only part of the entire serving she planned to give her. Viugra happily accepted, as the plate earlier didn't nearly fill her like she needed it to. Van initially felt that she shouldn't even get another helping since she ate without him, but he buried his aggression when Holly explained why she fed her early. With that being said, he realized that Viugra was still in the protective gear he gave her and rather aggressively clapped his hand on her shoulder to revert them back to her previous attire.

It was almost 9:30, and the three ate in near silence for several minutes. It was only after Viugra had finished her second plate that Van decided to speak.

"It's time I told you what you'll be doing for this trial."

"Well… yeah," Viugra responded, swallowing her final bite. She meant to sound sassy, but instead was timid.

Van set his finished plate aside, sat back in his chair, then crossed his fingers in his lap.

"Your first trial is the Trial of Pertinacity. This trial is meant to test your work ethic. As you know, I will be over your testing for this trial. Mori is also over your trial but will be watching at a distance as I am primarily in charge of this trial in particular."

"Okay..." Viugra said. She wished Mori was doing it all instead of this hot head.

"In order for you to pass this trial, you must earn my respect. This is absolute. This is also true for the rest of your trial administrators. And to earn my respect, you must prove to me you can survive in Nerezza without my help," Van said, sipping on his lemonade.

"That's it? Viugra said.

"Yes," Van began, "You'll have thirty days before–"

"Wow, really? This'll be easy!"

"...Will it now?" Van challenged, slightly annoyed about being cutoff. Viugra didn't even notice his mood shift.

"Uh, yeah?" Viugra said, "I'm not a slouch, y'know."

Van let out a stressed sigh.

"Okay then. I'll let you figure out the rest."

"Huh?" Viugra said.

"Okay then," Van said, repeating himself with emphasis, *"I'll let you figure out the rest."*

Holly watched Viugra carefully. She realized Viugra just annoyed him, and now he decided to test her on something already. Even though she was not part of Viugra's trial, she still couldn't say or do anything to help her out. Instead, she waited to see if Viugra would catch on.

"Alright..." Viugra said, not sure what he was meaning by that.

A slightly awkward silence followed. Viugra looked at Van funny, then sat back and closed her eyes.

Think... what would earn his respect?

Viugra peeked up at Van mid-thought. He had a steady yet fierce look in his eyes, which were fixated on Viugra. She flinched a little, but then felt challenged.

For the next several minutes, Viugra and Van had an undeclared staring contest, and Holly watched with her hand over her mouth.

Clearly, Viugra wasn't figuring it out and she was looking a bit goofy staring at Van. She was trying her hardest to try and figure out what Van was thinking while staring him down.

10:00 P.M. rolled by, and the two were still locked in a staring contest. Viugra started to get anxious.

I… I don't know what he wants me to do! I don't want to guess and get it wrong either! How many chances will he even give me to do anything? If only I had my powers, then I could just read his mind.

While she was struggling, Van remained calm. His stance was stalwart. Holly had placed her head on the table, pretending to be asleep from waiting.

Van knew it was about 10:00 P.M., but still checked the clock in the room. Viugra's eyes lit up and shifted to the clock as well. With his head still facing the clock, Van side-eyed Viugra as he made a statement to break the silence.

"You have thirty minutes before I go to my bed."

Holly peaked at Van when he said this, but when he caught her looking at him, she pretended to sleep again.

"O-okay," Viugra said.

Was that a hint?

Van nudged his sister. Holly lifted her head and looked at him. He tilted his head to her as if to signal something, and Holly nodded. Then he stood up.

A little panicked, Viugra finally broke the silence.

"W-Wait! Um…" she said, catching him before he averted his eyes.

"What is it, Valerie?" Van asked.

Man, what could he want? Viugra thought, *I have to try something! He wants me to do something, but I can't tell what! I'm just gonna have to make a guess…*

"W-would you… like me to… do the dishes for you?" Viugra asked with a nervous smile.

If I want to beat this trial, if I want to see my father, I have to figure this out!

"No, thank you," Van said, "I already agreed to do them tonight."

"Oh, okay," Viugra responded.

DARN IT! Viugra thought to herself, *What does he want? *huff*... If only I had my powers...*

As Viugra thought this and Van walked away to do the dishes, she faintly remembered something Mori had said to her the night before.

"You're a Charity Angel, and Charity Angels are naturally empathetic creatures! Just relax and focus. You'll know what to do because it's in your nature."

It's in my nature, Viugra thought, *Just... relax... and focus.*

Viugra closed her eyes and took a deep breath. Van reached the sink in the kitchen and began to run soap water to clean the dishes. As the water was running, Viugra opened her eyes and made her way over to the kitchen opening near the sink. As Van was focused on loading dishes into the water to clean, Viugra finally made a second attempt.

"What... do you want me to do right now, Van?"

Van stopped loading dishes. He stared at Viugra, then huffed. But this time, he smirked for what seemed to be the first time since Viugra had met him.

"You just did it."

Viugra nearly collapsed under her unnecessary expectations.

"Wait, what? I did?" Viugra asked, confused.

"Yes."

What did I just do? Viugra asked herself.

"...um... well... what did I do? Exactly?"

Van continued to smirk.

"You asked me a question."

Viugra couldn't believe his answer.

"*Are you serious*? That's all I had to DO?"

"I am serious, and that is all you had to do," Van said, finally standing up, "Took you long enough."

"Hey!" Viugra said, "Hold on, the first thing I did was ask you about the dishes!"

"True," Van said, "But that wasn't what I wanted you to ask."

"What kind of mess is this?" Viugra said, facepalming.

"The kind of mess you brought about for not listening," Van said.

"What are you talking about?" Viugra asked, mildly annoyed.

"Before I finished explaining, you cut me off. But you didn't even realize it until now, did you?"

"O-oh…" Viugra said, realizing that she had done that, "That's bad… isn't it?"

Van sighed again.

"You still don't get it apparently. Why don't you ask me why I wanted you to ask me what to do?"

"Okay," Viugra said. Then she asked the question, verbatim to avoid any more smart-aleck responses.

"Why did you want me to ask you what to do?"

"It's simple, really," Van said, "When you don't know something, you ask questions to learn. To gain information."

"Well duh!" Viugra said, "What's your point? And can't you give me a longer answer than that?"

Van continued loading dishes in the sink and washing them with a dish rag.

"You will never learn anything if you think like you know everything. If you want to win the war of survival here, asking questions is one of your greatest weapons. On top of that, you need to value the importance of listening as well. What good is a question if you don't listen and consider the answer given?"

"T-that's… true…" Viugra acknowledged.

"I'm glad you realize this," Van said, with a little sarcasm. He stopped for a brief moment while washing dishes and looked Viugra in the eyes. Viugra felt a nervous energy run through her body as if she knew what came next would sting.

"Remember this well. As a Charity Angel, your destiny is centered around how well you understand and execute communication skills. This is not only what makes your angelic race formidable, but what makes anyone cunning. If you ever hope to win this trial, if you ever want to regain your powers, and if you ever want to find your parents, then you need to get that through whatever brains you have left."

Van then returned to washing his dishes. Viugra was left with something spicy to digest. She gritted her teeth behind her pursed lips. For some reason, she felt a very strong urge to fight Van. It was so strong; she was finding it hard to stay focused.

That's when Viugra realized she was having a similar feeling as the moment the curse was first placed on her, when Chiara had asked her about seeing her father. It was the same spacey feeling she had back then, but it was the effect of a different trigger this time.

This feeling...! Viugra thought to herself, though they were a bit hazy, *Is this... what Mori was telling me... to check for?*

Because she caught it early, Viugra managed to control herself before the curse could affect her. Even so, it was taking a lot of energy to do so and she found herself breathing heavily to control herself.

As Viugra reached up to her chest where the curse's mark was, Holly noticed her movements but said nothing about it. Van continued to finish up the dishes. After she gained a bit of control, Viugra thought of a question she really wanted to ask him: a serious question from a state of sorrow. Little did she know that she would regret it soon after.

"...Why Van?"

"Why what, Valerie?" Van asked, finishing up the last dish. Viugra swallowed hard, then mustered the strength to ask her question.

"Why are you being so callous towards me?"

Van's smirk faded. Once again, he stopped washing his dishes and looked Viugra in the eyes. Viugra could feel in her gut that she wasn't going to like his answer. She could feel it in her chest.

"Because I hated your father."

Wish Upon a Young Star

Because you hated my father? How is that fair?

Viugra's late night thoughts fueled her insomnia, as Vulcanel's response earlier continued to kick her heart. After what he said to her, she didn't feel like conversing anymore and excused herself from the hall. The curse was starting to influence her way of thinking, and she knew she wasn't strong enough to avoid doing something she might regret. Van didn't force her to stay and talk either. Instead, he told Holly to escort Viugra to her room. The entire walk up, up until she flopped onto her bed, Viugra fought with the rest of her strength to keep from turning around and swinging on Van. And up until now, she was fighting to control the influence of the curse.

I don't understand everyone, she continued to think to herself, lying in bed, *Okay, so my father did something against the rules. What happened to forgiveness? Does it have to work differently for angels than humans? And how is hating my father any reason to treat me like this? You just met me earlier today for crying out loud!*

While in thought, a knock on her door briefly interrupted her thoughts. She sucked in her breath, hoping that whatever came next wouldn't reactivate the curse.

"Don't forget to take a shower," Van's voice sounded behind the door, "You still reek."

When Van walked away, Viugra sat up quickly and made a rather aggressive gesture towards the door. He was really getting on her nerves. Unlike Mori and even Bailey, Viugra knew he was coming from a place of hatred. This wasn't teasing or a tantrum to her anymore. This was bullying.

Viugra flopped back onto the bed. She hadn't felt this frustrated since Azariel cast her out of the Heavens.

I can't believe I thought that was just how he was. He really hates me! Just because of something my father did!

Viugra's eyes began to water a bit. *Here's a question: why couldn't I stay with Mori instead? At least he's nicer about the way he treats me.*

She let out a stressed sigh. As she continued to calm down, again, she rocked her head back and looked out the window with weary eyes. The lights of a distant airplane in the sky caught her eye. Seeing the lights on it moving through the night sky reminded her of a silly thing a little girl believed in.

When Viugra was sixteen years old, she was sent on a mission to answer this girl's prayers. The girl had a father who was very loving and wise. He also found great success in stock investments, which allowed them to become very wealthy after a while. Unfortunately, he eventually fell severely ill. Even though he was extremely wealthy, no amount of healthcare he paid for could rid him of his final stage of cancer. As his life was seemingly ending, the little girl saw a shooting star one night and made a wish for her father to recover.

This was Viugra's mission: to perform the miracle of healing this girl's father. But even though it was her only objective, Viugra saw the girl weeping and decided to stay longer to comfort her. She posed as a nurse who was taking care of the girl's father and spent some time with her.

After a loving heart-to-heart, Viugra and the girl looked up at the stars through the hospital window. It was then that the girl told Viugra about a legend that if you saw a shooting star soaring through the sky, you could make a wish in hopes that it would come true. She told Viugra that she had wished for her father's recovery.

But it wasn't this wish that caused Viugra to reminisce in her attic room. It was the other thing the girl wanted to wish for. Respect. Because of her wealthy status, other kids treated her as if she was too prestigious to hang with. And those who did only seemed to want a piece of that as well. The girl didn't want those fake kids around her, but the other kids unintentionally pushed her that way without trying to get to know how she really was. And when her father's condition worsened, other kids found out and began to bully her. The only reason she didn't wish for this was because she believed you could only have one wish at a time.

Viugra could relate well with what the little girl told her. While she was growing up with the other young angels, Viugra learned about her father and his achievements fighting against the demons. She was instantly captivated and had looked up to her father ever since. Even so, she noticed that she would be excluded from a lot of other angels' social groups and even heard some say nasty things about her father that were low-key about her as well. There were only a few angels who really respected and grew close to Viugra, even though one of them was currently on her bad side.

"I wish I could make a wish," Viugra said, as the airplane finally escaped the bounds of her window frame, "I wish I could just meet my father now and not have to go through this goofy trial."

She chuckled to herself as soon as those words left her mouth.

"They wouldn't even let me have that one. That would be too easy. At least let me have a friend to talk to."

As she said this, something slowly started to illuminate her backpack like a lantern. The glow faintly warmed the room until Viugra noticed it. She sat up in bed and reached for her satchel, curious as to what it could be. Slowly, she pulled the zipper open. Before she even got it all the way open, it clicked as to what it was.

A necklace. Specifically, the Reliquia Mori dragged her to VanHolly's to get made. She had forgotten all about it!

"Oh yeah! I forgot about this little guy!" Viugra said, eyes lighting up from excitement.

She pulled it out and examined it. It was a 22" silver chain with a slightly orange-yellow, ten millimeter gemstone shaped like a diamond attached. The silver chain is mostly thin but grew wider closer to the gemstone. Its glow was also yellow in hue.

I better let him out, Viugra thought, *I just need to call out to him, right? What was his name again... oh yeah!*

"Come on out, Astrel," Viugra said in a gentle and quiet voice. The pendant's light quickly grew brighter and dispersed just as fast. In its place, a single yellow ring appeared and glowed in a more concentrated manner around the gemstone. A light shot out and grew bigger in Viugra's lap. Once it reached a certain size, its glow began to disappear and shape into the form of an infant with wings curled into a fetal position. Astrel slowly opened his big eyes and looked Viugra in hers. Once he realized who it was, he began to grin with happiness to see her.

Viugra was touched by his joyful reveal. On top of that, to her, he was just too adorable to resist.

"Hey widdle guy!" Viugra said, now speaking in a babyish tone, "Aww, you so cute! You're happy to see me, aren't you?"

Astrel instantly looked at Viugra with disgust.

"Eheh... wh-why the face?" she asked nervously.

Astrel closed his eyes and shook his head.

"Please stop."

"WHOA!" Viugra freaked out, nearly dropping him.

"Whoa!" Astrel said as well, catching himself midair with his wings.

"You can talk?" Viugra asked, thoroughly surprised.

"You didn't know?" Astrel responded with a cheery voice.

"N-no, not at all," Viugra said, regaining her composure, "I mean, yesterday you weren't using actual words. If I didn't have my powers then, I wouldn't have understood a thing you were saying."

"Heehee!" Astrel laughed to himself. He gracefully floated back into Viugra's lap.

"So, what did you summon me for?"

"...well..." Viugra started.

For several minutes, Viugra vented her recent frustrations to Astrel. Astrel sat there and listened intently. He didn't say anything until he knew she was done.

"...Then he had the nerve to tell me to take a shower because I still smell! I feel like he wants to aggravate me."

"Uh-huh," Astrel said, signaling that he was still listening.

"So, then after that I looked out to the sky, wanting someone to talk to. Then you—er, your charm—started to glow. That's when I called you here."

"So that's it, huh?"

"Yep," Viugra responded, now lying flat on the bed.

"Alright," Astrel said. He then began to float around the room, thinking about what he was going to say next.

"Um... can I ask some questions?"

"Questions?" Viugra repeated, "Sure."

"Why do you think Van hates your father?"

"Well," Viugra started, "I figured it was because he was cast out of the heavens for breaking the rules."

"What rules did he break?" Astrel asked, floating closer to Viugra.

"He had sex with a human woman," Viugra said, placing her hands behind her head, "Angels aren't supposed to do that."

"What's sex?" Astrel asked.

"W-wait," Viugra said, feeling a bit anxious, "You... don't know what that is?"

"No," Astrel said, rubbing his cheek with a finger, "Should I?"

"Eheh," Viugra said nervously. Even though Astrel spoke as if he were older than he looked, he was still too young to learn about the birds and the bees yet.

"I'll... explain it to you some other time. All you need to know is that he had a child with a human woman."

"Aww, but now I wanna know," Astrel whined.

"Later," Viugra said with a smile on her face.

"Fiiiiine," Astrel huffed, "But I'm gonna ask again."

Sheesh, Viugra thought, *Did he get that from me?*

"Well, what's so wrong about having a child with a human?" Astrel asked.

"I... well," Viugra started. Funny enough, she hadn't even thought to ask herself that.

"Huh. I never thought to ask that. They just told me that we aren't allowed."

"Oh," Astrel said, "Well... maybe Van is so mean to you because he doesn't like rules to be broken."

"You might be right," Viugra said, "Still, that doesn't give him the right to be so mean to me. I mean, I didn't break that rule."

"True," Astrel said, "And as far as I can tell, you just want to help others. I don't see anything wrong with that."

"Exactly!" Viugra said, "Well, that and find my father."

"Why do you want to find him?" Astrel asked.

"Y'know," Viugra said, leaning up in her bed, "You're probably the first person to ask me that."

Viugra gently cradled Astrel closer to her chest.

"I want to ask him what happened myself. For the longest, the other angels told me he died in battle against demons a long time ago. But ever since I got sent here to do this trial, I learned that he was still alive. For years, I've wanted to meet my father. I mean, what child wouldn't want to see their parents? Also, I felt like the other angels were hiding something from me. So, I figured, if there was a way to ask him myself, I would. I want to hear his side of the story."

"I see," Astrel said. Then he noticed the concern in her face after she said this.

"What's wrong?"

"Well..." Viugra started, "I want to see him, and I will. But... he's in Hell. And I can't go there like this."

"Why not?" Astrel asked, "If you want to see him, why not just go?"

"If I go, I'll fail this trial," Viugra said.

"But you would see him, right?" Astrel said, "Is the trial more important than what you want to do?"

Viugra didn't answer right away. Astrel did seem to have a point. Why shouldn't she do what she wants? As far as she could tell, there wasn't anything wrong with wanting to see her father. It wouldn't hurt anyone for her to just talk to him.

"Then again," Astrel said, interrupting her thoughts, "Maybe that wouldn't be a good idea after all."

"Huh?" Viugra said, snapping out of her thoughts, "Wh-what makes you say that?"

"If you meet him like this, you might get stuck there."

Viugra let Astrel float out of her arms and to the window.

"Hell is… a very negative place," Astrel continued, "No hope, misery, pain, destruction… it's all there. And if you're not strong, it'll be the only thing you think there is. You could be stuck there forever."

"I suppose you would know," Viugra acknowledged.

"Well," Astrel said, "At least that's how momma said it."

"Momma…" Viugra wondered, "Hey, is your mother in Hell too?"

"Uh…" Astrel started, "Well… you could say that."

"What's her–" Viugra started to ask. But before she could finish, Astrel started to wobble in the air. Viugra quickly hopped out of bed and took hold of him.

"H-hey! What's wrong?"

"M-my head…," Astrel mumbled, "I just… got a little dizzy all of a sudden. I… think I'm fine now."

"Are you sure?" Viugra asked, genuinely concerned.

"Y-yeah," Astrel said, seemingly normal now, "I think I'm still getting used to this new life."

"Well, maybe we can talk some more later," Viugra said, "I didn't mean to tire you out."

"Maybe," Astrel said.

Viugra turned and grabbed the necklace. But before she used the pendant, Astrel stopped her.

"W-wait," he said, "Can I… stay out here for a little longer?"

"Um, sure," Viugra said, "But why?"

"Well," Astrel said, "I wanna watch the sky a bit longer."

"Okay then," Viugra said. She suddenly felt an impulse to breathe in a lot of air and exhale.

"Whoa, that was weird," she said, "I've never done that before. I do feel tired though. But I still have to take a shower…"

"Couldn't you do it in the morning?" Astrel said, "I'm sure you'll have time."

"Yeah… you're right," Viugra said, flopping onto the bed, "My energy is low anyways. Might as well rest up so I can shower later."

"Yeah," Astrel said, turning towards the window.

"Well, just make sure you go back in when you're ready," Viugra said, feeling another yawn coming on.

"I will."

"And… Astrel?" Viugra said before dozing off.

"Yes?"

"Thank… you…"

✲✲✲✲✲✲✲✲

Meanwhile, in the room across from the mess hall, Van and Holly were getting things ready for the next day of work. Van entered in just after telling Viugra to take a shower. The room they were in was a smaller woodshop area that Holly ran on Tuesdays and Thursdays. Woodwork was her specialty. When she noticed him walk in, she didn't waste any time bringing up what happened in the lunchroom.

"Done with the dishes, huh?"

"Yep," Van said, "What do you need to get done to prep for tomorrow?"

"I still need to sharpen all of the blades for tomorrow. You can start with the bandsaw blades on the table over there."

Van walked over to the table with several bandsaw blades sprawled about. He opened a drawer under the table to get the sharpening tools he needed to do his work. Before he even got started good, Holly began her questioning.

"Why did you tell her you were going to sleep soon?"

"You're still thinking about that?" Van said while picking the last tool he needed.

"Of course," Holly said. She was counting and sorting rivets, screws, and other binding pieces used in woodwork. There had to be hundreds, if not thousands, of little pieces she had to put up.

"I'm surprised she didn't realize you were making that up."

"I didn't," Van said, very defensively, "Once I'm done helping you out, I am going to my bed. Just as I said."

"That's not like you, Van," Holly said, "We both know that was misleading. The poor girl already has an assumption problem. She probably thinks you're going to sleep."

"If she does, that's her own fault," Van said, already finishing one of the blades, "I said exactly what I meant to her."

"Even the part about hating her father?" Holly asked, side-eyeing him from across the room.

"Even that," Van said, sighing, "Sis, what is this about? Clearly, you're bothered by how I'm conducting her trial."

Holly continued to work as she spoke her mind.

"I don't know, Van. You've just been more tense since she's been here. You haven't been like this with any of the other participants in the past."

"Hmph," Van said, "I just don't like lazy people. Charity Angels have a tendency to rely too much on reading people to get by. But what happens when they lose that power? They start asking 'why me?' and saying, 'this is too hard' and just whining about everything!"

Van finished another saw and placed it on top of the other one he finished earlier. Holly turned and walked towards Van. Surprisingly enough, she had finished sorting through the countless parts and taking inventory of everything.

"If you don't like how things are, then do something about it! Don't just sulk because it isn't going your way. That's why almost every one of them failed this test."

"Well," Holly started, now sitting across from him at the table, "What about that one girl from a while back? Chiara, I believe?"

"What about her?" Van asked, "She eventually figured it out, but she wasn't much different from Viugra. In fact, if she had lost her powers too, I think she would've still passed. Her downfall wasn't laziness, sis. It was a false love."

Van finished another saw and placed it in the pile. Holly finally spoke up about that.

"Y'know, you could make that easier for yourself if you just–"

"I already know, Holly," Van said, slightly annoyed, "You always say I can use the wheel or slow down time or something. But I prefer to do it the old-fashioned way, the way humans use to do it. By hand. That's just how I work."

"If you say so, sir," Holly said warmly, then continued on with the subject, "I just wish you'd be nicer to Viugra. She's a bit naïve, sure. But she's a sweetheart, I can tell. Can't you have a little patience with her?"

Van stopped sharpening the saws and looked Holly in the eyes.

"Holly, this world isn't patient. So, I'm not going to be patient with Viugra at all. You know why? Because I know what it takes to survive this damned world. She needs to understand what it feels like to fail, what it's like to be scared, what it's like to try everything and end up with nothing. Only then will she figure out what she needs to win my approval! And that's final."

Van picked up his tools and continued to sharpen the last two saws. Holly was stunned.

"Van… did you just cuss?"

"Damned isn't a cuss word, Holly," Van said, "It's only a cuss word when you use it as such. It's the same as saying 'this world is messed up.'"

"I know," Holly said, sticking her tongue out at him.

"Hmph," Van huffed.

Holly then stood up from the table, and began to head to the door.

"I still don't agree with your methods, but at least I know you care."

"What are you talking about, sis?" Van said, turning his head to see her.

"Don't play dumb," Holly giggled, "You know what I mean."

She opened the door and began to step out.

"Well, I'm going to my room now. I'm gonna write in my diary for a bit if you need me. Thanks for the help too."

"Alright," Van responded, turning back around, "And you're welcome."

Right as she rounded the corner out of sight, Holly remembered something before she got far. She peaked her head back into the room for one last remark.

"Oh, and Van?"

"What is it now, sis?"

"There's another pile of saws that need to be sharpened in the other room. You can see it through the window there."

Van looked through the windows into the big room in the middle of the floor. On one of the tables, there were several saw blades still lying about. The teeth were even more raggedy than the ones Van just sharpened. Growing angry, he snapped back towards the door Holly was standing in. She had long gone to her room. Van facepalmed, smiling behind his hand.

"I hate lazy people."

Mixed Messages

You must follow your heart.

"Huh?"

A little girl, lying on the ground, sat up to find the voice that spoke to her. No matter how hard she tried, she couldn't find its owner. All she could see were clouds miles high in the sky and along the ground, with castles and buildings of marble with gold trim throughout.

"Who was that?" The girl asked herself.

Curious to find out who spoke to her, she began to walk through the smokey alleys to find them. The further she walked into the kingdom, the more she became infatuated with its beauty. There was a happy and peaceful aura about it that could probably calm any beast.

She eventually came to a broad street that went on for what seemed like miles and dipped down to lower parts of the city. Looking to her left, she could see the tops of other buildings off in the distance with castle and cathedral-like buildings sprinkled throughout. It was a magnificent sight to behold.

"Whoa…" the little girl exclaimed, growing even more excited.

Suddenly, light shadows began to rush across the ground. The little girl looked up and saw colorful winged creatures with human forms and beautiful robes flying up from the streets and high into the sky. Angels!

They were laughing, singing, playing, and twirling around in joyful bliss. The little girl's eyes lit up in exhilaration, watching such beautiful creatures having so much fun.

"Wow! I wanna have fun too!" the little girl said.

Her slow walk turned into a brisk sprint as she found herself trying to chase after them. She ran as hard as she could. But the more she ran and jumped after them, the more she realized how futile it was to reach them. After all, she herself did not have wings to fly. After a few minutes, the little girl grew exhausted and slowed down to catch her breath.

"W-wait!" she tried yelling after them. The angels didn't seem to stop at all for her. She could've given up at that moment, but she was too determined now.

"WAAAIT! I'M COMING TOO!"

With a sudden second wind, she made another sprint towards them. She began to hop up in hopes of just floating up with them. She jumped several times, each after a few strides. After about a minute of running, the road began to go downhill. Seeing this only made her try even harder, though she was getting exhausted at this point. But her faith and determination might've paid off. Just before the big slope, a pair of wings suddenly sprouted from her back. The span of the wings immediately caught air, and the girl found herself gliding in the air a bit.

"I-I can fly!" she squealed in delight. Unfortunately, she was at her limit. Though she was a few feet off the ground, she couldn't find any energy to flap her newly-grown wings. So, instead of ascending, she descended back down to the streets and landed flat on her butt.

"Ow!" she whimpered, catching her breath. With saddened eyes, she watched the angels continuing to ascend and play without her. At this point, the girl was feeling abandoned and ready to give up.

It was then that one of the younger looking angels noticed her and swooped down ever so gracefully to greet her.

"How fare thee, m'lady?" he spoke to her.

"H-hello!" she responded, surprisedly.

"Oh? Doest thou not speakest the holy tongue?"

"Uhh," the little girl muttered, unsure of how to answer. This angel seemed a bit peculiar. He noticed the strange look on her face, then leaned in and whispered something to her.

"Don't worry, it's just an act. Play along maybe?"

He had her at play.

"Oh! Um… certainly?"

"Splendid!" He continued. He stretched his hand to her.

"I noticed your valiant efforts to make for the heavens. Such determination is due appropriate reverence. I would be honored to assist one of such…" he started. Before he could finish, several other angels that appeared to be as young as him hovering in the sky interrupted him.

"Come on, Lord Bautista! Lest we miss the warmth of day?" one of them said.

"Oh hush!" a female angel interjected, "The light never parishes in this land. Do go somewhere with that malarkey!"

The group of angels laughed at their humor. Clearly, they were in on the joke as well.

"Just a moment!" Lord Bautista answered, then turned back to the girl, "So, how about it? Can I give you a ride? It'll be fun!"

Once again, he had her at fun.

"Oh yes!" the girl replied, "Please, take me with you… uh, thee!"

"Indubitably!"

The male figure squatted down and turned his back to her with arms extended behind him. He was going to give her a piggie back ride.

The little girl delightfully climbed onto his back and hooked her legs through his cupped arms. The figure spread his wings to the sky, and in one powerful motion flapped them down and took off. In mere seconds, they were miles off the ground, piercing through the clouds at breathtaking speeds with his friends. The kingdom below was so vast and beautiful, brimming with shimmering light. It was as if stars filled every facet of the kingdom below. The little girl was in paradise, as they all danced amongst the clouds.

After a few moments, the angel known to the girl as Lord Bautista turned his head to her.

"M'lady?" Lord Bautista started.

"Yes, m'lord?"

"Might I ask a question?"

"Certainly!"

"Why did you want to be an angel?"

"I... I dunno," the little girl hesitated. Then, something resurfaced in her memory, and she quickly retracted her statement.

"No wait... I know! It's because of my daddy!"

"Your father?" Lord Bautista questioned. His tone seemed a bit funny, but the girl didn't seem to notice.

"Yeah! He always loved and protected everyone!"

"That is true," Lord Bautista muttered.

"Huh?" the little girl asked.

"Oh, it is nothing!" he covered up. He then did a twirl that tossed the girl into the air.

"Wheee!"

Lord Bautista then caught her and held her for a moment.

"Say, shall I teach thee?" Lord Bautista asked, "Teach thee the ways of an angel?"

The little girl gleamed. She went from lost and sad to overjoyed in mere minutes thanks to Lord Bautista. She couldn't possibly turn down his offer now.

It wasn't long before the little girl managed to work her wings again. And although she struggled for a bit at first, she soon kept up with the rest. In fact, she was becoming faster than most of them. It wasn't long before she had them in awe with her growth.

Time seemed nonexistent as the gang played among the brightly lit clouds. They played Aerial Tag, Lightball (Dodgeball with weak blasts of light), and more. But the favorite that they played longer than any was Imperium. It didn't matter how many wanted to play as it was a free-for-all game. The goal was to win respect from the other angels by getting them to surrender. You also had to follow role-play strategies determined prior to each session.

You could only choose one strategy, or role, to use per game which were called a Knight, Rook, and Bishop. Knights use offensive strategies, Rooks use defensive strategies, and Bishops use passive strategies. If you surrendered to an angel, you became their pawn and assisted them by zoning another angel until your leader commanded their respect. Pawns could not attack or speak, but they could defend their leader. When there were two angels left, the one with the most pawns was regarded as the King and the other as the Queen. Whoever conceded first surrendered the title of King to the other, which was declared the winner.

The little girl always chose to be a Rook, as she always wanted to be a protector like her father. She was surprisingly good at the role too. She would always beat this other female angel who struggled to play any role she chose. But she didn't mind being the little girl's pawn in the game. In fact, she did so often just to be on her team. They eventually became just as good friends as her and Lord Bautista.

Almost every game was won by Lord Bautista. The only exception was the last game, where the little girl used a move involving her voice to calm and lower his guard. It was one of the few techniques besides a shock arte and weapon conjuring that Lord Bautista taught her. Even so, she had gotten so good at Imperium that most of the games ended with her as the Queen. All of the angels were amazed with how quickly she had learned to play. None of them ever got mad at her either. In fact, they were elated that she was so good. They had a real respect for how well she played the game.

After that last game, however, she decided to sit out for the next one. A strange feeling swelled in her chest that was not at all pleasant. Hovering off to the side, she watched the other angels having fun. Lord Bautista decided to check on her while they started another game of Imperium.

"M'lady, doest thou farest well?"

"Yeah…" the little girl said. She was not at all convincing. Lord Bautista dropped the accent to take things more seriously.

"You don't sound too sure. What's wrong?"

"Well…" the little girl started, "I just… wish my daddy was here to see this. To have fun, too. I'm sad that he isn't here."

"I see," Lord Bautista said, "Well, you can still have fun without him. I'm sure he knows how much fun you're having."

The little girl pondered this for a moment, then shook her head.

"No… I… I can't."

"Of course, you can," Lord Bautista tried to affirm. But his push back was only agitating the feeling in the little girl's chest more.

"N-no… it's not the same," the little girl pleaded.

"Please," Lord Bautista said. He gently held the little girl's face in his hands. But his next words did little, if not the exact opposite, to calm her.

"Please. You must forget about your father."

"What?" The little girl said, surprised at what she was hearing, "No. I can't. I… I won't!"

"But you must!" Lord Bautista implored, "If you don't… you'll die!"

"I… I…" The little girl hesitated at first. The thought of death was sudden and uncomfortable. But with great conviction, she pushed away from Lord Bautista.

"I WON'T!"

That's right. Follow your heart.

The little girl held her chest. At the same time the voice spoke to her, the heaviness in her chest seemed to amplify. Lord Bautista noticed and inched towards her.

"What's the matter?" he asked.

"N-no..." she responded, "Just... stay away!"

The weight in her chest grew tremendously, becoming painful to the point where the little girl crumpled and began falling towards the ground. As she plummeted, the mysterious voice spoke to her again.

Follow your heart. Accept your desires. Remember your name.

"My... name...?" the little girl muttered.

"Azekah!" Lord Bautista yelled.

The little girl weakly opened her eyes as she descended to the ground below. The angels dispersed beyond the darkening clouds and Lord Bautista descended towards the girl, his friends calling after him in pursuit.

The air became warmer and humid, and the clouds condensed. Suddenly lightning began crashing into the kingdom below, disintegrating each building and structure. The sandy debris began to shroud the once beautiful streets, quickly turning it into a white desert land full of rubble.

Each strike became more severe than the last as Lord Bautista fell closer and closer to the little girl. He eventually reached her and held her close. But instead of flying back into the sky, Lord Bautista scowled at the sky, which was becoming more and more turbulent. The little girl continued to hold her chest while in his arms, too agonized to worry about him holding her anymore. Eventually they reached the ground, and Lord Bautista took off in a sprint.

Just seconds before the others reached the ground, the lightning began to sound different. The once heavy roar turned into sharp loud cracks that rattled the air. A bolt hit the angel who called Lord Bautista's name earlier. His lifeless body crashed into the sandy streets and didn't move.

The lighting was striking down Lord Bautista's friends. One by one, their bloodcurdling shrieks rattled the little girl's soul. Her new friends were being killed! Eyes wide in shock, the little girl cried out after them as each bolt pierced their bodies.

"NOOOO!" she screamed. Gusts of sand choked her words as she watched in horror.

The angels tried to fight back, creating arte circles to conjure powers with varying abilities. However, their efforts were futile. The lightning completely ignored their attacks, instantly frying them in their entirety. Each one was struck down except for the girl angel, who was on the little girl's Imperium team often. She ran alongside Lord Bautista. She looked at the little girl with great concern, as she noticed bleeding from her shoulder. Even she must have gotten nicked a little.

The environment had completely changed by now. Hot gusts of sand lashed against their faces as they reached a barely stable building to hide in. The once beautiful kingdom was no longer recognizable. All that remained was sand and indistinguishable debris. It was now almost pitch black, with powerful haboobs shrouding any light that would've shined through the sky, save the flashes of lightning.

Lord Bautista set the little girl down next to the other girl after they hid beneath a mound of rubble barely stable enough to be a shelter. He then stuck his hand in his pocket as he peeked around the corner of where they came.

But the little girl, now more hurt over the loss of her new friends, wasn't even sure if it was him anymore. He also appeared different now. He had on ragged clothing and looked even more beat up than her. Even his hair and head shape had changed, not to mention that his angelic assets were also gone. Surely his face must be different as well, but she couldn't make out all of his features in the dark.

"Azekah," he spoke. Even his voice was different.

"Wh-what?" the little girl spoke. The other girl looked up at him.

The desert winds seemed to quell when he spoke that name. The corrupted heavens might've known what would happen next because Lord Bautista pulled out a deadly looking pistol before answering the little girl.

"...Forgive me."

He raised his gun towards the little girl. Her eyes widened in disbelief, throat clogged with sand and fear.

No... why...?

The other girl jumped in front of her.

"No! Don't do it! NO!"

He pulled the trigger. The gun fired just as loud and powerful as the lightning strikes. The bullet pierced through both girls' chests, the force of which toppled their bodies to the ground. The little girl writhed in pain for several seconds, while the other girl barely moved at all. He then left the shelter of the rubble without a word. Then, silence.

The little girl, coughing up blood, realized the bullet missed her vitals. But she was still bleeding out and barely hanging on from passing out. But the girl who took the bullet first was in a much more critical state. The bullet left a gruesome cavity where her heart was. The little girl called out to her wounded guardian.

"Ez... rah..." she whispered, struggling to hold her consciousness, "Ez... rah..."

Ezrah stirred. The little girl could barely make out her face in the dark, but she knew Ezrah turned towards her.

"Aze... kah..." she coughed, barely audible.

"Ezrah... I'm sorry," Azekah cried weakily.

"No... You... didn't..." She struggled. But then silence. Azekah was scared that she was gone.

"Ezrah... Ezrah! she struggled to scream.

You didn't... deserve this...

The voice from before rung through Azekah's head. Suddenly, Ezrah's body sat up straight.

"Ez... rah?" Azekah muttered.

"You didn't deserve to live."

At that moment, Ezrah's head turned all the way around. Her mouth had stretched across her entire face and bright horns grew from her head. The glow illuminated her frighteningly decrepit face, as she closed in to consume Azekah.

"YOU DIDN'T DESERVE TO LIVE!"

✲✲✲✲✲✲✲

"AAAAAAAHHHH!"

Bailey woke up in her bed, eyes wide in fear and tears rolling down her cheeks. Her chest rose from her bed as she clenched the left side of it. The pain choked away her screams. She barely realized that she was back in her room before noticing she was having another panic attack.

But lucky for her, Mely was still home and heard her screams.

"Hang on, Bailey!" She yelled from her room.

Bailey couldn't even respond to her. All she could do was hold on for dear life until she made it to her room.

It was 5:04 in the morning when Bailey woke from her nightmare. Luckily for her, Mrs. Rooke was already up to get ready for work. After taking her medicine, she managed to completely calm down about fifteen minutes later. She was cradled in her mother's lap just like before.

"Are you okay?" Mrs. Rooke asked.

"Yeah..." Bailey said. Though she wasn't technically lying, she was still unnerved by the dream she had.

*What the h*** was that dream?*

"Did you have a nightmare?" Mrs. Rooke asked.

"Yeah..." Bailey answered, "Something... tried to eat me."

Mrs. Rooke giggled a bit.

"What's so funny?" Bailey asked, slightly offended.

"Well, never mind that," Mrs. Rooke said.

"Hmph," Bailey huffed, turning her head away.

"Always gotta be the rebel, don't we?" Mrs. Rooke said. Then her attitude became serious after she knew Bailey was better.

"You should stay home today."

"Why?" Bailey asked.

"I'm serious, Bailey," Mrs. Rooke said sternly, "This is the second panic attack you've had in just the last twenty-four hours. I know it was a dream, but your body is real. What am I gonna do if this happens while you're at school?"

"But... Mom," Bailey hesitated to say. She sat up as she spoke. "Today's the day for finals. The last day of school."

"I know, but your health is more important to me," Mrs. Rooke said, "You're very smart, Bailey. You can always breeze through it all again. But you can't breeze through death."

Bailey thought about her dream when the voices were speaking to her, and she thought about the girl who tried to save her at the end of it.

"...No, mom," Bailey answered, "I have to do this."

"Bailey..." Mrs. Rooke tried to protest.

"Don't," Bailey shot back. Mrs. Rooke started to argue but noted how serious she was and decided to hear her out.

"I am not about to do eighth grade all over again. You told me to finish school if I wanted to help anyone around here, and now you want to tell me to wait it out? And if you, your friend, or that other irritating bi..."

Bailey stopped, then noticed her mother's face. She was looking at her like she had better not cuss.

"...I mean tramp... won't let me go out and do that now, then I need to finish school. I can't keep waiting!"

"Bailey," Mrs. Rooke started.

"I know how it feels to be left to die," Bailey said, "And I'm not about to just sit here and pray, hoping they'll be okay. No, I'm gonna do something about it!"

Mrs. Rooke gritted her teeth behind closed lips. Bailey could see the stress that she was causing her mother, then let out a sigh.

"Look, I'll be fine. I won't have another panic attack."

"I don't believe that," Mrs. Rooke said, now standing up, "I can't. You just got in trouble because you couldn't control yourself."

"Well," Bailey started to defend herself, "I couldn't just let those... stupid girls tear that other one down like that! Someone had to beat their a**!"

"Bailey," Mrs. Rooke said sternly.

"Someone had to beat some sense into them!" Bailey rephrased with a huff.

"Maybe, but that isn't your fight," Mrs. Rooke said, "You have to let God work sometimes or you'll mess up what he's working on."

"And that's EXACTLY what I'm not about to do!" Bailey said, getting a little worked up, "Why wait? You'd just watch someone being slaughtered when you have the power to kill their assailants, wouldn't you? Wait, lemme guess, GOD will make a way somehow! F*** that, I'm gonna save them!"

"ENOUGH!"

Mrs. Rooke finally exploded. She grabbed the door and began to head back to her room. Before she did, she gave her last remarks before leaving her hard-headed child.

"I work so d*** hard to give you a better life, and yet you keep drifting back to this twisted world..." Mrs. Rooke muttered, then spoke up, "Fine Bailey, go to school! If that's what you want to do, you'll do it. But know this: they have no more tolerance for your antics at Duncan. If you do anything else crazy, they will expel you from the district. You go to school to finish your finals. Nothing else, do you understand?"

Bailey's lips were pursed. Mrs. Rooke was fighting for authority, but she held her ground.

"Do. You. Understand Me, Bailey?"

"Yesss," Bailey sighed.

Mrs. Rooke didn't say a word for several seconds. Bailey looked at her mother, seeing the amount of stress in her face from trying to contend with her. Though Bailey was unapologetic in her stance, deep down she hated to see her mother so stressed. Work was already eating away at her free time trying to find a response to the Animus Disease. And Bailey believeed the initiative was mostly focusing on making money from the situation rather than resolving it, taking advantage of those trying to find an honest cure. Even more reason as to why she wanted to take matters into her own hands instead of waiting around for the answer to come to Nerezza.

Bailey looked away from Mrs. Rooke, who then turned around and headed back to her room.

"I'm going to finish getting ready for work. Make sure you take care of yourself before you leave today."

"Sure," Bailey responded.

Once Mrs. Rooke left the room, Bailey laid on her bed and rolled to the side. Unable to sleep again, her thoughts retraced the heated debate that just transpired. Eventually, they drifted to the dream she just had about angels and death. Though the dream was vivid when she was asleep, its contents seemed harder to make out now. But what did stick out to her were the words that were spoken in her head.

Bailey eventually decided to peruse the internet on her phone until it was time for her to go to school. But the entire time she did, those last words lingered in the back of her mind.

Dive into the Heart

"Heeeeello, Sleeping Beauty! Ya gonna wake up, or do I need to kiss ya?"

After several squints, Viugra slowly opened her eyes to find the voice waking her up. When she was conscious enough, she realized something was off. Just as she noticed, some scorching hot liquid washed over her feet. Viugra jumped backwards and fell flat on her butt.

"Whouch!" she yelped.

As she sat up, rubbing her rear, confusion continued to sink in. Somehow, she ended up on the beach just behind VanHolly. It was still night, the beach illuminated by the glow of the waxing quarter moon. Her gaze dropped to the vast ocean in front of her. What washed over her feet must've been the ocean water. Although, the water seemed to have a darker hue than usual. It was almost a dark plum color.

Her eyes then darted about, analyzing the surrounding area. Clearly, she didn't understand how she ended up outside.

"Wondering how you got out here?" a voice spoke up, "Take a wild guess."

Viugra became alert, simultaneously feeling her heart sink in her chest like a stone in water. The voice sounded uncannily familiar, like the voice of a tantalizing woman who liked to toy with her prey.

"W-who's there?"

"Really girl?" the voice answered, "Don't play. You know who I am!"

Viugra then noticed a dark figure standing out in the water several meters from where she was sitting. She couldn't quite make out the silhouette, as it was too far and dark enough to obscure any details. But the figure seemed to be gently playing with the water with her feet. For some reason, a strange feeling of frustration swelled inside of Viugra watching this shadow playing in the water.

"...Why am I out here?"

"Ah," the voice spoke again, "I see Vulcanel's already testing your mental fortitude. Well between him, that special tattie I gave you, and those sclera lens the angels gave ya, you're gonna catch h*** sista. I'd give it until tomorrow night."

The mention of the *tattie*, which was referring to the curse mark on Viugra's chest, was undeniable proof who it was.

"...Chiara."

"Bingo."

At that moment, the shadowy figure on the water began to move closer to Viugra. The silhouette became more pronounced, revealing the shape of glowing horns, wings, a tail, and the checkered trench coat that defined her ridiculous outfit.

"To answer ya question, I dragged ya here. I wanna get to know my future business partner better."

When Viugra could visually identify Chiara, she took a step backwards. Then Chiara stopped.

"Wow. Are you scared of me? Aww poopsie!"

"Oh, p-please," Viugra tried to snap back. Unfortunately, she couldn't hide the trembling in her voice.

"*Ohhh please*!" Chiara mocked, "You're not fooling anyone."

Chiara smiled, the same one that ripped and stretched beyond her face.

"Don't worry. I ain't gonna hurt ya yet hun."

Chiara continued to walk closer to Viugra, who continued to take steps back. After a while, this started to annoy Chiara.

"...Would you stop walking away?"

In an instant, Chiara appeared right in front of Viugra's face. Viugra didn't even notice Chiara was so close until after she had her hand gripped around Viugra's neck, elbow in her chest, and was dragging her across the beach. Chiara slammed Viugra up against VanHolly. The impact created a crack in the building wall, sending excruciating pain throughout Viugra's body and possibly fracturing several bones in her torso. Viugra uttered a painful cry, coughing up blood from the internal damage.

"Yer gonna break mah heart," Chiara cooed, slightly tightening her grip.

"P-please... s-stop..." Viugra coughed, struggling through Chiara's grip. After a few seconds, Chiara chuckled and released her. Viugra fell to the ground gasping for air. While she was struggling to regain her bearings, she couldn't help but wonder where Mori and Van were to protect her.

Why aren't Mori, Van, or Holly here? They have to hear what's going on!

"So, tell me," Chiara said, looking towards the ocean and hand on hip, "How's my Cambion doing?"

"Wh-what...?" Viugra asked.

"My Cambion," Chiara angrily sneered, pointing a long sharp nail from her free hand down to Viugra's face, "You converted one of my Cambions into a Petta Angel last night—a special one at that! The least you can do is tell me what'cha did to'em!"

"You mean... Astrel?"

"Astrel, huh?" Chiara mumbled calmly to herself, "That's the name you decided to give him, huh?"

"Yes," Viugra said. She was close enough to Chiara to hear her mumbling.

Now that she had caught her breath, Viugra stood back up. The pain had her weak, but she remained standing.

"Such a traditional way of naming, you know?" Chiara remarked, "I gave him a different name. Something more... appropriate."

"You named him?" Viugra asked, surprised and curious. Most Cambion Demons are called by their classifications, such as imps.

Most demons don't go out of their way to name their underlings, which is why this surprised Viugra.

"What's his name?"

Chiara laughed.

"I'm not gonna tell you! Hah, you thought!"

Chiara slung her nail across Viugra's face, leaving a painfully large gash in her left cheek.

"Aaagh!" Viugra whimpered, holding her slashed face. Chiara continued to laugh while Viugra reeled in agony. The waves of the ocean in the distance seemed to grow more violent in sync with Viugra's pain. Chiara noticed the seemingly odd cause and effect.

When Viugra calmed down a bit, she spoke up against Chiara.

"Why are you hurting me?"

"Why am I hurting you?" Chiara snorted, "You said it yourself: I'm a deeeemon!"

"You're insane..."

"You're right," Chiara said, walking towards the ocean, "I am insane. I'm also weepy, irritated, thrilled, and... demented."

Viugra watched as Chiara admired her long lethal nails, the one extending from her index finger lightly coated with Viugra's blood.

"But you know what else I am?"

"Wh-what...?" Viugra asked regretfully.

"...Lustful."

Viugra swallowed hard when she said this.

Where's she getting at with this?

"Tell me something," Chiara continued, "Are you aware that some of your power has returned to you?"

"What?" Viugra said, surprised, "What are you talking about?"

"Clearly not," Chiara explained, "You should be more aware of the weapons at your disposal. Especially if you need to... protect yourself."

Viugra wasn't sure what she was talking about at first. But then it hit her: something weird did happen earlier. After Bailey bit her, she began to ask her about what she did after she screamed. Somehow, it calmed her down. It was her voice that Chiara was referring to.

"The voice of an Angel," Chiara said, retracting her nails, "The most basic form of defense of any holy being. And in your case, a spiritual S.O.S."

"Of course," Viugra said to herself, "I completely forgot I could do that!"

"Hmph," Chiara continued, "Let's get to the point of this little excursion, shall we?"

She then turned to the ocean and extended a hand towards it.

"You have something I want, Viugra. Just as I have something you want."

But Viugra wasn't really trying to listen to her. She was a demon after all. Anything she said was for the wrong reasons, right? So Viugra took a deep breath in. Chiara looked bored, as she noticed what Viugra was going to try.

"Don't bother. You're way too scary to hurt me. You can't even grasp your self-identity right now."

Viugra paused on her breath. She exhaled nervously.

"Wh-what are you–"

"Talking about?" Chiara finished her question, "If you just shut your a** up for a minute, you'd know. Course, we can just do this the hard f***ing way where I break every bone in your d*** body and…"

Chiara paused, then chuckled to herself. Viugra was not amused.

"What's so funny?"

"Don't worry about it," Chiara said. She could see the trembling in Viugra's body. Even if she tried to use her Angelic Voice to fight Chiara, she was too terrified to make use of it. And Chiara knew this, so she continued with her ultimatum.

"Here's the deal: I want half of your ocean?"

"My ocean…?" Viugra said. She couldn't tell if she was speaking nonsense or missing context.

"Yes," Chiara said, smiling creepily again.

Viugra couldn't comprehend a lot of things, as she used her powers to learn and 'store her memory' so to speak. But once Chiara brought attention to the ocean, Viugra started to connect dots about what was happening. From the burning ocean to the quiet city life atmosphere, she formed a theory of what was going on.

"You… this… this isn't even real, is it?" Viugra said. Chiara sneered.

"Of course, it is, hun."

"No, it's not!" Viugra shot back, getting defensive.

"Ooooh!" Chiara exclaimed, getting a little excited by Viugra's sudden energy, "Someone's buckin' up!"

"This place… it's all a dream, isn't it? And you… you're just a nightmare! I'm only seeing this place right now because it's the last thing I saw before I fell asleep!"

"Hmm…" Chiara thought out loud, "That's an interesting conclusion."

Suddenly, Chiara zipped directly in front of Viugra.

"If that's what'cha think… why don't we test that theory?"

Chiara grabbed Viugra by her left arm and began to drag her towards the ocean.

"H-hey!" Viugra flailed, grabbing Chiara's arm and trying to get loose. But her grip was immovable. She then took a chance and bit her arm. Chiara stopped, but not because it hurt. She was actually mildly amused.

"Pffft! Seriously? You're gonna try the child's move?"

With no other ideas, Viugra tried to use her last resort move: The Angelic Voice. With all her might, Viugra screamed at the top of her lungs. The sound echoed across the waters and open space.

But that didn't faze Chiara either.

"I told you," Chiara said, now looking annoyed, "You're too scared!"

With great launching power, Chiara chucked Viugra several feet into the ocean. Seconds later, Viugra was bobbing up radically and screaming from the agony of the wave's searing hot brine.

"Hahahaha! You should see the look on yo face! Hahahahah!"

"Aaaaa... *glub* ...ugh... aaaaagh!" Viugra screamed, as the water seared her flesh.

Wh-what's going on? She thought to herself, *Why's the ocean so hot?*

"Now tell me," Chiara taunted, "Does that feel like a dream? Or a living nightmare?"

No.... Viugra thought amidst her screams and frantic swimming, *I... I'm gonna die!*

"C'mon now," Chiara said, smiling evilly, "Just swim back. You can do it!"

I... can't... Viugra cried inside. The pain and fear she was experiencing began to weaken her conscious and strength.

"You look like you're having fun," Chiara said, squatting a bit, "Let me in on the fun!"

Chiara lunged several feet from the beach and slammed into the drowning Viugra. Viugra was just beginning to lose consciousness, as Chiara sunk her further down underwater with her hand over Viugra's curse mark. But even Chiara wasn't invulnerable to the burning ocean waters. Though enduring the searing of her flesh beneath the waves, Chiara sank further and further.

"Let's see if you come out of this alive or not."

No... I... Viugra thought, as her consciousness began to fade, *Father...*

☼☼☼☼☼☼☼☼

"GAAAASP!"

Viugra flew into the air and banked off the edge of her bed. She hit the bedroom floor with a loud thud, which could be heard all the way down the hallway. She opened her eyes slowly and realized that she was no longer drowning. She was back in her room. Calmly, she placed her hands around her body to assess the damages. But there were none: no broken ribs, scarred face, or burnt skin.

But despite the abrupt change in environment and the absence of her wounds, Viugra didn't appear to be surprised. In fact, she simply stood on her feet and walked towards the window to view the beach behind VanHolly.

As she seemed to expect, the beach was untouched. The waves of the ocean seemed clearer than when Chiara was there. There weren't any trails in the sand from when Chiara dragged her around or where they were walking and standing. And the waves were calm. Just the usual ebb and flow.

"What's with all the racket?" a voice broke the silence.

Viugra turned around slowly to see a frustrated Vulcanel standing in her doorway. The thud of her body on the ground must've triggered him. Even so, Viugra's response was calm.

"I had a nightmare."

"A nightmare?" Van asked, still frustrated, "You've been screaming like that off and on for the last hour!"

An hour, huh? She thought to herself.

"Well," Viugra began. But what she said next seemed to really shake Van, as he wasn't expecting the type of response she gave him.

"I'm sure you'll let me know how inappropriate making noise is at this hour and shout at me to go to sleep, because I have some long a** day tomorrow. But honestly, I really don't care right now."

Van couldn't believe the back talk he was getting right now. The look in Viugra's face was stone cold as well. She didn't appear sorry for anything she was saying. She just walked over to her bed and sat down on it, maintaining her icy stare.

"I'm going back to sleep now. And you don't have to ask me if I'm okay or anything. I know you don't care. I am my now-demonic father's child after all. Nothing to love about a tainted fallen angel, is there?"

"You have some nerve…" Van finally responded, completely taken aback by Viugra's unusual rebellious comments.

Van turned to walk out the door.

"You just earned yourself one strike on this trial. Keep talking like that when your day starts in a few hours, and you'll fail this trial faster than you got dragged out of the city last night!"

Van then proceeded to slam the door as he left.

"Hmph," Viugra huffed. She then flopped onto the bed. After the sounds of his marching footsteps disappeared, Viugra looked at her body once more. Then she proceeded to change her day clothes into some pajamas with her powers. Once in some fuzzy PJs, she got underneath the covers of her bed and turned to the side to sleep. Her eyes closed and her hands were clasped in a praying posture underneath her head. Viugra then smiled as she began to drift back to sleep. She smiled so hard that wrinkles began to form around her mouth.

And then… tears began to silently flow down her cheeks.

Premonitions

Out in the cemetery where Viugra landed, Mori walked amongst the gravestones. He seemed to reminisce on every other grave as if he knew each person. After a while, he stopped when he reached a grave with a cross and an angel headstone that came up to his waist. For several minutes, he stared at it. After a while, a voice broke the silence.

"Don't you ever do any work in your spare time? Or do you just like brooding all day?"

"Heh," Mori chuckled, looking to the sky, "Hello teapot. You're looking awful black yourself."

"Ha ha," the voice said sarcastically, as a man approached Mori.

It was Vulcanel. He walked up right beside him, standing in front of the grave together. They stood there in silence together, as if Van had come to pay his respects to whoever's grave it was. Once that time passed, he turned to Mori.

"Seems you were right," Van said.

"Told ya," Mori said, continuing to look to the sky, "So then... what will you do Van?"

Van closed his eyes as if pondering his response. Eventually, he managed an answer.

"Hope."

"Hoooope," Mori repeated, trilling his voice as if to tease him.

"You making fun of me, bone head?" Van questioned, gritting his teeth. Mori chuckled to himself.

"I'm sorry Vulcanel. Still getting used to you talking like that."

Van didn't share his amusement. In fact, he looked as if he would break the mandible right off him. But Van soon loosened up.

"Do you think she'll make it?"

Mori looked at Van.

"Well, that depends on you, doesn't it? She's gotta earn your respect."

"Hmph," Van huffed, "She may be the daughter of the once most respected angel of them all. But I can't respect someone who respects a cheater. I wouldn't dare give free power to a person who hasn't earned it."

"Oh, lighten up," Mori said, placing his hand on Van's shoulder, "Viugra may be spoiled, but that doesn't necessarily make her lazy. I'm sure she'll do the right thing when the time comes."

Van looked at Mori skeptically.

"You've only known her for a day, and yet you speak as if you've known her for years."

Mori didn't respond to this. After analyzing Mori's fiery eye sockets for a moment, Van closed his eyes and chuckled to himself.

"I see. So that's the game you're playing."

Van turned away and began heading out of the cemetery. Mori watched as he was leaving.

"We'll see if that theory of yours is right soon enough."

As Van disappeared beyond the hills, the sun began to rise from the opposite horizon. Mori sighed.

"And here I thought you would keep me company a bit longer."

He then faced the grave he was watching before and began speaking to it as if talking to its owner.

"All she has to do is persevere. The odds are already in her favor. Isn't that right?"

☼☼☼☼☼☼☼

Viugra woke up at 7:06 A.M. The bright and refreshing dawn was in stark contrast to how she was feeling. Holding her head, she sat up slowly and rolled to the edge of the bed. The world felt dreamlike and dizzying. But after a minute or two, reality felt stable, yet she herself felt miserable.

Ugh... Viugra thought.

She struggled to stand up, but when she did, she walked to the window. Her entire body felt heavy and difficult to move. Looking out the window, she watched idle ships. As her gaze swept across the waters, a very uncomfortable feeling stirred inside her. Though she couldn't quite make it out, it was like she felt the presence of another person in the room. One that was intimidating and yet ominously familiar.

Chiara...? Viugra thought to herself, paranoid.

"Hey Val? You're up now, right?"

A voice outside of Viugra's room startled her. It was just Holly.

"Van's out for a minute, but he'll be back soon. You better get ready before then."

"A-alright," Viugra mumbled. Holly probably didn't hear her for how low she responded, but Viugra didn't seem to pay it any mind. Her gut bothered and head throbbing, Viugra headed to the door and exited her room.

When Viugra stepped into the hallway, she heard Holly swiftly moving around the kitchen. Once she got there, Holly greeted her and prepared a plate of three pancakes, turkey sausage links, scrambled eggs, and a glass of orange juice. Though she had a taste of everything, Viugra barely managed to eat a quarter of her meal before deciding to get up and leave.

"Thanks for breakfast. Gonna head down now."

"Uh, Val?" Holly started, flipping the pancake on a skillet, "Are you okay?"

"Uh... well..." Viugra hesitated. Before she could finish, Holly set her skillet down and turned the heat off, heading over to check Viugra herself.

"You haven't been looking so good ever since you walked in here. And you barely ate your breakfast. Are you sick?"

Holly placed her hand on Viugra's forehead.

"You don't seem to have a fever. Did something happen last night?"

Viugra heavily sighed before answering her.

"I... don't know... I had a dream... a nightmare really..."

Viugra yawned for several seconds after she managed these words. Holly looked really concerned.

"Hmm."

Holly began backing up to the kitchen.

"Know what? Gimme a sec and I'll help you get ready."

"Huh?"

"You can't go downstairs when you haven't washed up yet. Plus, you're still in your pajamas."

"Pajamas...?"

Viugra didn't even realize that she was in pajamas. She thought she was still wearing her street clothes. This realization alone was enough to wake her up.

Wait... when did I change into this? I could've sworn I was wearing my street clothes...

Right after this thought, Holly zipped to Viugra with all kinds of feminine hygiene products. Viugra nearly tripped backwards from how fast she approached her. She didn't even notice her leave.

"H-how did...? When did you ...?"

"Come on, Val," Holly winked, "Let's get you cleaned up!"

She took Viugra by the arm and drug her into the bathroom down the hall. Once there, Holly began teaching Viugra the ropes for personal hygiene. She left Viugra in the bathroom to clean up afterwards, vowing to check up on her in ten minutes. She struggled to find the energy, but by the time Holly returned, Viugra had finished. Or at least, she thought so.

"Valerie," Holly said, a little disappointed. She noticed that Viugra put her pajamas back on."You know you can't go out there looking like that. Plus, you don't even have your shades on. You're gonna get weird looks."

Viugra sighed, more so from the exhaustion she was feeling.

"I'm sorry Holly. Truth is, I don't know where my other clothes are."

"Really?" she said surprised. Holly thought, then closely inspected Viugra's pajamas.

"You don't realize that you're still wearing them, do you?"

"What?"

"Your pajamas are your other clothes! You must've transformed them while you were sleepy."

No, that's not possible... Viugra thought, *I don't have the power to do that right now. But... I really don't remember... What's going on?*

"Well," Viugra started, looking away as if embarrassed, "I can't change them back."

"But how did–" Holly started to ask. But before she could finish, she checked the clock and realize that they were almost out of time before Van arrived.

"Never mind. I'll help you this once Val."

"Wait, won't you get in trouble?" Viugra asked, concerned.

"Only if you tell," Holly said with a wink.

She placed her hand on Viugra's shoulder, then forced her clothes to change into the street clothes she wore before.

"There. And I threw in a little extra express wash for ya, so they're practically brand new."

Viugra managed a smile.

"Thanks, Holly."

"No problem!" Holly said, handing Viugra her shades, "Now get on downstairs. Van should be here any minute."

As Viugra headed down the stairs and through the forge, she watched the workers coming to work. They all headed past her and up the very stairs she descended. Once she reached the front door, she saw a red pickup truck pull up to the entrance of VanHolly. It was Van.

"Let's go, Valerie! It's time to work!"

With an exacerbated sigh, she gripped her backpack straps and headed to the truck.

☼☼☼☼☼☼☼☼

The workday began with Van telling Viugra the day's agenda. Although she technically wasn't working for him, he mandated that she volunteered today so he could explain some basic things about Nerezza. In addition to this, it was part of his testing. Though her trial started yesterday with babysitting Bailey, this was Van's way of observing her directly.

Van explained his agenda as this: deliver finished products to several clients throughout Nerezza and have them complete the necessary paperwork. The VanHolly workers from yesterday had orders to rendezvous at some clients' locations for installation. Once Van arrived, they would unload the client's product and begin their work. As for Viugra, she would simply interact with the clients and have them sign off on paperwork for the final payment arrangements, warranties, and other miscellaneous contracts. This task seemed easy enough to Viugra, but Van warned her that it wasn't as simple as she might think.

"Don't get comfortable, Valerie. Remember that we live in Nerezza. Not all of my clients are honest. Stick to the script, no matter what. Don't bargain with them on anything. They just need to sign off. If it comes down to it, I will intervene and resolve the situation myself. *Only* if I think I need to. And don't take more than five minutes. Traffic will be tough getting around close to noon and the late afternoon. I need time to be punctual."

"Okay," Viugra responded.

"Remember, this is part of your trial. You could get a strike every time you disobey me or fail to complete the tasks I give you. You can also eliminate them by doing something right. But if you get three strikes, you fail this trial. And you know what happens then. So, I advise you to stay focused."

With that, 8 A.M. came and they took off. Traffic at this time was still mild compared to what it would be later. They started down the street closest to the coastline, giving Viugra a chance to observe the west side of the city a bit more. The industrial district extended for about fifty acres along the coast below southern Nerezza. Ten of those acres extended north of VanHolly into Nerezza. After a few minutes of driving, the street became lined with palm trees. Most of the buildings were less than three floors tall around here, and the shore was now like a recreational beach. She could see several umbrellas and lots of people already going to the water to play.

Shouldn't they be at work? She thought to herself.

As Viugra observed the people scattered about, she thought about the dream she had.

Was it really just a dream? I mean, my body is perfectly fine. My skin is intact, no scratch on my face, no bite mark…

Viugra suddenly realized that the wound Bailey inflicted on her yesterday was fully healed.

Wait…

"We're almost at the first place," Van interrupted her thoughts, "Get the first stack of paperwork ready."

"R-right," Viugra said, a bit startled. She grabbed the folder that Van gave her with the paperwork in it. He had organized everything in order of each destination on the route, so Viugra didn't have to look far to get the first client's paperwork. After a while, they turned down a street heading east, away from the beach.

When they arrived at their first stop, they both hopped out of the truck. The first client was a landlord for an apartment building by the name of Randy Wilcox. Van nodded to Viugra and told her to greet the man while he unloaded the delivery. Trying her best to shake her morning lull, Viugra approached him, who happened to be outside smoking while waiting for them.

"Good morning, Mr. Wilcox."

The man was clothed in a rather dingy turquois beach shirt, grey shredded shorts, and white sandals. He also donned a straw hat and shades similar to Viugra's. But, perhaps the most defining feature of this man was the reddish orange hair dye he had and the scar he had over his left eye. He was slightly shorter than Viugra, but stockier in width. When Viugra gained his attention, he lowered his shades to inspect this stranger coming up to him.

"You new?"

"Y-yes," Viugra answered, "I need your signature for the delivery, sir."

"You mind the smoke?" he asked before approaching.

"Uh, well," Viugra started. But Randy could read it in her face before she could spit it out.

"Geez, relax. I ain't gonna rip ya head off about it. Not unless you give me a reason to."

Randy tossed the cigarette down on the ground and stomped it out. Viugra handed him the paperwork once he came up to her.

This isn't that bad, Viugra thought to herself. Unfortunately, she thought too soon.

"What's your name?"

"It's Viu–" Viugra started abruptly. She nearly forgot to use her human name.

"…Valerie!"

Randy raised an eyebrow.

"Why you gotta lie about it? I just asked for your name!"

Crap! Viugra thought, *Why did I slip up like that?*

"Uh… I mean…" She struggled to find a truthful reason. But Randy wasn't about to deal with the bull she was trying to convince him of. Offended, he vented his frustration.

"You women nowadays… ain't no body tryin' to hit on y'all a**! You can tell me yo d*** name! That's just a courtesy! Stop actin' like men are the scum of the Earth, s***!"

Viugra, astonished by his sudden outburst, wasn't sure how to respond.

"Um... what are you talking about? I just–"

"Don't act f***ing dumb now," Randy interrupted.

He fiercely handed the paperwork back to Viugra. Out of impulse, she snatched it from his hand. He looked at her crazy.

"I know you ain't getting a f***ing attitude with me!"

"...It was a mistake..." Viugra said through clenched teeth. She was too tired to fight her urges effectively right now.

"Listen here, Valerie," Randy started, getting close to her face, "I deal with your type every day, all day. Thinking they can talk any kind of way and act any kind of way and expect me to bow down to their ignorance. And I've seen the worst of that s***, believe me. But I've got nothing but time, power, and heat if need be to deal with they a**. And little miss, you ain't no different."

Randy turned away and lit up a brand new cigarette as he finished his spiel.

"I'mma let this slide today, but you better learn some godd*** manners before you come back again. And I don't believe in puttin' my hands on women, but I ain't gonna let one beat the s*** outta me either. Got that?"

Randy walked into the building and watched the VanHolly workers install the doors he ordered. Viugra didn't even move. She felt a lot of frustration building up, similar to last night when Van made her angry. And yet, things were different this time.

Go ahead, a voice spoke in her head, *Slam his head on the desk. Punch him in his throat. Make him suffer for coming at you wrong!*

Viugra struggled to focus, as the rage was building inside her. She was feeling dizzy and nauseated. But with all her strength, she managed to overcome her odd immobility and sickness. She then headed towards the truck, holding her head.

N-no... I... I can't... it's not... right...

Viugra got into the truck and continued to hold her head until things finally stabilized. Luckily, the symptoms disappeared as quickly as they had come. Viugra looked up in distress and breathed heavily as if coming up for air.

Wh... what was that? That voice... Was that Chiara?

Not long after this, Van reentered the truck and prepared to pull off. Viugra glanced at him, then looked off. Van focused on pulling back out into traffic. Once he got going good, he finally spoke on the first delivery.

"Calm down, Valerie. We got it done. I saw what happened."

"WHAT?" Viugra shouted. Van shot her a fierce glare for being so loud, and Viugra nervously lowered her voice.

"Wh-why didn't you defend me? You said you would resolve the situation if you needed to!"

"IF I thought I needed to," Van said, "You need to remember everything I said if you want to argue."

"You didn't think I needed your help?" Viugra asked, trying to restrain her frustration.

"Did he try to put his hands on you?" Van asked.

"No."

"Then I didn't need to intervene," Van concluded, "The rest was vital to test you."

"You've got to be kidding me," Viugra said.

"Randy may be overreactive," Van said, as he turned a corner, heading south, "But he deals with some radical tenants. What he said was all true. A lot of his clients get into fights over there, many of which have ended in gunfights and death. He just had a long night dealing with a homicide in two of the apartments the day before you landed here. That's why he's so edgy right now. That's also why he's one of my frequent clients. Somehow the tenants always find a way to destroy his place. And that guy gets stuck with having to find a way to repair it."

Viugra started to feel sorry for him, but only a little bit.

"I suppose. That's still no way to talk to someone you don't know."

"Hmph," Van continued, "I'll admit, I'm surprised you had as much restraint as you did. However, you still earned yourself a strike."

"What?" Viugra said again, trying to catch herself mid-shout, "Why did I get a strike? I didn't do anything wrong!"

"You did," Van said, glancing at Viugra from the side, "You snatched the paperwork out of his hands."

"But that's because he pretty much shoved it in my face!" Viugra said, now a bit concerned.

"It doesn't matter, Valerie," Van explained, "By you grabbing the documents like you did, you exhibited wrathful behavior. Remember the teaching of being angry but sinning not?"

"N-no..." Viugra admitted regretfully.

"Well, that's your reason," Van said as he began pulling up to the next client's house.

Man! Viugra thought to herself, *I didn't think it would be this easy to get strikes! And I only get three chances before I fail?*

"Enough talking," Van said, opening the door of the truck, "You can clear that strike by doing right at this stop. Let's get a move on."

By the time they were halfway through the list of clients, it was about 11:30 A.M. They were headed towards the northern part of the city now. Viugra was getting stressed, as Van had to pull her away from three of the clients who were trying to smooth-talk her. Each time, she did well enough to dismiss a strike and bad enough to earn it right back. The strikes often came from her making mistakes she could've avoided had she paid attention to what she was doing. But it was difficult for her to focus, as she was still tired and with a headache throughout most of the day. And it didn't help with Van having an attitude the more the strikes occurred.

Despite being annoyed by his attitude, Viugra noticed that something seemed different about him. There wasn't the same level of aggression in his voice as it was yesterday. Though she couldn't pinpoint what she was sensing from him, Viugra definitely caught on to some vibe she was getting off of him.

At noon, Van pulled over so Viugra could grab a lunch for her lunch break. After she grabbed a sandwich from the back, she hopped back into her seat, and they took off. Between each bite, Viugra thought about the weird stuff that she had been experiencing ever since she woke up.

What is wrong with me? The nightmare I had last night, my clothes being transformed, the way Van's acting, and even this curse mark… I just have this weird feeling that I'm forgetting something. Something that might explain what's happening to me.

As soon as she thought these words, Viugra caught a glimpse of a person standing in the midst of the crowded sidewalk. It was a lady in ragged clothing, and she appeared to be staring back at her. Just as the lady moved out of view, she smiled at Viugra and waved. Viugra weakly smiled and waved back at her before she was out of sight.

The next half of the clients were from the residential districts along the northwestern coast, just beyond where the ship port was. There, big fancy houses and mansions were lined along the coast. They also had a beach, but there were far more people here than there were in southern Nerezza. But the time of day was close to noon, so more people were awake and ready to hit the sand.

The first couple of clients were surprisingly easy to deal with compared to the earlier ones. They didn't waste Viugra's time, as they were concerned with other business and wanted to quickly sign off and be done with their parts. The clients were wealthy after all. They had the money to pay everything off up front. The trade-off seemed to be that they were a bit condescending and prideful in the way they spoke to Viugra, but luckily, she didn't catch on to their sly microaggressions.

By 3 P.M., they were on their eighth client. This client lived in a very fancy mansion with a gate blocking the way to the front door. They had a courtyard with several floral patches lined along the driveway that snaked up to the house. There were several beautiful garden decorations, each which appeared to be baby angels playing with one another. Overall, the mansion's exterior gave off a classic Victorian feel with lots of floral décor.

Viugra flipped through the folder as they pulled up to the mansion. Once Van parked the truck, he got out and prepared to unload a special package, different from what they had been delivering before. VanHolly not only did practical iron and wood workings, but creative ones as well. This client in particular ordered a unique metal creation, most likely for decoration inside the home.

When Viugra got out, her head was on a swivel in anticipation of Chiara showing up again. While looking around, she noticed the client walking out of the front doors towards her. But something about her seemed familiar.

She looks familiar… but she can't be someone I know. I've never been to Nerezza before. And yet…

"Good afternoon, Van," the lady spoke, "I see you have someone new working with you today. Your name?"

Though the lady spoke with elegance, she didn't have the same haughty aura the other Northern clients had.

"Hello," Viugra introduced herself, "My name is Valerie. Nice to meet you!"

"Valerie, huh?" the lady said, now looking at Viugra's face intently, "Has… that always been your name?"

"Uh…" Viugra hesitated, "Y-yes?"

"Hmm… you look exactly like someone I knew sixteen years ago."

"Really?" Viugra said, "Funny… I was thinking you looked familiar too."

"Did you happen to work at a hospital in New York?"

"A hospital in New York?" Viugra exclaimed, "Well, technically yes. Wait a minute…"

"It is you, isn't it?" the lady exclaimed, "You're one of the nurses who helped take care of my father when he was fighting cancer!"

"Uh, yep, eheheh," Viugra said. She couldn't tell her that she wasn't really a nurse. Nonetheless, they both recognized who one another was.

"I know it's been years, but don't you remember me?"

"I do actually," Viugra said, "I just don't remember your name. Sorry."

The lady smiled.

"It's Leah. Leah Phelan."

"That's right! Now I remember!"

Just as Viugra uttered those words, she noticed a rather nasty glance from Van, who was unloading from the truck. Though Viugra couldn't understand his gesture, clearly, he was wanting her to get on with the paperwork. To Viugra, he was just being mean. Either way, she wasn't wrong.

"Seems someone's got their draws up their a**," Leah said, noticing Van's nasty look. Her whole professional demeanor seemed to dissolve now she knew who she was talking to.

"How do you know that?" Viugra asked, cluelessly.

Leah laughed.

"Girl! You still got jokes!"

She stuck her hand out to Viugra.

"Let me see that paperwork. I'd hate to get my favorite nurse in the world in trouble."

Favorite? Viugra thought, as she handed Leah the paperwork to sign.

"So, what'cha been up to all these years?" Leah asked as she glanced over everything and signed.

"Oh um," Viugra started to answer, "Y'know... saving the world..."

"Hahahaaaaa!" Leah laughed again.

That was funny? Viugra thought.

"Giiiirl!" Leah said, finishing up her paperwork, "You're on a roll today, aren't you?"

"Suuuure," Viugra responded, unsure about agreeing with her.

Despite feeling confused, Viugra was genuinely happy to see Leah again. Ever since Viugra first met her at the age of twelve, Leah had a very bubbly and yet mature personality. She reminded Viugra of another friend of hers from the heavens she spent a lot of time with. Just hearing her cheery voice brought her a moment's reprieve. And yet, at the same time, a strange, uneasy feeling stirred in her stomach.

That's strange, Viugra thought, *A feeling of happiness and… fear? But why?*

"You good, Val?" Leah broke into Viugra's thoughts.

"Oh!" Viugra snapped back to reality, suppressing her unease, "I'm fine!"

"Okie dokie," Leah responded, "Here's the paperwork back."

"Thank you," Viugra responded, retrieving the documents. Leah looked at her and shook her head. The look on her face had become suddenly serious. This change of expression instantly concerned Viugra.

"Why are you looking like that?"

"Val," Leah started, leaning in closer to her, "I… I don't know how to ask this really. But… I need someone to talk to. I've… been going through a lot the last few years after moving here. My emotions have been all over the place, I've been struggling to sleep some nights, it's just been crazy…"

Leah eyed Van glaring at them from the truck. He was clearly getting impatient. But Leah didn't care about his attitude. In fact, she did more than glare back at him. The look in her eye was almost murderous.

Viugra noticed that she was looking at Van and could somewhat tell that he was waiting for her to get in the truck and finish the deliveries.

"I-I see," Viugra said.

Before she could make her exit speech, Leah placed one hand on Viugra's shoulder and another on top of the other with paperwork in it. In a sly way, Leah slipped a piece of paper under Viugra's thumb.

"I know you have to go, Val. Not sure why you went from the hospital to iron working with this pain in the a**, but it's good to see you again. Just call me, and we can set up a time to meet."

"Y-yeah," Viugra said.

When Leah removed her hands, Viugra noticed the slip of paper with Leah's phone number on it.

"I don't think you will, but… please Valerie. Don't stand me up. I don't know if I can take much more of people rejecting me. I need you, Valerie."

Viugra, astonished by the shift in tone of the conversation, nodded her head.

"Don't worry, Leah. I won't abandon you. I'll call you later."

Leah smiled.

"I know you will."

Viugra briskly walked back to the truck, waving to Leah and stuffing the paper she handed her into her pocket. She was then whisked out of Leah's glorious front yard by a terribly furious man. Back on the road, Van was itching to let Viugra have it. Viugra was breathing heavily, waiting for him to shout at her at any moment. She didn't have to wait long.

"What did I tell you before we left out?" Van said through clenched teeth.

"To stick to the script?"

"That we're on a tight schedule!" Van yelled.

"I-I know that!" Viugra argued.

"Clearly not!" Van snapped back, "You already made us lose time with Randy earlier. But this time, I caught you wasting time conversing with this client! Now we're five minutes behind schedule!"

Viugra sighed heavily. That only added fuel to the fire.

"I know you didn't just sigh!"

Viugra was getting tight.

"So what if I did? I got the paperwork signed, why are you yelling at me? And it's just five minutes. I'm sure the other clients will–"

"We have a standard to keep, Valerie," Van cut her off, "You better take this time management seriously or you won't pass this trial!"

Viugra was about to lose it. The fact that he cut her off when he gave her such a hard time about doing that the night before pissed her off.

"Y-YOU JUST INTERRUPTED ME!"

"I sure did!" He admitted, unapologetically, "I'm not about to let you sit here and tell me what's alright and what's not!"

"THAT'S NOT FAIR! HOW CAN YOU CALL YOURSELF AN ANGEL ACTING LIKE THIS?"

Van hit the brakes hard when he reached a red light. Viugra's body rocked forward, hard into the seat belt. The sudden jerk hurt Viugra's chest where the strap came across. She slowly looked at Van with emotional and disbelieving eyes, unsure if he meant for the seat belt to hurt her. Van turned his head with fury in his eyes and calmly, yet very tensely, made a cruel statement.

"Angels have to uphold the high standards of the High One at all times, no matter how much sin may distract them from their task. If you can't learn to follow the rules AND respond appropriately when you're being tried and tested, you might as well give up getting back to your pseudo paradise. I'm doing what I'm supposed to do. You're not. Get your act together."

The light turned green, and Van faced the road again. As he accelerated, he finished his rant.

"You now have one strike."

"WHAT?" Viugra shouted, feeling a swirl of emotions all at once.

"Two more!" Van interrupted before she could say anything else, "...without making up for the first one, and I fail you. And just so you remember, you will be stripped of any of your angel power and status AND any memories associated with your angelic life. You will live out the rest of your days among the humans…"

Van paused, glancing at Viugra before finishing his statement. To her, the world seemed to slow down right before he finished. Despite having no predictive powers, she was terrified of what he would say next. For a brief moment, his expression was full of grief. Then, he looked back at the road and dealt the final blow.

"…and you'll never get the chance to meet your father."

With that, the curse mark on Viugra's chest immediately glowed. Her eyes grew wide before her consciousness precipitously fell into the void of her mind, her perceived world rapidly fading to darkness.

Sleight of Psyche

"V-Viugra…"

Viugra, unaware of what had happened, came to from the voice of a child. She found herself staring into the night sky surrounded by towering buildings. The air smelled foul, like the remains of trashed food marinating in their juices. Her face crumpled as she tried to respond to the voice.

"Where am I? Who's–"

Suddenly, she felt immense pain in several parts of her body and her head. She reflexively crumpled into a ball and began rolling around, holding her head, crying, and whining from the abrupt anguish.

"Aaaaagh! Haaaaaagh!"

For several minutes she wailed. Her screams eventually subsided into low moans of pain. By then, Viugra could finally endure it enough to sit up and search for the voice that called out to her. She recognized that she was in an alley somewhere on the north side of Nerezza, based on their design. Even though the alley was spooky, the lights from the inner city prevented any darkness from cloaking it.

In addition to splatters of blood and her shades around her, Viugra also noticed another tattered body lying on the pavement next to her. The red scrunchie tied around her hair signaled who it was, and Viugra was horrified.

"B-Bailey…?" Viugra uttered.

Bailey didn't respond. She seemed to have passed out from her pain. Fearing that she might've been suffering from another panic attack, Viugra pulled herself closer to Bailey to check her vitals. Her breathing was heavy and staggered, but it was from the pain she was suffering. Even so, Viugra couldn't tell the difference.

"Hey Bailey," Viugra spoke gently, trying to comfort her, "It's me. I'm here. You're okay, you're okay…"

"Aww, in't that sweet? But ain't it hard calming someone else when you're scared too?"

The unexpected words of a woman's voice alerted Viugra. Gritting her teeth, she was snatched up in a whirl of fearful emotions. Now familiar with her voice, Viugra knew who it was without a doubt.

"Ch-Chiara? Go away!"

"Hahahahahah!" she laughed, "I will. When I feel like it."

"J-just… leave us alone!" Viugra protested, setting Bailey down and standing to defend her.

Viugra gritted her teeth, frantically darting her eyes around in search of Chiara's location. No luck. She then started to feel faint, as her head was hurting so bad that she might as well have had a migraine.

"You'll never believe this," Chiara said, "But I didn't lay a finga on either of ya!"

"I don't believe you!"

Viugra didn't feel like hearing her excuses this time. She was so discombobulated from the extreme transition that took place that tears streamed down her cheeks. One moment, she was arguing with Van about the trials, the next she and Bailey are wounded in an alley with Chiara taunting her. Panicked, her chest began to expand and contract rapidly from hyperventilating.

"Careful sweetie," Chiara said, "A severe concussion and excessive breathing? You're gonna speed things up like that."

"Sh-shut up!" Viugra snapped, "Why are you hiding anyways? Y-you're scared too, aren't you?"

"That's precious. You think I'm scared of you? I could'a killed you two days ago. But I've got plans for you."

Suddenly, Viugra dropped to her knees. Whatever happened to her really left her wounded pretty bad, as the blood loss and the pungent smell in the alley were starting to make her lightheaded.

"Wh-what… is this?" Viugra asked, frustrated.

"I already told you a while ago," Chiara taunted, "At least, one of you! Hahahahah!"

"One of me…?"

At that moment, Viugra noticed the curse mark on her chest looked different than before. The design was more complex and appeared as if it had been finished.

The curse… don't tell me…!

"Hey, I'm not repeating myself," Chiara said, voice trailing off, "You wanna know what's happening… just ask yourself. Or should I say… your OTHER self?"

"W-WAIT!" Viugra cried in desperation, fists pressed into the concrete, "Just answer my questions!"

Chiara's voice dissipated, leaving an echo of laughter.

Viugra bowed her head in frustration when she realized Chiara had left. She was practically screaming in her head as she began to crumble under her stress. There was too much going on to process; the setting had changed abruptly, Bailey was present and injured, she herself was wounded to a great degree, and Chiara decided to torment her. Not to mention the stench of the alley was sickening. All of this was enough to start driving her mad. She couldn't even vocalize her distress because of her excessive breathing.

I… I can't keep up! Nothing… sense! No… answers! Why… WHY ARE WE HERE? What do I do? Wh-where's Van? Where's… Mori? It's not fair! Just… why me? …Why… m-me…wh… why…

Suddenly, her thoughts fell silent. Viugra's body went limp, passing out and slumping to the ground. She laid there with Bailey, now both unconscious and bleeding out. No one was nearby to help. Things weren't looking good for them.

Then, just when things couldn't get worse, the shadows around them began to move and take form. They morphed into yellow-eyed demons. Focused on Viugra, they crept to her body.

Just inches away from her, the demons were ready to pounce. Then suddenly, Viugra inhaled greatly and screamed with all her might. The power in her voice shook the demons' spirits, stunning them in place. She staggered up on her feet to a hunched-over posture. After taking a moment to wipe her tears away, she mumbled a single line.

"Star of wisdom and wonder, let your rays find truth and impale deceit."

Throwing her hands out to her sides, she conjured several daggers of light between her knuckles. She looked up with fierce conviction in her eyes, frayed strands of hair draped over her face. Then, in a flurry of arm movements, she implanted them in the foreheads of several demons. Some managed to avoid her onslaught, retreating to the shadows and disappearing. Viugra did not stop until she had banished or scared off every last one.

When she finally stopped, she turned to face Bailey who was still bleeding out. Viugra picked up her shades while walking to pick Bailey up. Once she lifted Bailey up, Viugra jumped up to the rooftops. As she hopped up the buildings and skipped across their roofs, she healed Bailey's injuries and her own, as well as her own clothes.

After jumping through the city at blinding speeds for several minutes, Viugra reached the Rooke residence. She opened the door and carried Bailey to her room, lying her down in her bed. She checked Bailey's vitals, and though she was still unconscious, her breathing had calmed down significantly.

Once Viugra knew she was okay, she searched and confiscated the 9mm pistol Bailey always carried and a uniquely designed rosary with a green bead in the center of it from her jacket and hand. Viugra, particularly intrigued by the rosary, looked back at Bailey.

"You're something else," Viugra said, with an oddly captivating tone of voice, "Where'd you even get this?"

With that, Viugra found a spot to sit, placed the items in her lap, and closed her eyes.

☼☼☼☼☼☼☼☼

"Wake up. I need to talk to ya."

Viugra, lying flat on her back, slowly opened her eyes. Once again, she found herself looking at the night sky. However, only a single star and a quarter moon which barely illuminated anything was there. The air was cool and refreshing. But odder than the absence of the stars was the absence of land. Somehow, she was lying atop the surface of an endless sea of water.

Where... am I? she thought to herself.

"Hey! I said wake up!"

That voice... there's no way...

Viugra sat up and looked around. Nothing but water and darkness.

"Finally. Look below yourself."

"Below?"

Viugra rolled over and looked into the dimly lit waters beneath her. At first, all she saw was her dim reflection. But as she looked closer, it began to move separately from her movements.

"Huh?"

"Relax," the reflection said, "It's just you."

"Relax?" Viugra said, now waking up fully, "How can I? I don't even know what's going on. And I'm talking to myself? I'm about to go crazy!"

Her reflection sighed.

"Just shut up, sit down, and listen. We don't have much time."

After a moment of hesitation, Viugra sighed, then sat upon the water with eyes focused on her reflection.

"Fine. I give up trying anyways."

"Good," the reflection sassed, "You try way too hard as it is, honey."

"Please, I'm not in the mood," Viugra stopped, "Just... get on with it."

The reflection frowned at Viugra, then walked away. After a few steps into the abyss of the ocean, it turned around. It was completely identical to how Viugra looked. However, some of the reflection's hair was covering the left half of her face. Plus, her expression was a bit more tantalizing than Viugra's normally would be.

"First thing's first. You and I are both the same and separate. I am your self-identity."

"My self-identity?" Viugra questioned, "How's that–"

"I'm not done explaining," the reflection interrupted.

"Oh, sorry," Viugra apologized.

"Accepted," the reflection continued, "You can see me because I'm using our power of introspection to speak with you right now. This place represents your subconscious, or psyche."

"Really?" Viugra said.

"Yes. It should be familiar to you."

"Well... if you mean like the dream I had last night..."

The reflection's expression became angry, then switched to sadness. Viugra noticed this brief yet strange moment.

"Wh-what? I didn't mean to make you sad!"

"Never mind," the reflection dismissed, "That's not what I meant. Just... I need your help. So, listen and answer my questions."

"O-okay," Viugra said, still wondering why her self-identity was fluctuating through different emotions.

"Do you trust yourself?"

Viugra, a little confused about the question, answered.

"Uh, I think so..."

"Hmm..." The reflection continued, "Okay... do you trust Leah Phelan?"

Again, Viugra was a little confused about the question being asked.

"Yeah… I mean somewhat. I know we're friends."

"I see," the reflection said, "One more question. That kid, Bailey. Do you trust her?"

"Bailey?" Viugra exclaimed, "I… I don't know. I feel like she doesn't like me though."

"Yeah… I thought so too."

Viugra couldn't hold back her wonder any longer.

"Hold on. You said you're my self-identity. Shouldn't you already know this stuff?"

The reflection brushed some of her hair back, sighing.

"You really don't remember anything, do you?"

"What do you mean?"

The reflection began to move her hands in explanation, first pointing to her chest.

"Remember the curse batwoman put on ya?"

"Batwoman?" Viugra questioned, looking at her own chest.

"I'm talking about Chiara. She didn't complete it the first time she placed it. However, that changed when she dunked your a** into the ocean last night."

"Dunked me into the ocean?" Viugra said, not getting it, "What are you–"

"Oh my god," the reflection growled, getting frustrated, "How are you not getting this? Just LISTEN! The ocean? That's me. I'm both your ocean and your reflection. Wanna know why? Because your self-identity is the source of your power! How did you forget that?"

Viugra held her head in her hand when her reflection said this. Though she was struggling to keep up, she recognized what she was saying.

"My power… that's… that's right! I did forget, but…"

"It finally clickin'?" The reflection continued, slowly starting to sound condescending, "But wait, there's more! That curse on you?

That ain't no alignment curse. Noooo, honey. That curse splits personalities! And now that it's complete, it split ours!"

"Split... personalities?" Viugra repeated, slowly making the connections, "Wait, if that curse splits personalities... that means you're–"

"...your alter ego."

Viugra gaped at her reflection in amazement.

"How can you be my self-identity and my alter ego? Shouldn't I be my self-identity?"

"That's the complexity of this curse," the reflection explained, "Simply put, Chiara used her spirit to 'pinch' your soul. Though we are somewhat separated, we are still connected. But the parts of your soul that contain your self-identity are concentrated on my half."

"I... see..."

"You still have fragments of your self-identity, partially due to you gaining even a sliver of your power back. That prevented the curse from completely splitting our soul in half. If it would've, we would be a vegetable."

"A vegetable?" Viugra asked, "How does–"

"It means death," the reflection answered, realizing Viugra didn't understand metaphorical talk, "Though our body would still exist, we ourselves would cease to."

"Oh..." Viugra said, feeling chills from the thought of that.

"So, congratulations. You now have Dissociative Identity Disorder."

"Whoa..." Viugra said, still trying to grasp everything.

"And you know what triggers the switch between us?"

Viugra shook her head.

"Whenever you react emotionally to someone else mentioning your father."

Viugra started to connect more dots, remembering back to when Chiara first put the curse on her. Right before she did, she made Viugra reveal her heart's desire which was to find her father. That was the moment she made her father her swap trigger. She also remembered the last thing Van said before things went blank. His words about losing the chance to find her father was what triggered the swap!

"I... I get it now... you and I switched. And while I was... switched... you... you were using my body!"

"You're finally getting it," the reflection continued, "And the only way you can switch back is when I lose consciousness again. So let me try to wrap this thing up for ya," the reflection continued, "We, like all other angels, were born with connections to the spiritual world. Our souls store that spiritual power. But do you remember how we unleash it?"

Viugra, still trying to get through the fact that she has an alter ego, tried to figure it out. She just couldn't remember.

"I... I don't remember..."

"Of course," her reflection said, slapping the water barrier between them, "That would be you. When that curse pinches your soul and I come out, your half of our soul contains the corrupted self-respect."

"I-I'm... my self-respect?" Viugra stuttered.

"Exactly. I define you, and you are the one who's to acknowledge and respect me. And the more you get to know and respect yourself, you're supposed to cling to that. And just like iron sharpens iron, others will test your hardness. Either they will sharpen your soul or cut you to the heart. That's how you get stronger."

"H-hold on, that's a lot to take in at once!"

"You should've remembered this on your own!" the reflection ridiculed, "But you over-relied on my power to think, remember, and communicate all these years!"

Viugra found the energy to argue back.

"But if that's true, you allowed me to do it! W-why didn't you stop me?"

"Why didn't I…?" The reflection nearly blew it, "Because I didn't have control over you! YOU have control over you! I was only a slave battered by your whips of doubt and unnecessary change!"

"…What…?" Viugra mumbled.

The reflection had tears rolling down her cheeks, fists against the water boundary between them.

"You are the dominant consciousness of this soul. Without the curse, I belong to you. I had no problem serving you. I was you, after all. But you created all of these false assumptions about yourself solely based on what others said about your father. And you tried to change me into things I'm not. What makes it even worse is that you couldn't decide if you wanted to be like your selfish image of your father or the opposite of what the other angels said about him. Do you realize how much that hurt me? I don't think you love me for who I am!"

Viugra flinched at this accusation.

"No… that's not true! I do love you!"

The reflection began backing up.

"I bet you don't even remember my name."

"…It's–" Viugra started, looking off as if trying to remember.

"Don't," the reflection interrupted, "I can't even read your mind, and yet I know you don't."

Viugra fell silent. The reflection turned its back to Viugra and sat down. A few seconds of silence followed. The reflection was using this chance to try and correct Viugra's way of thinking. Everything the reflection said seemed to hit hard for Viugra. There must be some truth to what she was saying.

After a moment to let her words marinate with Viugra, the reflection wiped its face and continued to talk.

"Well… thanks to that batwoman Chiara, I can be free of you for a change. A little added bonus to the effects of her curse. I'm honestly impressed with her abilities. Now I have my own self-respect. I don't wanna be constrained by you. I wanna be free to be myself. And the funny thing is, I feel like she understands that more than you."

The reflection lifted its head towards the waning crescent moon.

"While I still don't trust her, Chiara and I seemed to hit it off pretty well."

"But she's a–" Viugra started to say.

"Demon?" the reflection interrupted, "Maybe. But at least she's true to herself."

Viugra started to get nervous.

"Don't tell me you're starting to respect her!"

"And if I did?" the reflection snapped, "At least I'd be true to my heart! Something you ought to learn!"

"But I…!"

"…Don't you dare lie to me again," the reflection threatened.

A brief moment of silence followed. Then the reflection continued to talk.

"That so called dream of yours wasn't just a dream. It was this place we are in now. But because you were brought here in a dream, it looked different. Similar to the last place you saw in reality. So, ponder this: why was the water so searing hot?"

"…I don't know..."

"…you made it hot, Viugra. The ocean is your soul, containing your self-identity. Stop lying to me. I know you know why."

Viugra was shaking her head, wanting to lie. She didn't want to admit that her reflection was telling the truth. But she couldn't bear the pain of hearing the hurt she was causing her own self-identity. With sorrow and tears, she finally confessed.

"…because… I… rejected you…"

For what seemed like forever, their soul was still. So much just happened that neither knew what to say next. Viugra was overwhelmed by everything that had just happened, and her reflection had grown emotionally exhausted. No more words were exchanged on the subject. Viugra placed her hands over her face and cried for the duration of the silence. Though neither could read the other's minds, they seemed to understand that both needed another moment to calm down. Eventually, the reflection spoke again while Viugra was crying.

"I know who I am. But whether or not I like it, you are a part of me as well. I want to believe that you truly love me."

The reflection reached its hand out to Viugra.

"Please, Viugra. Please… just accept me for who I am. Cast aside those false beliefs of yourself. I am you."

Viugra cried for several more seconds before giving her answer.

"I… I'm… sorry…"

The reflection's expression grew sorrowful. Though she had a feeling of what was about to be said, she was hoping that her speech was enough to convince Viugra. But it didn't seem to be the case.

"I don't want to hurt you. I DO love you! But… I can't accept you. I can't. Not yet. I… I have to meet my father. It's the only way I can let those things go. It's the only way… I can confirm my identity. I need to know who he really is for myself. I need my father!"

The reflection showed grief but tried to hold in her disappointment from those words. She turned away from Viugra for a moment, then spoke.

"I finally gain a voice to try and convince you… but even after all of that… I thought I'd finally get through to you…"

Viugra lifted her head up with soft eyes. The reflection turned around, but her expression had changed to one of conviction.

"Fine. This is the path you chose to walk. I can't change your mind. But know this, Viugra. I will also walk my own path."

The reflection walked closer to the boundary between them.

"Since we have separate identities, I will have a separate name. From now on, you will refer to me as Vixen."

Viugra wiped her face and stood. The two looked at each other, studying each other's expression. A strange feeling washed over them both, one mixed with a little understanding, a little sorrow, a little disappointment, and a little frustration. But the strangest mixture in it all was the stalemate of respect between the two. They could neither accept nor deny respect of the other.

Self Reflection

Viugra's alter ego Vixen anticipated that Bailey might wake up soon. She gritted her teeth in frustration as if contemplating something uncomfortable. Viugra noticed her frustration but didn't inquire.

"...We... don't have a lot of time left."

Vixen sat down. Viugra's face scrunched.

"There's more?"

"Just listen," Vixen said, disregarding Viugra's distress, "Leah is... she's in danger."

Viugra turned towards Vixen in terror.

"Leah!? What the heck happened now?"

"I said listen!" Vixen growled, "Now shut up and let me get this over with. I don't wanna tell you just as much as you don't wanna hear it."

Viugra, eyes still moist and dreary from crying, sunk to her knees.

"When you wake up from this place, you won't have a lot of time to act. But you need to know what happened if we're gonna save her. So, let's start from the beginning."

✲✲✲✲✲✲✲

"...and you'll never get the chance to meet your father."

Viugra's eyes briefly jittered in response to Van's statement. In the same moment, Vixen's consciousness surfaced as Viugra's fell into the abyss of her mind.

"...I'll never get the chance to meet my father, huh?"

Van seemed to notice the strange change of tone in Viugra's voice. His eyes narrowed, still trained on the road ahead.

"That is what I said."

Vixen continued to glare at Van for a few more seconds, then smiled.

"That's an awful bold statement, isn't it? Even if I fail this trial, I'll 'never' get to meet him? I'm just gonna lose my memory and my powers, right? Would that really guarantee I won't meet him?"

Van didn't respond. Vixen smiled smugly.

"What? Cat got ya tongue? Or did I just catch you lying? That's not like you though, is it?"

Van still didn't answer. He turned a corner, eyes searching for the next.

"Actually, I think you're more of the misdirection type. Kinda like when you said you hated my father."

Van's eyebrows furrowed. He rolled the fingers on his right hand along the steering wheel back into a grip.

"...who are you?"

"Who am I?" Vixen said, playfully, "I'm Viugra. Obviously."

"No," Van refuted, "You sound and talk differently than she does."

Vixen huffed.

"What? You expected me to take all your crap and not defend myself? Just sit here and let you bully me because you claim to hate my father? No... that ain't my style."

Once again, Van fell silent. Seeing that she had him on edge, Vixen pressed further to make him uncomfortable.

"So, Van... Vulcanel... why don't you drop the façade and tell me how you *really* feel about me?"

Vixen studied Van intensely, as if trying to claw her way through whatever barriers he had around his mind. Van continued to focus on the road, his face muscles eventually relaxing. At the same time, Vixen adopted his previous expression.

"What's wrong, Valerie?" Van spoke after a moment.

Vixen looked like she was struggling, brows furrowing even more.

"You seem to know so much about me all of a sudden. Why can't *you* tell me how I really feel?"

Vixen lowered her gaze.

"...how are you doing that?"

"Doing what, Valerie?" Van said, now playing her game, "I just asked a question."

"You know exactly what I'm talking about," Vixen said accusingly.

Van found the next client's location and parked the truck. Then, he turned towards Vixen and got close to her face.

"I don't know what you're talking about, Valerie. I can't read minds like you can."

Vixen gritted her teeth behind pursed lips. Van stared at her for a moment as if to let his words resonate with her. Then he proceeded to get out of the truck.

"If you're done with this foolishness, then let's go. You still have a job to do, regardless of what you think of me."

Van opened the door and proceeded to the back of the truck. But before he closed the truck door, he remembered something.

"Oh. Come to think of it, I still owe you a strike for last night. That puts you at two, doesn't it?"

Vixen didn't say a word.

"You better get your life together, Valerie. Before we end up doing it for you."

Van walked to the back of the truck and retrieved the product that the next client ordered. As he was getting it, Vixen grabbed the paperwork that needed to be signed and stepped out herself. Then, she smiled. Somehow, she knew she managed to get under his skin.

✲✲✲✲✲✲✲✲

It was a little after 5 P.M. when they finished delivering to clients. Vixen did an outstanding job, approaching the rest of the clients with the utmost respect and a pleasant tone. The last client acted like Randy Wilcox, but even then, she maintained her composure. Despite her efforts, Vixen never got rid of the second strike. Even without reading his mind, Vixen could tell he did that spitefully. Regardless, Vixen wasn't about to let him toy with her emotions and get away with it like Viugra.

Shortly after they returned to VanHolly, Van went upstairs to prepare dinner. Holly was still managing the other woodworkers in the woodshop, so it was rather noisy. As for Vixen, she prepared to go to her paying job. A text came in from Mrs. Rooke, asking her to come in and babysit Bailey prior to their return.

It would've been appropriate to tell Van that she was about to leave, but instead she gave the message to Holly to relay to him. She looked confused that Vixen wouldn't just tell him at first, but after Vixen explained that things were tense between them right then, Holly agreed. When Vixen finally took off, she moved much faster than Viugra did. It only took her about thirty minutes to get to the Rooke's residence without moving too fast. Once there, she knocked on the door and Bailey answered. Bailey didn't look happy to see her.

"...come in," Bailey growled.

"Why thank you, B," Vixen responded slyly.

Bailey, who was about to head right back to her room, stopped dead in her tracks.

"Excuse you?"

"What?" Vixen said, smiling, "All I said was 'thank you, B.'"

"Who the H*** you calling a B?" Bailey snapped. She looked a bit surprised.

"You, of course!" Vixen said with no remorse, "Y'know, B for Bailey."

Bailey knew full well that wasn't what Vixen meant.

"My name is Bailey. You and I ain't cool enough for nicknames, Viagra."

"Well, that's not fair," Vixen toyed, walking towards the living room to set her backpack down, "You just gave me a nickname. That's a bit hypocritical, don'cha think?"

Bailey grew frustrated.

"Shut the H*** up! I'm going to my room!"

Bailey marched up the stairs and did exactly as she said. Vixen smiled and waved her goodbye.

"Bubye now!"

7 P.M. came around, and Bailey left her room to go to the bathroom. Vixen had been siting on the couch in deep thought about something up to that point (but she decided not to disclose this part of the story to Viugra). When she heard Bailey exit the bathroom, Vixen decided to mess with her. For some reason, she was getting a thrill out of messing with her. Plus, she was starting to get bored.

Vixen went up the stairs to knock on her door. Bailey must've heard her coming because she questioned Vixen before she even knocked on her door.

"What do you want?"

"To talk," Vixen answered casually.

"Go call your friends or something," Bailey responded, "I ain't got nothing to say to you."

"Oh, come now," Vixen toyed, "I thought we were friends."

"Friends?" Bailey laughed, "The F*** you get that idea from? I wish you weren't even here!"

"So hurtful!" Vixen continued to tease, leaning against the door as if she would faint, "No wonder you don't have any friends!"

"Don't you have something better to do than mess with me?" Bailey finally snapped, "I'm *trying* to ignore you!"

"I sure do," Vixen said, "I'm doing it right now! Boooonding!"

For a moment, silence followed Vixen's response. Soon after, the knob began to twist. Vixen backed up and stood with her hands clasped together as if happy to see Bailey come out of the room. One would probably guess Bailey would be livid at this point. However, she both looked and spoke as if she were confused.

"Seriously… what the f*** is wrong with you?"

Vixen smiled greatly, as if the ends could've stretched beyond her face.

"Nothing. I'm just so glad to see you today!"

"Bulls***," Bailey responded, "I always knew you could be petty ever since I had the misfortune of meeting you. But this… this is on a different level. You've never been this petty!"

Vixen laughed, finally dropping the act.

"Alright, alright. Ya got me. I just wanted to mess with ya."

Bailey didn't seem enthused.

"You're always so serious," Vixen said, "You gotta relax. It's not good for your health. Clearly."

Vixen pointed at her chest. Bailey frowned up, unsure of what she was getting at. Then, it clicked.

"…how long…?"

"Just a moment ago," Vixen answered.

Bailey wasn't buying it.

"There was literally nothing I did or said to possibly give that away. You're lying!"

"No, I don't think I am."

"You are!" Bailey snapped, "Who told you!?"

Vixen could sense Bailey was starting to get worked up.

"You might wanna calm down…"

"I will when you tell me the truth!"

"Seriously, I think you should relax…"

"Don't tell me what to do, B****!"

Vixen's expression changed drastically. Somehow, the energy in the room changed equally, and Bailey felt it in her bones. In her very spirit.

"I highly recommend you watch your word choice, Bailey. Things could get ugly if you don't. Wouldn't want you to have an… accident, now would we?"

Vixen struck Bailey with fear. Somehow, Vixen was using a power to suppress her attitude. Bailey took a step back, her eyes wide with shock. But even though she was being overwhelmed, Vixen noticed that Bailey was resisting her.

Amazing, Vixen thought, *This kid is stronger than she lets on to be. Even though I'm not forcing her to stand down, the strength of my will alone should've been enough to drop her to her knees. And yet, she continues to stand.*

Vixen dissipated her spirit, giving Bailey a chance to relax. Though her breathing was heavy, Bailey was calmed down. As she was getting her bearings, Vixen decided to return to the living room.

"Didn't mean for you to get so worked up. Guess I'll go back to the couch."

"Stop."

Vixen stopped. She could sense Bailey's spirit change.

"No more games, Viugra," Bailey said, now a different type of serious.

Vixen didn't move, standing at the top of the stairs. She read Bailey's mind before she even asked her question. Vixen was shocked about what she was going to ask. Realizing that she would have to think of an excuse, she waited until Bailey asked to formulate an answer.

"I can't believe I'm about to ask this… but… are you… are you an angel?"

Vixen waited a few seconds before answering Bailey.

"I am a human. Just like you."

"Humans can't calm people as angry as I was by simply screaming."

"Screaming?" Vixen said, genuinely confused, "I know I was harsh, but I didn't raise my voice at you."

"I'm talking about yesterday, smarta**," Bailey said, balling her fists.

Yesterday? Vixen thought, *She must be talking about the other me. That would explain the bite marks this morning…*

"You sure you weren't just feeling guilty for biting me?"

"N-no," Bailey said. She didn't sound so confident about it.

"I think you were."

"Was I guilty after the first time?" Bailey argued.

"Fair enough," Vixen smirked, "I woulda felt kinda dumb."

"Y'know what?" Bailey growled.

"Nope. What?"

Bailey thought for a moment, then made a proposition.

"Come over here and let me bite you again."

Vixen looked amused.

"Bite me again? You really don't like me, do you?"

"If I bite you hard enough, you'll scream again. Or I'll break my teeth. If you're human like you claim to be, you'll scream. Then again, if I feel weird like I did yesterday, I'll still think you're lying."

"And if I don't come over there?" Vixen asked, putting a hand on her hip.

"I'll tell my mother you were harassing me."

Vixen fell silent.

*H***... I didn't think that through. Well played...*

Vixen turned around.

"Alright, fine. I'll let you bite me."

Vixen walked up to Bailey, squatted, and stuck out her arm with her palm up. Bailey looked at Vixen with skepticism as she shifted her jaw around preparing to chomp her.

"You better not hold back," Vixen teased.

"Shut up," Bailey grumbled.

Bailey's focus went back to Vixen's forearm, staring at it with the focus of a martial artist about to break boards. Vixen could tell her breathing was heavy, even though Bailey was doing her best to control it.

With the swiftness of a shark, Bailey's mouth gaped and chomped into Vixen's flesh. Vixen's eyes tensed, her muscles following suit. She screamed in agony as Bailey's teeth punctured her skin and drew blood the same as the last time. Vixen dropped to her knees, snatching her arm away from Bailey's mouth and gripping it with her hand. Bailey's eyes widened in surprised at Vixen's reaction, simultaneously observing how she whined and moaned.

"Aaagh… s-see now?" Vixen spoke between cries, "I screamed… I… aaaugh… I'm bleeding… man, your bites *hurt*!"

Bailey's eyes closed and she turned her head.

"I can't believe this…"

"Seeing… is believing…," Vixen said, slowly getting use to the pain, "…now… would ya get… some bandages for me?

Bailey, seemingly disgruntled, went downstairs and grabbed the first aid kit. Once out of her sights, Vixen chuckled lowly between her affected tears.

☼☼☼☼☼☼☼

After Bailey fixed up Vixen's arm, she went back to her room quietly. Vixen could tell that Bailey was still thinking about what happened but didn't worry much about it. Instead, she returned to the couch and started to turn the television on. But before she cut the power on, she felt her phone buzz in her pocket.

Vixen pulled out the phone and saw she had a new message from Van. In so many words, he went off on her about leaving without talking directly to her and threatened to fail her for doing things disorderly. Vixen couldn't help but chuckle to herself.

Sooooo sensitive, she thought.

She slipped the phone back into her pocket but noticed a piece of paper that must've fallen out of it. She unfolded it and looked at what was written on it, which happened to be the phone number Leah had written on it for her to call.

Though Vixen wasn't aware of Leah giving her the number, she recognized the name from long ago.

Leah? I met Leah today? I guess that explains why Van was so irritated. I wonder if I was supposed to call her or something?

Vixen, feeling a bit bored, went ahead and dialed the number to call her. After a few seconds of ringing, the phone picked up.

"Who's this?"

The voice sounded unfamiliar. It didn't even sound like a woman's voice. And the voice was a bit gruff. Vixen raised an eyebrow.

"Um… it's Valerie?"

A little rustling came before Leah's voice continued the conversation.

"Val? I'm so sorry about that! That was my… coworker who answered the phone!"

Hmm… Vixen thought before responding.

"Don't even worry about it, girl! I'm just glad to talk to you again. So… what are you up to?"

"Oh, nothing important!" Leah continued, shuffling some stuff in the background, "Just taking care of some business. I'll tell you more about it later."

"Aww, you can't tell me now?" Vixen teased.

"Well…" Leah started, her tone slightly changing, "That depends on you. Are you able to meet up tonight?"

Vixen's eyes looked up towards the ceiling as if to peer into Bailey's room. She could sense that Bailey was unconscious, most likely taking a nap. Even though she had a job to do, Vixen believed she could step out for a moment if Bailey was unconscious. Besides, she wanted to see Leah again.

"Sure!" Vixen responded with delight, "Just tell me the place and I'll be there."

The Stench of Evil

Shortly after the phone call with Leah Phelan, Vixen snuck out of the Rooke's household. Leah told Vixen to meet her at her place on the north end of Nerezza. Vixen had to ask her for the address as she didn't know where her place was.

Before she got up and left, Vixen looked up the stairs to see if Bailey was up and about. She sensed that Bailey was a bit sleepy and was resting her body. However, her mind was still active. She seemed to be thinking about a fight that happened at school and some sort of necklace she picked up after. Random information about different necklaces started to fill her mind as well, leading Vixen to believe that she was researching something.

Before turning the doorknob to leave, Vixen paused in thought. Then she quietly crept up the stairs to Bailey's room. She then hummed a lullaby right next to the door just barely audible enough for Bailey to hear. Soon after, Bailey's thoughts became hazy until she fell into a deep sleep.

Just in case you decide to leave while I'm gone, Vixen thought.

With that, she departed. After entering an alley with no one around, Vixen hopped up to the roofs and began roof-hopping her way to Leah. She would reach Leah in no time. If she wanted, she would have time for a little excursion. And someone managed to convince her to do so.

Hey girly.

Vixen stopped several blocks away from downtown Nerezza, then looked around.

You know who it is. Let's chat.

Vixen sighed and rolled her eyes, then hopped down to the streets to the voice calling for her. The voice led her to an alley less than a couple miles outside downtown Nerezza. It was a long and narrow one lined with several small homes. People who lived here were out and about, socializing as the sun was beginning to set. After walking some distance, a woman in tattered clothing stopped her.

"Three days in and you're still coming out at night? You sure you aren't for the streets?"

Vixen placed her hand on her hip with sass.

"And here you are with me. What's your excuse?"

"Hah!" the mysterious cloaked woman laughed. She stood up, then removed the hood of her garments.

"I'm on a mission. To save humanity from getting divinely f***ed, I guess."

Vixen shook her head.

"You're doing a helluva job at that. What do you want, Chiara?"

"In a rush?" Chiara smiled.

"You know the answer to that."

"Why even bother coming here then?"

Vixen sighed.

"Because I know there's no point in running from you."

Chiara's smile widened, seemingly ripping her face to fit it.

"Well, aren't you brave. That, or a brash idiot."

Vixen smirked back.

"Y'know, it's strange. You wanting to meet around people like this. If you hurt any of them, or even took me out in front of them, wouldn't that cause a scene? If anyone's at a disadvantage, wouldn't it be you?"

"Hmm… I wonder?" Chiara played along.

"Besides. If you wanted to kill me, I'd be dust already."

"That's some pretty good logic," Chiara teased, her face muscles relaxing, "Doesn't it feel good? Being yourself around me, love? I think your alter ego should take notes."

Vixen's eyes narrowed.

"The other me and I are still the same, regardless of what you did to us. I'd appreciate it if you didn't disrespect her."

"Yeah, see, that right there's why I wanna talk."

Chiara walked up to Vixen and pointed at her own head.

"I can't talk to Viugra like I can you. Your other… consciousness… just isn't as witty as you are. No offense."

"Much taken," Vixen huffed, then started to walk away, "If that's what this is about, I'm out."

"Woooow," Chiara toyed, now walking to lean up against a wall, "You serious? You're angry at me for 'disrespecting' a person who doesn't respect their own self? I thought you wiser than that."

Vixen stopped.

"What's wrong? Hit a nerve?" Chiara sneered.

Vixen turned around and walked up to Chiara close enough to speak low and threateningly.

"Viugra's not stupid, you raggedy bat. She has more potential than you ever could. And she knows how to use it."

"She does? Or you do?" Chiara questioned.

Vixen gritted her teeth, then backed up a little.

"I can read your mind, y'know," Chiara said, gesturing with her hands as she talked, "And you know I have a point. Viugra lacks self-esteem. Good at hiding it, though. She allows what others say to alter the way she thinks far too much. It doesn't help that her father, the man she so greatly adores, was seen as a black sheep of the heavenly host and eventually kicked out of the flock. She loved the man of obedience, bravery, compassion, wisdom, and power. But what she hates is the man of curiosity, deviance, misdirection, and great prescience. And that's because she was taught to do so."

Chiara stood from the wall.

"She's gonna break under the pressure at this rate. And you'll shatter along with her. Once that happens, the angels will either mold you into the 'perfect servant' or discard you as a 'fallen saint.' But you know this. I'm just speaking your mind."

A brief silence followed. After processing what she was saying, Vixen had a response.

"...Sure, I got mad at my surrogate father. Sure, the other angels could've been better about talking about my father around me. And yeah, I do think their methods are ridiculous. But the love of those close to me is genuine. I'd be out of my mind to think they didn't care anything about me. In other words... you made that last part up."

Chiara chuckled.

"Just checking to see if you were paying attention, love."

"Yeah right. I think you were trying to manipulate me."

"You think or you know?"

Vixen fell silent. Chiara knew Vixen couldn't read her mind. Chiara began wrapping up her conversation and walking away.

"Aight, I'mma head out! I think that's enough talk for now. You do you, boo-boo! Just remember... I gave you an out. You are the key to your own shackles. Question is, will you use it?"

Chiara left Vixen in the alley. Vixen balled her fists.

*D*** Viugra... don't let her be right...*

...By the way...

Chiara's voice infiltrated Vixen's thoughts.

...weren't you heading to meet a Leah? I'd hate for her to get grumpy and... do something stupid...

Vixen's eyebrows scrunched.

You know what's going on, don't you?

Chiara never responded. Vixen shook her head in frustration, then darted out of the alley.

☼☼☼☼☼☼☼☼

After a while, Vixen reached Leah's mansion after eight. The lights in the courtyard around Leah's mansion were starting to cut on. With all of the floral decorations and the busts of mythological creatures and figures sprinkled throughout, it illuminated a fantastical scenery. Unfortunately, Vixen wasn't feeling the magic so much as animosity. And sniffed an odor akin to urine.

Sheesh… Vixen thought as she entered through the gate, *It smells… terrible! If Van smelled this earlier, I'd understand why he was pissed.*

Once she got past the smell, the fact that the gate was already open dawned on her. That confirmed that something was up. Looking up at the mansion, she noticed that there was a single vehicle parked by the front door.

Coworker's still here, huh? Strange, I only sense one person in there, though.

Vixen reached the front door and found that it, too, was already open.

Just left it open for me to waltz in unannounced, huh? Vixen thought, flexing her fingers before entering.

Once in, she saw a mess. There were all kinds of trinkets, clothes, and decorations sprawled about on the floors. The house had to have been like this for weeks. Even so, for how bad the smell of ammonia was, the junk on the floor couldn't equate to how pungent it was. But where one sees uncleanliness, laziness, and a lack of responsibility, Vixen seemed to notice a much more pressing matter. She immediately summoned her light daggers between her knuckles.

"Hey Leah," Vixen called out, now slowly creeping through the lobby, "I'm here. Do I need to take off my shoes?"

"Nah," Leah's voice answered, "Just come in. Ignore the mess, will ya?"

I'm trying, trust me, Vixen thought, nostrils flared.

She walked in slowly, checking each of the rooms lined against the lobby hall. The lights in the mansion were barely lit, leaving each room in a visible but eerie glow. As she approached the stairs, she continued to talk to Leah in a calm voice while still on guard.

"Y'know, this is some way to greet your guest."

"I know, I know. I'm sorry, Val," Leah apologized, still hidden somewhere, "I've just been so busy, I guess I've forgotten my guest etiquette."

"I see. Might wanna brush up on that."

"Tell ya what?" Leah bargained, "Meet me in the kitchen past the stairs and I'll have a drink ready for ya."

"Bet," Vixen answered, rounding the corner to the kitchen.

Vixen was just about to grab and turn the knob, but then Leah interrupted her.

"W-wait... umm... why not... explore first?"

Vixen raised an eyebrow, hand still on the doorknob.

"Oh, come on, Lee-lee! I came to see you, not the house!"

A short pause followed.

"Lee-lee... I haven't heard... that name... in years..."

Vixen smiled, then loosened her grip on her daggers.

"You said your father used to call you that. Right?"

"I'm surprised... you remember..." Leah said a little quieter.

Following this, Vixen could hear a little bit of sniffling behind the door she was about to open. Something was off with Leah, and Vixen was slowly figuring out what.

"Of course, I do. I also remember the loneliness I felt from you when you told me about school way back when."

A familiar loneliness, Vixen thought, briefly lowering her sights.

"That's what this is about, isn't it? I know you're counting on me to help you with something."

"Val..." Leah said, struggling to utter her name.

Vixen slowly turned the knob as she finished her comments.

"...And I'm personally counting on you putting that wine bottle down."

Vixen could hear a strong gasp behind the door. At that moment, she decided it was time to enter the kitchen. As soon as Vixen entered, she peered directly into the wide eyes of a tattered, messy-haired young woman. Her dress was soaked in liquor, blood vessels in her head were bulged, and her head and arms were perspiring. She was holding a bottle of Cabernet Sauvignon above her head, ready to clock someone with it. After their eyes met, Leah bit her bottom lip until blood appeared.

"C'mon Leah," Vixen spoke gently, "This isn't like you. Please put the bottle down."

Leah's expression feigned, and she dropped to her knees. The wine bottle hit the floor, shattering next to her.

"H-how did you know?" Leah asked.

"I'm kind of a mind reader," Vixen answered. She reached out to help Leah up, but Leah started moving away.

"Please, Val. Keep your distance. And... toss me that bottle on the counter."

Vixen looked around the kitchen to see what she was talking about. Sure enough, there was a bottle of medication sitting on the wet bar behind her. Vixen did exactly as she said, and Leah quickly popped a single pill after catching it.

"What are those?" Vixen asked.

"Drugs," Leah answered.

"Really, Leah?" Vixen spoke.

"Not that kind," Leah assured, "God, I hope not anyways."

"Shouldn't you know what you're taking?"

Leah, whose body was trembling from adrenaline, leaned up against the cupboards behind her. While Leah was getting a hold of herself, Vixen narrowed her eyes. She noticed that Leah's thoughts were getting a bit harder to read. Something was making it hard to do. Vixen didn't say anything about it.

"Tell me what's going on. I want to help."

"I know," Leah said, now propped up on her left arm, "This is hard to say... but... I think I have Animitis."

"Animitus?" Vixen asked.

"Yeah, the one that's been all over the news," Leah explained, "The mysterious brain virus that's been taking people out all over

Nerezza. Dr. Rooke thinks it's affecting people with mental problems. Haven't you been keeping up?"

Vixen hesitated for a moment.

"...no. Hadn't had a chance to."

Leah sighed.

"Well, I've been having... symptoms... of it lately. Started about a month ago. Work was starting to stress me out, trying to keep up with all of my investments. Part of the reason I moved out here was to get a better idea of how these people worked. Plus, something about the numbers was off. I wanted to see for myself."

"Hold on," Vixen interrupted, "What does this have to do with this... Animitis thing?"

Leah held her head for a moment, then continued.

"Let's just say... I took a personal tour of the docks. Something happened and... I lost consciousness. I woke up somewhere in the city and ever since have been struggling with bipolar tendencies."

"Bipolar, huh?" Vixen said, now taking a seat at the wet bar, "Is that what the medication is for?"

"Not exactly. Those aren't for the bipolar issues I've been having. They're for the Animus. Straight from Manna Labs."

"Pills for a virus that even they don't fully understand," Vixen realized, "These drugs... they're experimental, aren't they?"

Leah nodded her head.

"Yeah."

She began weakly walking to the other side of her wet bar where there were papers sprawled about.

"It didn't take long for me to realize my condition was abnormal. When I thought it was Animus, I called Manna Labs for help. The guy I talked to acted like I was a nuisance, but then Dr. Rooke took over. After hearing me out, she asked me to come by. I explained my condition, she ran some tests, then... she asked me if I could help her with her research."

Leah slid the paperwork to Vixen, then stepped back. Vixen

grabbed them and sifted through the stack. There were brain scans from different angles. They all showed abnormalities in the cerebrum.

Her brain... Vixen thought, *This Animus... it's slowly eating away at her gray matter. At this rate, it could kill her. But... there's something familiar about these patterns. Don't tell me...!*

"At first, I didn't agree to it," Leah interrupted Vixen's thoughts, "But then... she started explaining how serious it was. And... it reminded me of my father's condition."

"Your father?" Vixen asked, "You mean his cancer?"

"Yeah. Even though brain cancer behaves differently, it has similar effects on the brain as this Animus. Instead of causing rapid cell growth, the Animus eats away at your brain cells."

Eats away... Vixen thought.

Suddenly, Leah groaned and slunk to the ground holding her head. Vixen hopped out of her seat and to her side.

"Hey!" Vixen called out.

"S-stay back!" Leah pleaded, "P-please, Val!"

Vixen didn't listen. Instead, she sat on the floor and laid Leah's head gently onto her lap.

"Val, no! I don't...!"

But before she could finish, Val put her to sleep with her lullaby.

"Sorry, Leah. But I know why you called me here. And you can't watch."

Vixen closed her eyes and hovered her hands around Leah's head, moving them around it as if scanning it. Images of her brain began circling around Vixen's head. But they were different from the MRIs in hospitals. Red-violet coloration began to diffuse into her brain from Vixen's hands like food coloring in water. The coloration began highlighting what looked to be a thin but wide-spread vapor sitting on top of Leah's brain. It looked like a parasite, and it also looked like it was connected to something outside of her body.

Vixen traced the connection throughout Leah's house to her basement. There, Vixen saw the cloudy silhouette of something sinister. A swirl of ominous smoke with a bright orange light in the middle of it. It pulsated in sync with the tendril attached to Leah's head.

I knew it, Vixen thought in disgust, *The effects of the Animus, those brainwave patterns, and that foul smell… it had to be a demon! And it's my lucky day. It's just a sloth wraith.*

She gently laid Leah's head on the ground and conjured her daggers of light. With one of them, she slashed the tendril off from Leah's head. When it was severed, it vaporized into the air. Vixen then could hear the eerie shrill of the wraith from the basement.

"Scream all you want," Vixen said as she began heading towards the lobby, "I'm getting rid of you. How dare you try to consume her!"

But before she could even leave the kitchen, she was stopped by an unsuspecting guest.

"More like 'how I dare to interfere.'"

Vixen, alerted, turned around to see who was talking to her. But before she could get a good look, she was sent flying by a sucker punch, several feet from the kitchen into a wall in the lobby. The impact caused the wall to break and crumble on top of her. Vixen managed to peak her head out from the rubble, head slightly bloody.

"…Ugh… yeah, I do dare."

The mysterious figure grabbed Vixen by the leg and tossed her out of the house through the front doors. Vixen rolled along the ground but managed to roll in a way that would flip her up onto her feet. The man who flung her stepped out of the house after her. While trying to figure out who it was, Vixen coughed up blood.

Sheesh… why didn't I sense him? And… how is he so strong?

Vixen finished analyzing her assailant. And she was amazed to learn that he was human. He had on a dark brown beanie, a sleeveless biker jacket parted open, a rusty brown crew neck t-shirt with double Ls on it, three gold chains that were tucked behind his t-shirt, black biker gloves, black jeans, and black boots. On his right arm, a tattoo of a ram's head and a bangle with an orange gem in it.

On the other, a second bangle with a red gem in it. The red gem faded from a glow just as he stepped out.

Reliquias? Vixen thought angrily, *How did he even get his hands on those?*

"You must have some pretty strong rocks on ya," the man spoke.

"Well, that's rude," Vixen said, huffing, "First, you punch me. Then you call me a man? Who taught you how to talk to women?"

"...That's not what I–" The man tried to defend himself. But before he could even finish, Vixen was closed in on him with an open-handed haymaker.

"I know."

She clapped his head in her palm and slammed it into the ground with enough force to crack the ground underneath his body. When he didn't budge for a few seconds, Vixen began lifting her hand away from him.

Suddenly, his hands jetted out and grabbed Vixen's arm.

Crap! Vixen thought.

One hand pulled her closer as the other clenched her neck.

"Urk!"

"Nice tricks, Vixen," the man sneered, "You're a sly fox."

He began lifting Vixen off of the ground as he stood. In the midst of getting choked out, she noticed that there was a blue glow fading from beneath his shirt.

He's got a defensive one, too? Someone's getting kicked out of heaven for this...

His grip around her neck began to tighten. Vixen was quickly starting to lose air. While holding her, he got a good look at her eyes. The shades dropped off of her when she was knocked into the lobby earlier.

"Wow. Haven't seen eyes like that before! What are ya, a demon?"

Vixen couldn't respond.

"Doesn't matter. You can be a fox demon. Either way, foxes are a nice little snack for wolves."

*Sh-sh***, Vixen thought, feeling her strength slipping away from her.

Vixen opened her hand, then clapped it against the man's wrist.

"There's no point struggling," he said cockily, "You can't break from this!"

Soon after his statement, he felt a violent jolt surge through his body. Luckily, his grip loosened instead of jerking Vixen's neck. They both dropped to the ground, and the man convulsed from the paralysis arte she inflicted.

I'm glad THAT worked! Vixen thought while gasping.

After catching her breath, Vixen took the opportunity as a chance to book it to the mansion. She had her mind on getting Leah out of there. In a split second, she was already back in the kitchen. But surprisingly, Leah's body was not.

"Leah?" Vixen called out, now looking around frantically, "Leah, where are you?"

Instead of Leah popping up, Vixen came face to face with the soul sucking wraith from the basement. It screeched a terrible sound in her face, then lashed its limbs at her to try and capture her. Luckily, Vixen was quick enough to evade it. While doing so, she tried to locate Leah with her mind. She didn't have any luck.

Are you kidding me!? Don't tell me it…!

Though she was far quicker than the wraith demon, he was fast enough to keep her on her toes and made it hard for her to focus.

Great… I better get out of here for now. I don't know how, but she's gone. And I get the feeling these two have back up on the way.

Vixen conjured daggers and shooed away the wraith with them. Then she gunned it out of the mansion. On her way, her former assailant brushed against her leg with his hand. She avoided his capture and continued running towards the gate.

"Sorry. I don't have time for this anymore."

As she ran towards the gate, she noticed that it was slowly taking longer to reach it. When she reached the gate, Vixen noticed the sloth wraith caught up to her. The wraith extended a sharp bone and slashed at Vixen with tremendous speed, and she couldn't dodge it. The bone sliced through her stomach like a knife through butter.

"AAAAAAAHHH!"

Vixen fell between the gates, reeling in agony. As she suffered, the wraith drew closer to her. The wound was deep enough to be fatal if she didn't start healing it. She moaned in pain as she struggled to heal herself quickly enough.

Vixen noticed the thug atop the hill running at an unbelievable speed towards her. He looked pissed. She also noticed two more glowing lights from his body: one yellow from behind his shirt, and one orange from the bangle on his arm.

"No more tricks!" the man yelled, "I'm taking you out!"

His words came to her superfast and high pitched. Vixen soon realized she was under the influence of time manipulation.

You've... got to be kidding, Vixen thought, growing concerned for her survival, *I... I can't run... from this!*

"Peace out, B****!" the man said, now raising his hand. The pendant around his neck with the yellow gem began to glow again, and the wraith screeched as it closed in to deal a fatal blow.

Things were looking grim for Vixen, until the ram in the bush revealed itself. A powerful gunshot rang out and struck the man in the head. Without another word, he tumbled to the ground and to a lifeless halt. The wraith reeled backwards, screeching, and began flying around erratically high into the air. A small body emerged from the decorative trees on the side of the courtyard and approached the man who was laid out on the ground. It stooped down and appeared to check the man's pulse to confirm the kill. Then it stood up and spoke.

"...don't call her a B****."

Vixen couldn't believe her ears. As things began returning to normal speed and she healed herself enough to move, Vixen began moving towards the figure who had taken down her aggressor. The closer she got, the more she couldn't believe who her savior was. Just a few feet away from her now, Vixen gained visual confirmation of a girl with a 9mm pistol and a red scrunchie tied around her hair.

☼☼☼☼☼☼☼☼

"No... no, no, no... you're making that up!"

Viugra, wide eyed in shock, shook her head in disbelief as Vixen ended her story.

"Just because I didn't want to tell you this doesn't mean I'd lie about it," Vixen growled, now standing up, "I'm also not surprised you wouldn't believe me. You don't even respect me."

Viugra held her head with her hands.

"This... this is too much!"

"There's one thing we agree on," Vixen said, "There's too many factors at play here."

"Please... no more!" Viugra cried, "I haven't even had time to process what happened to... to us!"

"There is no us anymore, Viugra!" Vixen snapped, "We're just roommates in a single body! Unless you wake up from your delusions, that will never change!"

Silence followed. Vixen stared at her embattled half shaking her head in distress.

At this rate, she won't be able to function, Vixen thought to herself, *Maybe I told her too much? But I still haven't told her about...!*

Vixen's thoughts stopped as she began to feel Bailey waking up. Gritting her teeth again, she began walking into the abyss of their aquatic soul.

"It's time to go, Viugra."

Viugra, struggling with much fear and anxiety, noticed her walking away and began to plea with her.

"Please, don't walk away!"

"I don't have a choice, Viugra," Vixen said, without stopping, "You have the wheel now. And until the next time I come out, you need to figure out what you're gonna do. Cause if not, failing this trial of yours will be the least of your worries."

Intentions

Time crept upon 10 P.M. as a hesitant Viugra squinted her eyes open. She found herself sitting against the wall in a meditative posture, the same one Vixen was in beforehand. She noticed the items Vixen took from Bailey lying in her lap. With weary eyes, she looked up at Bailey who was on her bed. Despite being in her room for the first time, Viugra did not express any interest in viewing it. She didn't even look at Bailey for long before her gaze drifted to some place below the bed.

Seconds later, Bailey rubbed her head as she came to. When she was coherent, she seemed to realize something critical. She quickly sat up and grabbed at her jacket, realizing her personal belongings were gone. Her eyes immediately locked onto the absentminded Viugra sitting against the wall. A few seconds passed before Viugra finally noticed Bailey looking back at her. They remained locked in each other's stare for what felt like minutes. Growing tired of the silence, Bailey eventually spoke.

"...Well?"

Another brief pause.

"Say something."

"...I..." Viugra struggled, burying her head in her arms.

Bailey raised an eyebrow.

"...I can't..."

" The h*** you can't," Bailey wasn't buying it, "Spit it out already!"

"Spit what out?" Viugra shouted, "There's nothing in my mouth!"

"Wha–" Bailey said, confused, "Stop f***ing with me, Viugra! What are you thinking about?"

Viugra gritted her teeth.

"...What am I supposed to say, Bailey?"

Bailey swung her legs to the side of the bed.

"What do you mean?"

Viugra let out a sigh with traces of awkward laughter.

"How can I explain that I'm... I'm upset with myself? Without sounding crazy?"

Bailey's eyes widened, but she waited to respond.

"I... I've experienced all kinds of emotions. What I'm feeling now... I can't even begin describing it. There's just so much happening that I don't understand. And I'm... scared."

Bailey raised an eyebrow in disbelief.

"Scared? You scared?"

Viugra shuddered in her discomfort. Bailey sensed that Viugra was trying to shut down, but she wasn't going to let her.

"Look at me."

Viugra didn't budge. Bailey hopped off the bed, then knelt down in front of Viugra. She quickly, but gently, took hold of her head under her chin. Just before she lifted her face, Bailey felt Viugra stiffen.

"...I already saw them. They're black, right?"

Tears began to trickle down into Bailey's palm. Feeling this, Bailey sighed and softened her tone.

"You can talk to me. I won't judge you. Just... you better not be faking those tears."

Viugra sniffled, then after a moment of consideration allowed Bailey to lift her head up. Her hesitation to open her eyes took up a couple of minutes. The entire time, Bailey held a solemn look on her face. When Viugra's eyes were finally open, Bailey nodded.

"Thank you. Now... why are you scared?"

"I..." Viugra struggled, "I don't... want to let anyone down."

Bailey looked confused.

"How would you be letting anyone down?"

"...by being myself."

Bailey's eyes widened. She couldn't believe what she was hearing.

"Listen," Bailey said, trying to comfort Viugra. "I don't know what you're not trying to tell me. But there's nothing wrong with you being yourself. Whoever told you that is probably trying to control you."

"No... that's not it," Viugra said, finding some strength to speak, "Everyone's expecting me to be great. And... I tried to in my own way. But they kept saying things when they thought I wasn't around. Because I didn't do what... what my peers did, I was seen as a deviant. They said I would never reach my potential if I... if I could never control myself..."

Bailey gritted her teeth behind pursed lips.

"I'm gonna stop you right there. I've only known you for about two days now, and unless you were pretending, you being you seemed to work. Did anyone tell you to save those goons from me? Or did you do your own thing?"

"...my own thing," Viugra muttered, "But–"

"No 'but's," Bailey interrupted, "You're probably more capable than you or any of these other idiots think you are. But no one is gonna see that until you show them. And no one will really respect you until you do."

Hearing the word respect in this context brought Viugra back to what Vixen was telling her in her mind. Things were starting to connect.

"And if they still don't respect you... f*** 'em! It's better to live your truth than to live theirs."

"Truth..." Viugra muttered back.

"Exactly!" Bailey said, getting pumped, "H***, it sounds like they were comparing you to someone else. Who were these people comparing you to?"

"Uh... well..." Viugra stammered.

But before she could answer, Viugra felt a strange sensation wash over her body. It was akin to the feeling of gallons of heavy water being dumped on a person, threatening to uncontrollably sweep one off their feet.

"Ugh..."

"Viugra?" Bailey asked, unaware of what was happening.

Viugra's body began to tremble harder. Her face was slightly contorted, as if she were about to have a stroke.

"Hey! What's wrong?" Bailey called out to her.

Viugra suddenly grabbed Bailey's shoulder.

"I-I'm... sorry, I..."

Viugra couldn't finish her statement. She choked on her last word, soon falling silent. Viugra's hand slipped off of Bailey's shoulder, and her head dropped.

"HEY!" Bailey said when she realized Viugra wasn't responding.

Frustrated, she took Viugra by the shoulders and shook her a bit. Viugra's eyes were open, but she was unconscious.

"Don't go to sleep on me!"

Some of Viugra's hair drooped down in front of her face. Just as this happened, she finally became responsive.

"...ugh... you've got to be kidding me..." she mumbled, her voice strangely low.

"Huh?" Bailey muttered, stilling her hands, "What's going on with you?"

Viugra then firmly grasped Bailey's wrists and removed her hands from her shoulders. Little did Bailey know, Viugra was no longer in the room with her. Instead, Vixen's conscious had surfaced.

In her next move, Vixen grabbed Bailey by her shoulders and picked her up.

"HEY! Let me go!"

Vixen didn't listen. She stepped towards Bailey's bed and dropped her on it.

"I guess I'll have to discipline you myself," Vixen growled, "We need to talk about what happened tonight."

Suddenly, Vixen found herself looking down the barrel of a Glock. Vixen's eyes opened wider with surprise. She thought the gun was left on the floor.

"Touch me again, and I will kill you," Bailey said sternly.

Her tone had changed dramatically. Bailey's whole demeanor had changed from a fiery anger to an ominous calm. Her deadly focus was palpable. Vixen could tell that she was serious. For a moment, the two stared at each other, feeling each other out. It was just like in the alley a couple days ago. But this time, Vixen couldn't read Bailey's mind. Vixen narrowed her eyes.

This is the third time I failed to read someone's mind today... But why this time? She's just a human child. Unless...

Vixen noticed one of Bailey's hands was behind her back. She was hiding something. Odds were that it was the necklace Vixen confiscated earlier.

"I guess you were pretending," Bailey finally spoke, "We were just talking a moment ago. Unless you meant something else?"

"...not at all," Vixen responded, "I just need to know who I'm dealing with."

"Didn't realize we were on the same page," Bailey said dryly.

A moment passed in silence.

"...Let me ask again," Bailey asked, "And if you lie to me again, I'll make sure it's your last. Now... *Are you an angel*?"

Though she couldn't read her mind, Vixen could tell Bailey was serious about pulling the trigger. Something about the energy she was giving off was cold and murderous. Vixen sighed and walked back to the wall she was sitting by. She leaned against it, all while Bailey kept her gun trained on her head.

"First of all, I didn't lie to you earlier. So, I'll say it again: I'm human."

Bailey started to squeeze the trigger.

"I'm not finished," Vixen said quickly, "Secondly… well, truth is I'm not supposed to tell anyone."

"Why?" Bailey asked.

Vixen shrugged.

"Honestly? I don't know. I guess my folks like to keep secrets. You understand, I'm sure."

Vixen flipped her hand out as if wanting Bailey to set the answer to the next question in her hand.

"So… why ask such an oddly specific question?"

Bailey thought a moment before answering.

"…everything about you has been inconsistent since the first night we met. First, you were this bold, goody two shoes with inhuman muscle strength. The next day you were dumb, and I drew blood when I bit you for the second time. And today, you've gone from a home invader to a girl in a midlife crisis."

She did talk to Viugra then, Vixen thought.

Bailey stood from her bed.

"If anyone needs to explain themselves, it's you. I don't trust you in my home right now. So go ahead and give me a reason to cap your a**."

"Fair enough," Vixen said, "But I still don't–"

"Hey," Bailey interrupted, waving her gun, "I'm asking the questions."

"Y'know, I have reason to not trust you, too," Vixen shrugged, "You're far too edgy for a child your age, especially with as much skill as you have with a gun."

Bailey's eyes narrowed.

"…we take turns. I'm next."

"Okay then," Vixen smiled, "What's your next question?"

"Assuming you *are* an angel, why are you babysitting me?" Bailey started, "Shouldn't you be out healing people or something?"

"Heh," Vixen chuckled, "Nothing you said about me suggests anything angelic. A serial killer, a psychopath, heck a monster even! But an angel? That's oddly specific, Bay-Lay."

Bailey's grip tightened.

"Answer the question."

"Relax, sheesh," Vixen started to explain, "Simply put, I got in some trouble recently. So, to prove myself, I've been tasked to take care of you. It's almost like my punishment is being your guardian angel! If we're assuming I'm an angel anyways."

"What's that supposed to mean?" Bailey said, scrunching her eyebrows.

"Hey," Vixen mocked, "If we're both asking questions, isn't it my turn?"

Bailey gritted her teeth. Vixen smiled.

"I assumed you were asleep earlier. How did you find and reach me so quickly?"

"Because I can," Bailey said, "My turn."

"What kind of answer is that?" Vixen asked.

"A f*** you, that's what," Bailey retorted.

"You're so mean," Vixen whined playfully.

"I don't care," Bailey said, "Next question: why have you been acting like two different people?"

"Well, there are two minds in this head of mine. You could call it Split Personality or Dissociative Identity, even though that's an inaccurate simplification."

Bailey looked annoyed.

"Are you serious?"

"I haven't lied to you once this whole time," Vixen said, "That's up to you to believe."

Vixen sat up from the wall.

"My turn. How many people have you shot and killed recently? Was it just the one?"

"The LL is the only one I've killed," Bailey said calmly.

"You said that so casually. You know that's not normal, right?"

"Ask out of turn again and you won't have to worry about that," Bailey threatened, "Why did you leave the house?"

"Sheesh," Vixen briefly explained, "Long story short, a friend of mine was in trouble. So, I went to go help her."

"Hmph," Bailey said, "That's actually a reasonable answer. You should've told me."

"What, so you could leave the house without getting in trouble?" Vixen shrugged, "I don't think so. My turn. What makes you think I'm an angel?"

Bailey and Vixen stared at each other for a moment longer. Eventually, Bailey responded.

"You're persistent."

"And you're stubborn," Vixen replied, "If nothing else, I guess we have that in common."

"I'll tell you if you answer my next question," Bailey bargained.

"Aren't you twisting the rules a bit?" Vixen teased.

"My operation, my rules," Bailey said, getting tired of Vixen's playfulness.

Clearly, Vixen wasn't taking this interrogation as seriously as she was. But the next question Bailey asked her soon changed her attitude.

"Your father… what was he like?" Bailey asked.

"My… father?" Vixen asked.

"Did I stutter?" Bailey threatened, waving the Glock, "Answer the question."

Vixen looked off, expression turning frustrated as she answered.

"I would tell you. But I've never known either of my parents. I had surrogate parents."

"Surrogate parents?" Bailey inquired.

"Did I stutter?" Vixen lightly teased, continuing quickly before Bailey decided to pull the trigger, "I had two people step up to raise me. They're the only parentals I've ever known. Although, one of them made me mad recently."

Vixen placed her hands on her hips.

"I've seen him more like an older brother or cousin. But that didn't stop him from spending time with me and disciplining me like a father would. He also made things clearer when my teachers were confusing. Even proper etiquette and self-defense. That enough for ya?"

"...keep going."

"Some operation you're running," Vixen huffed, "Well, there was this one game I played with him and his friends. We used to always be the last two standing, but he'd always kick my butt in the end. Defense isn't always the best offense with him."

Bailey's eyes softened a bit.

"Some days, I'd asked him about my real father. He would always give me a short answer and change the subject. That or find some other way to avoid telling me."

Vixen's tone started to change. The emotion in her voice wavered between anger and sadness.

"Between that and hearing others around me talk negatively about my father, I—my other self rather—started to abandon me. But that's because she wanted to be a people pleaser. We showed behaviors similar to that of our father apparently, and they didn't like that. Said we were following the path of deviants. Soon, they stopped hanging around us. Honestly, her fear of abandonment is probably what started to separate us. Then one day, our stand-in father and the other me got into an argument. It didn't end so well, especially when he told her to forget about our real father."

"Hold on," Bailey interrupted, "Is this your opinion or the other one's?"

"I guess it does sound a bit convoluted," Vixen acknowledged, "Back then, we were one and the same. It was only recently that our personality was split."

"I see," Bailey said.

Vixen sensed that Bailey wanted to know what caused the split. But neither bothered to explain or inquire further. Instead, Bailey lowered her gun and dropped the big reveal.

"Your surrogate father... did the others call him Lord Bautista?"

Vixen's eyes lit up in shock.

"...H-how did–"

"A dream. From last night."

Vixen thought for a moment, then it clicked.

"...the S.O.S...."

"That's the angelic voice thing, isn't it?" Bailey further asked.

Vixen narrowed her eyes.

"So that's why you... how much do you know?"

"Enough to know you're an angel," Bailey said, now switching the gun to safety, "The basics, I guess."

"I see," Vixen said, "And seeing that you locked your weapon, I'm guessing you trust me now?"

"Hardly," Bailey scoffed, "But at least I know who I'm dealing with."

Bailey placed the gun in her jacket. The other hand that was behind her back slipped into her rear pocket. At the same time, Vixen could sense the cloud over Bailey's mind dissipating. On top of that, she could tell that Bailey's aura was returning to what it normally would be.

I knew it, Vixen thought, *That thing was blocking my powers. But for her to put it up now seems a bit reckless if she still doesn't trust me. Hmm...*

Vixen began asking Bailey more questions.

"What was that in your other hand?"

"Interrogation ended when I put the safety on the gun," Bailey answered.

"Y'know I can just read your mind to find out, right?"

Bailey sighed.

"It's a long story... but I fought this kid bullying someone today. He and his two accomplices ran off, but he dropped a necklace on the way. So, I took it."

Some random kid had a Reliquia? Vixen thought, *How in the world did so many of these things get in the hands of humans, let alone a child?*

"Funny… I never imagined you to have someone following you around. Anyways… shouldn't you give that back to Shaun?"

"Would you keep your f***ing mind to yourself?" Bailey snapped, "And I'll give it back when I feel like it. That idiot doesn't need something like this."

Vixen sighed.

"Honestly, you shouldn't have it either. That's… something that belongs to angels."

"Oh really?" Bailey said, raising an eyebrow, "In that case, I'm definitely not giving it to you."

"That's terrible logic," Vixen smiled, "But considering what's going on in this city, you might need it."

Bailey looked skeptical.

"You're not serious…?"

"I was gonna take it from you. But on the account that you keep slipping out at night, I figured it might be best for you to hold onto that. It might be the thing that saves your life."

"Hmph," Bailey huffed.

Vixen looked out the window. Remembering Leah, she realized that time was of the essence.

"I don't have much time left to chat. Like I said earlier, I was going to help a friend. I think her life is in danger."

Bailey watched as Vixen stooped to pick up her backpack.

"A word of advice: stay home. You can't see them, but there are countless demons circulating through this city."

Vixen's face grew serious.

"You are the only one I'm telling this to. You might as well know, since you know so much already. If there are more demons around like the one I fought earlier, they're the cause of your so-called Animus Disease."

"W-what?" Bailey said, astounded, "You made that up!"

"Like I said before, I haven't lied to you once," Vixen shrugged, "It's up to you to believe me or not, kid."

Bailey looked annoyed. Vixen raised an eyebrow in response.

"For the love of God, stop treating me like a kid, d*** it! I'm older than I look!"

"I already knew that, but okay."

"Thank y–"

Bailey stopped abruptly.

"...how would you know?"

Just as Vixen gave her response, Bailey eased her hand into her rear pants pocket.

"I just do. Don't worry about it," she answered.

"Bulls***," Bailey growled, "Tell me the truth."

Vixen sighed.

"I don't think I need to explain. Considering you reached for that necklace, you must know the answer already."

Bailey gasped.

"Don't look so surprised," Vixen said, looping her arms through the backpack straps, "You're not the only one who needed to know who they were dealing with."

In one swift motion, Bailey pulled the gun out on Vixen and switched the safety. But unlike before, desperation took control of Bailey's face. Vixen noticed her aura becoming more erratic.

"Leave. Me. Alone."

"Whoa! Hit a nerve, did I?" Vixen responded with snark, "If you're so uncomfortable, why don't you 'flip that switch' in your head that suppresses your emotions?"

Bailey gritted her teeth.

"Surely, you didn't think I wouldn't notice?" Vixen smirked, "One moment, you're a basic edgy teenager. The next... a trained assassin."

"How... how much do you know?" Bailey asked, breathing growing heavy.

"Enough to know you're no angel," Vixen smiled smugly, "The... basics I guess."

"F*** off, Viugra!" Bailey shouted, body shaking from nervous energy.

"Oh, for the record, my name is Vixen," Vixen corrected, her voice growing more spiteful.

"I don't care!"

"Of course not."

At this point, Vixen seemed to have forgotten her urgency. She was more concerned with digging into Bailey's business.

"While we're on that, what made you change your name?"

Bailey's face tightened ever more. She didn't answer. She simply turned away from Vixen.

"The question isn't rhetorical, Azekah," Vixen called after her.

"Shut up..." Bailey muttered under her breath, holding her head with her other hand. Bailey's struggle to breathe was slowly worsening.

"If you tell me yourself, then I will," Vixen bargained.

Vixen waited to see if Bailey would do it. But Bailey remained trembling in silence. Sensing that Bailey wouldn't cooperate, Vixen pressed on. She pointed at the portrait on Bailey's dresser. Bailey looked at it without turning around.

"The day this picture was taken, you and your fellow comrades lost your lives. But by some miracle, you came back from the dead. And who was there to resuscitate you but both of your new parents?"

"Please… shut up…" Bailey muttered again.

"You were lucky to make it out of that place alive. You were the only survivor of that massacre. You were protected, Azekah. But you feel like you failed to protect those around you! All your comrades died trying to get you out of there. And you blame yourself because you were too crippled to help. So, tell me, is that why you changed your name?"

"Please… stop..."

But Vixen did not stop.

"You also lost two of the closest people you ever knew in two devastating ways. Betrayal and death. But what makes it so bad, is that you wished it was you who–"

"STOOOOOOPPPP!"

Bailey whipped around towards Vixen with a blood curdling screech that disrupted Vixen's invasive rant. As if snapping out of a demented trance, Vixen's eyes widened at Bailey's cacophonous cries. It was as if Bailey stopped Vixen with her own Angelic Voice. No longer caught up in her trance, Vixen finally realized what she was doing to Bailey. Immediately, shame welled up within her. But it was too late.

"Bailey I..." Vixen whispered, reaching out to her.

"LEAVE ME ALONE!"

A crazy look flashed across Bailey's face. She improperly aimed the Glock at Vixen with one hand, emotions soaring through the roof. Then... she emptied the magazine. Each 9mm bullet crashed into Vixen's body. The sting of each bullet left painful bruises, causing Vixen to flinch and stumble back to the wall she was sitting against. One by one, the bullets wandered from a lethal point to random parts of her body. After the seventeenth round, the iron shower subsided.

Slowly, Bailey stopped pulling the trigger and lowered the gun. Her breathing was irregular and heavy, her gaping eyes inflamed with tears. Vixen, also wide-eyed in shock, screamed in agony.

"AAAAAAAAGH!"

The pain Vixen felt was excruciating, like being stung by the most painful hornets one can think of. Vixen slid down the wall and crumpled on the floor as she endured the pain. Surely, if Viugra had taken the blows, this would be the end of her story.

The hyperventilating Bailey took a couple of minutes to realize what she did. Several expressions of emotions flashed across her face before addressing Vixen.

"AAAAAAGH! I F***ING HATE YOU!"

Vixen managed to open her eyes a bit. Bailey bared her teeth.

"LEARN TO SHUT YOUR F***ING MOUTH! D***!"

Vixen felt terror in response to this declaration. She was not expecting Bailey to go this far.

"B-Bailey..."

Overwhelmed with emotion, Bailey fell to her knees. The Glock fell out of her hands as well. Tears streamed down her face, and her choked speech sounded ugly from the raw pain coming from her.

"YOU HAVE NO F***ING SELF CONTROL! THAT'S WHY NO ONE LIKES YOU! YOU'RE EVIL!"

Vixen closed her eyes in shame. Then tears began to roll down her cheeks. She really messed up. And she started to consider why Viugra was pushing her away.

No... control? Could that be why... No...

Bailey found it harder and harder to breathe as she continued to vehemently roar at Vixen.

"I want to die! That's what you wanted to hear, right? There, I f***ing said it! You pulled it out of me! While you're at it, why don't you grant my wish?"

Bailey chucked the Glock at Vixen, which bounced off her head. Though the Glock was empty, Vixen sensed that Bailey was serious. Even in the midst of her emotional craze, Vixen felt Bailey's desire to want to end it all.

That's when Vixen realized something important. Something she nor Viugra considered when they landed on Earth. And the realization vigorously churned the humiliation blazing in her stomach.

Bailey began losing control over her breathing, her panic attack now in full force. Vixen stood and limped over to Bailey. Bailey choked on a sudden intake of breath when Vixen approached her. Unable to scream at Vixen any longer, she started scooting back from Vixen with her hand out between them.

Bailey backed right up to her bed, unable to move any further. Without permission, Vixen gently caressed Bailey's face. Bailey tried to move her head away from her but found herself too focused on breathing.

Surely, Vixen should've been locating the medication Mrs. Rooke gives to Bailey to calm her down. But Vixen had a better remedy in mind. She began singing, with all her heart. With a euphoric warmth, Vixen sung of purpose, empowerment, and perseverance. Her voice imbued with all her power; she began healing Bailey's very soul with these words:

Shadows of night may cloud your day
And shroud your blue skies with sinister gray
But look to the gleam that lit your way
And know it's the reason you survived the fray

Evil may reign in your darkest hour
But the morning shines hope to all
Through the light of power

Strength to endure the sins of the night
And love to curate humanity's blight
Celestial glow wash over our sight
And remind us of why we endured the fight

Beyond our sunset our hearts will elope
The purpose of life veiled in twilight's
Dawn of hope

Once Vixen finished, the negative energy in Bailey's heart was suppressed. With it, the panic attack subsided. Bailey's face expressed shock, but a certain amount of serenity and peace were present as well.

Vixen then embraced Bailey, and they both sat there for a while. Eventually, more tears began to trickle down Bailey's face as she finally spoke up.

"...wh...what was...?"

"F-feel… better…?" Vixen grumbled.

Vixen felt Bailey's head slowly nod into her shoulder. Vixen smiled weakly, then her embrace weakened. Vixen slumped to the side, nearly falling to the floor if Bailey hadn't caught her.

"H-hey!"

"I-It's… okay," Vixen struggled, "I just… need to rest."

Bailey nodded.

"…why? Why hurt me then heal me?"

Vixen smiled.

"Bailey… I'm so sorry. I… I didn't mean to hurt you…"

Bailey didn't respond to this. Instead, Vixen explained herself.

"The day we met… you made a wish on a shooting star… didn't you?"

Bailey's eyes lit up.

"…y-yeah."

Vixen then turned to the window in Bailey's room. She studied the moon and the few stars she could see in the night sky.

"That wasn't a shooting star. That… was me."

Bailey's eyes widened.

"You?"

Vixen nodded.

"I was sent here to prove myself. But only now did I realize… that I was also sent here to answer your prayer."

Vixen sat up and maneuvered herself next to Bailey against her bed.

"They didn't even tell me… if I had known, I wouldn't…"

Vixen paused.

"No… maybe I would've still messed up. I can't believe I'm saying this, but maybe my other half has a good reason for deserting me…"

Bailey thought for a moment, then gently elbowed Vixen in her arm. Vixen looked up at Bailey, confused as to why she did that.

"Don't talk like that," Bailey said, "There's nothing wrong with being you. You just have to be careful of your intentions."

Vixen pondered her words, then nodded.

"You're right."

"And she shouldn't abandon you," Bailey continued, thinking about her past, "That only leaves you to start doubting yourself. You'll never be able to live your truth if you let her keep you down."

"Heh," Vixen chuckled, "You're wiser than you let on."

Bailey blushed, then looked off.

"I'm just saying."

Suddenly, Vixen's expression grew serious, and she looked out of the window.

"...that wraith..."

"Huh?" Bailey said.

Vixen began standing up, but she did so slowly. Bailey followed suit.

"That's my lead," Vixen said, "I need to go."

"Hold on," Bailey said, wiping the remainder of her tears from her face, "You're too weak right now. You'll just get hurt."

Vixen shook her head.

"I've lost a lot of time as it is. I need to find out what's going on with Leah."

Vixen turned around and placed her hand on Bailey's shoulder.

"That song was a hymn that can dispel any negative spirits in a person's heart. But it all depends on the singer's spiritual power and the listener's openness of heart. Unfortunately, I'm not strong enough to purge everything right now. I'm sorry, Bailey."

"It's... fine," Bailey said.

"No, it's not," Vixen corrected, "You've been waiting for healing for a long time. I promise, when I get my full strength back, I will heal you."

Bailey hesitated, then she nodded.

"But for that to happen, you have to promise me something," Vixen said.

"What?"

Vixen looked Bailey dead in her eyes.

"You have to trust me."

Bailey opened her mouth, but then shut it.

"I know," Vixen acknowledged, "I have some nerve asking you to do that after what just happened. But that's the only way the song will work. A doctor can't stitch you up if you're covering the wound."

Bailey pondered on this for a moment.

"I... can't make that promise right now. But... I'll try."

Vixen nodded.

"...that also means no more cussing."

"Oh h*** naw," Bailey jumped away, "You just threw that in there for the heck of it, didn't you?"

Vixen sighed.

"You're feeding into that negative energy doing that. It won't make it any easier for me to work my magic. So, you have to stop cussing. Same thing with killing people. You don't want to live that life any longer, do you?"

Bailey started to say something but retracted her tongue. Vixen didn't get a clear definitive answer from her, but she took what she could get.

"That'll do for now, I guess."

Vixen turned around, then opened the window of Bailey's room. Before she lifted herself up to it, Bailey grabbed her backpack strap. Vixen peered behind herself.

"Vixen..." Bailey started to speak.

Sensing what Bailey was concerned about, she tried to assure her once more.

"I know I don't look like I'm up to the task right now. But it won't take long for my power to come back. Trust me, I'll be careful."

"...fine," Bailey gave in, "But before you go, tell me... what was the name of that song?"

Vixen smiled.

"Aurora Spei."

Wolf's Deception

"We need to talk, Moriel."

As Moriel finished eliminating a horde of demons in Northern Nerezza, Vulcanel had contacted him via telepathy.

"Uh oh," Moriel said, casually twirling his scythe, "Are we breaking up?"

"I'm not in the mood for jokes, Moriel," Van growled.

"Relax, Vulcanel," Moriel chuckled then sighed, "I know it's about Viugra."

Vulcanel fell silent.

"Give me a moment."

Moriel flashed his scythe out of existence, then power jumped to the height of the highest skyscraper in mere seconds. Once there, he twirled himself over to its edge and sat on it gracefully. Once situated, he returned to his call.

"Look," Mori began, "You know I'm not at liberty to tell you how this will end. You'll just have to trust the process."

"I know how to trust a process," Vulcanel replied, "What I don't know is if I can trust you."

"That's a fair statement," Moriel agreed, "Honestly, I don't know if I can trust myself. That's the fate of a Death Angel."

Van's sigh echoed through Mori's cranium.

"There's major interference with her trial. I won't even say how it makes me feel. But I'm concerned that she might not make it to the next one. She's already got two strikes with me."

"Wow," Moriel said, "You're really being hard on her, aren't ya?"

"I'm supposed to be," Vulcanel said.

"Of course. Well, at the end of the day, whether she passes or not depends on you. She has to earn your respect."

"I know that already," Vulcanel growled, "What I don't know is why there's so much interference. Honestly, it's killing me that I can't do anything about it."

Moriel's head drooped a bit. After a moment of silence, Vulcanel sighed.

"Please Mori, for peace of mind, can't you tell me if she'll be okay?"

Mori rubbed his cheek bone with a single finger.

"Geez man… That may still be too much information."

"…I see," Van said in a low disgruntled tone.

A strange nervous energy resonated in Moriel's voice.

"…before you jump to conclusions–"

"Relax Mori," Van said, "I know this is how he operates."

"…r-right," Mori responded, "Everyone's doing their part. Whether they realize it or not. Even Bailey has a role in Viugra's reawakening. But as unnerving as it sounds, Viugra's fate now depends on her. The 'other' her."

"Right," Van said, sighing.

Right after Van said this, Moriel picked up on something approaching him.

"Gonna have to cut this convo short. I think boss man wants to talk."

"Alright," Van agreed, "Keep me posted."

When the line between him and Van had ended, Azariel instantly appeared before Moriel in the sky.

"Moriel."

"Yellow?" Mori playfully answered instead of 'hello'.

"You can never take things seriously, can you brother?" Azariel sighed.

"Only when you take them too serious, bro," Moriel teased, "Anyways, to what do I owe the pleasure?"

Azariel closed his eyes.

"I've come to inquire about Astrel."

✲✲✲✲✲✲✲

Minutes after departing the Rooke's residence, Vixen found herself heading west towards the coast of Nerezza. Though the sloth wraith seemed to be wandering earlier, it was now heading along a straight path. Vixen figured that it showed up near the Rooke residence because of Bailey's episode. But since she calmed her down, the wraith seemed to lose interest in her. But that alone wasn't enough for Vixen to wonder.

Even if I cleared Bailey's distress, that demon should still be wandering, Vixen thought. *But now, it's flying away with purpose. Something specific has its attention. That… or someone is calling it back.*

As Vixen pursued the wraith, she noticed that it left victims of its attacks throughout southern Nerezza. Some of the scenes were pretty disturbing, as the victims appeared to have suffered from agonizing brain damage. One group of victims consisted of the guys who snuck pictures with a frozen Viugra the day before. Though Vixen had vague recollection of this, their contorted faces retained some resemblance to what she remembered of them.

This is terrible, Vixen thought, *They all look like they had massive seizures and strokes. These kids didn't deserve this…*

Vixen looked to the sky.

I can't believe no one's come to stop this wraith by now. It's been a couple of hours since it's been loose.

Just as she did with the other murder victims, Vixen ran out of the alley the boys were in and used her powers to influence others to aid them. Once she was sure that the pedestrians saw the boys, Vixen continued her pursuit of the wraith.

A few minutes later and she neared the docks. The wraith had vanished somewhere behind the shipping yard. Sensing that this was also strange, Vixen cautiously entered the docking area.

The yard area was well lit with shipping containers stacked three to four high. As Vixen walked between each block of containers, she noticed there were gaps between the blocks every four columns. Judging by the size of the gaps, the routes of transport vehicles probably traversed between them.

Vixen read some of the company names on the containers. One of the names grabbed her attention more than the rest. It was a dark purplish color with the letters "PSI" painted on it. There were several crates in one block with this name on it. But what caught her eye was the design of the logo. Unlike the others, this shipping crate's logo had a wolf's head incorporated into it. It was more inventive than what the other shipping containers looked like.

A wolf logo, huh? Vixen thought to herself, *I wonder…*

Suddenly, a single shot of gunfire cracked through the ambient sounds of the dock area. The bullet crashed against Vixen's head, causing her to fall over from the surprise attack. While it didn't pierce through, it did cause bleeding. The pain caused her head to ring as if it had been hit by a mallet. She wanted to yelp from the pain, but managed to hold it in.

Ugh… How many times am I gonna get shot tonight? Vixen screamed in her head.

After a few minutes of lying on the ground, Vixen heard several footsteps approaching her. She remained motionless, planning to play dead until the right moment to make a move. As they approached her, Vixen remembered that she wasn't wearing her shades. She closed her eyes just before they were close enough to see her do it. Once close enough, a couple of them began talking.

"You told me you wouldn't hurt her!" a woman's voice said.

"Did I? I must'a forgot," a man's voice replied sarcastically.

Vixen recognized both of the voices, much to her discomfort.

"You better hope she's not dead or I'll kill you myself!"

The man slapped the woman, then hemmed her up. Vixen's muscles tensed at this.

"You were supposed to kill her your own d*** self! You oughta be thanking me for my help!"

The people surrounding Vixen began laughing. The loading of a rifle silenced them.

"Two shots to the head. Confirm the kill and we'll accept you."

The woman hesitated for a moment, then she lowered the muzzle of the weapon to Vixen's temple. There was a moment's hesitation before the man next to the woman jostled her to hurry up. Just as the woman was about to pull the trigger, she heard Vixen's voice in her head.

Don't be an idiot... Leah.

V-Valerie? Leah thought.

"What's wrong? You'd rather die, huh?" the goon standing next to Leah said, reaching for something in his pants.

Leah gritted her teeth, then pressed the rifle against Vixen's face more.

I'm... sorry Val. This isn't personal.

Yeah, I'm sorry too, Vixen replied, *I'm sorry that I'm gonna have to beat some sense into you!*

Suddenly, several quick shots cracked through the air. But it wasn't Leah. One of the goons surrounding Vixen fell to the ground. Someone was shooting at them!

Leah and the man who gave her the gun exchanged glances.

"You two," he called out his goons, "Go handle that situation."

Vixen, surprised, immediately searched the minds in the area and picked up on who was shooting. When she learned who it was, her heart sank.

Bailey? Vixen communicated through thought, *What the h*** are you doing?*

...Did you just cuss? Bailey thought.

That's what happens when I'm dealing with defiance! Vixen screamed in her head, *Why aren't you at home?*

I do what I wanna do, Bailey snapped back, *I couldn't let you handle this by yourself.*

You need to leave! Vixen tried to plea, as the goons neared Bailey's position, *You're gonna get yourself killed!*

If you don't do something soon, then I just might, Bailey said, carefully peeking around the corner, *I know I can't take them down. That's why I tried to give you a chance to do something.*

Vixen gritted her teeth, as Bailey checked her gun. She then quickly peeked around the corner, then withdrew behind her cover. Bailey couldn't have looked for more than a second.

If you're still in my head, then listen up, Bailey thought to Vixen, *There's ten people on the ground, four of which are heading my way. There's two on top of the containers, the one in front of your face and one behind your head. Twelve people total. Also… I'm assuming the lady in a raggedy dress holding the rifle to your head is Leah.*

How did you–? Vixen thought, truly astonished at Bailey's analysis and deduction skills,

Just before I got to the mansion, I saw her leaving with these LL goons, Bailey thought, *If I had to guess, she was about to use you for a "rite of initiation."*

Figures… Vixen thought to herself.

Vixen was so disappointed with Leah that she could've slapped her herself. How Leah seemed now wasn't what Vixen and Viugra knew her to be like years ago. Leah wanted to do things right despite having little to no friends and being bogged down with the spoiled rich girl stereotype her peers pushed onto her. She strived to do right. But this, this was all wrong.

The four are almost on me, Bailey thought, *You better do something after I take my next shots. Or we're both done for.*

Wait, don't–! Vixen tried to warn.

Bailey did not wait. In one swift and focused movement, Bailey peeked the corner, iron sights trained on her first target, and pulled the trigger. Four shots rang out, each hitting the goons somewhere in their legs. Two fell in pain, while the other two powered through it.

"I-it's a kid! She's g-got an auto!" one of them yelled.

"A kid?" The guy next to Leah yelled.

The two LL on top of the shipping containers turned towards Bailey's position. With everyone's focus on Bailey, Vixen had a perfect opportunity to catch them off guard.

Swiftly, Vixen opened her eyes and lifted her body enough to swing her legs into the back of Leah's kneecaps. Leah, taken by surprise, was forced to her knees and fell on her side. The man next to her turned to face Vixen. By then, Vixen had already planted her foot in a way that she could lunge at him. Before he could even react, she pushed him with an open palm into a nearby shipping crate. The impact slightly dented the container and caused the ones stacked above to shake a bit. The goon up top, caught off guard by the wobbly footing, lost their footing and fell over. The other four goons who were still watching over Vixen prepared to aim and shoot, but Vixen was too fast for them.

She scooped up Leah and dashed between the containers nearby. As she ran, Vixen heard several gunshots hitting the pavement behind her. When she got far enough, she gently set Leah down against the crates. Leah lifted her head to briefly exchanged looks with Vixen. Vixen made sure she could read the utter disappointment in her face. But Leah took in more than just that.

"Y-your… eyes!"

"Don't you dare move," Vixen commanded looking off towards the gunfight, "This convo isn't over."

Leah nodded with hesitation, then Vixen switched to talking to Bailey.

Bailey! Vixen screamed in thought, *Stop shooting at them!*

Then you better do something, Bailey threatened. She then retreated behind cover. The two that were still approaching her were simultaneously shooting at her. Unfortunately for them, Vixen zipped over to them and knocked them all unconscious. Hearing the sudden silence after Vixen subjugated the thugs, Bailey peeked around the corner once again.

"You can come out now," Vixen assured.

Bailey raised her gun at Vixen.

"...You missed one."

Before she could react, Bailey pulled the trigger once more and hit the last thug on top of the other crates behind Vixen. Vixen, surprised that she didn't pick up on their presence, whirled around to see the man drop his weapon and crumple.

"Bailey!" Vixen commanded, now speaking normally, "You promised you wouldn't keep killing people!"

Bailey snapped out of her assassination mode, then snapped at Vixen.

"I didn't kill them! And why are you mad at me for covering you?"

"Because you shouldn't be here!" Vixen yelled back, "Do you want the pain to go away or not?"

Bailey gritted her teeth in frustration. She was so tempted to cuss, but she remembered her promise with Vixen.

"Can't you just say thank you or something? I said I wouldn't kill'em and I didn't! I just crippled them! So be happy... d-dang it! It was them or you, Vixen!"

"You aren't exactly wrong," Vixen facepalmed, "Ugh, whatever. Come on."

Vixen and Bailey walked past the LL lying about, and as they neared the ones who were conscious, Vixen knocked them out. The closer they got to Leah, Vixen realized the goon she launched was the same one Bailey had shot earlier.

"Well, well..."

"Isn't this the same one I shot earlier?" Bailey asked, "I thought I killed him!"

"Apparently not," Vixen said, checking his vitals, "If I had to guess, he probably had one of his Reliquias activated when you shot him. Figures."

"If I didn't know better, I'd think you wanted him dead," Bailey teased.

"I'm still mad at you," Vixen glared.

Vixen then turned her attention to Leah, who was beginning to stand up holding her side with one hand.

"Leah," Vixen started with an upset tone, "Is this what you wanted my help with? A gang initiation? I thought you wanted medical help!"

Leah looked at Vixen with tired eyes.

"...I'm ...sorry."

"Sorry?" Vixen snarled, while she and Bailey walked closer to Leah, "You're gonna have to do better than sorry! What are you trying to do?"

"Okay..." Leah said.

She leaned against the containers.

"I told you that my father made stock investments, didn't I?"

Vixen nodded.

"Well... turns out his reasons were deeper than I thought."

Leah looked up at one of the shipping crates across from where they were with the PSI name on it.

"Phelan Shipping International. Turns out, it's a family company founded in the late 1900s. Skoll Phelan, my father's uncle, founded it. He wanted to create a new network for innovative minds around the world to share, inspire, and innovate new ideas. Artwork, inventions, movements, you name it. And the shipping industry is how he planned to do it."

Leah balled her fists.

"My father invested in the company naturally. He even gained additional financial support when they found out we were family. But... he knew something was off. And recently, so did I."

"What do you mean?" Vixen asked.

Leah looked Vixen in her eyes with conviction.

"That extra financial support had nothing to do with being family. It was bribe money to keep my father's mouth shut about something. But my father couldn't do it."

Vixen began piecing everything together.

"So, your father snitched?"

Leah didn't answer right away.

"Don't lock up now," Vixen said, "If you want to keep my trust, I need to know the truth. The whole truth."

Leah nodded.

"...he tried to expose whatever they were up to. He couldn't let them get away with whatever evil they were doing. But... he got caught."

"Where is your father now?" Vixen asked.

Leah closed her eyes.

"...he's ..."

Vixen could tell from her hesitation what his fate was. Holding back her frustration, she continued to question Leah.

"What did they do to him?"

"...it was the cancer," Leah answered.

"The cancer?" Vixen asked, "Didn't it go away?"

Leah shook her head.

"It came back."

Leah approached Vixen and gripped her shoulders. Vixen could tell how hard it was for her to recount everything by how vigorously she clamped her.

"But nothing could treat it the second time. And it worsened more rapidly than the first. The medical staff couldn't do anything for him. But I know something was off! None of the treatments even phased the cancer! And it came back way too aggressively!"

Leah lowered her head and tears trickled down her face.

"They poisoned my father, Val! Someone in PSI poisoned him to shut him up for good! I know they did!"

"Hold on," Vixen tried to calm her down, "That doesn't make sense. How could they give him cancer?"

"PSI ships to countries all around the world," Leah explained, "And each city of the ports the ships dock at is experiencing the same Animus problem Nerezza is."

"The Animus?" Vixen repeated, following her train of thought, "Are you saying… that there might be some other disease that causes severe cancer?"

Leah looked up at Vixen with a strong stare. Her eyes confirmed Vixen's deduction.

I see, Vixen thought, *Aside from Nerezza, I did learn of other cities that have been giving angels problems across the world. Come to think of it, I feel like I've learned about a miasma that causes cancer like symptoms.*

"What does this have to do with you and the LL?" Vixen asked.

Leah sighed, letting Vixen go.

"The LL like to hang out by the docks at night. But I've seen them making exchanges with PSI associates. I think they've been hired to guard some illegal shipments. But I got caught one day. If it weren't for them recognizing that I was part of the Phelan family, I probably would've been killed. Instead, they forced me to join their gang."

"I see," Vixen said while placing her hands gently around Leah's face. She wiped her tears with her thumbs.

"I'll be honest, I don't buy everything you just told me. But it's clear these guys and PSI have hurt you and your father. Lee-lee, you shouldn't do so much reckless stuff on your own. Dealing with these guys alone is suicide."

Vixen looked out into the open area where the goons were lying about, then looked back at Leah. She embraced her lovingly.

"You might be a bit crazy, Leah. But… I think I understand. We'll figure something out."

Leah shook her head.

"…I'm sorry Val. But there can't be a 'we'."

Just as Vixen let Leah go, she sensed another presence that snuck up behind her. Just like at Leah's mansion, Vixen didn't even notice him until he made his presence known. Without thinking, she shoved Leah out of the way as the brute slugged her. Vixen flew a couple hundred meters away, skidding along the ground to a halt.

"Vixen!" Bailey shouted out, finally managing to get her mouth free from this massive man's headlock.

Vixen fought for her consciousness, but to no avail. The brute hit her harder than a loaded semi-truck. Vixen's thoughts faded, as she lied on the ground motionless.

Nephilim's Cry

The time was nearing 11:30 P.M. when Viugra woke up in complete darkness. She couldn't see anything, only felt the cold wooden planks beneath herself. Just like the first time she went under, she was confused and discombobulated. Her head was throbbing from recent blunt trauma.

"Ungh... Now what's going on?" she spoke aloud.

Viugra crawled around, feeling for whatever might be nearby. After a few feet, she felt some rough fabric reminiscent of jean material against her hands. Viugra patted it more to reveal the shape of an arm.

"A denim jacket?" She spoke, "The arm is kind of small."

She gently tapped up the jacket to the shoulder, eventually feeling a face and hair. Viugra discovered the person's head. Being very careful as to where she placed her hand, she felt the hair a bit more as she was piecing together who she was with. The revelation came when she felt the hair was tied back with a scrunchie.

"B-Bailey?" Viugra yelped, "Oh no, Bailey! Are you okay? Say something!"

Bailey was unresponsive. Viugra gently tapped the side of her face to try and wake her up but stopped in horror. Immediately, she felt something wet dripping down from Bailey's lip. And Viugra feared it wasn't sweat.

"Oh god, no," Viugra feared, "Please, no. Bailey, wake up!"

Viugra tapped her face vigorously, fearing the worst. Still no response. Viugra gently set her head down, then pressed her ear against Bailey's chest. To her slight comfort, she was still breathing. Viugra also heard her heart beating slowly as if she were sleeping.

"Oh, thank God," Viugra exhaled.

Viugra then placed her hands on Bailey's stomach and closed her eyes. She was trying her hardest to heal her. Again and again, she tried to prime her powers.

"C'mon... work, please," Viugra grunted.

To her surprise, a faint glow emanated from her palms. Viugra's eyes briefly lit up in relief, then she focused her strength in trying to heal Bailey with what little power she had. For several minutes Viugra sat beside Bailey in the dark, slowly mending her wounds. Suddenly, the clanking of metal bars being unlatched cut through the ambient silence. Lights from the outside filled the container. Viugra stopped healing Bailey for a moment and turned around towards the light. She struggled to identify the two figures standing in the doorway, as her eyes adjusted to the sudden illumination. But once they did, she felt several negative emotions at once when she saw who was there.

"Give me a minute, Declan."

"I told you no name drops!"

"...it doesn't matter if she's gonna be killed, now does it?"

Declan gritted his teeth, then stepped to the side.

"Just hurry the h*** up."

Viugra sat up, eyeing the woman approaching her with disbelief.

"L-Leah...! Wh-what's...?"

"Val," Leah spoke, kneeling and placing a hand on her face, "I'm sorry about all of this. I really am. This wasn't how I wanted things to happen."

"What *is* happening?" Viugra asked, "What are you even talking about?"

Leah scrunched her eyebrows.

"You seem... different from earlier."

Viugra gasped, then turned her head all too late.

"Listen Val," Leah sighed, "It didn't take seeing your eyes to know you're not human."

"Huh?" Viugra spoke.

Leah looked down at Bailey, still unconscious.

"I've known for years now. My father was at stage four. At that point, the cancer could only be cured by a miracle. You are literally the only one who managed to get rid of it out of all the doctors and nurses he's had. And now, knowing the truth behind his sickness, I realized that you had to be special."

Leah looked Viugra in the eyes.

"That's why... I had to use you. You were what they wanted. It had to be you."

"Hurry it up in there," the man known as Declan rushed, "They're on their way back."

"I don't blame you for hating me," Leah said with guilty eyes, "You and I learned so much from one another. I only wish that you could understand why I'm doing this."

"Wh-what are you planning?" Viugra asked.

Leah grabbed Viugra's arm and looped it through her backpack strap. Then Leah wrapped Viugra's fingers around a coin.

"My backpack!" Viugra said, questions ever growing in her mind.

Leah held a finger up to Viugra's mouth. Viugra, frustrated, slapped Leah's hand away. Shocked at her own reaction, Viugra's eyes widened.

"Leah... I don't know what's going on, but it sounds like you're doing something stupid! You're stronger than this, aren't you? What happened to doing what's right no matter what?"

"Val," Leah answered, "...I can't let them get away with hurting so many people. Sometimes seeking justice pits you against those who don't understand. Even those you respect the most."

Leah stood and headed towards the cargo crate doors.

"I won't apologize. Not until this is over. Until then... this is goodbye."

"Leah, no!" Viugra pleaded, struggling to get to her feet.

Leah made it outside of the shipping crate. Declan noticed her fists were balled up so tight that they were turning red.

"Cutting it close, aren't we?" Declan complained.

"Just close it," Leah said.

Without another moment's hesitation, Declan did as she commanded. Viugra reached them just after they were locked. Once again, Viugra was in the dark both literally and figuratively. And as she slid down the doors, she felt her sanity sink even further.

"AAAAAAAGGGGGHH!"

Viugra screeched in frustration. She began pounding and kicking the walls of the crate, disregarding the bleeding she caused herself. After a while, her hands were shaking from the damage. She held them up in the darkness as the pain reminded of her mortality. She hit the wall one last time, but with less energy. Tears trickled down her face. Then, she heard a voice amidst her whimpering.

"...are you... done... throwing a tantrum?"

Viugra, startled, looked up towards the voice that called out to her.

"...Bailey...?"

"Who else...?"

Viugra immediately turned around and crawled over to where she was. She bumped against Bailey's foot when she reached her.

"Agh!" Bailey yelped, "Watch it!"

Viugra disregarded her warning and hugged her.

"AAAAAGH!" Bailey yelped again, "That hurts!"

"I'm so relieved you're okay," Viugra cried weakly, "I was scared you'd died, and I'd have to explain that to your mother and to Van, and I didn't know if I could bear to live with that and losing my mind and–"

"Okay, D***!" Bailey yelled, "Get'cha mammaries off of my f***ing face!"

"S-sorry..." Viugra apologized, letting Bailey go.

"Geeze," Bailey complained, "Acting like that, you're definitely not Vixen."

"Vixen?" Viugra asked, "H-how do you know about her?"

"Let's just say we had a 'passionate' conversation. I know almost everything about you two."

"No way..." Viugra said, heart sinking to her stomach, "I don't believe you..."

"You're an angel. She's your alter ego. They call your 'father' Lord Bautista. You can read minds. Your voice can affect people's minds. Need I go on?"

Viugra's mouth was gaped. She couldn't believe Vixen told Bailey everything!

"I'm so screwed..."

"Gee, what makes you say that Viagra?" Bailey said sarcastically, "The blood on my face or us being trapped in a container?"

"You don't understand Bailey," Viugra growled, finally scooching against the wall next to Bailey, "There's no point in hiding it now... It's against our laws for humans to know our identities. The fact that not only you know but Leah and potentially whoever else is out there knows what I am means I broke that law. And once they find out... I'll lose everything."

"You're being dramatic," Bailey claimed.

"No," Viugra said softly, "If I fail this test, I lose my powers and my memories. And I'll be stuck down here on Earth."

Bailey fell silent for a moment.

"... Viugra... I mean, Valerie..."

"It matters not the name thou dost choose to call me," Viugra responded in her Elizabethan accent.

"...Why are you talking like that?" Bailey inquired, "Now's not the time for jokes."

Viugra sighed.

"There was a game I played with Lord Bautista and others where–"

"I know that stuff already!" Bailey shook her head, "...you're uncomfortable, aren't you?"

Bailey could tell by the energy in Viugra's voice that she was. On top of that, she could feel Viugra shaking with nervous energy next to her. The random Elizabethan accent was just the cherry on top.

"Listen, Viugra. These other angels you're talking about don't know about it yet, right? They won't know to fail you if you don't tell them, right?"

"It's not that easy, Bailey," Viugra shook her head, "I was a very strong angel, but there are hundreds, no, thousands, much stronger than I was. And one of the seven strongest is the one overseeing my trial, Lord Bautista."

"He's running this trial?" Bailey said.

"Yeah."

"How strong is he?" Bailey inquired.

"I can't quite picture his strength anymore. But angels as a whole oversee the order in the universe. You'll just have to use your imagination."

Suddenly, the metal bars to the crate began turning. The doors of the crate opened once again, but this time only an arm peeked inside. Viugra watched closely, as a yellow glow flashed from its hand before withdrawing from the crate. Immediately, an eerie and unnatural moan rattled their spirits.

"Wh-what was that?" Viugra asked.

Bailey started crawling to the back of the container, eyes wide in shock.

"I don't know, but it sounded like a ghost or something."

"A... ghost?" Viugra asked.

Then she remembered what Vixen told her before she woke up.

"That's not a ghost."

Viugra and Bailey were stiffened in the darkness of their metal dungeon, unsure of how to navigate the invisible demon before them. With few tools at their disposal, and Viugra's inability to see it, things seem rather grim for their situation. But Viugra couldn't cling to her fear any longer. Instead, she began falling into a place of hopelessness.

"I guess... this is how we die," Viugra smiled goofily, "I guess this was my fate from the beginning."

"What?" Bailey said, "I know you aren't giving up yet!"

"Why not?" Viugra said, "I can't fight this thing. If Vixen had a hard time with one earlier, then I probably don't stand a chance against this one."

"Seriously?"

Bailey crawled towards Viugra slowly. The demon made another low moan as if threatening Bailey to stay back. But despite her initial fear, Bailey didn't stop. When she reached Viugra's ankle, she reminded Viugra of something Vixen did earlier.

"Aurora Spei. That name ring a bell?"

"Aurora Spei?" Viugra exclaimed, nearly snapping out of her depression, "I wouldn't say it rings any bells, but I remember the song a little. How do you know it?"

"Vixen sang it to me earlier," Bailey said, "If you two are supposed to be the same person somehow, don't you know that song too?"

"I... I do, but..." Viugra started.

"Then sing that! Maybe you'll calm it down or something!"

"I don't remember all of the words!"

Bailey gritted her teeth.

"Oh, come on! Don't you love that song?"

"I do, but that doesn't mean I–" Viugra started explaining.

The demon began stirring again, interrupting her spiel. It seemed like it was getting ready to try something against them.

"Man..." Bailey grew concerned, "Look, I'll help you. Shadows of... night? Might... cover your way?"

"No," Viugra said, "It's 'may cloud your day.'"

"See?" Bailey said, "Sing it! You know the words!"

"But I don't! I only remembered that much because you reminded me!"

"Ugh!" Bailey sighed heavily, "Just... come on!"

Together, the two tried to remember the words to Aurora Spei. For several minutes, they fumbled over words and finished each other's statements to try and get it together. Eventually, they figured it out. To their surprise, the demon never attacked them while getting it together.

"You got it now?" Bailey asked.

"Yeah, I think so," Viugra said.

"How come that thing hasn't attacked us yet?" Bailey asked, "If it was giving Vixen such a hard time, we should've been diced a long time ago."

Viugra thought for a moment.

"I wonder if it's the same sloth wraith… oh!"

"Oh what?" Bailey asked.

"It's a 'sloth' wraith," Viugra emphasized on the word.

"Okay… and?" Bailey said, annoyed she didn't finish explaining.

"Sloth means lazy. If it's the same one Vixen was fighting, then it's probably tired!"

"What, so we have nothing to worry about?" Bailey asked, trying to stand up.

"Well… not exactly," Viugra continued to explain, "It can still kill us if we don't get away from it soon."

"Well, get to singing then," Bailey hurried, "You're our ticket out of here!"

"But… I'm not a ticket…"

"Shut the heck up and sing!" Bailey said, irritated.

Viugra took a deep breath, then started to sing the song. Her vocals were beautiful but weren't nearly as powerful as when Vixen sung it. Something was missing. And the wraith made sure to let them know.

Near the last line of the second verse, Viugra felt something cold rub against her arm.

"Eeeek!" she screeched, falling onto her butt.

"Hurry, scooch towards my voice!" Bailey said.

Viugra obeyed her command, and it was a good thing she did. The wraith must've slashed down into the spot where Viugra was, because the container shook and the sound of wood shrapnel clanged against the metal.

"Whoa…" Viugra huffed, "That… was close."

"I don't get it!" Bailey said, "I know you can't sing like Vixen, but how did you agitate it?"

"I didn't mean to!" Viugra pleaded, "I don't know what happened."

"Hold on," Bailey thought aloud, "This won't work unless you put some emotion into it, will it?"

"…uuuuh…"

Bailey facepalmed.

"And there it is. You aren't singing it from the heart!"

"I can't do that!" Viugra said.

"And why no–" Bailey started to ask. But she was catching on to Viugra's lack of understanding and doubled back to explain what she meant.

"When I say, 'from the heart', I mean the song doesn't mean anything to you! You don't even know what you're singing about!"

"O-oh…" Viugra said.

"UGH!" Bailey growled, slamming her fist against the door, "You have *got* to stop acting so d*** hopeless! Vixen sang this song to me, and I felt its power! It's all about never giving up! Remembering why you succeeded as much as you did! The purpose of your life! And reminding you of why you should never give up on life! Doesn't that mean anything to you?"

"My… purpose?"

Viugra's eyes widened. The purpose of life? What was her purpose for living? Why did she do the things she did and feel the way she felt? It was something she lost sight of long ago because she was so focused on what others wanted for her.

"What… what's my purpose?"

Suddenly, a light began glowing from Viugra's backpack. It was faint, but enough to be noticed.

"What's that?" Bailey asked.

"Astrel…" Viugra mumbled.

Viugra scrambled to the backpack before the light faded, grabbed it, then hurried back to the back of the crate. The wraith remained still. Unsure of what she was about to do, Bailey waited to see instead of asking more questions.

"Come out, Astrel. Speak to me," Viugra summoned quietly.

In just a few seconds, Astrel appeared before her in a ball of light.

"I felt you were really sad again," Astrel said, "What's wrong?"

"Hold on," Bailey interrupted, "That's not your child, is it?"

"What?" Viugra and Astrel said in sync, "No!"

"Okay, sheesh!" Bailey said, snapping back.

Just then the light faded from Astrel, and they were in the darkness again.

"Wh-why's it so dark in here?" Astrel asked, a bit unnerved.

Viugra sighed.

"We're in a bit of a bad situation. I have an idea of how to get out of it, but for it to work I have to remember something."

"Oh," Astrel asked, "So, you think I might know what you forgot?"

"Yeah," Viugra said "I've… I've forgotten my purpose in life. You wouldn't happen to know what it could be, could you?"

"Wow, that sounds deep," Astrel said, "Let me think…"

For a while, they sat in silence. It must've been making Bailey uncomfortable because she broke the silence with a snappy tone.

"…well? Does it take this long?"

"Oh, sorry," Astrel said, "The truth is, I have no idea. You've never told me yourself, Viugra. I can't remember something I never knew."

"Oh…" Viugra said, disappointed, "I see…"

"I'm sorry," Astrel tried to comfort.

"No, it's not your fault," Viugra said, "Still… now what do we do?"

Bailey thought for a moment, then spoke up.

"I know you're just a child, but how about this? What is the purpose of life for you?"

"My purpose of life?" Astrel asked

"Yeah."

"Hmm…"

"…please don't think too long," Bailey pleaded.

"Oh, okay," he responded, rubbing his cheek with a single finger.

It didn't take long for a response.

"Actually, I do have an answer for that."

"Really?" Viugra said, surprised, "That's a pretty difficult question for someone as young as you."

"I don't think so," Astrel said, "It's not hard for me anyways."

"Well?" Bailey interjected, "What is it?"

"The world is still new to me," Astrel began explaining, "There's so much to see and do. I guess I want to learn as much as I can and enjoy it as well."

Viugra and Bailey didn't make any remarks for a moment.

"I sense surprise from you two," Astrel said, "Was… that too much?"

"N-no…" Viugra said, "I'm just surprised at how simple and mature that answer was."

"Seriously though," Bailey said, "Are you sure he's just a child?"

"Not anymore," Viugra responded.

"Aww, you two," Astrel said, blushing.

"But… I'm still not sure about your answer," Bailey challenged, "Life isn't always fun and games. It's full of unfairness, lies, and all kinds of mess. You can easily get lost in the chaos and lose your mind if you're not careful."

"Wow," Astrel said, "Really?"

"Trust me, I've been there," Bailey said, "How can I enjoy life when there's always something ruining it?"

"Bailey…" Viugra muttered.

"That's… a good question," Astrel said, "But… still not hard to answer I think."

"Seriously?" Bailey said, now sharing in the shock of Astrel's young wisdom.

"Yeah. If something is ruining your life, why don't you stop it?"

"It's not that simple," Bailey stated.

"Why not?" Astrel said.

Bailey balled her fists. Viugra noticed that Bailey was getting uncomfortable. She reached out to her and placed her hand on her.

"…why are you patting my head?" Bailey asked.

"Oops," Viugra said, realizing it wasn't her shoulder.

Bailey removed Viugra's hand.

"I'm fine," Bailey said, then answered Astrel, "Sometimes… no matter what you do, you just can't stop the chaos happening in front of you. You're just… not strong enough. All you can do is watch. Helplessly."

"Oh…" Astrel said, sensing the dread in Bailey's heart, "It… it can get that bad?"

"Yeah," Bailey nodded.

Astrel thought a moment longer. As he did, the wraith began stirring. It sounded as if it were becoming livelier with each passing minute. Hearing its moans, Bailey felt anxiety trying to creep up on her.

"So, what are we gonna do? Any minute now, this thing is gonna get ravenous."

"I… I don't know what to say," Astrel said, now unsure of how to answer Bailey.

Slowly, dread began to shroud Viugra's heart.

"So… I guess there's nothing I can do…"

Bailey and Astrel looked in the direction of Viugra's voice with disbelief. Just before they said anything, the wraith began to growl. He seemed to be getting enough energy to do something. Viugra sat in misery, while Bailey and Astrel's anxieties were on the rise. But then, a voice rang out in Viugra's head with a hint.

...search your heart...

"Ah!" Viugra said.

Though no one could see them, her eyes lit up.

"W-what?" Astrel asked, a bit startled.

"What did you just say?" Viugra asked.

"I didn't say anything!" Astrel exclaimed.

"Me neither," Bailey agreed.

...Vixen? Viugra thought.

Then, the words of the voice in her head called forth a memory from the previous day. Something important that Moriel said to her:

When the time comes when you feel lost, search your heart for the answers. And when you find the truth, follow it relentlessly. It'll keep you honest.

The... truth... Viugra meditated, *The... truth... what does it mean?*

For a moment, Viugra pondered. Then, something finally clicked. Viugra opened her eyes, dreary with understanding. Viugra stood up, feeling a strange energy of certainty and defeat. The wraith's moans became agitated, as if in response to Viugra's change in energy.

"Astrel," Viugra said, "Thank you. You should return now."

Bailey felt a little sick hearing Viugra's tone. Just a few short moments ago, she was wallowing in misery. But now, she seemed to have a grim resolve.

"Uh... sure," Astrel agreed.

He also felt the change. It was so palpable that he thought there wouldn't be any point in questioning it.

Viugra held up Astrel's pendant, and for a moment, the glow reformed around him and swept him back into the Reliquia. Once he was inside, Viugra placed the pendant in one of her pants pockets. As she did this, she spoke to Bailey.

"Aurora Spei won't work," Viugra explained, "I just… don't understand it. The words don't make sense to me right now."

Viugra withdrew the coin Leah gave her and fiddled with it.

"Earlier, you told me to live my truth and not others," Viugra acknowledged, "I still don't know if I agree with that. But… I don't want to die like this."

She stopped messing with the coin.

"I'm letting go."

"What do you mean?" Bailey asked.

"The moment I stop fighting myself… may be the moment things become clearer," Viugra said, "It's inevitable that I'll fail this trial. But if this is it…. I want it to end knowing my truth. I want to be free… of the deceit."

After a moment of quiet, Viugra began to speak words aloud that Bailey hadn't heard before.

"…star of wisdom and wonder… let your rays find truth and impale deceit."

Suddenly, light from her right hand erased the darkness in the crate. The light extended from her hand and took form in the shape of a slim sword. Bailey was startled by the sudden illumination.

"Whoa."

The wraith squealed, withdrawing to the back of the crate. The big thud they heard against the doors across from them gave it away. As it squealed, Viugra realized that she could see a faint silhouette of the demon now.

Focus still on the wraith, Viugra spoke to Bailey one last time before confronting the demon.

"To me, truth is everything."

The wraith seemed to get more agitated, as the light of the short sword she conjured stirred it. Viugra positioned herself to attack the wraith.

"Viugra, wait!" Bailey cried.

It was too late. Viugra lunged forward, aiming the tip of her light sword at the wraith. She impaled it nearly to the hilt of her light blade. The wraith swung it's scythe-like talons at Viugra out of impulse. Viugra side stepped out of the way, snatching the blade from its body. However, it still gashed into her side. She collided with the side of the crate. The wraith went in for another slash. Viugra remained focused, despite her flesh wound. She fell to the floor, the wraith missing her completely.

"Haaaaaaa!" Viugra screamed with all her strength.

She thrust the sword with as much strength and speed as she could muster. But the wraith avoided her attack. After receiving her attacks, it seemed to be fully alert.

In the same motion it dodged, it flew towards Bailey.

"No!" Viugra yelled. She wasn't going to make it to her in time.

Bailey held her breath, but she did not move. Then suddenly, Viugra's sword of light dissipated.

"Huh?"

At the same time, the wraith demon slowed to a halt. Viugra was confused. But Bailey seemed to know exactly what she was doing. She smiled, then removed her hand from behind her back. In it was the necklace she used against Vixen.

"That demon isn't attacking, is it?" Bailey asked.

"N-no," Viugra said.

Then she realized what was going on.

"Wait… that's a Reliquia, isn't it?"

"A what?" Bailey asked.

"Never mind it," Viugra dismissed.

She looked at her hand as she tried to conjure her weapon again. Failing to do so made her realize what it could do.

"I see," Viugra said.

Viugra thought for a moment, then came up with a plan. She tapped the doors behind her to test how hard they were.

"I've got an idea. Turn that thing off."

"Are you *kidding* me?" Bailey complained, "This thing might decide to spill my guts if I do that!"

"I won't let that thing hurt you. Trust me."

Hearing Viugra ask her to trust her reminded Bailey of what Vixen asked of her earlier. With great hesitation, Bailey agreed.

"...alright."

Viugra raised her hand, positioned as if about to throw a javelin. Bailey stopped the Reliquia. Just as it did, Viugra's light sword came back. Viugra wasted no time throwing the sword at the wraith. The blade managed to skewer the wraith in its back, causing it to shriek in anger. Immediately, the wraith flew at Viugra rapidly. Viugra dropped to the floor milliseconds before the wraith slammed into the shipping crate's doors. The force of the impact caused the crate to lift off the ground, robbing both Viugra and Bailey of their balance. In the process, Viugra dropped the coin she was carrying.

While the wraith did manage to dent the doors, it didn't have enough strength in its charge to break them open. The wraith turned around and began slashing at Viugra again.

It didn't work... Viugra thought.

She bobbed and weaved, simultaneously trying to form her sword again. But to her surprise, she only formed a small dagger.

"Wh-what?" Viugra uttered in shock.

The light of the dagger illuminated the area, and Bailey noticed the coin glinting in its glow.

"Bailey!" Viugra called out to her, "Move!"

Without hesitation, Bailey did as she was commanded. Viugra flew into the back of the cargo crate next to Bailey. The wind was knocked out of Viugra for a moment, causing her to cough for air.

"Viugra!" Bailey said, then activated her Reliquia.

She was a bit too slow with it. Viugra noticed, grabbed Bailey, and jumped past the wraith before it collided where they were.

While they slid to a halt, the wraith stayed in place once again. Viugra finished catching her breath, and Bailey sat up in irritation.

"This is getting ridiculous…" she said.

"I don't understand," Viugra said, flexing her hands, "I can't make a sword?"

Bailey thought about it, then connected the dots.

"The coin!"

"The coin?" Viugra asked.

"You dropped a coin on this side of the crate before you got launched. I bet that's what gave you that extra strength!"

Leah… Viugra thought.

"We need to find it," Bailey said, already patting the floor for it.

"Right," Viugra agreed, "Just keep that Reliquia working."

Both Viugra and Bailey started patting around the crate for the coin. But Viugra noticed something faint as they searched for it. The smell of ammonia started to permeate the air they were breathing. Just as she noticed it, Bailey got her finger on the coin and picked it up.

"Got it!"

"Quick!" Viugra tried to warn, "Hold your breath!"

To her dismay, it was too late. Bailey began feeling uneasy, and her Reliquia's power gave out. Wide eyed with despair, Bailey crumpled to the floor.

"Bailey!" Viugra exclaimed, leaning over her.

The wraith, free from restraint, closed in above them. It was ready to skewer them with its talons. But Viugra didn't hesitate. Out of instinct, she stepped in front of Bailey just as the wraith came down. The wraith's talon pierced through Viugra's stomach. Its talon protruded through her back.

"AAAAAAAAAHHHHHHH!"

Bailey was startled by Viugra's blood curdling scream. Though she looked up to see what had happened, she could only imagine what was happening.

"Viugra...!" Bailey shouted.

"Ah... hah..." Viugra coughed, blood spewing from her mouth with each hack.

Though she couldn't see what happened, she knew Viugra had been severely hurt. But being affected by the miasma, Bailey was reminded of the death of her friend years ago. In that moment, Viugra was Ezra taking a bullet for Azekah.

Bailey's breathing became heavy and unsteady. She attempted to reach out to where she thought Viugra was but found herself immobile. This only worsened her anxieties.

Meanwhile the wraith began lifting Viugra up, claw threatening to rip through her body. Viugra continued to whimper as the pain of being lifted caused her to be woozy. She could feel its talon threatening to slip through her flesh like a hot knife through butter. If it were moving any faster, she would've been split in two. But divided or not, she felt her life slipping away.

This... feeling, Viugra thought, consciousness fading, *Am I... dying...? It hurts... so bad...*

Now on the brink of oblivion, Viugra felt her energy slipping away. It was getting difficult to think, and the fringe between cruel reality and eternal slumber beckoned for her crossing. But just as the life began leaving her, a voice cried out from deep within her psyche.

Use your voice.

V-Vixen? Viugra thought.

You must use your Angelic Voice.

There's... no point...

Have faith... trust me...

Suddenly, Viugra felt a hand take hold of hers. A fear-stricken Bailey had managed to take hold of her. In between their hands was the coin Leah had given Viugra. With her struggling breath, Bailey pleaded with Viugra.

"Don't... die...!"

Viugra felt the strain in Bailey's voice. Filled with compassion and her inner wisdom, Viugra weakly opened her mouth. Her weary eyes gleamed with the spark of hope once more, as she struggled to take in all the air she could. With all her being, she let loose a war cry that shook the spirits of everyone in the crate.

The wraith shrieked a terrible cry, writhing in agony from the power of her heart. Bailey's clouded mind became clear. As it flailed about, it slung Viugra towards the back of the crate. Upon impact, Viugra lost consciousness.

"VIUGRAAAA!" Bailey screamed.

Suddenly, the shipping crate doors flew open with great force. The wraith slowed down immensely to a complete halt. Then, the stiff wraith was sucked out of the crate. Just as it reached outside, it was immediately ignited in flames. Bailey turned around to the blinding light. Standing between her and the fireball in the air was a shadowy figure of a tall man with several rings on his right fingers held high.

In Search of Truth

"...you gonna lay there forever?"

Awakened by Vixen's voice, Viugra opened her eyes. She quickly sat up and looked around, anticipating another attack from the wraith. But none came. Little did she realize that it was defeated by a mysterious figure. Besides, it couldn't physically harm her in the place she was in.

Viugra was in her subconscious world of water and night sky. No one else was

there besides her and Vixen in her reflection. The night sky was filled with nothing but a quarter moon and two twinkling stars.

"Vixen..." Viugra finally spoke back, "Why am I here? Am I... dead?"

Vixen chuckled.

"No. You're not dead. That was a close call though. You had me worried."

"Worried?" Viugra couldn't believe, "I thought you were upset with me."

Vixen sighed.

"I was. I might still be. But no matter what I think, the truth remains that I am you. At least, your identity."

"Hmm," Viugra thought, "...in other words, you only care because you need me to live."

"Seriously, Viugra?" Vixen scowled, "That way of thinking is what made me mad with you in the first place. Stop that!"

Viugra smiled.

"I'm just messing with you."

Vixen's eyes lit up.

"Heh. I should've seen that coming."

Vixen shook her head.

"I want to believe that you finally accept yourself, accept me, for who we are. And yet… I can't tell if that's really the case."

Viugra bowed her head and closed her eyes.

"To be honest, I don't really know. But… I did realize something important."

"What's that?" Vixen asked.

"This whole time, I've been relying solely on others for direction. And when they wouldn't give me any, I'd use my powers to syphon their knowledge. That way, I'd know what they'd want me to do. What I thought I should be doing."

Vixen was listening intently, though she wasn't sure if she liked where Viugra was going with this.

"Ever since we started going through these trials, I've been restricted. And ever since you came about, I haven't had my powers at all. When that happened, I felt vulnerable. And recently, I realized that's because I had turned my powers into my own protection. Without them, I thought I was going to lose myself. After being attacked by Chiara and dealing with so much happening at once, I guess I felt like I was losing myself."

"Viugra," Vixen interrupted, "When you try too hard to save your life, you end up strangling it. You'll end up choking it to death."

"I'm… not sure what that's supposed to mean," Viugra acknowledged, "But if I had to guess, it's what I had been doing to you this whole time."

Vixen's eyes lit up in surprise.

"Well… yeah actually."

Viugra nodded.

"At the end of the day, I realize I had been too harsh on myself. On you. And in those last moments that I thought I might die, I finally realized what was truly important to me."

Viugra stooped down towards the water.

"It was you."

Vixen's eyes lit up in emotion. But as soon as she reacted, she turned her head in disbelief.

"Please. Don't feed me lies to make me feel better."

"I'm not… feeding you lies?" Viugra responded, confused about Vixen's phrasing, "I'm being honest."

"…prove it."

Viugra looked off, thinking of how to do just that.

"…this whole thing started because I wanted to find my father. I still do honestly, but I don't know if that'll happen anymore. At first, I just longed for my real dad to tell me who I was. His words were the only ones I thought I could trust. Ironically, I doubted the very knowledge I… I stole from others."

"I wouldn't call it stealing from them," Vixen corrected, "You were learning from them. Even if a lot of it was their bias."

"Perhaps," Viugra agreed, then sighed.

"What's wrong?" Vixen asked.

Viugra looked up and around at the vast ocean she sat upon.

"You know that we love knowledge. The excitement of learning something new and the thrill of figuring things out on our own? That's what gives us joy."

Vixen thought about what happened between her and Bailey.

"Yeah. It's also what gets us in trouble."

"Huh?" Viugra asked.

"I have a lot to catch you up on," Vixen briefed, "But long story short, I told Bailey about her past. I… brought up a lot of painful memories."

"Vixen…"

"I know, Viugra," Vixen cut in, "I messed up."

Viugra nodded, showing that she understood.

"I still think knowledge and wisdom is good if used correctly. But there's something I've learned from all of this."

Vixen listened closely.

"I want to continue learning the truth. But… I want to do it on my own. Without anyone forcing me to learn what they know. Without the bias. I want to form my own view of things without being told how. I'm tired of that. I'm *so* tired."

"I see," Vixen thought, "But… what does that mean for me?"

Viugra turned back towards Vixen. She hadn't thought of that.

"Well… I don't know…"

They sat in silence for a moment. Then Vixen made her statement.

"Viugra, I think I believe you. Even though I can't feel if you're genuine, your words seem sincere. With that being said… I would be at peace if we continued to do things separately."

Viugra's eyes lit up.

"But Vixen, how would that work? We share the same body still."

Vixen smiled.

"Don't worry. I promise I won't interfere with your life. Though, in a sense, I'll always be with you."

Viugra sat with her mouth open in disbelief. But Vixen wasn't done yet.

"Besides, we may end up forgetting one another once you wake up."

"Oh… right," Viugra said, remembering the situation they were in.

Vixen pressed her hands against the surface of the water.

"There is… one thing I want to say though."

"What's that?" Viugra asked.

"I promised Bailey that I would fully heal her heart when I got my strength back," Vixen admitted, "She prayed for that. I believe we were sent here to fulfil her wishes. Just like the shooting star wishes."

"Wow," Viugra said aloud, "Now that you say it, it makes sense. But why didn't the angels tell us?"

"I hope I find out," Vixen said, "That and the reason why Leah betrayed us."

"...yeah," Viugra agreed, "I can't believe she did that..."

The two sat there in silence for a moment, then Viugra spoke.

"Hey, I'm curious. Why Vixen?"

"That's a good question," she responded, "Someone called me that. They said it like it was a bad name, but I like it. It sounds... diva-ish."

Viugra chuckled.

"It sounds bad alright. But, I like it too."

Vixen smirked.

"Of course, you do."

Suddenly, the water began to ripple. Though Viugra wasn't sure of what it meant, Vixen was aware.

"Looks like someone's trying to wake us up."

"Yeah," Viugra said, "So... which of us is going up?"

Vixen smiled.

"I think you know the answer to that."

✲✲✲✲✲✲✲✲

"Come on, Viugra. It's time to get up."

Squinting at the bright lights above her, Viugra opened her eyes in response to the call. As her eyes adjusted to the light, she noticed the tops of stacked shipping containers and yard cranes. Then she turned her head towards the figure that called out to her. And to her surprise, it was Vulcanel sitting with her head resting in his lap with a solemn expression.

"V-van...?"

Van looked away for a moment.

"How are you feeling?"

"I feel... fine."

"And your head?"

Viugra nodded.

"...then it's time to stand up."

Viugra nodded, then sat up. As she did, she noticed his hands without gloves. She also noticed several rings with elaborate designs and different colored gemstones in them equipped on his fingers. Each finger has at least one ring, and the middle and ring fingers had two.

After she sat up, she noticed several people were nearby. Moriel, Hephasteya, Bailey, and... Azariel. There was no need to inquire why he was there, however his presence brought about a subtle feeling of dread.

"...where's the wraith?" Viugra asked.

"I... got rid of it," Van spoke up, turning his head away, "Although... it didn't take much effort. You wounded it quite a bit."

Viugra noticed a slight change in his voice. She found this interesting but decided not to ask.

Azariel reached out to her, inviting her to step closer. Viugra did as she was asked without question.

When Viugra stepped up to Azariel, her head was hung in woe.

"Viugra," Azariel said.

"I know why you're here," Viugra stated, "Just... get it over with."

Azariel hesitated on a thought.

"I'm sorry, Viugra. I wish it didn't turn out this way, but I am sworn to abide by the rules. There's nothing else I could or can do for you."

"I know."

Azariel sighed.

"You were a very gifted angel, one with great potential to be a member of the higher choirs. To say that I am utterly flabbergasted and perplexed that you have failed and in such a short period is an extreme understatement."

Viugra didn't answer back.

"I just want to know one thing," Azariel said, gently raising his hand to her forehead, "Why did you tell the child what you were?"

Viugra's eyes drifted to Bailey, who was still in Hephasteya's arms. For several seconds, her gaze was locked there. Bailey then shook her head as if to tell her not to talk.

"Well?" Azariel asked again, breaking Viugra from her trance.

Viugra looked back to Azariel, a gaze of divine frustration covering her face.

"... Because. I felt she needed to know."

Azariel's spirits grew woeful. These words seemed to stir Vulcanel's spirits as well. He turned away from her and Azariel, dreading what might happen next.

"Viugra... you know that is against our rules. Our law."

"It doesn't matter anymore, does it?" Viugra stood her ground, "In a moment, those rules won't apply to me any longer, will they?"

Azariel began to grow frustrated, lowering his hand for a moment.

"Rules are rules, but it's about the principle of the matter more so. Have you forgotten that?"

"Maybe I have," Viugra answered, "It wouldn't be the only thing I would've forgotten after I was cursed."

Bailey, watching what was unfolding, felt that something was familiar about the way Viugra was talking.

Wait... is that really Viugra? Or...?

"Honestly, I don't even understand this trial. What was I supposed to learn from it? Or can't you tell me that either?"

Viugra's frustration was beginning to show. The bold expression on her face indicated a rebellious posture. Contrary to hers, however, Azariel's face was stern but steady.

"Considering that your trial will soon be over, I suppose telling you presents no problem."

"Alright then," Viugra urged, "Tell me why."

"All who face the trials must do so without the assistance of any heavenly host."

"Really?" Viugra said, sticking a hand in her pocket, "Why?"

"The trial requires the individual's current knowledge and skills to complete and theirs alone. Any help would be seen as interference."

"Okay, but why though?" Viugra asked again.

Azariel narrowed his eyebrows.

"Are none of these answers good enough for you?"

"Honestly, no," Viugra responded, "Isn't it our job to keep humanity on track? If we Fallen Angels—no, Nephilim—are supposed to be living as humans, it would only make sense for angels to help us."

"Help would only give you the right answers without finding them yourself," Azariel said.

But this statement made Viugra even more annoyed.

"Find my own answers? You of all people should know that I tried that in the heavens! But I was silently ridiculed for it!"

"Viugra, I thought I told you to stop reading everyone's minds," Azariel sighed, "Is that what this is all about?"

"Not anymore."

Viugra looked at Bailey again.

"It's about me. I can't live like I want to when I've been trained to ignore who I am. I'm a compassionate being. I want to help people, whether they're deserving or not. That's a part of my purpose!"

"Enough," Azariel commanded.

"I'm not done yet," Viugra snapped back.

Hephasteya gasped. Bailey looked at her, then back at Viugra.

"You and Archadeya both helped raise me. I'm grateful for that, even if you do get on my nerves. But something isn't right about these trials. Maybe it's just the guy who's running them. But they need to be fixed."

"I said enough," Azariel repeated.

His spiritual energy increased, and it caused Viugra to drop to her knees.

"Viugra!" Bailey called out to her.

Moriel turned his bony head towards her and held a finger up to his mouth. Bailey gritted her teeth, struggling to do just that.

"I will not tolerate your disrespect, Viugra," Azariel spoke boldly, "Whether you would lose your memories or not, you should never speak to me like that. I am an Archangel, and you will adhere to the etiquette the angels have established for my choir."

Viugra struggled to move. She was nowhere near strong enough to even think of resisting him.

After a while, Azariel eased his spiritual power. Viugra found herself catching her breath, as the pressure was nearly suffocating. But as she was doing so, Azariel warned her with a much more tender tone.

"Please, Viugra. Do not make this any harder on me than it already is."

Viugra took a few more seconds to catch her breath, then she stood up.

"Fine. But know that forcing me into submission won't earn you my respect."

Azariel narrowed his eyebrows.

"So be it. Before I finish, I need all of your Reliquias and angelic items. Your clothes will simply lose their power, so there is no need to relinquish them."

Viugra reached into her pockets and placed Astrel's pendant and Leah's coin in Azariel's hand. She then lowered her arms, but hands balled in fists. After receiving the Reliquia, Azariel teleported it somewhere out of his hand. He then proceeded to place the tips of his fingers on Viugra's forehead.

Bailey began to squirm in Hephesteya's arms.

"No! This isn't fair!"

"I'm sorry," Azariel said, "It isn't meant to be fair, child. It's meant to be right."

Suddenly, an unbelievable wave of spiritual energy washed over the area. Bailey, being the only one there completely vulnerable to it, was so overwhelmed by the strength of it that she felt her own breath stifle.

Upon Viugra's head formed an Arte Circle full of intricate designs. Without a second to waste, Azariel muttered words that Bailey couldn't comprehend. Next, an uncountable shower of small balls of light flew out from Viugra's head and across the sky. One infused itself into Bailey's head. In that same moment, Bailey felt as if something was sucking away at her mind. She couldn't focus on anything, as reality became unclear to her.

After only a few seconds, Bailey felt her memories of Viugra beginning to slip away. As the gap in her mind widened, she watched as the lights retraced themselves back into Viugra's head. Viugra closed her eyes as she accepted her fate, the Arte Circle lighting up from the lights returning to her head.

As the Arte Circle was glowing more intensely, Azariel and Viugra exchanged one last glance. It seemed as if they were communicating with their eyes just how resolute they were with what they stood for. But in their final moments, Azariel uttered his final remarks to her.

"Viugra, I will always love you."

Viugra stared at him, contemplating a response. The man who wore several hats in her life, that being a father, a brother, and a friend, was the same man responsible for putting her through such a ridiculous trial. And yet, with tears trickling down her face, she found the strength to return his sentiments with an uncanny smile.

"I love you too, 'father.'"

Then the arte circle dissipated. Viugra fell unconscious, and Azariel caught her body before it hit the pavement. Bailey followed suit, slumping in Hephasteya's arms. Moriel bowed his head.

A moment followed, as both Azariel and Hephasteya lowered

the girls to the ground gently. When both were certain that Viugra and Bailey were unconscious, Azariel broke the silence.

"It is done."

"Y-yeah..." Moriel confirmed.

"Moriel," Azariel ordered, "You know what must be done next. I will entrust the rest to you."

Moriel nodded.

"And Ms. Zelos," he continued, turning to Hephasteya, "Thank you for your assistance."

"My pleasure, Lord Bautista."

Azariel prepared to return to the Heavens. But just as he was about to, he noticed Van's distant behavior. Before leaving, he called out to him as well.

"Vulcanel. I commend you for upholding the commandments of this trial, despite your personal feelings towards the outcome. As we always say, obedience is better than sacrifice."

Vulcanel didn't respond.

Without waiting for a response, Azariel disappeared into the night sky. Once he was gone, Moriel approached Vulcanel. Vulcanel didn't budge. Hesitantly, Moriel gently placed his hand on Vulcanel's shoulder. To his surprise, Vulcanel's body was trembling. Mori had never seen him like this before.

"...I'm sorry, Vulcanel," Moriel tried to comfort, "In the end... this was the only way."

Vulcanel suddenly grabbed Moriel's hand fiercely. Though he meant to chuck his hand away, Vulcanel showed restraint and gently lowered it instead.

"...don't," he muttered, "...not right now..."

Then Vulcanel disappeared without warning.

"Van?" Hephasteya gasped.

"He'll be fine," Moriel assured, "He just needs a moment to cope. After all, the daughter of the man he respected the most just lost her powers and place amongst the heavenly host."

Hephasteya nodded, then picked up Bailey.

"I guess we better finish things up here. It won't be long before we lose our memories as well."

"Yeah."

Moments later, Hephasteya disappeared as well, with Bailey in her arms. All that was left was Moriel standing over a sleeping Viugra. Despite the intense moment that transpired just a while ago, she seemed to be asleep peacefully as if there was nothing to worry about anymore.

Moriel knelt, then he lifted her up as a knight would his princess. Before he followed suit to place her where she needed to be, he began to sing the few lines he knew of a lullaby to her. It was the only song they both had memories of.

"Fallen stars from the heavens above, you'll one day return to respite. But stray away from the luminous void; yield not to the alluring black light..."

Epilogue

A Week Later…

"Thanks again for watching Bailey. It really helps me out."

Mrs. Rooke took hold of Valerie's hand and placed her check in it. The two were at the front door of the Rooke residence saying their goodbyes for the day. It was in the afternoon, and the sun was just setting beyond the beach waves.

"It's no problem, Mrs. Rooke," Valerie responded, "I should be thanking you honestly."

"Please, I told you to call me Mely," Mrs. Rooke scolded.

"Oops," Valerie covered her mouth, "I'm… still working on that."

"Yeah, yeah," Mrs. Rooke teased, "By the way, how's that migraine you had?"

"Oh that?" Valerie acknowledged, "It's fine. Honestly, I don't even feel it anymore. It must've gone away this morning."

"Ooookay," Mrs. Rooke said, skeptically, "Just make sure you're eating three full and balanced meals every day. And drink plenty of water."

"I am, don't worry!" Valerie assured.

"Good."

Mrs. Rooke then peered closer into Valerie's eyes of which were a vibrant violet color.

"I still can't believe you have such beautiful eyes. No wonder you were wearing shades so much. Probably got tired of people staring at'cha."

"Uh," Valerie awkwardly responded, "I suppose so."

"You don't have to tell me if you don't want to," Mrs. Rooke assured, "I'm just speculating here."

Mrs. Rooke turned from the front door towards the stairs.

"Bailey! Get down here and say goodbye!"

"I don't feel like it," Bailey growled.

"Ugh, I swear that child," Mrs. Rooke grumbled.

"It's okay, I don't mind," Valerie calmed, "I'll see her tomorrow anyways."

"It's not okay," Mrs. Rooke said, "She needs to learn how to show some respect to people."

Soon, Valerie departed from the Rooke's residence and headed home. On the way, she greeted several people on the streets with a warm smile. A few senior pedestrians crossed the street with her, so she made sure to walk with them until they were safely across.

Before she went home, Valerie stopped by a small store that sold affordable food items and bought several small sandwiches. As she was getting rung up, she noticed the news was playing on the radio behind the counter.

"...the police have not released any further info about the LL gang members who strangely turned themselves in last night. All that is known is that the victims they assaulted will live to see another day..."

"Weird, in't?" the man ringing Valerie up said, "The LL don't usually rat themselves out like dat. 'specially when it involves killin.'"

"Yeah, I suppose so," Valerie agreed, "I only recently moved here, so I wouldn't really know. But still, that is weird."

"Hmm," the man said, "By the way, ain't this a lot o' food for one young lady as yourself?"

Valerie chuckled.

"Nah. I can handle this."

The man shrugged.

"Well, here's your change."

Valerie thanked the man, then left the store. But instead of heading home, she made a detour. She cut through an alley where many homeless people were encamped and handed a sandwich half to everyone there.

"Oh, bless your heart young lady," a woman nearly skinny to her bones complimented, "Truly, this is a blessing!"

"It's no problem at all," Valerie said, "Every bit helps, right?"

"You and that other girl do more for us than anyone else around here," she smiled.

Valerie smiled back.

After handing out food to everyone there, she had a few left over. She decided to keep them for herself when she got back to her apartment. Valerie felt that she might need all the energy she could get to deal with her absurd neighbors.

✲✲✲✲✲✲✲

"Well done, Chiara."

The demon chained up somewhere in the hells complimented her.

"No thanks needed," Chiara bowed, "It was… child's play."

"Continue to obey me, and I may even have my other pawns release your child early."

"That would be delightful, my liege," Chiara smiled.

"The girl is no longer an angel," he boasted, "This pleases me. And yet… it does not please me enough."

"Shattering her heart wasn't good enough for ya?" Chiara asked.

"No," the being said, looking off into the distance.

His attention seemed to be focused on another place in the distance.

"That isn't enough. She needs to suffer more."

"You're quite the sadist."

"It comes natural."

The demon stretched his hand forth.

"Return to Nerezza and continue to torture her. Make her life miserable."

"As you wish, so it shall be," Chiara pledged.

Chiara then exited his chambers. She walked down the stairs with a confident smile. It seemed like forever for her to reach the bottom of the tower, but just as she did, her smile worsened.

"You're quite the fool, you know that?"

☼☼☼☼☼☼☼

Bailey watched outside her window as Valerie headed home. When she was out of sight, Bailey flopped onto her bed.

"Babysitter gets on my nerves sometimes, I swear," she grumbled to herself.

She rolled to her side and pulled her phone off her nightstand. Today, her pass time consisted of keeping up with the news. Headlines showed updates on PSI's lead in the shipping industry, the progress of medication development for the Animus Disease, and the strange incident with the LL turning themselves in.

When Bailey reached the latter article, she stopped midway through reading it. She suddenly had the urge to pull out a letter she received in the mail a few days ago. Bailey set her phone down for a moment, clicked on her nightstand light, then reached in her drawer for the letter. When she withdrew it, something fell out of the drawer.

"Ugh, dang it," she grumbled.

She slid out of the bed and grabbed what fell out. Before returning it to her drawer, she examined it for a moment.

It was a pendant with a green gem in it. But it was unique in design, signaling that it must've been very expensive to make. Or, at the very least, very difficult to craft.

After examining it a bit, Bailey finally rested it back in her drawer. She then crawled back into bed and withdrew the letter from its envelope. The contents of the letter read as follows:

Dear Bailey,
Please read this letter thoroughly. This is not junk mail. This is a commission. You are about to play an important role in saving humanity from needless destruction. Sounds crazy, I know. But this is not a joke.

You have shown exceeding resilience to hardships you should never had endured. In due time, you will be healed of the pain and trauma that haunts you. But the promise keeper, the one by the name of Valerie Evangeline, does not yet remember.

Until then, you must help educate her on how to survive in your society. But most importantly, you must help her grow her network of respectable individuals. She has no idea how to take care of herself. She needs you, as you do her. And the world will soon need you both.

Forgive me for not disclosing my identity, but it is necessary to avoid compromising my cover. In the future, when Valerie regains her memories, you will remember me and all that we discuss. But for now, record everything that you notice that's off about her. In doing so, you may reveal the truth about her identity and the key to her remembering who she is.

May your light shine forth,

Spectrum Oblivionis

P.S.: When she finally remembers, give her this pendant. Humanity is not the only world she's saving.

No matter how many times she tried, Bailey just couldn't figure out who the 'Spectrum Oblivionis' was supposed to be. And no matter how many times she read it, the letter sounded like a prank.

And yet, for some reason she felt, deep down, that she needed to keep it to understand.

Bailey returned the letter to its envelope and opened the drawer. But before setting it in, she rustled through the drawer and pulled out another pendant. The design of this one was different than the green one, as it had a yellow gem in it. But the designs on the chain suggested that it was like the green one she put away earlier.

"Hmph," Bailey huffed, then placed the pendant in the envelope, "Why do I suddenly have to be the main character?"

Now feeling tired, Bailey decided to go to sleep early. It was summer break anyways. She had the whole month of August to do what she wanted. But getting rest now seemed necessary, as things seemed like they were about to get very interesting.

THE END

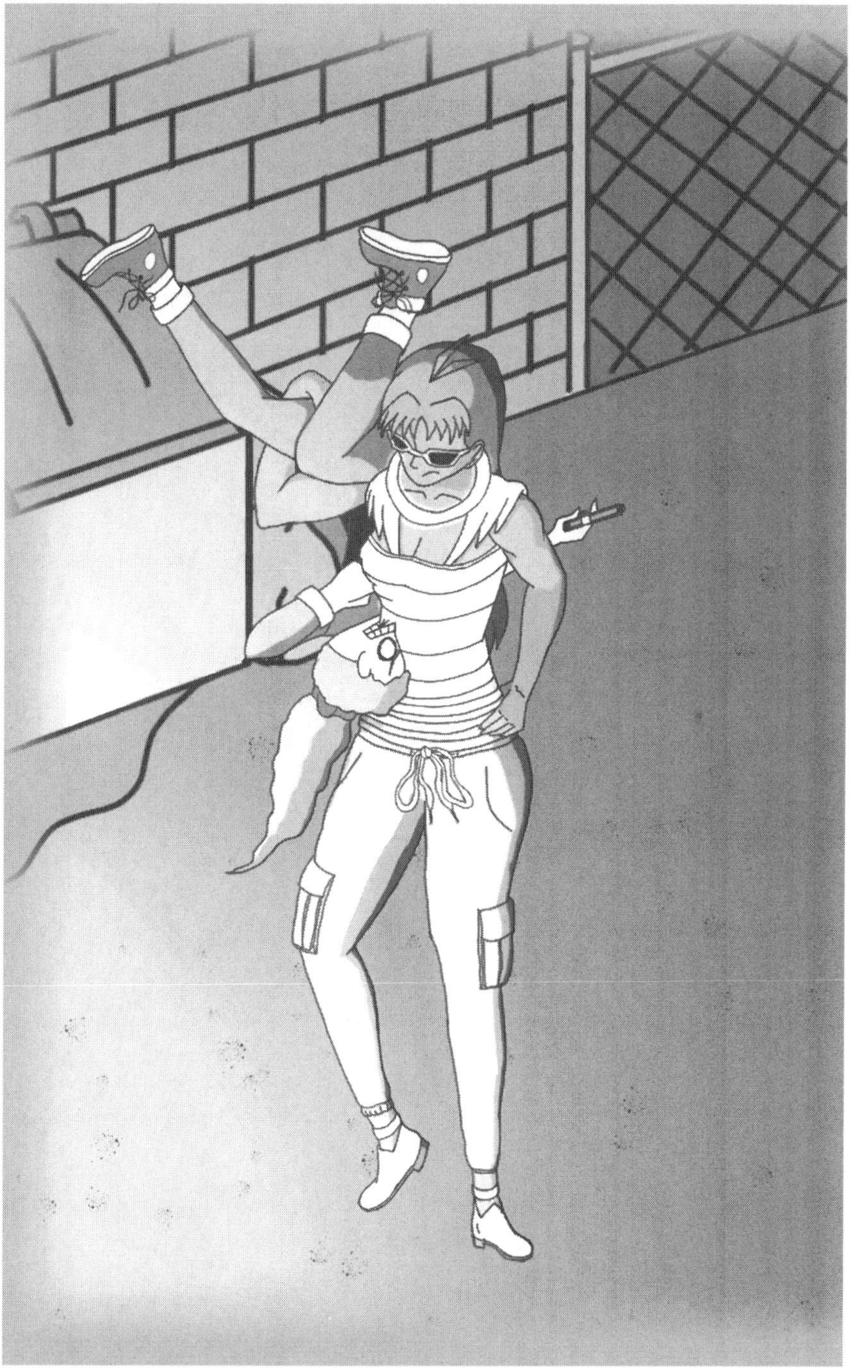

Concept

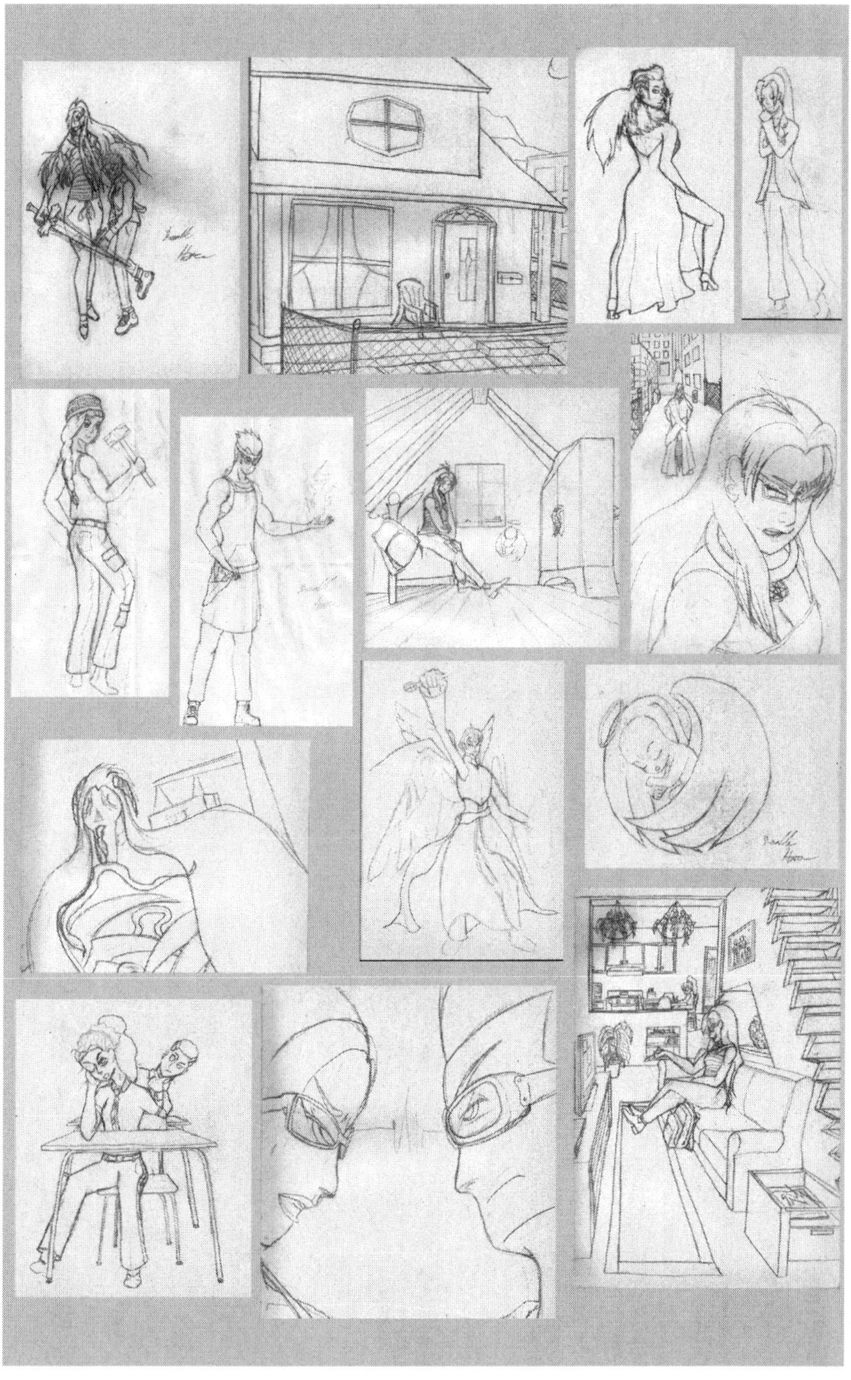